THE FIND

Books by Venezia Miller:

THE FIND SERIES

THE FIND
EVIL BENEATH THE SKIN
RETRIBUTION

COMING SOON:
THE STORM

THE FIND

Venezia Miller

THE FIND

For information contact: Venezia.Miller@gmail.com

Book and Cover design by K. Vanhalle
Pictures: www.pixabay.com

ISBN: 9798503331141

First Edition: April 2020

CHAPTER

1

HIS **WARM BREATH** drew a circle of condensed water vapor on the dirty cabin window. It had stopped raining, but the forest road looked muddy, and the air was still damp, leaving him with some resistance to go outside. The dried-up streaks of dirt and dust on the glass irritated him, but not as much as the dog who had become restless, scratching, and barking continuously.

God, the dog is so annoying!

The noise was so loud. It bounced from every wall. It pounded in his ears and saturated every one of his senses.

Maybe he should go outside. The fresh air would do him some good. It was too cold inside, anyway. The small electrical heater didn't provide the comfort he wanted. Most of the warmth was seeping through the cracks of the wooden panels. The cabin was old, bought by his parents in the eighties and, apart from minor improvements, never well-maintained. Pests had compromised the integrity of the front porch and the platform at the back, leaving the boards to decay. He had tried to mend some, but it demanded a more professional intervention to fix all the problems.

Alexander gave in to the dog's ceaseless excitement, and five minutes later he was struggling to find his way through the mud and fallen leaves. It was chilly for the time of the year. The air was already rich with the fragrance of early fall, but in the background, birds were singing, and the wind was blowing through the leaves, with every gust sending a melancholic song through the wood. Far away there was the sound of running water from the brook. It was peaceful, yet full of activity. He welcomed the serenity in his head. The image of his dead father kept ghosting through his mind, and the nightmares, he had been suffering from since his teenage years, had come back in full force, almost driving him insane. It was the same dream over and over again. What did it mean?

The dog had taken a different path than usual. The trail was tough, twisted, and winding through the trees. This part of the forest was new to him. It was dark, with little sunshine coming through the thick foliage. The road in front of him was now practically impassable by broken branches and rocks, and he couldn't see the dog anymore.

"Spark, Spark, where are you?" Alexander said, but he heard nothing. Spark was a stupid name, although it hadn't been his choice, but his father's. His dad loved that dog, probably more than he had ever cared for his own son.

He reached the edge of a small ravine. The heavy rain of the last days had caused a mudslide dragging trees and even rocks down with it. Several conifers, hanging over the rim, were about to fall over. When he glanced around, he spotted the dog a few tens of meters away from him, vigorously sniffing and scratching the soil. He wasn't standing close enough to recognize what Spark had found. The icy wind made him shiver, and he really wanted to go back to the cabin as fast as possible, but Spark didn't listen.

"Spark, come here!"

No reaction. He should just leave him and go back alone, but a strange sense of guilt prevented him from abandoning the dog, and he walked toward him.

"What are you doing?"

He put his hand on the dog's back and kneeled next to him. Spark was too busy to notice. He looked down to figure out what the object of Spark's undivided interest was. As his mind finally understood what was in front of him, he fell backward in terror. Bones partially buried in the mud ... a skeleton. He knew enough to grasp that these weren't animal remains. He saw the skull. These were the remains of a human being. He had seen nothing like this before. But the skull, remarkably clean and shiny, had a hypnotizing effect on him. He reached out to touch it, but it was almost like an invisible force pulled him back. A disturbing sensation, something he couldn't place properly.

Meanwhile, the dog, unaware of the gruesome scene, continued digging and stirring up the earth, slowly exposing the full skeleton.

Why didn't it upset him more? Most people would be terrified, but then again, he wasn't the average person.

* * *

Chief inspector Isa Lindström slammed the door of her car harder than she should have. It bounced, and the bottom edge landed against her lower leg. She could barely suppress a cry of pain. The car, a fifteen-year-old Volkswagen, had once belonged to her grandmother and although environmentalists would not agree with her nowadays, the sentimental attachment to the car was far more important to her than any awareness to reduce her ecological footprint.

It was one of those days: a fight with her boss in the morning, a suspect they had to let go because of lack of evidence, a pile of files on her desk that seemed to grow with every minute and that was even more harmful to her perpetual procrastination, and now this horrific discovery that was keeping her away from a good book and a warm bed.

As she pulled her coat more firmly over her shoulders and neck, she strode toward the group standing near the trees. She was a handsome, but intimidating woman, in her mid-thirties, brilliant but unconventional in her police work, and some would even call her wild and reckless. Most men and women knew her only by reputation, which instilled fear rather than admiration.

Night had fallen, the crime scene was heavily lit, and people were running to and from. Some of them were police officers, others in their white coveralls were members of the forensic investigation team.

"Can someone bring me up to speed?" she said annoyed.

A young policeman looked up and walked toward her.

"Sorry, boss, I didn't realize you had arrived. I wasn't sure if you'd come. The local police are here and ..."

"So?"

The man wanted to continue, but before he could finish the sentence, she interrupted him again.

"Where the hell is Magnus?" she asked. "I need him here." Quickly she turned around, scanning the surroundings for her partner.

"I haven't seen him yet."

"As usual! So, what's the deal?"

"Around 4 p.m. a hiker, walking his dog, found the remains of a person - or at least that is what we assume - buried over there."

He pointed at the site where most of the activity was concentrated. The lights illuminated the small tent the forensic investigation team had put up to protect the bones and any remaining evidence. It also safeguarded the investigators from the harsh weather. It rained again and, more than ever, everyone who was standing outside felt the icy wind penetrate through the layers of clothes with such savagery it felt like cutting through flesh and bone.

"Where is he?"

Her direct and somewhat erratic questions threw the inexperienced policeman off balance. It all made sense in her head, but it was a challenge for her conversation partner to keep up with her reasoning.

"Who?"

"The hiker. Where is he?"

The impatient tapping of her foot, the frowned eyebrows and the constant turning of her head, gazing at the surrounding people, wasn't helping his increasing stress, and he took a deep breath before answering.

"He's in the cottage, ten minutes walking uphill. That's where he's staying. Two police officers went with him to take his statement."

"I also want to talk to him, and, afterward, I'd like a chat with Dr. Olsson. She's running around over there, right?"

"Correct ... but it's best not to disturb her ... she's still examining the remains," the young guy replied with some hesitation.

"That's fine ... I'll be back later," Isa said and gave him a forced smile, and then walked in the direction of the cabin. It took over fifteen minutes before she reached the front porch. It was a challenging walk because of the darkness and emerging fog that hung low against the ground.

The warm air came out to meet her as she opened the door. The cabin was rather ordinary with a minimalist interior design: a tiny kitchen on the left, a small living area with a dinner table and four chairs on the right-hand side and a comfortable leather armchair in front of a TV, which was probably the only item in the room that somewhat reminded her this was 2017.

When she entered, a policewoman nodded as a sign of recognition and handed her a piece of paper.

"Alexander Nordin, thirty years old, researcher," Isa read out loud.

"Yes," he answered, and for an instant, the young man, sitting at the table and staring at her with his blue eyes, surprised her.

What a beautiful man!

He emanated sensuality and an air of intrigue, without even knowing it. Every line, every shape of his body and face was so well-proportioned, that, for a moment, she couldn't believe he was real.

"Uh ... so what are you researching?" she asked and immediately realized this was not the strongest question to start with. She needed to put order in her thoughts. He already distracted her.

"Mathematics, I am working on my doctorate at the University of Uppsala."

"I see ... I am chief inspector Lindström and I'll be leading this investigation. So, can you tell us what happened today?"

"But ... I already told your colleagues everything I know," he said with a certain reluctance.

She grabbed a chair and sat down facing him.

"And now, you'll explain it ... to me."

He found her intimidating. So much that it was hard for him to look at her, and instead he stared at the hands in his lap. A safe option.

"Nothing much to say ... I walked the dog around 4 p.m. It had been raining before. By chance, we took another route than usual and ..."

She interrupted him. "Why?"

"Don't know ... I guess the road was too muddy because of the rain, and I just followed the dog."

He could feel how her eyes were fixed on him. It was unsettling, and that got reflected in the way he was talking. He had never been a gifted speaker, but now the words were failing him completely.

He continued in a quiet voice: "The dog spotted the bones."

She was treating him like a criminal. She didn't believe him. Why? Did he seem so unreliable to her?

"They're human ... aren't they?"

The peculiar fascination he had noticed at the moment of discovery still puzzled him. That wasn't normal. Why did he feel like that? How should he behave?

"What ... what happened to ... the person?"

She didn't answer. It was her prerogative to do so.

"You're far from home. What are you doing here?"

"This is my parents' cottage. I stay here sometimes ... maybe once or twice a year, to take a break. I am going back this Sunday."

"You know the area well. Yet, you are not familiar with the site where you discovered the remains," she pointed out.

There was an almost sadistic pleasure in seeing him getting more nervous and pressured. She did it with all witnesses, but especially with him. It was her classic reaction when faced with a handsome man. It irritated her how beautiful people moved through life with such ease and arrogance. Though with him, she missed the typical lofty, arrogant attitude she expected from men. There was something about him, a strange blend of mystery and aloofness, intertwined with such an overt sensuality. She wanted to see past the superficial, but she couldn't help herself. Finding a decent balance between dislike and desire had always been a struggle for her. Typically, she gravitated to one of the extremes. It was black or white. There was no in-between.

"No," he said.

"Any neighbors?" she asked and wrote a few lines on the paper the police officer had given her when entering the room.

"A few, but it's at least five to ten minutes by foot."

"Can you give me their names?"

It was the first time during the entire conversation he had gathered enough courage to glance at her. She had a soft and kind face, which clashed with her hostile attitude.

He reflected about the question. Admittedly, he only knew few by name. He rather kept to himself. Much more socializing happened years ago when he came there with his parents. They knew everyone in the neighborhood: the young and the old, parents and grandparents ... but the older generation rarely came anymore. Some of them had died, and he didn't particularly like to hang out with the younger folks.

"Let's see, there were Olav Bergqvist and his family ... but I believe he died some time ago and the cabin has not been used ever since. No, I'm mistaken ... I think one of his daughters was here last summer with her family. On the other side, half a kilometer to the east–you can take the road uphill–is the cabin of Mats Norman. He still comes here now and then, occasionally with his wife Annette, sometimes with his grandchildren. Mostly during summer."

He sighed, and for a second, he looked sad, almost tormented.

"They were good friends of my parents," he said.

"Is that all?" Isa asked while still writing down the information he had given her.

"No, there is a younger couple ... in the neighboring cottage. But I can't remember their names, and I haven't seen them for a while. The house is empty most of the time."

He stopped and stared at her, waiting for a reaction from her side, but there was none. She was still occupied by the sheet of paper in front of her. The conversation faded into an uncomfortable silence. Alexander just wanted them to go away and leave him in peace.

"Okay," she started again," that's all for now. Thank you for the statement. We have your address and cell phone number in case we need to ask you more questions afterward."

She gave the report to the police officer who had been moving around the room during the interview and was now standing close to the door.

"Do a background check on him," Isa lowered her voice.

At that same moment, a dark-haired man briskly entered the room and startled her. Alexander estimated him to be mid-forty, handsome but arrogant and self-righteous. The man wore a long black coat, burgundy trousers, and fashionable boots. Obviously, he took good care of himself and loved the attention he received from people around him. The admiring glances of the policewoman, standing next to Isa, had not gone unnoticed.

"Jesus, be careful Magnus!" Isa snapped at him.

"You'll survive," he laughed," are you done here?"

He saw Alexander staring at them. It always amazed Magnus how you only needed a few seconds to form an impression about someone. He didn't like this man in the cabin. In fact, he was pretty sure he detested him.

"Is he the guy?" he asked with a certain disdain, pointing to Alexander.

"The guy? If you mean the witness who discovered the remains ... yes. But we're done here. Let's go outside."

She grabbed his arm and almost forced him through the door. As she left the lodge, she turned around and quickly glanced at Alexander, who felt more comfortable now they were leaving. Yet, inspector Lindström intrigued him, and as she took off, he got up from his chair and walked to the window, trying to catch the last glimpse of her. She was tall and slender, with medium-long, light-brown curly hair, which she held up with a hairpin. Wet from the rain, it now fell in messy wisps along her neck. He stared at it until the policewoman called his name. She wanted him to sign his statement about the events.

* * *

"Magnus, where have you been?" Standing on the porch outside the cottage, she wanted to lecture him about being late.

"There was stuff I needed to finish and ... you know how hard it is to get here!"

She looked at him with a growing feeling of anger and frustration. These days, he wanted to spend more time with his family, but work was work and there was no room for his personal problems.

Isa hadn't forgotten her break-up with Magnus, and how he was now back with his wife after their two-year affair. He still owed her an explanation. Things had stayed civilized, no fighting, no hard-hearted accusations had been thrown back and forth, but underneath the surface, the indignation and disappointment over the rejection were boiling. It would burst at some point.

"Okay, okay," she sighed. She was tired of arguing about it. "Did you have the chance to talk to Ingrid?"

"No," he shook his head," she was still busy, but let's see if she's available now."

They strolled downhill to the site where Dr. Ingrid Olsson had worked for nearly four hours to recover the bones. Ingrid was the police forensic anthropologist. She had worked for the department for more than a decade, being a witness to how not only science but also investigative practices had changed over time to incorporate more forensic methods and technology. It had been an interesting evolution.

"What do you think about this case?" Magnus asked Isa after an awkward silence. He knew why she had been so angry with him, and it wasn't because he was late.

"What is there to say? The hiker gave us nothing useful. His dog dug up the remains during a walk. The area is relatively desolate. Maybe it's an old crime or an accident."

Dr. Olsson approached. She was wearing protective clothing over her regular clothes, including a face mask she quickly took off.

"This will be tough," Ingrid started. "The skull is fairly unscathed. The bones are human, female and rather young, probably a teenager, but I need to examine them more closely in the lab to get a better idea about the probable age. No soft tissue. I estimate that the body must be there for more than five years. But it's not an archaeological skeleton. I guess the body was buried quite deep, but the rain and the recent mudslides have exposed the bones. They are reasonably untouched with limited damage from scavengers ... few bite marks from the dog, but that's all. The identification will be challenging; we found pieces of clothing, but not a lot. I will need to use the teeth, skull, perhaps bone DNA typing and other markers on the bones to identify the body."

"Any clue about the cause of death?"

"There are no obvious signs of violence, but I can tell you more after I have examined the bones in detail. We need to do more digging, but the weather is terrible. We must stop for today and continue tomorrow."

Isa was staring at the trees and the tent. She couldn't explain it, but an awful feeling of panic and horror froze her on the spot. This was not a good omen. Magnus had noticed the change in facial expression. She looked horrified.

"Isa, what's wrong?" Magnus asked.

"I don't know...," she said without looking at either of them. "There is something wrong."

"What do you mean?" The words puzzled her colleagues.

She turned around. As reality sunk in and she realized what she had been saying out loud, she mumbled: "Never mind." She dismissed that sudden moment of anxiety in her head as irrational and speculative. She shouldn't think about it any further.

CHAPTER

2

WHEN MAGNUS DROVE HOME that night, he also couldn't shake the feeling something was wrong. Who was she? What had happened to this girl, buried in a forlorn area of Sandviken?

The city was located 190 kilometers north of Stockholm, near Storsjön, one of Sweden's four largest lakes. In winter it attracted mostly skiing fanatics, and in summer the lake and its amazing surroundings were the favorite places for hikers and nature lovers. Detached suburban homes enclosed by the greenest grass you'd ever seen, and rows of terraced houses and condos painted yellow, red and green, contrasted with the more industrial area around the steel mill. Nothing exciting ever took place here. Until now.

The ethereal music playing in the background carried an air of melancholy, and his thoughts wandered to his wife and kids. The bones ... This person was someone's child. Were the parents still searching? Had they given up?

He had met parents of missing children before. The uncertainty was often worse than knowing someone had killed their loved ones. There was no closure. The rare cases where they found children alive after years of incarceration gave them hope ... but that took its toll. Little by little, there was nothing left to live for except that tiny sparkle of hope.

The drive back to Gävle took almost an hour, although it was only twenty kilometers. The road was terrible, poorly lit, and the heavy rainfall made driving even harder. The windscreen wipers couldn't handle the amount of rain.

When he parked the car, it was after four in the morning. The house was quiet. He undressed downstairs and went up to the bedroom. His wife Sophie woke up when he got into bed.

"And?" she asked, barely able to keep her eyes open.

"I'll tell you later, just go back to sleep."

"I wasn't sleeping," she said. A long yawn followed.

"You only came back now?" He sounded surprised.

She turned around.

"No, we came back at ten, but I couldn't sleep."

He stared at her with a tenderness and compassion he rarely showed for anyone else. His fingers ran down her cheeks, gently removing the strands of hair from her face.

"What did the doctor say?"

"This time it's serious. They want to change his meds. Not sure when...," she paused and wanted to see his reaction, "and even if we can take him home."

It was one of the best-hidden secrets of the entire police department. Only his superintendent knew about his son's devastating mental illness: schizophrenia.

"It's time," she said with the softest voice he'd ever heard, "it's time to think about it."

The words came out hesitantly. Magnus had been against admitting their son to a mental hospital. It was defeat; it was acknowledging they couldn't manage. But now? Now things were different. In one of his psychotic episodes, Toby had attacked his older sister Anna with a knife. She was unharmed, but the number of hallucinations had increased, and it had become increasingly more difficult for him to distinguish delusion from reality. Magnus had to admit this situation was no longer tenable, and he gave in.

"Yes, it's time. You're right. When you visit him today, talk to the doctors and check what our options are."

She lifted her head from the pillow and kissed him. There were mixed feelings. In truth, she had given up on Toby a long time ago. It was something she could only admit to herself. Magnus would never understand these emotions, and she couldn't bear the disappointment on his face. Toby was a stranger to her, someone else's child, not hers. She couldn't connect with him, not even in his more lucid periods. Hatred was a strong word, but it was exactly what she felt for him some days. She blamed her son for the failure of her marriage. It never occurred to her that this was partly her fault, because of the distance she had created between herself and the rest of the family. This was not the woman Magnus had married, that cheerful girl, full of life, radiant, open-minded, an optimist with big plans. The change had come gradually. It started after Anna's birth. She didn't want to be just a wife and mother. Where were those glorious dreams she had aspired before? Her identity was gone. She only existed in relation to someone else.

But she couldn't take the step of leaving them. It was too terrifying. They had never talked about it, but Magnus knew. He'd hoped his affair would somehow prompt her to reflect on their prospects as a couple. But she had forgiven him, with such ease it had surprised and disappointed him at the same time. Duty-bound to give his marriage another chance, Magnus had returned to his role as a loving husband, but he knew it was a hollow picture of a marriage that couldn't last.

* * *

"Really," Ingrid yelled as she got out of the car. The weather had been even worse than the day before. The rain came down in buckets, and the team struggled to hold up the tent. Part of the surface had started to slide again. They had put in place safety measures to support the overhanging trees to prevent them from falling, but she didn't feel safe at all. She had expected to complete the excavation by noon, but the mud had covered the remains again and they almost had to start from scratch. The continuous bad weather would significantly shorten the hours of sunlight and it forced them to work quickly to get everything finished by end of the day.

She saw the cabin at the top of the road. Hardly discernible, the distant figure was Alexander Nordin standing on the front porch. The activity surrounding the macabre discovery intrigued him. He had barely gotten any sleep, and felt nervous and scared, although he couldn't really explain why. It would have been better for him to leave immediately and go home, but somehow, he felt responsible. He wanted to know who this person was and how he or she had died. The dog, locked in the house, became anxious again. When the barking started, he went in. Ten minutes later police officers saw him walking up the trail, with the dog in front of him.

"Where are the remains that have been retrieved from the site?" Ingrid asked a police officer, standing just outside the tent. The raincoat he was wearing had not been enough to keep him from feeling cold, and he was jumping up and down when Ingrid approached him.

"Your colleagues put them on the table near the big van," the young man said, continuing the rather strange-looking exercise of keeping himself warm.

She turned around and saw a second, smaller tent next to the big white van parked near the site. With the hood of her heavy raincoat pulled tightly over her head and a thick scarf around her neck, she walked toward the vehicle where most of her assistants were standing.

"Dr. Olsson, everything we could recover so far is in separate bags and has been labeled. I'll send them to the lab for analysis."

"Excellent work," she said, looking at the items displayed on the table in front of her. The table was not sturdy and, with its legs resting on uneven ground, it didn't seem very stable. Afraid it would tip over Ingrid urged the team to put the remains in the secure boxes.

She picked up some transparent bags and placed them carefully in the van. One of the plastic bags, already in the box, suddenly caught her attention.

"This can't be right," she called out. The rest of the team stopped their activities and looked at her in surprise.

"What's wrong?" one of the young women asked.

"I found a collarbone in the box," Ingrid said, "are you sure this is from the site?"

"Yes, everything here was retrieved from the area near the hiking trail. I don't see a problem with the collarbone?"

"Well, I do, since there are two more on the table over there. Three collarbones seem a bit too many to me. These bones are not coming from the same person."

It took a few seconds for this new reality and its implications to sink in.

* * *

After only two hours of sleep, Magnus dragged himself into the office. He needed coffee. He usually avoided caffeine. It made him edgy and hypersensitive, but this time his entire body was craving for that cup of steamy black coffee, even if it was a bad one. On his way to the espresso machine, he passed by Isa's office. The austere room wasn't very inviting. People usually had the impression they were sitting in an interrogation room instead of an office. But it was how Isa liked it. Freed from all distractions, it allowed her to be more efficient, and that was why people rarely saw a lot of papers or files lying on the desk. This time it was different. When he glanced through the open door, she seemed lost in thought. The papers and pictures were scattered over the desk, with Isa looking at them and, now and then picking up a few and putting them down again as if she were searching for something.

He hesitated, knowing she probably wanted to be left alone, but he entered anyway. It impressed him that she looked so fresh and alert, knowing she'd slept even less than he had.

"Hey," he said.

She looked up. For a moment, she almost didn't seem to recognize him and stared at him without really seeing him.

"Hey," she said softly, "you got home alright?"

He nodded.

"I'm just tired. Have you heard anything from Ingrid?"

"Nothing, but she sent pictures. What do you think this is?"

She pointed at a photograph displayed on the desk.

He came closer and for a second, she felt uncomfortable. It disturbed her that this insignificant gesture could bring such strong feelings to the surface, and she took a step back.

He picked up the photo and brought it closer to his face. Between the bones and the dirt, there was something more colorful.

"It looks like a piece of paper or cloth."

"Yes. Clothes or maybe something else? It reminds me of something."

"Of these Ikea plaid blankets ... you know the one everybody had ... with red and green stripes."

The pupils of her eyes widened, and she said: "Yes! That's what it is. They found bits and pieces among the remains. I wonder if someone rolled her up in it."

"Perhaps."

"We need to get a sample of this material."

"Why? What will this tell you?"

"You don't think the blanket can give us more information?"

"Dream on," he said, "they've probably sold millions of these things ... there is nothing unique about it."

She stared at the photo for a while.

"If he wrapped her in a blanket, it's a sign of remorse. A heartless killer would have just dumped her, but not him. He wanted to cover her up. It's an act of compassion."

The sound of Isa's cell phone startled them. While she took the call, Magnus made his way out of her office to the coffee machine. He poured himself the cup of hot coffee he so desperately needed.

"We have a problem," said a voice behind him. He jumped up and nearly dropped the cup. It was Isa, all agitated and almost out of breath.

"What's wrong?"

"It was Ingrid. It's not just one body. They found the bones of a least two more victims. And there are probably more ... many more."

* * *

The diener pushed the last gurney into the postmortem room. The top part was covered with a white canvas. With a particular deftness, acquired during years of practice, he removed it and pulled the remains, which they had put in a gray sealed bag, from the gurney onto the autopsy table. For a moment, he stood there looking at the other tables in front of him: two rows of four and five tables respectively, each covered with a gray bag. Small and large bags. Nine dead bodies. He felt a deep sadness. It was a feeling he rarely experienced these days. The humdrum work of every day had made him numb to the tragedy and suffering of the people he lay on these tables. The silence was interrupted by footsteps rushing down the hallway toward the room. They were in a haste. The woman and the man who entered the room were surprised to find him there.

"Where is Dr. Olsson?" the woman asked, then sighed and didn't wait for the answer to cross the room to glance at the tables with the remains.

"She'll join in a few minutes," the assistant said, showing no sign of the emotion he had experienced the moments before they had arrived. He continued folding the canvas and left the room when done. It didn't take long before Ingrid Olsson came in.

"Isa, Magnus, I didn't expect you to be that early."

"This is a high-profile case. The chief wants to see results. We need as much information as possible and as soon as possible."

Isa almost sounded out of breath.

With an almost annoying calm, Ingrid put on the latex gloves. She wasn't impressed with the way her friend put pressure on her.

"And I need more time. The condition of the bodies is very diverse from victim to victim. We have three bodies where only bones and some pieces of clothing are remaining and six where we can use soft tissue to identify them, but it's uncertain. I have sent samples to the lab for DNA typing, but it will take several days or even weeks. For the others, we can only use the clothes and other accessories for first identification. Bone DNA typing will take weeks and ideally, I need some DNA of female relatives to compare it to. Bones contain little nuclear DNA and then we need to use mitochondrial DNA, which is solely inherited from the maternal bloodline."

"Jesus, Ingrid, nine bodies! Are we dealing with a serial killer?"

"It's probably the same murderer. He wrapped all victims in the same kind of blanket, but the way they died is different. Two of them were shot in the back of the head, execution style. Some show signs of multiple fractures all over the body and in some bodies the bones were almost intact."

"Maybe several killers working together?" Isa asked.

"It's too early to make any claims," Ingrid said. She sighed and looked at her friend. Ingrid felt Isa was on an emotional rollercoaster ride. It would be difficult to curb her.

"It's rare," Magnus continued, "I wouldn't count on that theory."

Isa frowned and bit her lip.

"They are all female. Looking at the stage of the epiphyseal plates of the long bones, I'd say all of them were teenagers, roughly between twelve and eighteen years old."

"Any signs of sexual assault?" Magnus asked.

"I examined body number seven. It's the most intact in terms of tissue, organs, and bones. I found no traces of semen on clothes, pieces of the blanket and inside the body. It doesn't rule out sexual assault, but so far, I cannot confirm it."

"Body number seven is intact, you said?"

"Yes, we can probably do a facial reconstruction to identify her. This body has been buried there somewhere between six months and a year ago."

She started unzipping a bag and wanted to show the body, but Magnus stopped her. This was typically something his stomach didn't handle well, and if he could avoid it, he would.

* * *

Isa stood leaning against the wooden desk in her office. Magnus, sitting in the chair a meter away from the desk, flipped through the file, his eyes scanning every written line and every picture as if he were trying to memorize it. The other eight files were scattered over the desk.

"The killer has experience with the region. It's a dense, wooded area and the trail where the bodies were found, is not used very often by hikers. It's deserted, so he can easily bring in the bodies and bury them without the risk of being seen."

There was not much luminosity in her voice, and while talking she had difficulties to suppress a yawn. She turned and looked at the half cup of coffee standing between the papers. It was cold by now.

"But the risk is not zero, nor is the terrain easily accessible," Magnus said, eyes still fixed on the photos. "The question is: why wasn't he seen? Ever? Why could he get away with this for so many years? And why there?"

"Who says no one has seen him? He can be a local. Then it's not so unusual for him to hang out there."

"Like ... what's his name: Nordin?"

The strange statement surprised her. "Alexander Nordin? Maybe ... although he doesn't actually live there, and he is too young to be the killer as some bodies have been buried there for over twenty years."

"Did you do a background check on him?" he asked.

"That was clean. Nothing special. He has lived his entire life in Uppsala, where he went to school and university. He started his doctorate at the university more than five years ago but took a two-year sabbatical to take care of his father. He has no criminal record. Not even a parking ticket."

"What's wrong with the father?"

"I don't know, but his father died last year. His mother is still alive."

Magnus couldn't help it, but he disliked Alexander Nordin, from the first moment he had laid eyes on him, sitting at the table in the cabin, all naïve. He was competition. Competition for what? He didn't know. Isa? That story was over, or at least he was trying to convince himself of that. Yes, there was still passion. He hadn't ended the relationship because he no longer loved her. But that was why he couldn't bear the idea she would move on with someone else. He wanted her to desire him and no one else, even if he was unavailable. It was selfish, but he didn't care.

A silence followed as Isa sat down behind the desk. She turned to look at the photos and felt a sudden surge of fear and despair. For the first time in her career, a case of this magnitude had come her way. It was a great opportunity, but she didn't see it like that. Her superiors expected results quickly, which she felt she couldn't deliver. But it was usually the enormous pressure she self-imposed that blocked her. The slightest comment or question seemed to put her in a state of anxiety and prevented her from thinking rationally. She hadn't slept properly for days.

"Isa, we need help," Magnus said and closed the file before putting it on his lap, "it has been five days and we still don't have an idea what we're dealing with. No idea who the victims are, not even solid evidence this was done by the same killer."

"We'll get an additional five people coming in from Uppsala to help us," she said, "but there's nothing we can do until we get the DNA report."

Magnus got up.

"Do you mind if I take this file with me?"

"No, go ahead."

Superintendent Anders Larsen entered the office. He was a tall gray-haired man, an imposing appearance, close to retirement, but still as driven and passionate about his job as his first day on the police force.

"I just got off the phone with the superintendent in Uppsala. Those vultures are eager to get their hands on the case, but I got them to work with us. The additional people will probably arrive tomorrow on an indefinite assignment."

"Great, we can use all the help we can get."

"Magnus, Isa, I really need your full focus on this. People in Uppsala and Stockholm are getting nervous. So far, the media has no clue, but once this gets out, the pressure will be even ..."

He stopped halfway through the sentence. Isa saw him staring at a picture with increasing astonishment and confusion. He picked up the photo and continued to examine it.

"What's wrong?" Isa asked.

Magnus, on his way out, turned around and walked over to Anders.

"The Belgian girl," Anders whispered.

Isa and Magnus looked at each other in surprise.

"Do you know who it could be?"

"Yes, I recognize the necklace." He pointed at the golden pendant in the picture. It had a peculiar design of small rings centered around what looked to be a letter 'K'.

"It's an old case from the time I was working in Göteborg," he explained while the hand holding the picture started to shake. The emotions were overwhelming.

"We never managed to solve the case, although we had a suspect, but he was later acquitted."

"Göteborg?! My God, these victims come from all over the country," Isa said.

"Even from different countries. I think we've probably found the body of Katrien Jans, a fifteen-year-old Belgian girl who disappeared in

2002 in Göteborg while on vacation with her parents. We need to contact the Belgian authorities."

CHAPTER

3

THE RUGGED TEXTURE of the wood lay beneath her fingertips. Gently, she put the rest of her hand on the door. She waited and looked at the handle. For an instant, she hesitated, but she didn't want to enter. Never. That moment of fantastic ignorance had kept her going all these years, but it absorbed all of her energy. She slid down against the wall and sat on the floor for a while. The tears always came. Fifteen years. With every day, every hour, every second, she missed her more and more. Her life was an endless routine of sitting in front of her daughter's bedroom, crying, sometimes sleeping on the floor, and dreaming of times when she was still there. Everything else was pointless.

Downstairs, resting in his chair, André heard his wife crying, but he did nothing. He lived in another world he had created after his daughter disappeared. It was a universe of daydreams and painful memories, interrupted by watching TV and spending hours in the garage with his model planes and ships. He didn't talk to his wife anymore, not really. For years they had just been living side by side.

The doorbell rang. It startled him. They rarely had visitors anymore. He shuffled to the front door. Before opening it, he tucked in his shirt. It was stained with small spots of paint. Inspector Reynaert, accompanied by a young policewoman, stood before him. With the gray hair and the pronounced wrinkles on his forehead and around the eyes, he looked older than the last time they had met in the Leuven police station. An achingly long second, there was utter silence.

"Inspector, what brings you here? Do you have news ... after all these years?"

His mind started racing.

There must be ... otherwise, why would he visit them?

"Can we enter?" the inspector asked.

"Yes, of course," André said and opened the door wider, allowing them to come in.

It was a simple terraced house near the center of Leuven. Thirty years ago, it had been just them, newlyweds with no children. They had dreamed of something bigger, more modern with a large garden for the children, but gradually they had appreciated the neighborhood, the vivacity, and juvenility of the students living in the area. And after a while, they hadn't seen it as a temporary stop anymore, but as their home. A place that suddenly didn't feel like a home anymore after Katrien's disappearance.

He offered the police officers a seat on the living room sofa. Anticipation tingled through him like tiny sparks of electricity as he saw the inspector open his mouth, almost in slow motion, and say, "Where is your wife?"

Why couldn't he just say what he had to say?

"She's upstairs. Shall I get her?"

"Yes, if you don't mind."

In the meantime, his wife Liesbeth had come down. There was a sickening feeling in her stomach as she slowly walked into the room and sat down in the chair next to her husband.

The inspector sighed, took a photo from the pocket of his jacket, and handed it to André.

"Do you recognize the necklace?"

The photograph showed the golden chain they had found near the first body.

"Yes, yes," Liesbeth shouted, "this is the pendant I designed for her and gave her when she was twelve." She pulled the photograph from her husband's hands. The rush of excitement dazed her, and she could barely breathe.

"Please sit down, Mrs. Jans," the policewoman tried to calm her.

Liesbeth looked at them. Why weren't they more excited? Why so serious? And suddenly she knew. She knew it was not the message she had expected. In that split second, all hope was gone. Forever. The photo fell to the floor.

The inspector took a deep breath. He knew the family well. He had lived with them for years through their pain and suffering. In the background he heard the ticking of the wall clock. Tick, Tock. Why had he never heard it? Had it been there before? It was like the ticking of a bomb in the chilling silence before it went off.

"The Swedish police have sent us this photograph. They found the necklace near ... a body they found in the woods north of Gävle."

There was an awkward silence. He continued, without taking his eyes off them. "We don't know for sure it's Katrien, but everything ... the necklace, the pieces of clothing, indicates ... it's her. I am very sorry."

At every word, he saw them cringe. Liesbeth held on to the arm of the chair. It was like someone had thrown her under a truck. It crushed her with an incredible, unmatched power that left hardly any room for recovery.

"Where is Gävle?" André muttered.

"About 500 kilometers north of Göteborg."

"We weren't even looking in the right area ...," his voice broke. Once the tears came, there was no way to stop the flow. Liesbeth got up, kneeled next to him, caressed his hand, and put her head on his shoulder.

"Why, why?" he stammered.

She kissed him softly.

"Shh ... we finally know," Liesbeth whispered as she wiped away his tears. Her fingers were so soft. She felt the lines of his face for the first time in years.

"How did she die?" Liesbeth asked.

"We don't know yet. It will take a while before they can tell you what really happened to her. The forensic lab also needs some DNA from you, Mrs. Jans, to confirm that this is truly Katrien."

She nodded.

"André, Liesbeth, I am so sorry. I wish I had better news. If you need help, please let us know and we can refer you to a psychologist."

"I'd like to see her," André blurted.

Inspector Reynaert and the policewoman exchanged a brief glance.

"That's not a good idea," the inspector said.

* * *

July 2002. It was going to be a great summer. The family Jans planned to take a long vacation, traveling through Northern Europe by car: Norway, Sweden, and Finland. André, a brand manager, was married for sixteen years to high school teacher Liesbeth. They had three children: Katrien,

Thomas, and Emma. All teenagers. Katrien was fifteen, a beautiful young girl with dark brown hair and blue eyes. Although she was in that difficult age, trying to find her place in the world, she was close to her parents and siblings. She played guitar, sang in the church choir and was popular at school. She dreamed of becoming a medical doctor. Her brother Thomas was thirteen, still a playful boy who loved football and hanging out with his friends. Emma was the youngest, just finished primary school. She admired her big sister and wanted to be just like her, but as befits sisters they often had their fallouts and quarrels over - what Emma only realized later - trivial things.

After two weeks of driving through Norway, they arrived in Göteborg, Sweden's second largest city, on the west coast.

An avid fan of ancient warships and history, André decided to visit the Maritiman, a floating maritime museum on the Göta Älv river. The children didn't like the idea, and it took time to convince them. That day, it was sunny and comfortably warm. The museum was crowded with people enjoying the beautiful weather. Moving from one vessel to the other, André and Liesbeth had quickly lost sight of the children who were scattered across different ships and boats. But they hadn't been worried. Everywhere they saw families with children, young and old, and their laughter and noise made them feel safe. They saw Thomas walking in front, while the girls had taken the lead and were way ahead of them. Thomas had been very reluctant to come, but he enjoyed it. After a few hours, Liesbeth decided it was time to move on if they wanted to see more of the city itself. Thomas was there, but they hadn't seen the girls for a while and André walked around to fetch them. He found Emma near the gift shop, planning to buy postcards for her friends. Katrien was gone. He did the entire tour a few times while Liesbeth was waiting with Thomas and Emma in the gift shop. When he still couldn't find her, he frantically started running through the different vessels, calling her name. It took another two hours for the museum staff to call the police. Few witnesses had seen the dark-haired girl, and no one could remember seeing her leave. They put an inexperienced inspector on the case. In the days after the disappearance, they also investigated the residents of the neighborhood, without luck. She had just disappeared.

The family left Sweden a month and a half after the disappearance. Days turned into months and years, and the world seemed to have forgotten about Katrien until the case was reopened five years later. Inspector Anders Larsen inherited the cold case. In the five-hundred-page long file, his interest was sparked by the testimony of a woman who had seen one of the museum staff members, one Josip Radić, arguing with the young girl.

Josip's parents were Croatian immigrants who had come to Sweden in the mid-1980s. Josip was a smart kid but had experienced problems getting accepted at school, and by the end of high school he got involved in drugs and petty crime. The police arrested him at nineteen for robbery. It was a wake-up call. After that, he promised his parents to turn his life around. When he got out of prison, he went back to school and found a part-time job at the museum. He met Lisa during evening classes and immediately fell in love with her. They got engaged six months later. On the day of Katrien's disappearance, his life was back on track. Five years later, married, with a young son and a second child on the way, he no longer worked at the museum. He was an accountant for a big pharmaceutical company in Helsingborg. Life was good, but everything changed when the police questioned him about Katrien Jans. That day, five years before, he had confronted her about damaging museum property. He had been impatient and easily irritated, and their conversation had rapidly escalated to a shouting match. But she had run away, and he hadn't seen her after that. Anders didn't believe him, as some witnesses had seen him running after the girl, which he denied. A month after they reopened the case, the investigators searched his home and found evidence of child pornography on his computer. With no sign of Katrien and only circumstantial evidence, they couldn't prosecute him, but the damage to his reputation was done. He was fired, lost his wife, children, and home. In 2017, he was only a shadow of the man he had once been. He spent most of his time drinking and dwelling on the past, in a small apartment in Uppsala.

* * *

"Clara Persson, disappeared June 1987 ... Anna Falk, December 1990 ..." While calling out the names, she put the photographs of the girls on the magnetic board. Beautiful girls, smiling, with so many dreams and hopes for the future ... a future that was brutally taken away from them. The days before, Isa had stared at the photos for hours. The pictures had only been a snapshot, the capture of a brief moment in their existence. Maybe they hadn't been happy at all, maybe they hadn't aspired to any glorious dreams. But she couldn't think like that. This idealized image of them was all that remained and would live on in the minds of everyone involved. Even their family and friends had polished the rough edges of their personalities and had forgotten the conflicts, fights, disagreements, and nuisances that seemed so futile in hindsight.

Nearly a month after the gruesome discovery, the forensic investigation team had finally identified each of the victims. It had been a wild ride with many heated discussions between the forensic team who didn't want to be pressured into making statements and conclusions, and the team of investigators who wanted quick answers. But there were no quick answers. It was shocking to learn that the victims had been so spread in time: a serial killer who had been active for thirty years, right under their noses, and they had no idea until now.

She continued: "Ida Nilsson, January 1992. Anna Berg, January 1995. Katrien Jans, July 2002. Lise Ekström, June 2004. Ella Nyman, January 2008. Elin Dahlberg, May 2010, and Stina Jonasson in September 2016."

She turned and looked at the twelve people in the room. Each of them was a senior investigator tasked with solving these murders and bringing the killer to justice. A team of extra police officers had been provided from Uppsala. Now they clustered in the back of the room. Their integration had been difficult. From the beginning, their haughty attitude and prejudices toward the Gävle team caused the friction between the two teams. Isa thought they were of little use, and she didn't trust them.

"We believe these are the victims of the same killer. Someone buried them close together. Each of the bodies was wrapped in the same type of blanket. But the cause of death is not the same. Three victims were shot in the head: Clara Persson, Anna Falk, and Lise Ekström. How the other victims were killed, is still unclear, but many of them showed signs of beating, malnutrition, and starvation. We believe the murderer probably abducts his victims, holds them captive and abuses them for years."

Magnus stood at the back, lost in thought. He didn't notice how her eyes narrowed and the brows were molded in a deep frown. These days he prompted these feelings of annoyance in her a lot. Isa wondered what was going on. Something was occupying his mind, but he hadn't confided in her and that upset her even more.

Everything was going too slow. The Uppsala guys would certainly take the case out of their hands if they didn't show results soon. She continued the briefing.

"The first abduction dates to 1987. Clara Persson, thirteen years old, disappeared on the last day of school. She left school around noon but never arrived home. The family was living in Uppsala. Neighbors, family friends, school friends, teachers were questioned, but they never arrested a suspect. It has been a cold case up to now. Lars, Berger, I want you to take this case. The parents have died, but the brother and sister of Clara still live in Uppsala. I want you to take the second case too: Anna Falk, a sixteen-year-old."

She pointed at the photograph on the board.

"She disappeared at a New Year's party she attended with her brother in Stockholm. Also, a cold case that was never solved. Plenty of witnesses saw the girl leave the party, but no one could tell the investigators where she had gone. The family also lives in Uppsala."

"Have the families been informed?" Lars asked.

"Yes, of course." She hesitated before continuing: "For most, it was actually a relief ... to know after so many years what had happened to them."

"What about the blankets?" a young woman asked.

"Good point," Isa said, "Ikea sold these blankets between 1990 and 1995, and they were very popular. It's not possible to find out who bought these particular plaids, but it might indicate Clara was still alive in 1990 as pieces of the cloth have been found between her remains. We believe the killer may have abducted Anna after Clara's death to replace her."

"Nina," she turned to the young woman again, "Elin Dahlberg is your case. She went missing after visiting her aunt."

Nina nodded, and it was clear she would dive into the problem with all the determination and fierceness she had shown in her previous assignments.

Magnus, woken up from his reverie, walked to the front and took over: "Janus, Herbert, the Ida Nilsson and Anna Berg cases are yours."

The two young men were sitting in front and seemed very pleased when chief inspector Magnus Wieland called their names, like little schoolboys who just got complimented by the teacher. Isa didn't like them. They were always sucking up to Anders and Magnus.

"Both girls, living in Stockholm, were fourteen when they went missing. They never came home after school. In Ida's case, witnesses saw her get off the bus and walk in the direction of her home, which was just two blocks away from the bus stop. She never arrived there. The police interrogated a man, who had been driving around the area in a rather suspicious manner, but he was released later."

"The case Anna Berg is something else," Isa said. "Most of you don't remember, but this was a huge media circus. At least that's how I remember it. I was a little younger than the girl. Anna's father was a very influential lawyer, who had plans to go into local politics. He put quite some pressure on the police to find Anna, and eventually a suspect was arrested and convicted, although the girl was never found. To this day, the perpetrator continues to claim his innocence."

"So, a case of wrongful imprisonment," Nina pointed out.

"Maybe ... for sure it's a sensitive case."

Isa was exhausted and leaned against the wall. Emotionally, this took a much heavier toll than she expected. Her entire body felt empty of energy and excitement. But this was not the time to falter. The people at the back would be all too happy if they failed. She cleared her throat and continued: "Magnus and I will take the Jans' case and Stina Jonasson. Nils and Sara are handling the remaining two cases."

Magnus said nothing. He was off in his own world again.

Magnus, damn it, do I need to do this alone?

But the message had come across loud and clear. The intensity of her gaze needed no words. They were in this together, as a team. Not the team she wanted, but a team altogether.

Magnus strolled over to the board. For a moment he stared at the photos. Girls with similar features: dark long hair and blue eyes.

"Lise Ekström went missing in June 2004 after visiting a friend. They found her bike two weeks later in a deserted field on the outskirts of Kristianstad. And Ella Nyman never showed up at a party in 2008. She was sixteen. According to her friends, she was really looking forward to the party that would be a joint birthday celebration for three other girls and herself. She left that evening at eight to go to her friend's place, but never showed up."

He pointed at the photographs.

"All these girls deserve justice and have their murderer found. We need to be successful, there is no room for mistakes. Isa and I count on all of you!"

After a pause - to give the words a certain flair of drama - he started again: "You will report to inspector Lindström and myself. We will have a first read-out tomorrow at ten. Make sure you have something."

* * *

Isa was still leaning against the wall after all the men and women had left the room. She couldn't shake the intense feeling of panic and fear. The last few days, she had been cycling through incredible ups and downs, not knowing how to control it.

"What's wrong?" Magnus said.

He stood before her. His face was so close to hers. She pulled him closer and kissed him. Not a tender kiss. No, it was wild and desperate. She wanted more than a kiss. At first, he didn't push her away, but then he quickly realized it was wrong.

"Is, I..."

She caressed his lips and neck, and slowly her hands moved down to his loin.

"Isa, stop!"

He pushed her away.

She, heated by the moment, stared at him in disbelief.

"You don't mean that," she said, "I need you and you ... want me."

She took his head in her hands and kissed him again. The men she had picked up in nightclubs over the last few months could never match him. Their names had been erased the moment she had let them out the door the next morning.

"I am here ... but as your colleague. We really can't. They need me ...

at home."

She pushed him away and turned her back on him. The humiliation. The disappointment. What had she done wrong? Why would he prefer that plain nobody over her?

"Is ... I ..." The words were failing him.

"I can't do this, I don't know where to start," she whispered.

"Are you talking about the case?"

She didn't answer.

"Of course, you can. You've done this before. Isa, what's wrong?"

She didn't know. Everything was so intertwined with her personal life. She longed for someone ... she longed for him. Why couldn't it be him? The break-up had been so devastatingly difficult. How had it gone wrong? One moment they had made plans to move in together, and the next day he had announced he was going back to his wife. The stability in her life was gone, causing her to fall back in a series of meaningless relationships, periods of doubt and moments when she could hardly control the clamor in her head. Magnus knew how to temper these swings, but he was no longer there to contain her erratic behavior and those feelings that sometimes unexpectedly rushed in and overwhelmed her.

She looked at him and said: "You need to take charge of this investigation. I'm not sure if I can really take this responsibility."

She waited for a sign from his side. Finally, he said, "The families of these girls need you ... us. We work on this together. But you are the boss. You can do this."

He was right. She had to get her act together. Her problems were so insignicant compared to the agony of the people those girls had left behind.

When he saw her leave the police station that evening, Magnus realized they had never really talked about the break-up. He had never told her about Toby. How guilty and helpless he felt. He owed her an explanation, but how could he tell her she was the one he loved and that his son had been the reason for choosing Sophie over her? Did he love his wife? Not really, not anymore. He felt responsible for them. But Isa wouldn't understand.

CHAPTER

4

THE NEXT MORNING, Isa and Magnus drove to Enköping to visit
the parents of Stina Jonasson. They did the two-hour drive to the
small city north-west of Stockholm in complete silence. Neither of them
wanted to rake up the unpleasant conversation of the previous day. While
Isa drove south on the E4, Magnus thought about his son. It wasn't going
well. His recovery was slow, and in the last weeks there had been no
progress at all. Trapped in the hell of his own mind, Toby desperately
tried to escape the isolation, but he couldn't. Sophie was still reluctant to
visit him. She didn't understand his behavior. The world he tried to
describe with his faltered speech was too terrifying.

They were out to get him. Yes, they would come for him, and she was part of the plot. He couldn't trust her. She wasn't his mom. She looked like her, but she was an imposter, and she was controlling his mind.

How could she ever connect with her son? She couldn't hug or touch him. No, everything about him scared her. The look he gave her, the mumbling, the sudden verbal lash-outs, the endless repetitive movements. He misinterpreted the simplest word in his twisted beliefs. So, it usually took her a mere ten minutes between entering Toby's room and storming out of the hospital to get home as fast as possible.

Everything was falling apart, bit by bit, slowly but unquestionably. Magnus couldn't fix the relationship with his wife, no matter how hard he tried. She had forgiven him, she said, but the words didn't match the way she'd been acting lately. Their love life was non-existent and every time he mentioned Isa's name, he saw how she froze and tried to hide in the silence, which had become a comfortable way not to confront anything. That silence was the worst. He wanted her to take a swing at him, to fight with him, he wanted to see and feel the passion. He wanted to know if there was anything left to fight for, but there was nothing.

* * *

Isa parked the car in front of the building. It was a quiet street with three-story apartment blocks on one side, in colors alternating between white and light pink. White balconies, many of them with satellite dishes and occasionally one or two garden chairs. On the other side of the street, trees, partially covered in snow, and several small garage boxes. The Jonasson family lived on the second floor of the building where Isa had left the car. A small woman opened the door, mid-forties, medium-long brown hair with streaks of gray, and a kind but sad face. A warm glow met them as they entered the apartment. It was a pleasant contrast with the icy wind blowing from the north. Temperatures would drop significantly in the coming days, and more snow was coming.

She had expected them. On the table stood three cups and a plate full of cupcakes, tartlets, and chocolates. While Mrs. Jonasson poured the coffee, Isa skimmed her gaze over the place. The room was tidy, maybe too tidy. Except for the photographs of Stina, it felt impersonal. Stina had been an only child and Isa could imagine that these days her mother's main preoccupation, having no job and plenty of leisure time, was to keep the apartment clean and organized. The room radiated no joy. The photos were important. They occupied a prominent place in the interior. It was nostalgia and grief, but at least they were there. For many families, it took years, sometimes decades before they could look again at pictures of the children they had lost, or even think about them, without the overwhelming and debilitating pain that overshadowed every aspect of their lives.

"I am sorry we need to talk about this again, but since we know now that Stina is one of the victims, we need to get as much information as possible. It might seem unnecessary to you, but we have to make sure we overlooked nothing."

"That's okay. As long as you find the person who did this ..."

Her voice broke. Eyes glassy with tears, about to roll down, she took a deep breath. The walls, which she so desperately wanted to keep up, were about to collapse. She couldn't let that happen, not now, not in front of them.

The pause brought some relief.

"Is your husband here?" Magnus asked.

"No, he's at work. I thought one of us would be enough and ... I don't think he can handle another conversation about Stina. He ... he doesn't talk much about her these days."

"That's fine, Mrs. Jonasson. Thank you for having us here."

Isa continued: "The Gävle police are officially in charge of the investigation, but we are working with the various police departments in Uppsala, Göteborg, Stockholm, and Kristianstad."

Mrs. Jonasson nodded her head in confirmation.

"Stina disappeared on 7 September 2016. Can you walk us through the events of that day?"

"She had started seventh grade a few weeks earlier. That day ... Wednesday, it was a Wednesday. My husband couldn't drive her to school and pick her up in the afternoon, so she took her bike. And I was okay with that ..."

The smothered tears came back as soon as she started to talk about Stina: "We know she arrived safely at school, and she was there until noon but coming back she passed by her friend's house. I got a call from her around noon to check if that was okay. She'd be back home around five. When she was still not home at seven, I got worried, and I went to her friend's place. When they told me she had left two hours earlier, I panicked and called the police."

She stopped again because the emotions were too intense, and she had a hard time keeping herself from crying.

Be strong! These people don't want to see your tears.

"Mrs. Jonasson, please take your time," Isa said.

She tasted the salt of the tears on her lips as they ran down her face, and the slight stutter was barely noticeable as she took deep breaths. It was so painful to watch the mother break down before their eyes. Magnus could almost feel how her muscles tightened to keep the sobbing in check, her fingers clutched in the armrests of the chair, so tightly as if she were looking for a physical pain more grandiose than the emotional one, she was already experiencing.

"They found your daughter's cell phone a few hundred meters away from her friend's house, next to her bike. It was too damaged to recover any information. As far as we understand, few witnesses saw her that day. In the days before her disappearance, did you notice anything strange, out of place ..."

There was no reaction. Mrs. Jonasson saw his lips move and heard the sounds come out, but it was as if there was a delay in processing the information.

"Mrs. Jonasson?"

"Uh ... like what exactly?" Mrs. Jonasson asked.

"Like strangers hanging around the neighborhood, unfamiliar cars parked along the street ..."

She took a moment to think about this. Everything seemed to go in slow motion. Then she shook her head and whispered: "No, nothing really comes to mind."

"Stina didn't mention anything was out of the ordinary?"

"No, she didn't," her mother answered.

"How was she doing in school?"

"No high-flyer, but an average student. We had concerns about her choice for the natural sciences program, but sixth grade went unexpectedly well, and she was very motivated. Sara, her best friend, has helped her a lot."

"And did she have a boyfriend?"

She shook her head.

"Mothers are always the last to know, but she was still so childish, naïve and innocent in the way she approached things."

Isa stared at Stina's photo on the table next to the sofa. The teenager was smiling and had her arm around another girl. It was summer. Clear blue sky and in the background trees, forest and something that resembled a lake.

Stina had done something unexpected the day of her disappearance. It hadn't been her daily routine. How could the kidnapper have known she was visiting a friend? He must have followed her or ...

"Mrs. Jonasson, why did Stina visit her friend's house? Why didn't she come home right away?"

For a moment, she stared at Isa. Yes, why didn't Stina come home? And why did she, her mother, not know?

"When she called me that day, I didn't ask. I assumed it was because of a school assignment. I think Sara had mentioned something like that to the police officers. Why? Do you think something is wrong?"

"But she never told you beforehand?"

What was this? Did they accuse her of something? Of neglecting her daughter? Of not showing interest in her?

"No, I just told you."

A gnawing feeling of irritation got hold of her.

"Is this Sara?" Isa continued and pointed at the other girl in the photo.

"Yes, that's Sara," Mrs. Jonasson confirmed.

"Did Stina do this often?"

"No ... yes, I mean. Sara and Stina were best friends since first grade and they literally did everything together, including all school assignments as they were in the same class. It was nothing unusual."

"They had the same interests?"

Mrs. Jonasson confirmed the statement.

"Stina had a Facebook account?"

"Yes, like most young girls and boys," the mother said.

"And she was often online?"

"Not more or less than any other child, I guess."

"Do you know if she had met new friends online?"

"I don't know, but we often had discussions about this. I tried to warn her not to trust everything that is posted on the internet. Do you think she met the wrong friends?"

"We can't rule it out," Isa said and leaned back before dropping a bomb on the mother: "One more thing: how is your marriage? Any tensions?"

The irritation suddenly went through the roof, and Mrs. Jonasson jumped up.

"I don't see how this has anything to do with my daughter's

disappearance and murder," she replied.

"I want to check if Stina would have had a reason to run away from home."

Mrs. Jonasson's breathing was fast and shallow, and with her fists clenched tightly, she screamed: "How dare you? Of course not! Stina was happy. We are all very happy ..."

She stopped. There was no Stina anymore. They had taken her beautiful and innocent daughter. How hard she tried, she couldn't cope with that.

How many times she had opened the window and imagined what it would be like to jump. It was only two stories high. She would surely survive. But maybe her husband would finally realize she wasn't as strong as she pretended to be, that she needed help, that she needed him. Her marriage wasn't strong enough to survive this. Her husband secluded himself more and more, while she wanted to talk about Stina, think about her, even though it was painful. They had been at a different pace in processing the drama. She had so many doubts and fears about what her life would be in the years to come. The progress she had made over the past year in accepting her daughter's death was slipping away at a ferocious pace, and she couldn't stop it.

* * *

"What do you think?" Magnus asked as he opened the door of the car.

"The mother knows nothing. She believes Stina was a good, zealous, and innocent girl."

"But you don't?"

Magnus saw how she put the key in the ignition.

"No, girls that age typically have secrets, usually little secrets, that they don't want to share with their moms. But what if the secret is much bigger than that? I think the only one who knows is her friend Sara. She lives close by. We can visit her. School is done. She should be home."

"Why do you think the girls were lying?"

"Just a hunch," she said and started the engine.

It took only five minutes to get to Sara's house. The family lived in a detached house with a small garden on a quiet street where many families with young children lived. School had just ended and even with the low temperatures, many children were playing outside in the snow. This confirmed Isa's suspicion. It was difficult to go unnoticed here. If Stina had visited her friend the day she disappeared, many people - especially children - should have seen her. But where did she go then? Why did she tell her mother she was at her friend's place?

Sara opened the door. In many ways, she resembled Stina: blue eyes, brown hair she wore in a simple bun for convenience, same posture, and gentle features.

"Sara Norberg?"

The dark-haired girl with braces nodded.

"Is your mother or father home?"

"Yes, mom is home," she said.

"Can you get her, please?" Isa asked.

The girl disappeared, leaving the door open. The interior of the house was modern, white, with an abundance of light. A slim, tall woman came toward them. Sara had clearly inherited much of her mother's good looks.

"Yes?"

"Mrs. Norberg, my name is inspector Isa Lindström, and this is inspector Magnus Wieland. We are investigating the murder of Stina Jonasson, and we want to ask your daughter some questions. Is this okay?"

"It's Ms. Bergqvist. My husband and I are divorced."

She wasn't good at hiding the glimpses of anger and frustration over her failed marriage.

"Ms. Bergqvist, can we come in?"

"Can I see some identification first?" she asked with a stern voice.

She studied the badges carefully and then gave them back.

"Okay, but Sara has already told your colleagues everything she knows," she opened the door and let them in, "... though, it's awful to hear they found Stina. Sara is all shook up about it."

She invited them into the living room. The house was in chaos, with books and clothes lying on the tables and chairs. It was difficult to maneuver between the many cardboard boxes scattered around the hallway and living room. Ms. Bergqvist cleared a few chairs at the big table for the inspectors to sit down.

"Sorry, we're in the midst of moving ... the divorce, you know? We're going back to Uppsala. Would you like something to drink?"

She quickly got up.

"No, Ms. Bergqvist, we don't want to take up too much of your time, but can we talk to Sara?"

Ms. Bergqvist walked to the doorway and called her daughter. The young girl came in and sat down next to her mother at the big dining table.

"I know this is tough, Sara, but we need to ask you a few questions about Stina. I think you can give us important information to find her murderer."

Isa paused and looked at her carefully. The girl wiggled back and forth in the chair.

"I've told everything I know," she said softly.

"Are you sure, Sara? You were best friends, right? I think she may have entrusted you with things she wouldn't have told anyone else."

She continued to observe the young girl. Sara avoided eye contact with the inspectors and continue to stare at the floor.

"Sara, I think you know more. Help us find out what happened to your friend!"

No reaction.

Should she say something? Stina ... stupid Stina ... why did she put her in this situation?

Isa thought it was time for more creative measures.

"We found the Facebook account."

Magnus turned to his colleague, puzzled by the words she had just said. What was she up to?

But the words had been very effective. The girl looked up. The fear in her eyes was striking.

"Sara?" Her mother couldn't believe it. Her daughter had kept secrets.

"It was just a joke," Sara yelled in panic, tears rolling down.

"Sara, it's okay. Just tell us everything from the start."

Isa's voice reassured her and gave her the impression that everything was not as bad as she expected. This secret had weighed so heavily on her peace of mind; it was a relief it would be out in the open now.

"It was just fun," Sara started, wiping the tears from her face. Her mother, still flabbergasted, was sitting next to her. But the silence was pretense. The nails of her fingers, hidden under the table, were about to pierce through the flesh of her palms, her lips so tightly pressed together, trying to prevent her from letting go of the held-back frustration and disappointment.

"It was just fun," Sara repeated. "At least we thought it would be fun. Stina came up with the idea of creating a fake account on Facebook, to chat with boys ... older boys. We pretended to be eighteen. But it was disappointing. Most guys were really stupid, and they were sending idiotic messages. I wanted to quit, but then Stina became all obsessed about a guy who had been texting her regularly. I think she loved the compliments he gave, and the way he wrote about her ... which was actually sweet. She showed me a few of the messages."

"Do you know his name?"

"No ... sorry."

"And when was this?"

"Two months before she disappeared."

"Did she have plans to meet him?"

Sara sighed and then continued in a soft voice: "Yes ..."

She bowed her head. Why hadn't she stopped her that day? She knew something was wrong.

"Yes, they had agreed to meet after school the day she disappeared."

"Where?"

"I don't know. She said it was a secret."

"So, you never saw her that day?"

"Except at school, no ... she never came here. I tried to call her, and I sent her messages, but she never replied."

"Sara, how could you ..."

"Ms. Bergqvist, please," Isa intervened.

Her mother couldn't hide it anymore. Frustration, but worst of all was the disappointment.

"How did they communicate?"

"Facebook Messenger."

"Which account was she using?"

"But I thought you knew," Sara stammered.

It had been a trick, a stupid trick to get her to talk. And she had fallen for it. But the feeling of relief was good. It had been such an incredible burden. For a while she had told herself that it wasn't her fault, that it hadn't been her responsibility to tell the police, but the more time passed and Stina still hadn't been found, she knew she had made a mistake. Maybe they could have found and saved her. But it had been too late.

"Her account name was Sara243," Sara said, "that was my idea."

"Thank you, Sara. You helped us a lot."

She touched Sara's hand. With eyelashes wet with tears and a red-stained face, the girl smiled. It was a faint smile. The nagging unrest that had been spooking through her head for the past year was still there. Was she responsible for her friend's death by keeping quiet?

* * *

It was dark when they left the house, and it was now quieter outside than when they had arrived. Only the dim light of the lampposts illuminated the road and sidewalk. Thin snowflakes fluttered down. It felt like the temperature had dropped ten degrees. Isa pulled her coat tight over her chest and neck and tried to pull up the collar to protect her ears.

"Let me drive," Magnus said and took the key out of her hands. She let him.

As they hit the road home, they both sat in silence for a while, reflecting about what had just happened. The snow was coming down more heavily than when they had left Enköping. A few times he felt the car slip, but he managed to keep it on the road without too many problems. He was an excellent driver. That was why he was behind the steering wheel. Isa was too reckless, and it wouldn't be the first time he demanded to stop the vehicle and let him drive.

"This was interesting," he started.

"Yes. The timeline is all messed up. He didn't kidnap her around 5 p.m., but hours before. We need to get our IT team on the account. Though, ... I'm not sure we'll find anything. If the killer is skilled enough, he probably covered his tracks."

"Are we sure it's the murderer?" Magnus answered. "Maybe it's just a boy ..."

"Do you really believe that?"

"No," he said, "I don't believe in coincidences. Still, it's interesting because if this guy is our man, he's a serial killer, active for over thirty years, who uses social media to lure his victims."

"Somehow, I feel he has done this before. I mean, this is in line with his modus operandi, just a different time, a different medium."

"You're probably right."

"Maybe they knew him?"

"A route worth considering," Magnus said as they headed back to Gävle.

CHAPTER

5

MATS NORMAN WAS a good-looking man in his sixties, distinguished and charming. He strongly reminded Isa of someone, but she couldn't immediately put her finger on it. He had invited them to his beautiful house on the outskirts of Uppsala. The villa was impressive. It had a majestic driveway lined with trees, now bare and covered in snow, but you could imagine that in springtime the colors and scents of the blossoms would be magnificent, a real treat for all senses. On the right, behind the trees, was a small pond. The garden was enormous, mostly comprising grass. The house itself was two stories high, painted white, with a large gabled dormer in the center, and the wooden panels of the outer walls were still visible, which gave it a typically rustic look.

His wife was absent as she was visiting friends and family up north. These days, his mother-in-law was not well, being in and out of the hospital. But he didn't mind being alone. The "me-time" was precious. Since his retirement, there were small frictions between him and his wife when it came to the household, he laughed. Nothing serious, but enough to get his irritation levels up now and then.

"So, my dear inspectors, I think I know why you're here," he smiled as he sat down in the comfortable chair near the electric fireplace. The style of the room was surprisingly modern, with lots of black and white accents, a theme that continued throughout the entire house. The many pictures and framed certificates displayed on the walls gave it a certain status. The older man noticed how Magnus had been scanning the room.

"I was a physics professor at the Uppsala University. I am retired now, but sometimes I still act as an advisor when asked by my former colleagues."

"Impressive," Magnus said.

"Professor ...," Isa started.

"Please call me Mats," he said.

His smile was very pleasant, and a little teasing. He must have had many female admirers in his younger years, she thought, and even now, he could probably charm the skirt off most women.

Hot teachers and teenage crushes. Isa knew all about it. Looking back at her own teenage indiscretions, the silly and humiliating things she had done to get the attention of a handsome teacher, she wished she could erase them from her memories.

"Mats," she corrected, "as you may ... and obviously already know, we have discovered nine bodies in the woods near Sandviken."

"Nine?" Mats asked, terrified. "They told me it was only one body. Nine, my God!"

He looked genuinely upset.

"Who told you?" Isa asked.

"Irene Nordin, Alexander's mother. She doesn't live that far away, and she's good friends with my wife. We spent many summers together in those cottages in Sandviken. Ah, sweet memories! I've seen Alexander grow up there. Brilliant kid, so intelligent! But sad though ..."

His expression suddenly changed and became more serious.

Alexander Nordin. Yes, that was it. He looked a lot like Alexander Nordin. It was the way he talked and moved. Those same blue eyes.

"Why sad?" Magnus asked.

"Peter Nordin, Alexander's father ... he had mental problems. Depression ... or was it bipolar disease? Anyway, it weighed heavily on the family. I can't say I ever saw Alexander and his mother truly happy. There was always some sadness hanging over them. Irene was afraid Peter would hurt himself or his family. She took care of him to the end. Brave woman ... though he finally killed himself. Perhaps for the best."

Magnus kept looking at the wall. The pictures were focal points to distract him from what Mats was telling.

Keep staring at them! Don't let this get to you.

This felt so personal. These people had gone through such an ordeal for so many years, and it had almost destroyed them. That was confronting. What about his own family? Would they survive his son's illness?

"He killed himself?" Isa asked.

"Yes, last year. Alexander found him. He hung himself from the handrail of the staircase in the entry hall. The boy was devastated."

Boy? That was a strange way of referring to someone who was thirty and way beyond being a boy. Alexander Nordin was a man, a very fine man. She had hardly been able to get that handsome appearance out of her mind.

"Alexander put his Ph.D. on hold to help his mother take care of his father, but I think it was just impossible to help him. My wife and I went to the funeral. It was just so sad."

A moment of silence seemed right to all the people in the room.

"These are all your children?" Isa finally asked, while pointing at a photo on the mantelpiece.

In the photo, they could see three boys and one girl. The girl and two of the boys were teenagers, while there was an age difference with the much younger boy who tried to hide behind the girl.

"Yes," he answered.

"Four, wow," she called out.

"No, three," he corrected himself, "oh, I see you're looking at that photograph."

He got up and took it off the mantelpiece. He pointed to the children in the photograph and said: "This is Michael, a corporate lawyer, my daughter Tessa who lives in the US – she's a physics professor at Stanford - and my youngest Simon, a jazz musician. He was a lousy student, but ever since he was a child, he was so obsessed with music ... and now he travels the world with his band."

"And the young boy?"

"That is actually Alexander Nordin. The photo was taken more than twenty years ago ... in Sandviken. The children loved to go there. How time flies by!"

He looked at it again, and an elusive melancholy appeared on his face. Gently and with great precision, he put the photo back. It took him a few trials to get the picture exactly where he wanted it to be.

"Prof. Norman, we came here to ask you some questions about the cabin," Magnus continued. He wanted to get out of there as soon as possible, and he didn't care too much for useless chatter about family and summer vacations.

"Yes, of course," he turned around and faced the inspectors again.

"In all the years you've stayed in Sandviken, do you remember seeing anything strange ... unknown people with a particular interest for the area?

Have you seen anyone late in the evening wandering around, acting suspiciously?"

"God ... not really, the summers ... ten years ago, were always so lively. The area is popular. I would say it's challenging to kill and bury young girls without being seen."

He got up and paced the room.

"Sorry, my back ... you know. I need to get up now and then. As I wanted to say: we were four families who always spent at least one month together in Sandviken: the Nordin family, Olav Bergqvist and ... what was the name again: Radić or something. A Slovak ... no, Croatian family."

Isa quickly exchanged a glance with her partner. Josip Radić, the suspect in the Katrien Jans case! Was this family?

"Is there something wrong?" the old man asked.

"No, please continue."

"Nothing special. The Croatian family sold their cabin about ten years ago. There was a problem with one of their sons. He was involved in a criminal matter and arrested but later acquitted. I think Olav Bergqvist died more than a year ago and his children sold the house. After the mother fell ill, they rarely came anymore. And Nordin ... as you know, Alexander tried to maintain the house as best as he could the last years when his father became too ill to take care."

Suddenly he seemed so downhearted.

"It's such a difference from the times when the children were young, when we were all young. Those days are gone. What happened?"

He missed playing cards with Peter, Olav, and Ivor, discussing every topic from the latest political developments in the world to the school choices for the children. The children, even though they were so diverse in age, always found a common interest. Those were unforgettable moments building treehouses, chasing each other through the woods, hiking and swimming in the lake. Wonderful times!

"I don't know what else to tell you. It all seemed normal. A killer, burying young girls in the area near the cabins, is the last thing anyone expected!"

Josip Radić. The name was buzzing in Isa's mind ever since the professor had mentioned him. She tried to get more information from Mats, but he couldn't tell them anything more than they already knew.

* * *

Overly excited, Isa left the house after the nearly two-hour interview.

"Let me review everything I've just heard, so it's clear in my head," she yelled, while she almost slipped on the sidewalk outside the house. Magnus took her arm. It didn't stop her from rattling on about the visit. She was almost out of breath when saying: "Did I hear it right? The person who was arrested and almost convicted for the murder of Katrien Jans spent the summers during his childhood in the area where we found the girls. I don't know what you're thinking, but this must mean something."

"But what?" Magnus tried to calm her down. "He's not old enough to have committed all these crimes."

"Sure, but you have to agree, this is intriguing! Something strange is going on here."

"Isa, you need facts, you need evidence. And I am still not entirely sure what you want to prove with this?"

"Maybe he is covering up his father's crimes?"

"Is … don't go all obsessive on this! I know you and I remember what happened last time."

The excitement and energy dazed her. It wasn't far from reaching dangerous levels. A few years ago, that dedication turned into an obsession when she stalked the suspect in the murder case she was working on and got suspended for a while.

"Then let's pay Josip Radić a visit," he continued. The only way to control this was to guide that vigor toward the correct goals. She had to see and feel for herself what was real and rational, and what intrusive and destructive thoughts were about to take hold of her mind.

* * *

Alex Nordin closed the laptop and put his glasses on the desk. He ran his fingers through his hair and sighed. All day he had been working on a journal paper he wanted to submit before the evening. It was intense. He had the tendency to go into too much detail, sometimes losing sight of the goal. The paper had been written and rewritten so many times he couldn't count it anymore, much to the annoyance of his supervisor who had finally given him a deadline to turn in the paper.

It was quiet. The offices were empty. Everyone had already left for the evening. He wanted to put his head on the table and close his eyes, just sleep. That warm, blissful feeling when you are in that transition between wakefulness and sleep, in which you can let yourself sink away, was so tempting. But he had promised his mother to visit her and help her clean his father's stuff. His father ... it was only one year. It was too soon, but his mother was resolute. He would be lying if his father's death hadn't been a relief, but there was the disappointment and guilt that he had failed in helping him. There had been great times. He had his fair share of problems and his father had always been there for him, every time, but he had also seen his father at his worst. And there were plenty of those moments. He hoped that in time those memories would find a place in his life and that he would understand them.

He rubbed his eyes and got up. Sleep was a luxury these days. The nights were filled with terrifying images. It was the same dream, repeatedly, and he didn't understand it. It didn't feel like a memory, and it had nothing to do with his father. But it was so vivid it had pushed him into a cycle of self-imposed insomnia.

He walked to his mother's house. Outside, it was freezing, but it had stopped snowing and he loved the silence of a town that had come to a standstill. Few people were on the street. Most were in a hurry to get back to the warmth of their home. It was a familiar route he had taken many times in recent years. While he was walking, he thought about his future. It was the first time in years he dared to think about it. Sweden was not the country where he wanted to continue his research. Except for his mother, there was no reason for him to stay. In the US, there were several appealing post-doc positions he was applying for. However, telling his mother was something he had avoided. He wasn't sure she would allow him to leave. On the other hand, Irene Nordin was not a woman hungry for affection and love. She had learned that the hard way when she was a child and later when she was married. That love could leave the deepest wounds, both physical and mental, wounds that sometimes were beyond mending. She cared for her son, but she had always kept a distance. The affection between mother and son had remained superficial. For years, he had wondered if the fear that he might have inherited the same mental disease as his father had caused the distance between them.

It scared him. It was sometimes so crowded in his head. So many thoughts, so many things he saw and wanted to do. It exhausted him and preoccupied him all the time, to the extent that he was talking to himself like a madman, oblivious of the world around him. He had blackouts. Sometimes he couldn't remember how he got from his flat to the university or what he was doing in the library. But was this mental illness? Had it started like this for his father?

And he couldn't deny it: in the past, even as a child, he had given his mother plenty of reason to worry. Those times he had tried so hard to leave behind him, but the emotional and physical scars, only he could see, reminded him of the defeat every day.

After a twenty-minute walk, he reached the house where he had, on and off, spent almost thirty years of his life. He had moved out after his father's death. It had given himself and his mother some breathing room, something they had desperately needed. At least that was what he thought, but recently his mother had been talking obsessively about moving back home.

The building was a simple terraced house, nothing special, just enough for a small family. He looked at the left window on the second floor. It used to be his room. Probably he had spent more time there than the average kid. Watching the people on the street, imagining what their lives were like, imagining what his life could be and then the disappointment when he realized it was an unattainable dream. He had been so alone with his fears, his thoughts, his nightmares, and those grand emotions that overwhelmed him ... so much that ... Coming here was never good for him. The pain of everything was still there, and it was wearing him down.

He had been standing outside for a while when his mother opened the door. The face of the small woman with short gray hair lit up when she saw her son.

"Alex, what are you standing there for? Quickly, come in! It's way too cold."

He had to gather all his courage to smile at her, and he stepped inside, saying nothing. The sadness grew deeper with every step as he entered the house. She took his coat and put it in the closet of the entry hall.

He couldn't help but look up at the staircase where he had seen his father hanging from the railing. A nauseating feeling took hold of his stomach as he quickly entered the living room where the warmth of the fireplace overwhelmed him. As usual, his mother had turned up the heat so much that it didn't feel comfortable anymore. He saw the boxes on the floor. There were about ten relatively large cardboard boxes, which seemed to be mostly filled with clothes, judging by the pieces of fabric that partly stuck out. For a moment, he stared at them. Was this what was left of his father? He didn't understand why his mother wanted to get rid of this so quickly.

Irene noticed her son's dismay.

"Alex, he's not coming back," she whispered. He turned around and looked at her.

"Mom, how can you throw his stuff away?"

"I am only getting rid of his clothes. That's all. Try to understand! It's also difficult for me to see his pants and shirts hanging there every time I open the wardrobe."

She tried to hug him, but he stopped her. He felt the tears roll down his cheeks. He had intended to be strong and not give in to any outward display of emotion. Especially not toward his mother. Was this really because of his father or because of something else, this undefinable feeling of anguish that grew stronger every day? His mother looked disappointed and confused. He had rejected her so openly that it even shocked him. This is not what he wanted, and he took her in his arms. As he wiped the tears from his face, he sighed and asked: "Where do you want the boxes?"

"It would be great if you could put them in the car," his mother said as she sealed some with tape. "I parked the car in the side street. You have to go outside again."

He put on his coat, took the car key, and carried the first boxes outside. He was almost running on automatic pilot. He couldn't think. It was all a blur in his head. Maybe he should talk to someone. It wasn't going well, and he knew how bad the outcome could be if he left it lingering. He had no friends, at least no real friends. Who was there to talk to? Doctor Wikholm?

He put the boxes in the trunk of the car and went back inside to get the next load. The box felt heavier than the previous one, and before he could reach the car, the bottom of the box was ripped open, and the content fell to the floor. When he looked at the clothes spread over the dirty snow, he was stunned. This was more than just shirts and trousers. In front of him, he saw the hardcover of a photo album and the photos scattered around it. He leaned over to pick them up. He had never seen them before: his father, mother, Mats Norman, and Olav Bergqvist sitting around the table. He tried to collect the pictures and put them back in the album. As he picked up the clothes, he saw a thin little black book lying on the sidewalk, close to the car. It had a leather cover, and it looked old. When he opened it, he recognized his father's handwriting. It was a list of dates and places. Now and then he found comments written next to them.

"Driving around for three hours," he read out loud and shook his head. What was this? He didn't understand, but he felt this was important. Instinctively he put the booklet and photographs in the inside pocket of his jacket when he heard the footsteps of someone approaching. He grabbed the album and the clothes and quickly put them in the partially damaged box before closing the trunk. It was his mother.

"Alex, what are you doing? I was worried."

"I had a problem opening the trunk, but it's solved now. Don't worry."

He didn't want to confront her about the reason she wanted to throw these old photos away and what the black book was about. At least not now. He went back to the house to get the last boxes, and she followed him, seemingly satisfied with the explanation he had given her.

* * *

Alex was eager to go home and have a look at the black booklet, but she wanted to talk to him. She poured herself a cup of tea to warm up while she said: "Christmas is coming."

He didn't respond. As she walked from the kitchen to the living room, he followed her.

"Do you have any plans?" she continued.

"You know I don't." His voice was full of fatigue.

"Mats and Annette have invited me to spend Christmas and New Year with them. You should come too."

"No, thank you. I don't want to impose."

"I am sure it's no problem. They would love to see you. You know they are fond of you."

"No, I'll be fine on my own."

"Jesus, Alex, you are as social as a monkey in a ... field full of zebras!"

He laughed at her unusual comparison. It also put a smile on her face.

"But seriously," she said, "I do worry about you."

He could only stare at her. From the silence that followed, she could only conclude he didn't want to talk about it any further.

"Okay, something else: have you heard anything about the body in Sandviken?"

"Bodies," he corrected.

Surprised, she looked up and repeated: "Bodies? How many?"

"It was on the news a few days ago. Nine."

"Nine ... my God," she reacted and put the cup on the small table next to her. Her son was sitting on the sofa in front of her.

"Have they contacted you for more information?" she continued.

"No. I'm not sure how much more I can tell them."

She observed him for a while, in silence. The sniffing and scratching of the dog, locked in the storage room, were the only sounds that echoed across the room. Irene preferred to keep the dog out of sight.

The way she observed her son, with those bright blue eyes that almost pierced through him, was intense and it was as if he couldn't hide anything from her.

"Are you sleeping okay? You don't look well. What's wrong?"

"I am okay, mom," he answered, but she knew he was lying. When he tried to hide something from her, he usually avoided looking her in the eye and he had a nervous tic, fiddling with the strap of his watch.

"I don't think so. Is it the Sandviken thing?"

He shook his head.

"I know you. It has been running through your mind."

"No, it's fine," he said, irritated by the persistence with which she started to question him, "just leave it."

"Why don't you stay here? You don't have to live alone."

"Why?" he sighed, "I am thirty ... it's about time I stand on my own two feet."

"Yes, but I don't think you can."

Her words were harsh and, as always, the attack came out of the blue. That's the way it usually was.

"I don't want to be the one picking up the pieces anymore," she continued.

Her face showed no emotion. He knew it was better not to respond. She just wanted to provoke a confrontation that typically ended by him being hurt and humiliated.

"I have to go," he said and got up.

She said nothing and saw how he left the living room to pick up his coat in the hall.

"So, you run off," he heard her say. He closed his eyes. The inner balance was gone.

Calm down! She can't hurt you anymore. This is now entirely in your hands.

"I have to work. I'll call you tomorrow."

It was nearly eight o'clock when he left the house and walked back to his apartment. This usually took about ten minutes, but this time he had to stop on the way. The emotions were just too much. It was so unfair! Why couldn't she just let go? What did she want from him?

He felt the booklet in the inner pocket of his coat pressing against his ribs. The black book, the mysterious legacy of his father.

CHAPTER

6

THE APARTMENT HE RENTED was small, but enough for a bachelor like him. The living room had a sofa, TV, and a wooden desk he used as an office. The kitchen was equipped with a microwave and a larger oven with cooking hobs that he rarely used. Opposite the bathroom was a bedroom, barely big enough to fit a single bed and closet.

As Alexander ran up the stairs to his apartment, he took out the black book and nearly lost some photos along the way. He couldn't wait to take a closer look. The coat fell to the floor as he walked to the other side of the room and put the leather book on the desk.

The jacket is on the floor. It doesn't belong there. Pick it up! It's not right.

He took a deep breath to suppress the nagging unrest in his head.

The book was not exactly in the center of the writing mat. He was so close to taking out the ruler and measuring the distance from each side to put it where he wanted it to be.

Put it right!

He felt the anxiety grow. It had grown over the past year. He could hardly control it anymore.

The ringtone of his cell phone startled him. Where was the phone? He was such a scatterbrain sometimes! Most of the time he barely knew where he put the damn thing. The pocket of his coat. There it was.

There was no other way. He had to take the coat from the floor. It wasn't his fault. He needed the phone.

It was such a relief! He put the jacket on the hanger of the coat rack, with the buttons facing the window. The sound kept going, persistent, with a noise level that seemed to get louder with every cycle.

"Alexander Nordin," he said.

It was silent on the other side.

"Alexander Nordin," he repeated and waited.

He heard someone breathe.

"Who is this? I'll hang up if ..."

"Alex," a man's voice interrupted him.

It was as if the person wasn't sure whether to continue or not. There was again a long silence. Who was this? He didn't recognize the voice.

"Alex," the man repeated, "it's me ... Josip."

Alex didn't know what to say. He was stunned. It had been ages since he had seen or spoken to Josip.

"Josip, how ... why?"

"I am sorry, but I need to talk to you ... urgently," Josip said.

His voice sounded more confident than it had been a few moments ago.

"How did you get my phone number?"

"That doesn't matter. I need to see you. Can you meet me

tomorrow?"

"But why?"

"Tomorrow? It's urgent and I don't want to talk about this over the phone."

"Yes, okay, I guess," Alex said hesitantly, "where?"

"I'll give you the address. Come tomorrow evening around 8 p.m. And don't tell anyone!"

Alex wrote the address down, and the conversation was over. He stared at his writing for a while. It was somewhere outside the city center. That neighborhood had a reputation for being unsafe, and a certain feeling of anxiety arose just by looking at the scribbles on the paper.

Josip Radić. His childhood friend during those summer vacations in Sandviken. Why would he want to talk to him? Josip was six years his senior, but he had always felt a connection with him. But, one time, he hadn't been a good friend to him. He had let him down when Josip got into trouble with the police. It wasn't one of his finest moments. What did he want after so many years? This mystery wasn't good for his paranoia, especially now, after the Sandviken incident.

He didn't feel at ease after the phone call. It was best not to go to the appointment the next day, but the conversation had sparked his curiosity. He decided to sleep on it and make a final decision in the morning. The black book, not perfectly positioned, was still lying on the table. It took him five minutes to place it right before he could open it. It was still wet and a bit dirty from the snow. That irritated him.

Don't touch it! It's contaminated.

And the book wasn't symmetrical. How could he read it? He closed his eyes. Where would it end? The anxiety clouded his thinking. This was all in his head. Inhale, exhale. The sound of his own breathing calmed him.

Things don't have to be perfect! Touch it. Nothing will happen.

He looked at the yellowish pages. The ink was almost gone, and the handwriting, although his father's, seemed to alternate between a calm and regular writing and hasty, erratic, and almost illegible scribbles. His hands trembled as he turned the page. The first entry dated back to 1984. On the left side of the margin, "19 June 1984" was written and on the right side, he read Sandviken. The line at the bottom of the page caught his attention. A big circle was drawn around the date "26 June 1987", and "Uppsala" was written next to it. What did this mean? There were at least fifty more pages of dates and places, but only a few specific lines were marked.

On one page, he saw his own name. "1992," he read aloud with his stare fixed on the year. There was something. It was important, but the memories were so vague and elusive. It was a whisper, soft and quick, almost audible, but gone by the time he could grasp what he had seen.

Why was it important for his father to keep this list? He stared at the pages one more time, but he couldn't figure it out. Finally, he gave up, left the book, nicely centered on the desk, and went to bed, but he had trouble falling asleep. His mind went into overdrive. His father's death, the bones in the woods, his mother's behavior, the booklet, Josip Radić. Sleep came only three hours later, but it wasn't a refreshing rest. The dreams quickly turned into more sinister scenes. Images of Josip, his family, and the other children changed into the nightmare he had experienced before, over and over, perhaps his entire life.

* * *

Like so many nights, he woke up frightened, disoriented and in a fight-flight mode that almost made him jump out of bed. His heart was racing. The details of the dream were so fleeting that although the emotions were there, he couldn't really grasp the meaning.

The red LED number display of the alarm showed it was six o'clock. Too early to go to work, but he got up and stumbled to the kitchen.

Caffeine would do the trick, as always. As the excitement of the dream faded, he felt extremely tired. The simmer of the coffee machine bounced in his head and echoed from one ear to the other. It sparked the onset of a headache.

While he waited for the coffee, he took his laptop from the drawer in the living room and placed it on the desk next to the black book. There was a dried-up stain from the melted snow on the writing mat. He should replace it.

By the time he took his first sip of coffee, his laptop was ready to use, and he opened the Google search engine. He typed: "26 June 1987" and "Uppsala". Links to books on archeology, history, and justice appeared, but nothing that looked interesting enough. He scrolled down and clicked on the second page. He stopped at the top entry.

"Family and friends commemorate the disappearance of Clara Persson twenty years ago."

He opened the article and continued reading. The newspaper article dated back to 2007 and talked about a small ceremony in memory of a local girl who disappeared on 26 June 1987. The photo showed a young girl with long dark hair and remarkable blue eyes, wearing a blue and white striped sweater. The article was short and didn't say much. 1987! She disappeared just a few days after he was born.

He closed the link and looked through the book to find the next line that was marked.

"31 December 1990." But there was no place next to the date. He sighed. Links enough, but probably no useful ones.

Maybe this was nothing, and maybe his mother had been right to throw this away. Disappointed, he closed the laptop.

* * *

It was still dark outside when Alexander left the apartment to head to the university. The headache was getting worse. He had an appointment with his research promoter at ten o'clock. It usually stressed him out. Professor Werners didn't like him, he never had, but that was fine. After years of frustration, doubts about the quality of his work and the attempt of his promoter to end his Ph.D. after Alex had announced he'd take a sabbatical for family reasons, he had made his peace with the realization that he would simply never be good enough for the man who considered himself the God of artificial intelligence and had little empathy for people who dared to challenge his ideas. He just had to survive another six months, get his Ph.D. and then he would be gone. Mats Norman had agreed to help him. He valued the opinion of the once highly regarded physics professor a lot. Yes, it was true, the Norman family always had a soft spot for him and his mother. Was it pity? Probably, but he didn't care. It was time to use Mats' extensive network to get what he wanted.

It was quiet when he arrived. There were only a few people in the university building, including his office buddy Robin Gilmore. Alex wondered if Robin ever went home. He always seemed to be there. Completely absorbed by the article displayed on his computer, he hadn't noticed Alex. Robin was an American exchange student, originally with a plan to spend only a few months in Uppsala, but those months had now turned into almost two years. Alex didn't understand why he had chosen to stay here. The research level could certainly not meet his colleague's expectations. Only 25 years old, and yet Robin had already published in several high impact journals. Alex envied his brilliant mind. Something he felt was missing in his own case. He was average at best. It upset him that it took him so long to grasp the simplest concepts while Robin juggled them around so easily. Maybe he wasn't good enough to go to the States.

"Hey, Alex, how did it go?"

Alex turned around in surprise.

"What do you mean?" Alex asked.

"The paper ... did you make the deadline?"

"Oh, yes, I did," Alex replied and took off his coat.

Buttons facing the window.

"Good, we should celebrate this evening," Robin said and gave his desk chair a twist, so he faced Alex.

"No, I can't. I have plans."

Robin stared at him and shook his head.

"No, I don't believe you. Alex Nordin never has any plans. You are the most asocial person I know. By the way, what did you do? You look like crap."

"I didn't get much sleep," Alex mumbled as he opened the drawer of his desk.

He didn't find what he was looking for.

"Where are my glasses?"

"So, what do you think? Are we going somewhere this evening?"

"No, I really can't," Alex answered and got up to get his coat. As he searched the inside pocket, he didn't find the glasses but the photos he had taken with him after yesterday's visit to his mother. The man in the photo was Mats Norman, holding a baby, smiling. Alex recognized the background. It was the living room in his parents' house. The sofa was different but the wallpaper, the cupboard and the paintings on the wall hadn't changed. The other photographs had been taken at the summer cabins in Sandviken, but he hadn't just brought photos with him. Between the dozens of photographs was a folded letter. He put it back in the pocket and turned to Robin.

"Sorry. Maybe tomorrow?"

"Could work. After work then."

Robin was satisfied with the answer and concentrated on his work again. An hour later, Robin left the office to attend a seminar and Alex finally got the chance to read the letter. It confused him. Addressed to his father, it said: "*Dear Mr. Nordin, we regret to inform you we could not use the samples you provided for analysis. Please send us new samples within the next two weeks. Yours sincerely, Dr. Freya Linn."*

The letter was dated 20 June 2016 and GenoOne was the name of the company mentioned in the header. It was a commercial lab that specialized in DNA testing.

DNA testing? Why did his father contact this lab?

The mystery got bigger. Was there any way to find out what the letter was about?

He called the lab later that day. The woman on the other end agreed to put him in touch with Dr. Freya Linn who had written the letter. A soft and calm voice answered, "Dr. Linn speaking."

"Uh, my name is Alexander Nordin and ..."

"Oh, yes, Mr. Nordin. What can I do for you?"

He could have told her he wasn't the Nordin she had corresponded with, but it was better to have her believe he had been the requester of the analysis.

"I sent you the samples a while ago to rerun the analysis. I was wondering if you could send me the outcome."

"Yes, I remember. We discussed this more than a year ago. Would you like to question the result again?"

"No, no ... well, I'm not sure."

He got nervous. The letter hadn't been the only correspondence between his father and Dr. Linn.

"My conclusion remains the same. There's no match."

Alex didn't know what to do with this information. Which match? Who or what should be a match?

"Okay ... but I didn't receive your report on this analysis," he lied.

Silence. He heard someone typing on the keyboard of a computer.

"Dr. Linn?"

"We sent the report to you on 7 September 2016, after we discussed it over the phone the same day. I believe you are not exactly truthful. Mr. Nordin?"

He dropped the phone. 7 September was the day before his father died. Did this have anything to do with his death? Was this the reason he had committed suicide? And where was the report?

CHAPTER

7

"WHERE DO YOU LIVE?"

She hesitated. The man, whose arm dangled through the half-open window, had been following her for several hundred meters in the red car. He looked nice and friendly, but she kept walking, trying to ignore him.

"Look, I am really concerned ... a young girl, all alone. Let me take you home!"

Why was he so interested in her? This couldn't be right. She heard her mother's voice in her head telling her not to trust him. Her stomach tightened with tension. The area was deserted. No house for kilometers. It was the first time she had been so aware of it, and she had gone that way many times on her way home from school.

Keep walking!

She quickly glanced at him. He pushed the accelerator slightly to keep up with her increasing pace. Strangely, he fascinated her. Fine facial features, radiant smile, and the sparkle in those beautiful eyes. He was very handsome. Confusing.

"I am going in that direction anyway," he said, "I have to take my son to the doctor."

Only then she saw the sleeping baby in the back of the car. He was so tiny and cute.

"What's wrong with him?"

The man turned around and looked at the child in the carrycot. The car stopped. She stood a few meters away and watched them.

"Fever, coughing ... he's sleeping now, but it was a tough night," he whispered. The blanket hung over the edge and the baby's leg and arm were uncovered. The way he looked at the baby was genuine. His eyes radiated concern as he leaned forward from behind the driver's seat and tucked him in.

No, don't be fooled! Keep walking!

"Okay," she sighed.

"You can sit next to the baby," he smiled.

He continued instantly: "Actually if you don't mind ... I'm worried. Can you keep an eye on him while I drive you home?"

She nodded and opened the car door.

Stop. Go back.

The voice in her head grew louder. But she got in. Everything would be fine. He didn't look like a criminal. He was just a father, concerned about his son, trying to be friendly by offering a lonely girl a ride home.

"Are you okay there?" he said and looked in his rearview mirror.

"Yes, I'm fine," she said.

There was a slight tremble in her voice. Maybe she didn't trust him after all.

Suddenly, he got out of the car.

"I forgot his stuffed animal," he said and walked to the back. She heard him open the trunk. The nagging feeling that something wasn't right crept back in. Why was she in this car? It wasn't too late to get out.

No, it would be okay. Just drive. Take me home.

"I think he's fine," she said and looked at the child, still perfectly still, unaware of what was going on around him. It was so quiet outside. Sunny weather. Nothing but flowers, knee-high grass, buzzing bees. It was so peaceful. It put her mind to rest.

And then the door on her side was opened.

"I know, Clara."

How did he know ...

It was too late. The hand over her mouth. The sweet smell of chloroform. Panic. She tried to get the handkerchief away from her face, but he was too strong. She felt the blood racing through her veins. The breathing was shallow and fast. The baby's cry was the last thing she heard before the warm, blissful intoxication took over.

* * *

For the last ten years of his life, Josip Radić had been drunk, but today he was sober and worried, deeply worried. Alexander Nordin was the man he needed to talk to, as fast as possible. It was as if someone had lifted the fog and he could see everything clearly now. Well, clearly, that was maybe a bridge too far. There were still so many questions remaining, and it was doubtful he would get the answers from Alex. But with the newly acquired clarity came the guilt and the realization he had done his friend wrong ... terribly wrong. What he wanted was forgiveness.

It was nine o'clock in the morning. The smell of freshly brewed coffee invited him to the kitchen. He hadn't slept much the last few weeks. There were dozens of empty bottles in the kitchen sink. His entire life in a bottle of Scotch. He reached out and let his fingers run over the smooth glass. Could he have another one? He deserved one.

Drying out was painful. He had gone through it many times and had failed every time. So, disaster was again written all over it. That was how it usually ended. Why should it be different now? More grief for everyone, more promises that couldn't be kept. He took a step back. No, this time it had to be different. Yes, he was angry and disillusioned, but determined to make amends. It was important, not only to him but to so many others. If only he had said something ... if only they had done something, some girls could have been saved and so many lives wouldn't have been wasted.

There was a soft knock on the door. Who was this? He expected no one. He froze, and only the sound of his own breathing gusted through the room. His hands were sweating. There was a second knock. Slowly he walked to the door and looked through the peephole. He didn't recognize the man and woman.

Just leave.

He waited. Silence.

"Josip Radić, police! Can you open the door? We know you're there."

He sighed. Of course, he was the usual suspect. He slowly opened the door, the chain still on the slide track.

"How did you get in, the front door is ...," Josip asked.

"Inspector Isa Lindström," the woman said, showing her badge and completely ignoring his question, "and this is inspector Magnus Wieland."

"Why do you want to talk to me?" he asked, seemingly surprised.

"Can we come in? We would like to talk to you about Katrien Jans."

"Look," he said, irritated, "I have nothing to do with her disappearance; I have been acquitted."

He was determined not to let them in.

"Well, that's not entirely true, is it," Magnus replied," they dropped the charges for lack of evidence. That doesn't mean you're innocent."

The expression on the man's face changed from mild irritation to anger. Isa saw it wasn't going well and tried to calm him down: "But we are not here to throw new accusations at you, Mr. Radić, but we believe you can help us."

She gave Magnus an angry look. He tended to scare off people with his direct and often insensitive approach. It wasn't the right way to convince Josip Radić to talk to them. The man, hyper-vigilant by the alcohol withdrawal symptoms and his general lack of trust in people, had immediately taken a defensive stance and only Isa's words had kept him from slamming the door on them. There was still doubt visible on his face, but he finally slid the door chain and invited them in.

The apartment was small and hadn't been cleaned for months. Clothes were thrown everywhere: on the floor, over the sofa, and on the table. Empty beer cans were standing on the coffee table, and in the kitchen dozens of dirty dishes were lying on the counter. The air smelled of stale sweat and mold.

"Had a party?" Magnus remarked when he entered, pointing to the empty bottles. There was no answer. Josip pushed the clothes aside and invited them to sit down on the old and dirty sofa. He slumped down in the one-seater sofa on the opposite side. Magnus glanced at the shabby-looking man sitting in front of him. The hand tremors and the bloodshot eyes. He had seen it all before. An alcoholic in rehab.

"Mr. Radić, we would like to talk to you about the disappearance of Katrien Jans."

Josip let out a sarcastic chuckle and said, "I knew it."

Isa ignored it and continued: "We found the bodies of nine girls. They were buried in Sandviken, near the area where you and your parents spent the summer holidays years ago."

"Oh." Josip seemed surprised.

"Your friend Alexander Nordin found the bodies," she continued, "this can't be a coincidence."

He sat there in silence, scratching his arm and shuffling back and forth.

"We have witnesses who saw you in Sandviken a week ago and they claim you are a regular visitor to the nature park. You used to rent a cabin there. Why?"

He felt cornered. How could he tell them he went there to drink and to try to end his life? How many times had he put the gun to his head and tried to pull the trigger? His life was worthless. No one would care if he were dead. Just a part of some obscure statistics. Forgotten.

"I just wanted to get away. I go there on holidays."

"On holidays? Strange for a man who has no job and no family to take care of."

"I ...," he said, "I'm going there to drink."

"Alone?" Magnus asked.

"Yes, alone."

"Not with your father?"

"No, why? Did anyone say my father was there?"

He sighed and looked down, before continuing: "My father is just an old man. He has done nothing wrong."

"I'm not so sure about that," Isa said and flipped through her notebook.

"Do you know why your father came to Sweden?"

He stammered: "Because he wanted a better life for his family ..."

"We've been looking into your family's history. It's strange: before 1984, there was no record of Ivor Radić ... anywhere. It's as if he never existed before that time."

"Perhaps most records were lost during the Yugoslav civil war," Josip said, "Dubrovnik was badly damaged during the war."

"That's strange," Isa said and looked at him closely, "on his application form for Swedish citizenship he claimed to be from Vukovar, not Dubrovnik."

He looked at her in disbelief. This couldn't be right. He remembered his father telling them stories about their life in Dubrovnik before coming to Sweden when Josip was three years old.

"Now, who lived in Dubrovnik and disappeared with his family in the eighties, is a certain Igor Rajković ... convicted criminal and accused of abusing a fourteen-year-old girl before he vanished."

How could his father have kept that secret from him and his brother? For sure he had noticed inconsistencies in his father's stories about their life in Croatia, but he had attributed it to old age and a lack of memory. Maybe it had been more than that.

"We have contacted the Croatian authorities so we will know soon if Ivor Radić is actually Igor Rajković," Magnus added.

"I am sure there is a perfect explanation for it," he got up and paced around before saying: "But instead of harassing my family, I suggest you take a closer look at the others. I can tell you a few things about Olav Bergqvist and Mats Norman."

"Mr. Radić, I am all ears," Isa said and leaned back on the sofa, notebook and pen in hand. She didn't have much hope of getting new information from him, although she had to admit Josip Radić was more intelligent and coherent than she had expected.

"There were rumors," he began, "about Olav Bergqvist. He supposedly raped a girl while he was still in high school. He has never been convicted, though. The family settled with the girl's family, and they sent him off to boarding school in the UK after that. When he returned a few years later, there were again rumors he had assaulted several girls in England."

"Interesting, who told you? How do you know?"

"I don't remember. Friends, acquaintances."

"What about later?" Magnus asked.

"I don't think there was anything after he got married. Although, I remember always feeling like there was something wrong with his wife

Margot. She was always very reserved. Quiet. Never mingled much. And at some point, she started wearing those big sunglasses everywhere, outside and inside. Then my mother got suspicious. She thought Olav abused her. He had a temper, and he could be verbally abusive, but to be honest, I've never seen him hit his wife or daughters. Anyway, my mother confronted her with this."

"And?"

"Margot was furious. She claimed there was nothing wrong, and it wasn't my mother's business. They had been very close before the incident, but after that, there was a distance between them, and it remained until Margot died five years ago."

"When did the argument between your mother and Margot take place?"

He sighed and shook his head: "I don't know. It must have been mid 1990s ... just before I got arrested the first time ..."

"And what do you know about our Professor Mats Norman?"

"I don't understand how this guy is still married. He's a womanizer. Every summer we spent in Sandviken, he had a different woman, or shall I say, mistress. He sometimes disappeared for days and left Annette alone with the children. When he finally showed up again, he was bragging to everyone about the young women he had spent the night with. Still, it always puzzled me how Annette looked up to him. She adored him. He was her God. And she forgave him again and again while he so openly humiliated her in front of their children and friends."

"That seems more innocent than Olav's story," Magnus claimed.

"And there were rumors ... about him and Irene Nordin."

"Oh. Tell us more."

"They were always friendly to each other, nothing more ... but Alex had caught them kissing once. He told me. Though ... I don't know if his interpretation of what he saw was correct. He was still young ... five or so. And he has probably forgotten it. I'm not sure ... none of us have ever seen any indiscretions between the two. But Alex was quite upset. I managed to ease his mind. We were such good friends. I think I was his only friend. He was a timid and vulnerable child."

"You were friends? Not anymore?"

"We haven't seen each other in years. I can hardly say we're friends now."

There were mixed feelings. His best friend had given up on him. Alex should have known he couldn't have done the horrible things they accused him of.

"And Peter Nordin?" Isa asked.

"Peter Nordin ... he usually kept to himself. It was as if he wasn't really there. Do you know what I mean?"

"Not really, explain."

"He came every summer with his family, but often he separated himself from the rest, scribbling away in that black book he was trying to hide from everyone. I once had the opportunity to glance through it, but I couldn't make sense of it. Weird. He was mentally not well, you know. Depression or something else. We never noticed much of it, but I know Peter and Irene had many arguments and fights about his condition. Alex then usually fled the cabin and hid at ours. Now and then, he talked about the situation at home."

"Now, Mr. Radić, you know an awful lot about other people, and that's interesting, I agree, but what about yourself? I still don't think it's a coincidence you were a suspect in the disappearance of a girl we later found back near the cabins where you have spent most of the summers during your childhood."

He went to the kitchen and poured himself another coffee. There was silence for a while until Isa became impatient.

"And," she asked, "anything to say?"

"Nothing in particular," Josip said," you have my file. I have nothing more to say."

He looked again at the bottles on the kitchen counter. This had been his life for so long because of that one day. One stupid day, one moment. Everything destroyed, so much time wasted. It made him sad and scared. Scared he couldn't change this time either. This was his last chance.

"Can you tell us again what happened that day at the museum in Göteborg?"

"Jeezes, for the millionth time ..."

He sighed and looked down. How many times had he told this story? To the police, to his parents, to himself, over and over again, in his head until it almost drove him mad.

"I had to keep an eye on the visitors that day. The girl, Katrien, was an arrogant little ..."

He realized that scorning the victim would not earn him the sympathy of the inspectors sitting in his living room.

"She touched the panels. They are very fragile, and I asked her to stop, but she didn't listen. And she ignored my request a second time. I don't know what happened, but I must have pulled her away. The so-called assault a woman witnessed. She also claimed I was shouting at the girl, but I swear I didn't. I pulled her away from the exhibits and I wanted to talk to her, but she ran away."

"And did you go after her?"

There was a slight hesitation in his voice before he replied: "No, I didn't."

Yes, he had run after her, but not immediately. And he had seen her talking to someone outside the museum. Someone he hadn't immediately recognized, but now, after so many years, he kept wondering why he hadn't put two and two together. And then there was the red car he had seen again not so long ago in the woods of Sandviken. He had been so naïve to think everything had stopped after ...

God, this was planned so well. He had everyone fooled ... all this time.

Or maybe not? Maybe there was a perfect explanation. Blackmail had crossed his mind. All he wanted was to clear his name so his children would be proud of their father again. Then why didn't he tell the inspectors what he had discovered?

"You didn't," Isa repeated, and he confirmed.

She had felt that momentary hesitation in his voice. But Magnus intervened: "Where were her parents?"

"Well ... nowhere to be seen," Josip answered and took place again on the sofa.

"Four more girls disappeared after Katrien Jans. I wonder where you were at the time of their disappearance?"

He looked perplexed.

"How am I supposed to know? I don't even know when they went missing and how can anyone still know what they did so many years ago!"

"Ella Nyman disappeared on 18 January 2008. The same day they released you from custody in the Katrien Jans case. Your father picked you up at the police station in the afternoon and a few hours later Ella was never seen again. If I were to consider the other cases, would I find similar coincidences?"

He couldn't say anything. How could he explain this? He couldn't, he didn't understand.

Magnus continued, "Mr. Radić, you are hiding something from me, and I'll find out what it is. We're done here ... for now."

He signaled to Isa who put pen and notebook in the pocket of her jacket, got up and walked to the front door, with Magnus behind her.

"If you think of anything else, here's my card ... you can always contact me," Magnus said and handed him the business card.

* * *

After their departure, Josip stared at the wall for a while, trying to organize his thoughts. Could it be a set-up? If so, he was in more danger than he thought. And not just him. He couldn't stay here. Finally, he got up and took a small package from the cupboard in the kitchen. It had been hidden between the pans. How he craved for that glass of whiskey right now! Feeling the warm glow of the alcohol trickling down his esophagus. His hand touched the bottle. No, there was no time. He opened the package and took out a brown envelope, quickly wrote a few lines on the front and put it back in the package. A few minutes later he left the apartment and headed to the center of Uppsala on foot.

From behind the dashboard of the car, Isa and Magnus saw him walking down the sidewalk, away from them. They waited a few minutes before getting out of the car. His pace was slow and easy to keep up with. They were walking a few hundred meters behind him. He was so lost in thought he didn't notice it. The walk lasted ten minutes and ended in front of a bank. When Josip entered, he still didn't know Isa and Magnus were right behind him. They waited outside for a while. Light snow was falling when he came out thirty minutes later. He made his way toward the river Fyris through Gotlandsparken. He crossed the river, passed the cathedral, to end up a few blocks further in a bar where he spent the rest of the morning and afternoon. The lure of the alcohol was too strong, and again he lost himself in its soothing daze.

After one hour of waiting, the inspectors went back to check out the bank branch where Josip had first stopped on his journey through the center of Uppsala. The office was small and at the counter, there was only one clerk.

"May we ask you something?" Isa approached the lady and showed her police badge. The woman, in her late forties, rather disinterested and bored, suddenly was nervous and stammered: "Yep ... I mean yes."

"Have you seen this man?" Isa asked and showed her a photograph of Josip Radić.

"Yes, that's Josip. I know him well. He was here, an hour or two ago. Why? Did he do something wrong?"

Isa got straight to the point: "What did he want?"

The woman, still excited by meeting the police officers and in doubt about what she could reveal, stared at Isa for a while, before answering: "He wanted to put something in his safe deposit box."

"You have safe deposit boxes here?"

"Yes, we have some," the woman said.

Isa sighed and looked at Magnus. They needed a search warrant if they wanted to know the content of the box.

"I guess we need to do our homework first," Magnus laughed. Isa threw him another angry glance. He was particularly annoying today.

CHAPTER

8

HE WAS HALFWAY UP the stairs when Irene said, "What's so urgent that you can't even say hello to your mother?"

Alex turned around. "Sorry. Hello, mom. I'm in a hurry. I need something from my old room." She said nothing and strolled to the living room.

At the top of the stairs, he stopped. It was so quiet in the house. What was wrong?

"Where's Spark?"

With her hand on the door handle, she looked up and said without showing the slightest emotion, "He's dead."

Alexander was flabbergasted.

"Uh ... what? How? What happened to him? He was fine yesterday."

"My fault. I opened the door, and he ran into the street. A car hit him. It happened this morning. His body is in the backyard."

Cold, distant, as if she were talking about a business contract. It wasn't the first time. When he was a child, she used to punish him by flushing his goldfish down the toilet or by letting the parrot die a gruesome death in the sweltering veranda. Was this another of her psychological games?

Calm. He had to stay calm, just like the evening before. But he couldn't ignore the impact she had on his peace of mind. From one moment to the next, she could push him so easily in a downward spiral of self-doubt and depression. He took a deep breath. The control was slipping away.

His mother had disappeared into the living room. There was nothing more to say, and he made his way toward his father's office. The GenoOne letter and the black book kept playing through his mind. Would he find more information in his father's old files?

The curtains were closed, and there was a musty smell in the room. The light poured in when he opened them. It was so strong it blinded him for a moment. The snowfall outside made the light even more intense. The room itself was small, just big enough to accommodate a desk, chair and a few bookshelves and cupboards near the walls. The smell, the light, everything reminded him of his childhood. How many times had he passed by the study on his way to his own room and had seen his father sitting at the desk, in the early days going through papers scattered on the table, and later, after some convincing it was finally time for him to enter the digital era, behind the laptop? But there was also the screaming, the books his father had thrown at him, the corner of the room, between the bookcase and the lamp where he had grabbed him by the throat and had almost choked his son. His fingers ran over the spine of the book. It was still there. War and Peace. As he felt the air being squeezed from his lungs, the only thing he could remember was the coarseness of his father's hands and this book, seen from the corner of his eye.

He didn't know how to deal with those memories. Painful as they were, they were a part of his father. For years, he had tried to rewrite the memory in his head, making it less traumatizing, less about his father and more about himself. Curled up in the corner of his room, trembling with emotion and fear, weeping, his mother had lectured him. It had been his fault. He had triggered the outburst; he hadn't been considerate enough. His father needed tranquility. Now, so many years later, Alex still had problems coming in here.

He turned around. At one end of the desk, there was a neatly stacked pile of papers. He sat down and tried to open the drawer on his left side. There his father kept the laptop and the most important documents. But to Alex's surprise, someone had locked it. There was usually a spare key behind a book in the cupboard by the door. The books had disappeared, but the key was still there.

The laptop was the only item in the drawer. The startup of the computer was very slow, and while waiting for the intro screen to appear, he flipped through the photo album lying next to the pile of documents. Photos when he was a baby. His parents in Sandviken. Christmas celebrations. Birthdays. But nowhere in the book there was any sign photos were missing. Where did the photographs he had found that evening on the snow-covered sidewalk come from? Who had taken them? What was so special about them they had ended up in the cardboard box for disposal?

He looked at the screen of the laptop and entered the password. His father's personal folder was still there, but it contained very few files, and some of them were encrypted. Strange. Alex didn't think his father was able to encrypt files. He had been barely able to open and save them. But the encrypted files would be no problem. He might have given up on his illustrious career as a hacker, but he hadn't lost the skills.

He set the laptop aside. The rest of the time he spent searching the old archive of papers. Most documents were related to his father's work as an Ikea sales representative. There was a second, smaller stack of papers on his illness: hospital records and psychiatric evaluations. Most of it was uninteresting, except for one transcript:

"The patient insists that he has no psychiatric condition. He is convinced that he is being poisoned. These delusions suggest that the diagnosis of depression needs to be re-evaluated. It is my recommendation we should run new tests to rule out schizophrenia and bipolar disorder."

Dr. Wikholm, the psychiatrist who had been advising his father since 1991, had written the document.

The black book, the letter. The scribbles and thoughts of a man, erratic, unpredictable ... his behavior and mind controlled by delusions. This could explain his father's aggressive behavior, which had escalated over the years. He understood his mother's reaction. His father was gone, but it was hard to forget the pain, frustration, and fear that man had caused his own family.

But what if his father had been right? What if someone had poisoned him? Who and why?

* * *

He put the papers back, closed the curtains and took the laptop. Slowly he walked down the stairs and gently opened the door of the living room.

"Mom, I am leaving now," he said.

His mother looked up from the book she was reading.

"Are you coming for dinner later? It's been a while since we've had dinner together, and ... I should apologize. I didn't mean what I said yesterday."

He noticed how lonely she looked. The attitude of superiority and arrogance was gone and instead, he saw an old, sad lady sitting in a chair.

For a moment, he felt sorry for her, but he knew all too well that her mood could change quickly, and then he would be in the line of fire again.

"No, not tonight, I'm meeting someone this evening," he replied.

Was it because of that nagging sense of unrest and danger in the back of his mind, and because he wanted to be reassured, he decided to tell her about the strange phone call? Or was it something else?

"Do you remember Josip Radić?"

"Yes, of course," she said, surprised.

"Well, the strangest thing happened: he called me yesterday and said he urgently needed to talk to me. I've agreed to meet him tonight."

She got up and walked over to him. The look on her face told him she didn't like the idea.

"Why does he want to talk to you? Alex, be careful! He's a criminal. I never liked him, and history has shown I was right to mistrust him. Are you sure you want to go?"

Of course, he wasn't sure, but curiosity had gotten the better of him and ignoring all his inner senses, he had agreed to meet Josip.

"Yes, I'll meet him in his apartment. I'm sure it's nothing. I'll be fine."

He kissed her and wanted to leave, but she grabbed the sleeve of his coat and pulled him back.

"Alex, when were you going to tell me?" she asked with a stern voice, looking him straight in the eye. It scared him. What had he done wrong now?

"Uh ... what?"

"When were you going to tell me you want to go to the US?"

He was speechless. How could he tell her she had been one of the reasons for his decision? It was strange. She seemed genuinely offended. Sometimes he thought he had her all figured out, and then she did something that didn't fit that image at all. Those expressions of care and genuine interest in his life alternated with moments of sheer jealousy, reproach, and anger. Anger, a lot of anger.

"How do you know?"

"Annette Norman. She helped me with your father's stuff this morning, and she told me you asked Mats for advice."

She waited a second before continuing: "Looks like you can talk to Mats about this, but not to me?"

He sighed.

"Mom, I've been thinking about this for a long time, and I haven't made up my mind yet. Yes, it's a great opportunity, but honestly, I didn't know how to tell you."

"You thought I wouldn't understand?"

What was he going to say? Was she really expecting an answer?

"I know it's time for you to go your own way. You need to build up your own life, instead of worrying and taking care of your parents. I understand. But I would be lying if I said I wasn't worried. And it would have been nice to be consulted about it. To help you."

This was such a contradiction with her behavior the day before, and he didn't trust it.

"Mom, you're right. I'm sorry. I asked Mats because he knows the academic world. He has connections, and he knows what my chances are. So far, I have only spoken to him about it once. That's it."

"And?"

"In principle, I could start in the summer. I can finish my dissertation by then and come back for the defense at the end of the year. It should be workable."

"So why haven't you decided yet?" she said in a low voice.

He lowered his eyes. Everything was so messy in his head. Maybe she was right, and maybe he just wasn't capable of living alone. Going to the US was a big step.

"Alex, your father is gone. I know he never wanted to hurt us, but he did anyway. You're in pain, but that shouldn't stop you from living your life. There is nothing here that should hold you back. I'll be fine. I have my friends and my sister. You are so smart. You should amaze the world with your talent. Take the job."

Why couldn't she always be like that ... this loving and supportive mother? He had rarely seen this side of her. Now it seemed unnatural, fake. How could he believe everything was okay? It wasn't okay. Nothing was fine in his life.

"Are you serious?" he asked.

She nodded and took his hand.

"Okay," he kissed her on the cheek, "we'll talk about this later. Now I really have to go."

She let him leave. He took the laptop from the table in the hallway and left the house. The snow was coming down heavily. Instead of going back to the university, he went to his apartment. He needed to know what was in those files.

* * *

When he entered the flat, it was cold. The bedroom window was open. He had forgotten to close it in the morning. The snow, flown in, had left a pool of water on the floor which he, a prisoner of his OCD, had to clean up first. He turned the temperature up and put the laptop on the desk next to the black book. Decoding the encrypted files was done in no time. Hacking had been one of his favorite hobbies as a teenager when he had been hiding in his room from all the fights between his parents. Hiding from his father's erratic behavior and his mother's bullying. He had been part of several internet communities specialized in cryptography, and had learned the ins and outs of hacking, coding, and decryption.

Most files were disappointingly boring and uninteresting, except two. There were scans of a birth certificate - his own - and a lease contract for what appeared to be a house. It was difficult to read. The name on the document, Nikolaj Blom, meant nothing to him. Why were these files left on the computer and why were they encrypted? He felt frustrated. He had gotten more questions than answers. The GenoOne letter, sticking out from the pages of the black book, caught his attention again. How could he have put it in so casually? The symmetry was lost. He removed the letter and placed it, nicely aligned, next to the laptop. He entered "GenoOne" in the Google search engine. The browser history hadn't been deleted. A few months before his death, his father had searched for labs that could do DNA sequencing.

"DNA, paternity testing ... why were you looking for that?" he whispered.

It could only mean one thing. He closed the laptop and paced the room. Had his father seriously thought he wasn't his son? Why? And who was his father then? Should he confront his mother with this? The thought alone turned his stomach.

He went back to the desk, picked up the book and flipped through it again. The lines of dates and places still didn't mean anything to him. The comments were sometimes illegible or made little sense. He looked at the clock: 5 p.m. Three hours before the meeting with Josip Radić. Maybe his childhood friend could give him more answers.

CHAPTER

9

ONLY THE CRACKING OF SNOW beneath his feet could be heard as he walked through the empty streets of Uppsala to Josip's apartment that night. It was almost full moon. Without a cloud in the sky, the moonlight, reflecting off the historic buildings and snowy landscape, brought a certain idyllic and mysterious ambiance to the city as Alexander began his walk from the center toward the outskirts of the town. As he moved north, the buildings became simpler, more structured, and industrialized. All houses looked alike and lacked identity and creativity in his mind. Few people were on the street. Through the open curtains, he saw the light from the TV reflecting off the walls and windows. People seemed motionless, dull, uninterested, depressed. It breathed a tone of indifference. A vague sense of unrest settled in his mind, and he accelerated his pace. He should have taken the bus, but walking helped to clear his mind and these days there was a lot to clear. The events of the last days had left him even more insecure and vulnerable than ever before. The constant rumination exhausted him, and he desperately wanted some sleep, some nice refreshing sleep. He stopped and looked around. It was so quiet. Ever since he had left the apartment, he had the feeling someone was following him. Everything looked strange, and behind every shadow, menace seemed to lurk. The sense of imminent danger grew stronger with each step. Maybe he should just go home? It was not too late. But his curiosity got the better of him, and he continued on his way.

After thirty minutes of walking, stopping, and doubting whether to go back, he finally reached the apartment building. It was a six-story high-rise building with two apartments per floor. Josip's apartment was on the fourth. He pressed the buzzer and waited. There was no response, and he pressed it again. An icy wind numbed his face and ears. He put the collar of his coat up to get warm. Ten minutes passed and still no response. Disappointed and a little worried about his friend's no-show, he decided to go back, but stopped when he saw a young woman walking to the front door with a stuffed shopping bag in one hand and a laptop bag on the other shoulder. She didn't seem to mind that he sneaked in behind her. The elevator was old and took a while to come down. She kept looking and smiling at him, saying nothing. As always, he didn't know how to react.

The woman got out on the second floor, and he continued his way up to the fourth. When he got out, the hall was immersed in darkness. The light switch was broken and after a few tries he gave up trying to get it to work. In the dim light of the moon, pouring in through a small window, facing the street, he saw the two doors of the apartments on either side of the elevator. One door was open, and a bright light shone from behind the door. He walked slowly to the door and, without thinking, pushed it open. Someone had thrown pieces of papers on the floor, chairs were knocked over, drawers half opened and thrown on the ground. The place had been burgled. What possessed him to enter when all his inner senses were screaming to go back?

"Josip, are you here?" he whispered.

There was no response.

Suddenly he heard a soft sound behind him, and he froze. It was so stupid to enter like that. He should have left and warned the police, but now it was too late. The person who had done this was still in the room, behind him, slowly emerging from the dark. He held his breath. His brain was overloaded and shouted conflicting instructions. He didn't know what to do. There was a hard blow to the head. The sharp pain pierced through his skull, stopped his breathing for a moment and made everything turn black before his eyes. It was as if every system in his body shut down at the same time. He fell to the floor.

* * *

When he woke up, everything was blurry, and he touched his head. His fingers were stained with blood, his own blood. He tried to get up but couldn't. His head felt heavy and there was an invisible force that kept pulling him down. With the greatest difficulty, he dragged himself to the door and crawled out of the apartment, before passing out again. Images of a bearded man staring at him alternated with memories of his childhood. Josip and himself. Happy memories, fun, and laughter, and then suddenly changing to desperation and terror. The face of a girl, crying, begging for her life. Tearful eyes, first terrified, then acquiescence and compassion. When the pain came, reality took over, and he heard a man's voice calling his name. Then footsteps running away from him, down the stairs. He tumbled back in a dreamlike state.

All his senses were disturbed. The hearing came back first. The voices, which at first seemed so distant and unintelligible, became clearer and he understood they were calling his name. Opening his eyes was more difficult. When his eyesight finally got back to normal, he realized he was lying in an ambulance with a paramedic leaning over him.

"Ww, where am I?"

The dizziness made it impossible for him to sit up.

"Mr. Nordin, please lie down, you have a severe concussion," the woman said and gently pushed him back onto the gurney.

"What happened?" he asked.

"A resident found you on the floor in front of his apartment when he got home. The other apartment has been broken into. The police may want to talk to you later, but now you should rest and lie down."

The headache was getting worse, and he still couldn't see clearly, having problems focusing. As he lay in silence, he felt a soothing relaxation coming over him. For the first time in a long while, he could let his mind go blank. But the moment of peace was short-lived and suddenly interrupted by a familiar voice.

"Mr. Nordin, so we meet again."

He opened his eyes and saw the face of a woman. He recognized her: inspector Isa Lindström. It took him a while to get up. The nausea was getting worse. He heard one of the medics say: "Inspector, he has a severe concussion. He needs to rest."

"I'm sure he'll be able to answer some questions," Isa said with confidence. She turned to Alex. The young man was struggling to keep his focus on the conversation.

"I know you're not feeling well, but I need to know what happened here," she said.

"I, I ... I don't know," he tried to explain.

"Okay, let's start with ... why are you here?" Isa asked and took her notebook. She sat next to him in the ambulance.

"I ... I ..."

It was so hard to find the words and make a decent sentence. His head felt heavy, and his thinking was so slow. He wanted to lie down again, but instead he supported his head with his right hand.

"Mr. Nordin?"

"Uh ... I got a phone call from Josip Radić yesterday."

He took a deep breath and continued, "He wanted to talk, and we agreed to meet at his place at ... seven. No ... 8 p.m. But ... uh ... when I arrived, he wasn't there, but the door was open. I think ... I went in and saw the mess. The burglar must have hit me. From that moment on, I remember nothing."

"Did you see the face of the man who attacked you?"

He shook his head no. He wasn't sure what had been real or what had been a hallucination and a figment of his imagination when he had been lying on the floor and had seen the strange man's face.

"Do you have any idea why Josip Radić wanted to talk to you?"

"No, no ... but he sounded very agitated. I haven't seen him in years. It's strange."

"Do you think it has anything to do with Sandviken?" she asked and wanted to see his reaction.

It had crossed his mind. But what did she know? Why would she ask this?

"And?" she was waiting for an answer.

"Maybe ... really, I have no idea what he wanted to discuss," he replied, irritated by her persistence and lack of concern about his condition.

"Well, that didn't get us anywhere," she sighed and continued almost immediately: "We will need your fingerprints to distinguish them from others at the crime scene. Did you touch anything?"

"No, I don't think so ... although ... I really can't remember what I did after I got hit."

He paused for a moment and touched his head with both hands again. With every heartbeat, he felt the pain pounding in his head and growing stronger. Only then, she noticed the bruise and cut on the right side of his forehead, running along the side of his head toward the back.

"Inspector, can I do this tomorrow?" he pleaded.

Maybe she was too hard on him. He really didn't look good. She left the ambulance and went to the paramedic standing a few meters away.

"His injuries are ...," Isa started and turned around. He was still sitting on the stretcher, face hidden in his hands. She couldn't take her eyes off him.

"Severe," the paramedic completed.

"Yes," Isa nodded.

"I think someone hit him with a sharp object ... about ten centimeters long. He really needs to go to the hospital. A 24-hour observation is necessary to rule out bleeding in the brain. He shouldn't be left alone."

"Of course," Isa agreed.

"But ... he refuses to go to the hospital."

"Okay, I'll make sure someone takes care of him."

She took the phone out of her pocket and quickly dialed a number.

"Thomas, where is Radić? Is he still in the bar?"

The voice on the other end hesitated for a moment and then said: "We've lost him."

"What do you mean you've lost him?"

"We waited outside the bar for a long time, thinking he was still there. When we went in, he was gone. He must have left through a different exit. I'm not sure how long ago ..."

"Come on, guys! Amateurs! You should have known this could happen."

She yelled at him. Why had she tasked the juniors of her team with this? An error in judgment?

"So, he could have been here, in his apartment. Find him! He's hiding something."

She put the phone back into the pocket of her coat, threw her head back, and sighed. She felt exhausted.

A few police officers in uniform approached.

"Yes?"

"Are you inspector Lindström, Gävle police?" the eldest asked.

"Yes, what can you tell me?"

"We have done a first sweep of the place."

"And?"

"Many fingerprints, but it's hard to say whether they all belong to the owner of the apartment or not. He's in the system, so we should know soon. No sign of the weapon that was used to attack Mr. Nordin, and at first sight, nothing was stolen. TV, radio, even money was still there. Do you think this has something to do with the case you're working on?"

"Maybe. Did the neighbors see anything?"

"No, the man across the hall came home around nine. He was the one who found Mr. Nordin. When he left the apartment in the morning, everything seemed fine. However, he doesn't interact much with his neighbor. Mr. Radić is a bit of a loner."

"I see. The burglars were looking for something ... but what? Nothing has been stolen. But we can't assume they didn't find what they were looking for. And we can't ignore the timing of this incident." And she looked at Alex, still sitting in the ambulance.

It was well after midnight when she decided to drive home. The inspection of the apartment had yielded no additional information. On the side of the street, on one of the concrete blocks that marked part of the sidewalk, she saw Alex sitting, cell phone in one hand, and touching the head wound, meanwhile patched up with a white bandage, with his other hand. The ambulance was gone.

"Why didn't you go to the hospital?"

He remained silent and stared straight ahead. The cold was piercing through his clothes, and his hands and feet felt stiff and numb. He had been sitting still for too long.

"How will you get home?" she asked.

As he looked up, he said: "I'm trying to contact my mother, but she's not answering ... I don't know."

It puzzled him.

"She should be home."

"Come on. I'll take you."

* * *

They drove in silence. The man next to her had his eyes closed and was trying to support his head with his right hand. She wasn't sure what to do when they would get to his place. The medic had asked to keep an eye on him, but it wouldn't be professional of her to stay. She planned to get hold of his mother as soon as they reached the apartment. The drive took only five minutes, but she had trouble finding a parking space. A good twenty minutes later they entered the apartment building. With some effort, he climbed the stairs, followed, and watched closely by Isa, afraid he would pass out and fall down the stairs.

"I think it's best to lie down," she said, taking his coat as they entered the living room. He nodded but said nothing. With stiff and cautious movements, almost like an old man, he sat down on the sofa. His responsiveness and reasoning had slowed down by a factor ten. The wound had started to bleed again.

"Your head ... it's bleeding again. Not much, but we should clean it. Do you have disinfectant and bandages?"

He touched his head and saw the bloodstained fingertips.

"The bathroom is behind you, to the left ... you might find something in the closet."

The bathroom was the tidiest she had ever seen. Everything was meticulously placed and ordered. The entire apartment was like that. The amount of furniture was minimal. It felt impersonal. No photos or memorabilia anywhere.

She found some iso-Betadine to clean the wound. When she entered the room, his eyes were closed. For a moment, when she saw him lying there, so still, she thought he had slipped into a coma. She touched him, and he jumped up, startled by the sudden and unexpected push.

Their faces were now so close she could feel his breath on her cheeks. His face had this amazing symmetry. She followed the lines from his lips and cheekbones up to his blue eyes. For a man, he had long eyelashes that made his eyes stand out even more. So beautiful.

The tension between them was unbelievable. He felt it; she felt it. It was like a hurricane racing through her entire body. Every cell, every nerve, every blood vessel resonated with longing for him. It took her by surprise, and she gasped for air. This wasn't supposed to happen. She looked away and took the bottle of iso-betadine.

"You really should go to the hospital," she whispered as she cleaned the wound. Her touch was gentle. The whole time he looked at her, her beautiful face, the slightly curly hair that fell a little messy on her shoulders. He wanted to touch her face.

But then she saw the scar on the inside of his left forearm. A vertical mark, running from the wrist about five centimeters up the arm. She stared at it in shock, and when he saw it, he quickly pulled the sleeve of his shirt down to hide it, as he always tried to do. Those moments were awkward, and he hoped she wouldn't ask about it. But she remained quiet, turned her eyes away from the arm, and continued to focus on the wound.

"I can't stay with you all night," she said with a soft voice, "but someone should be here. Shall I try to call your mother again?"

"Yes ... that would be nice. Thank you."

It was almost one o'clock when she tried to contact Irene Nordin. The old woman arrived at her son's apartment half an hour later. Alex, meanwhile in bed and slumbering between consciousness and sleep, was unaware of his mother's presence. Isa left ten minutes later. During the journey home, all she thought about was that one sizzling moment of pure longing. Alexander Nordin. He was a problem.

* * *

Her son was sound asleep. That night, the sofa would be her bed. Irene wasn't that tall, so she would fit perfectly. Alex always kept extra blankets in the closet, and she knew exactly where to find them. While she was setting up her temporary overnight stay, her eye fell on the black book lying on the desk by the window. She recognized it.

"I thought I had thrown it away ... why...," she whispered. This was one of the things she had put in the boxes and had asked Alex to put in the car. Why had he kept it? What did he know about it?

She took the book in her hands and flipped slowly through the pages. She had seen the notes before. Did he know what it was about? For a moment, she was tempted to take it. It wasn't good for him. It would only add stress and confusion, but she finally put it back in the same position as before and crawled into bed. The night would be short.

That night, Alex's nightmares came back in full force. The image of Josip, standing over him, alternated with images of summers in Sandviken. Voices, laughter, a sense of happiness, suddenly interrupted and replaced by a long black tunnel. He heard a young girl sobbing. A force pushed him through the tunnel. At the end, there was a faint light and as he walked slowly toward it, his anxiety rose with every step. The light came from behind the gaps of the closed metal door. The sobs were louder now. It was scary, and he hesitated for a moment. Should he go in? There was someone behind him. He felt the hand on his back, pushing him forward. His heart was racing. The door opened, and the light blinded him, but when he could finally distinguish features, he saw nothing but red, red spots on the wall and a pile of blood on the floor ... a hand, a foot, a body. She was still alive. The sobs turned to screams and a man's voice said: "What are you doing here?" It was a deep voice he didn't recognize. The scene was so gruesome he screamed and wanted to run back into the tunnel as quickly as possible, but he couldn't. Someone grabbed him and pulled him back into the room.

He screamed and jumped up in his bed, wildly swinging his arms. His mother was sitting next to him.

"Alex, Alex, it's okay ... it's okay," she tried to comfort him. It took him a while to realize it had been a dream ... the same dream as always, although this time it was different. The blood, the screams ... it was new, and it was more terrifying than before. His entire body was shaking uncontrollably, and he was about to throw up.

"Mom ... is that you?" he asked after he calmed down.

"Yes, I'm here. It's okay ... you got hit on the head. It's normal."

"No, that's not it."

He wanted to explain to her how terrifying these dreams were, how exhausting and sleep-depriving they had been for such a long time, but the details, so vivid and clear just seconds ago, had faded and seemed elusive and surreal. Instead, he looked at her and said, "Why are you here?"

"Inspector Lindström called me and asked to keep an eye on you. When I arrived, you were already asleep. Don't worry. I'll stay here the whole night. Try to get some rest and go back to sleep."

He remembered the attack in Josip's apartment. Yes, in the dream, Josip had been there and had talked to him, and he now believed he had seen him while lying on the floor in the hallway. He had to talk to inspector Lindström about that. There was no point in keeping it a secret.

He put his head on the pillow, and his mother put the blanket over him. Before she left the bedroom, he asked her: "Where were you this evening? I tried to call you several times, but you didn't answer."

She turned around, astounded by the way he had addressed her. It felt like an interrogation.

"I was with Annette Norman. She's having a hard time with her mother in the hospital and so ... anyway, I didn't notice you had called."

With his back turned to her, she couldn't see he wasn't entirely satisfied with the explanation. Where had she been so late at night? Was she telling the truth or was she hiding something? Was she with her lover? His real father? It had been haunting his mind ever since he had found the letter.

"Alex ...," she said hesitantly. There was something bothering him. She felt it, but she couldn't find the words to help him or make him feel at ease to open up to her. She never could, and maybe she didn't want to.

"I'd like to go to sleep now," he said.

She left the room. For the rest of the night, he struggled to fall asleep again, afraid the images of the dream would return, with all the grisly details, burned into his mind, unable to wipe them away this time.

10

"**HE'S NOT DOING** well," the doctor said and looked at the two people in front of him, Magnus and Sophie Wieland. There was a lot to take in. Despite many attempts to have their son Toby admitted to a specialized psychiatric hospital, he was still in the university hospital in Uppsala, for almost two months now. His mental health had deteriorated so quickly that his doctors didn't consider it appropriate to transfer him to an unfamiliar environment.

"He had at least two major episodes this week, and he tried to assault a nurse. We had to sedate him."

He waited a few seconds before continuing.

"Mrs. and Mr. Wieland, we often see that the support of the parents can help … so, what I am trying to say is that it can be helpful if one of you visits him more often. It can really make a difference."

"Doctor, I know … but I have this big case right now … I am trying to spend as much time with him as I can … but it's hard to see him like that."

Magnus sighed and then continued, "Sophie is here almost every day. Is that not enough?"

The doctor turned to Sophie, who quickly looked down at the hands in her lap and said nothing. Magnus noticed the tension in his wife's body. The cramped shoulders, the constrained movements, as if she were pinned to the chair, avoiding eye contact. She was hiding something.

"Sophie?"

She had increasingly delayed visits to the hospital. How many times had she been sitting in the car, with the key in the ignition, about to drive to the hospital, with Anna in the back? And then, overtaken by sheer anguish, she had stepped out again.

"I may have skipped a few," she mumbled. The expression on the doctor's face didn't change, but he knew that only Magnus had visited Toby in the past weeks.

"Mrs. Wieland, as I told you before, your support is crucial in your son's healing process."

With glassy eyes, the tears about to run down, fists clenched, she started, "You talk about healing, but you and I know that there is no healing in this case, ever. We are … he is condemned to a life like this forever. Don't talk about support! You don't know what I've done and what I've been through all these years!"

She couldn't stay there any longer. How could that man just sit there and judge her like that? And Magnus? What a saint! The perfect father. And she … the failed mother. With a tearful face, she got up and ran out the doctor's office.

"Doctor, sorry, I have to go after her," Magnus said and rushed out the door. He found her in the hallway, a few meters from the exit. People, passing by, gave her a strange look. Sophie was crying violently, head against the wall. Magnus took her arm and gently turned her around, so she would face him.

He said: "Isa ... I'm sorry."

He stopped, shocked by his own words. In that split second, he realized there was no way to take it back, no way to ever make it right.

"Isa? I see."

There it was. Isa. Beautiful, exciting, sensual Isa. Everything he wanted, everything she wasn't.

"Sophie, I'm sorry. It doesn't mean a thing. I swear."

"No, it means everything ... she's still in your head and in your heart," she said. "Maybe you should just go back to her."

Magnus fought back. She couldn't put this all on him. Where was her part in all this mess?

"You gave me no choice, Sophie," he said with a stern voice, "you didn't want me anymore."

But before she could respond, he continued immediately: "Why haven't you been visiting him? Why?"

That was a question she couldn't answer.

"You may not love me anymore, but he is our son. He needs both of us. Why is it so hard for you to love him? He's not the perfect child you had hoped for, but he's ours. We are responsible for him."

The perfect father. The perfect husband, but not for her. Not anymore.

She touched his face and ran her hands through his hair. Here and there a few gray hairs started to sprout. It made him look more distinguished and sexier. His tanned skin was glowing. What a beautiful man! That's why it was so hard for her to finally admit: "We want different things in life, Magnus. I'm not sure I still fit in this marriage. I'm sorry."

She broke free of his grip, and without looking back she walked away and out of the hospital. He could only stare at her. She had finally said it out loud. This was what he had wanted all along. Now he could move on without her. But why did he feel so defeated? Was this really what he longed for? Sophie was gone, maybe forever. His family ... well, there was no family anymore.

* * *

Almost on automatic pilot, he went back to the doctor's office. The conversation lasted for another twenty minutes, with the doctor explaining to him the new treatment he was planning for Toby, but Magnus heard nothing. In his head, he was still going over the conversation with Sophie.

"Mr. Wieland? Are you okay?"

The words slowly seeped through.

"Look, I wish I could tell you that everything will be okay, but most marriages in this sort of situations struggle and rarely survive without proper guidance. I see it all the time. As I have often suggested to your wife, we are willing to provide psychological counseling to you and the entire family. It may be good to talk to other families. I'll give you the number to make the first appointment."

Magnus was still trying to grasp what had happened in the past half hour. He was in doubt. A marriage of twelve years, just gone! Yes, they were so disconnected from each other and the rest of the world. He realized that now. It had happened unnoticed, gradually. In the past few years, they had invested nothing at all in their relationship. It had been so much easier to find love elsewhere.

He had to believe he had tried, that Sophie had tried, but maybe not hard enough. Strangely, Sophie's rejection and the doctor's words gave him renewed energy to continue and not give up. There was still doubt.

But hopefully, it wasn't too late.

The doctor handed him the card with the counselor's name and telephone number.

"Thank you, doctor. It has been very difficult for us, especially for my wife. We are grateful that you take such good care of him. I'll try to visit Toby as often as I can."

They arranged for a new meeting and then said goodbye. Outside, in the parking lot, he tried to call Sophie. Her car was gone, and all attempts to reach her failed. She had switched off her cell phone. Maybe it was best to give her space and time, but he was eager to talk to her. He had to explain. But what would he say? Should he convince her it was over with Isa? He didn't believe it himself. Isa, she was everything Sophie wasn't or wasn't any more. Passionate, adventurous, wild, carefree. It was so different from his seasoned relationship with Sophie. After twelve years, he missed the thrill of new love, the attraction, the flirting, and the chase.

But who was he kidding? That wouldn't last either. He would get tired of Isa, or rather, she would get tired of him.

He needed time to think. Isa, Sophie ... the doubt, the guilt. It was all there, like the pendulum of a clock swinging one way and the next moment going the other way. And then there was work. This murder case took up so much of his time. It wasn't going well. After two months, they still had no clue about the killer. Isa was right. Perhaps this was beyond their capabilities. Compared to the teams in Uppsala and Stockholm, they were just a bunch of amateurs. How on earth could they have ever imagined they could solve a case of this magnitude?

He tried to call Sophie one last time, without success. Then he drove off to Enköping where he had an appointment with Marian, the eldest daughter of Olav Bergqvist.

* * *

The meeting of the police officers on the case was taking place in Isa's office. Nina, sitting quietly in the corner of the room, was clearly bored and annoying everyone by continuously flipping through the pages of the file in her lap. Berger was leaning against the desk, as always, with a wait-and-see attitude. It was young and ambitious Lars who started by saying: "Where are our Uppsala friends?"

Isa gave him a quick, angry glance, just enough to make him change the topic of the conversation.

He continued: "The IT team is still working on the Facebook account. I'm not sure why it's taking so long. And Berger and I have paid a visit to the family of Clara Persson."

"And?" Isa asked.

Lars loved to bring his narrative with a good drama, and he usually started with cryptic, tension-building sentences as if he were going to make the most shocking revelation ever. But today his audience was tough. The frowned eyebrows of his boss were cues to tone it down and get to the point as quickly as possible. She was in no mood to hear long speeches.

"Her brother and sister were very helpful. They mentioned that in the few months leading up to her disappearance, Clara thought someone was stalking her. The house was burgled a few weeks before she went missing. Nothing was stolen except some underwear of Clara. The police were brought in, but the case wasn't exactly at the top of their priority list and the investigation was quickly closed."

"Let's go back to the stalker. Why did she think someone was following her?"

Berger continued the story: "Her sister said she had received short notes and presents from an admirer. And Clara had told her mom that someone had followed her a few times when coming back from school."

"Did she see who it was? Did she describe him?"

"No. Besides, her parents didn't believe it. She was a needy child, always looking for attention."

"But the notes and presents were real," Isa remarked.

"Yes, that's what the sister said, but for a thirteen-year-old, she had many admirers, and it doesn't have to point to a stalker," Berger said.

"Nina, what do you think?" Isa said and turned to the girl, barely listening to the conversation. Awakened from her reverie, Nina jumped up.

"Uh ... well, I don't think Clara was a random victim. It's likely the killer followed her for a while before abducting her. He probably took every opportunity to get close to her. Where would he have the best opportunity to do that? I wonder if he didn't approach her at school."

"Are you thinking of a teacher?"

Isa's interest was sparked. This was why they had hired Nina in the first place. She always came up with a slightly different point of view, and most of the time she was right.

"Yes, maybe, but I certainly would look at neighbors around the school and home, and maybe even parents of children who went to school there."

"Great. Berger, Lars, check which male teachers were present at that time ..."

"You assume she was kidnapped by a man," Nina remarked.

They all looked at her in surprise.

"There were no obvious signs of assault. So, in fact, we can't rule out that our perpetrator is a woman."

"You're right, but statistically men are more likely to abduct young girls than women."

"Just saying ...," Nina sighed.

Isa continued to address the young men: "Also talk to neighbors, classmates, and parents. Maybe they might have noticed something ... although it happened thirty years ago."

Nina wanted to intervene again. It was her suggestion. Why hadn't

Isa asked her?

Isa interrupted her: "I need you for something else, Nina."

She turned to the two men: "Lars, Berger, anything else?"

"Anna Falk," Lars said, "we went to talk to the brother about the night Anna disappeared."

"The brother, then eighteen, wanted to attend the New Year's party at his friend's house. Those days, the family was temporarily living in Stockholm because of the father's work assignment. Anna had insisted on coming. The parents initially refused, but she got her brother to convince them to let her join. This guy has been living with a tremendous feeling of guilt since his sister disappeared. The relationship with his parents is bad … they still don't talk to each other. Anyway, they arrived at the party around 8 p.m."

"How many people?" Nina asked.

"It was a big party with about fifty, sixty people or so. Mostly youngsters."

Berger jumped in, although Lars was eager to continue his story. There was a healthy competition between the two men in trying to impress the boss. Both had been with the police for almost five years, and they were determined to climb the career ladder as quickly as possible. But none of them liked Nina, the brilliant, energetic young woman who had joined the team six months ago. She had an exceptional way and intuition of looking at cases, and they clearly felt threatened by her.

"Her brother said she was very nervous and kept looking around as if she were looking for someone. She denied it, but he knew she was lying. He lost sight of her, and when he wanted to go home, he couldn't find her anymore. With some friends, they searched everywhere, inside and out, but she was gone. It's not clear when exactly she went missing. It could have been hours before her brother noticed the disappearance."

"Let's go back to what you said before," Isa interrupted. "Why did she insist on going to the party?"

"She was going to meet someone," Nina replied immediately, "and she didn't want her family to know."

"Exactly," Isa said and smiled at the young woman.

"There is something more. Weeks before the disappearance, someone occasionally left flowers at the front door of the family house. No note, no sign of who had left it there."

"So, another stalker," Nina said.

"Yes, but it wasn't stalking. She knew him, and she was looking for him at the party. They probably agreed to meet there."

Isa got up and paced the room.

"The modus operandi is very similar for these three girls: Clara, Anna Falk, and Stina. He follows these girls for a while, contacts them and gains their trust. And when they least expect it, he strikes."

"We need to check if this applies to the other girls. How far are the others in their investigation?"

Nina was right. The killer likely would have used the same way to approach them.

"I don't know," Berger said, "I haven't talked to them yet."

"I want to see them this afternoon," Isa said," it's really not going fast enough."

"I think the Uppsala guys have been meddling," Lars said carefully.

"What do you mean?" Isa turned to him.

"Inspector Finn Heimersson of the Uppsala police department was here yesterday, and he tasked our guys to turn over all the information to his team. I thought you knew."

"What the f...," Isa yelled and jumped up, "this isn't ... no, he can't do that ..."

"Is this official?" Nina asked.

"No, it's not," Isa said.

"Maybe Anders can talk to him," Berger suggested.

They all stared at Isa who, deep in thought, was pacing around the room without purpose. Anders had warned her. It wouldn't take long for the Uppsala team to take over. But nothing was official. It was just a power game, who would shout the loudest. They just had to carry on as if nothing had happened. But she would tell inspector Heimersson exactly what she thought of his attempt to undermine her investigation.

"Elin Dahlberg," Nina started, "I looked at the Elin Dahlberg case."

"What?"

Isa sighed, shook her head, and tried to focus on the conversation again.

"So, what did you find out?"

"It's a tragic story. Her mother died of a drug overdose five years ago. Her brother is in prison, sentenced to ten years for his involvement in the murder of a police officer in Stockholm. At the time of her disappearance, the girl was living with her grandmother in Eriksberg near Uppsala. The grandmother died shortly after Elin's disappearance at the end of 2010. I spoke to the neighbors. They remembered her as a friendly and very intelligent girl. Elin had cut all ties with her mother and brother after the mother had beaten up the girl in a drunken state. Her grandmother had taken her in and had provided some stability. They told me that after Elin's disappearance, the health of the old woman took a bad turn, and she died six months later."

"So, nothing new," Isa interrupted.

Nina nodded and took a moment to continue: "I think Elin was a mistake."

"Why do you think that?" Isa said, surprised.

"Well, she had the same physical features as the rest, but according to the neighbors and teachers, she was confident, mature, and smart, unlike the other girls, who were naïve and pretty self-centric. Maybe he thought she was a broken girl, abandoned by her family, and that she was looking for someone to love her."

"If she wasn't his type, why did he abduct her?" Lars asked.

"Good question," Nina said. "It means he took her randomly, on a whim, or he didn't have enough time to get to know her."

"He was pressed for time?"

"There were only two years between Ella Nyman and Elin Dahlberg," Lars remarked, "maybe Ella died too soon."

Nina hadn't thought of that. It made sense.

"He isn't a patient man, and he can't live without abducting a girl for too long. Stina died in 2016, a year ago ... so...," she said.

"He has already kidnapped another girl," Isa completed Nina's reasoning.

"Or he is looking for a new one," Berger corrected.

"Or maybe he's dead," Nina said.

Isa looked at the two men: "Lars, Berger, check the missing person reports for teenage girls who have disappeared in the past twelve months and check any reports about stalking. That's it for now. You can leave. I'll talk to both of you tomorrow. And Nina, you stay!"

Reluctant and frustrated by the fact Isa didn't want to include them in the secret conversation, Lars and Berger left the room.

* * *

Nina and Isa were alone in the office now.

"Nina, I want you to investigate the Nordin family."

"We've already done a background check on Alexander Nordin," Nina replied.

"Yes, there was nothing, but do you think we can get his medical records?"

"Inspector Lindström ... you know these fall under the doctor-patient confidentiality. The only way to get access is to have a warrant, but he's not a suspect. So, no chance. Why are you so interested in him? He couldn't have killed them. He's too young."

Isa had heard none of Nina's comments, absorbed by her own thoughts.

"What if I were looking for reports of domestic violence or ... a suicide attempt? Wouldn't that have been listed in the police records?"

"Uh ... yes, unless he was a minor at that time, and then the files would be sealed. Suicide attempt?"

"Okay, okay," Isa sighed and stared at the floor for a moment. It had nothing to do with the case. It was this strange fascination with Alexander Nordin that took over her thoughts at the most random moments. Her heart sped up every time she heard his name. She wanted to know everything about him.

"Does this have something to do with the murders?"

No, but she couldn't just admit it. Or maybe it had? Why would anyone attempt suicide?

"To be honest, I don't know, but I want you to investigate the father, Peter Nordin. I have the feeling this family may be at the center."

"I'll get on it," Nina said determinedly.

She got up and wanted to leave the room when Isa stopped her from opening the door.

"Has Alexander Nordin come in yet? We need to take his fingerprints to have an idea of who was in Josip Radić' apartment."

Nina shrugged her shoulders: "I don't think so. It's still early. Shall I contact him?"

"No, no, I'll do it," Isa said. That way she could hear his voice again. Just him and her. Just the thought excited her.

Nina left and Isa went through the files again. Magnus would return from Enköping later that day. She didn't know what she was looking for, but maybe they had overlooked a small detail that could be crucial in solving the case. Even the smallest thing could lead to the murderer.

But she got distracted by Alexander's file. There was nothing spectacular in it, but she couldn't stop looking at it. This wasn't good at all.

Focus, Isa, focus! But not on him.

* * *

That morning Alexander woke up with the faint sunlight shining on his face. The curtains of his bedroom were half open. It was past ten o'clock in the morning. The dizziness was still there, but the headache was less. He got up and went to the living room. His mother was busy making coffee in the kitchen. When she saw him, she smiled.

"How do you feel?" she asked.

"Okay," he said and stumbled to the bathroom. The dried bloodstain on his forehead annoyed him. It was dirty. There was probably blood all over his bed cover. It had to go. The bruises were spectacular: blue and green, slightly swollen, and his face looked so pale.

What was he thinking to go in like that? Why? To play the hero? Stupid. He could have died.

At least he had seen inspector Lindström again. He looked at his reflection in the mirror. Why was he smiling when he thought of her? She wasn't his friend. He was probably a suspect in her eyes.

Finally, he gave up trying to clean his face. It was too painful.

"Alex, come and sit down," his mother yelled from the kitchen, "coffee is ready, and I've made breakfast."

He went to the kitchen. The small table, just big enough for two, was filled with plates and baskets full of croissants and toast, and a warm, nice smelling cup of coffee. What was this? This had never happened before, and he didn't trust it.

"I'm not so hungry."

"Nonsense, you still need to recover from yesterday's ordeal. Sit down."

His mother sat down next to him.

"I'll take you to the doctor in the afternoon," she said as she poured herself a cup of coffee.

The sudden expression of concern and affection felt out of place. He was waiting for her to yell at him about how irresponsible he had been, but the "I told you so" didn't come. With an iron calm, she handed him the bread and jam.

"You don't have to. I'll be fine."

The last thing he wanted was to depend on her. Somehow it would backfire on him. It always did.

"No, you're not okay, and we have to go to the police station. I promised the nice female inspector to drop by. They have to ask you a few questions and you have to give your fingerprints."

He suddenly looked up and saw how carefully she was watching him. The nice inspector. No, he didn't want to see her. Not like that. She made him feel ... what exactly?

"I don't want to go to the police. Maybe tomorrow, but not today."

"Alright then ..."

She spent the rest of the breakfast babbling about her friends and sister, and what she had been up to the last days. He said nothing. This wasn't his mother. Something was wrong. A pleasant conversation at the breakfast table had been an unattainable dream for as long as he could remember. It was something normal, but nothing in his dysfunctional family had ever been normal. Why now?

"I'll be back later," she blurted out and got up, "I have to go home for a while. I'll be back this afternoon. Call me if something is wrong!"

"Okay."

It took her only five minutes to leave. His stress level dropped as soon as he heard the door close. He cleared the table, put everything back in the cupboards and walked back to the living room. His head felt heavy and painful. Work was impossible. Maybe it was best to lie down and sleep. He spotted the black book on the desk. It had been moved from its original position by at least half a centimeter. Someone had looked at it. Had it been his mother? Why hadn't she said anything? Or might it have been inspector Lindström?

CHAPTER

11

BLOOD. **SO MUCH BLOOD.** It was everywhere. The average adult has about five liters of blood circulating through his veins. Were these five liters? Splashed on the floor and the walls. The sweet metallic nauseating stench was mixed with the musty smell of mold. He had spent an hour looking at the corpse, mesmerized by the shiny coagulating drops that slowly spread over the floor, and the stillness of the person lying at his feet. Was she really dead?

He kneeled and gently touched the side of her pale face. It felt so cold. The eyes were wide open and stared at him. Her mouth, all twisted and frozen in a weird grimace by the starting rigor mortis, made her almost unrecognizable, as if she were wearing a mask. It had taken her by surprise. She had been so perfect, but now the big gaping wound in her neck and head destroyed it all. He gently ran his fingers down her arm and shoulders, down her breasts to her thighs. Never again would he make love to her, hold her in his arms, caress her, and feel her warm naked body against his. Clara ... sweet, beautiful Clara!

He got up and sat down in the wooden chair in the corner of the room. It was time to be practical now. How could he get rid of the body?

There was so much blood. It would take hours to remove it, but she had to go first. The blanket on the bed was just big enough to wrap the young girl. He put it carefully on the floor. But it was more difficult than expected, and he had to pull her arms and roll her over a few times before he could put her on the blanket. The blood stained his shoes and trousers. He stopped and looked at it. It felt dirty.

Wipe it off. No, not now. There was no time.

The physical labor was beyond anything he had ever done before, and it had drained all energy out of him. Panting and snorting like a dog, he sat down again on the chair. He was in such a bad shape. The cadence of his own breath brought a certain calm. He closed his eyes. It was so quiet. So soothingly calm.

And then ... What was that? There was a soft noise coming from behind the door. Suddenly, all his senses were on high alert. How could he be so stupid?

The door opened slowly. Paralyzed, he was just a mere bystander who saw it all happen, unable to intervene. But no one entered. The door was ajar, and he heard someone running away through the tunnel. He had to go after them. This was such a mess!

The tunnel, connecting the room to the entrance, was poorly lit. He only heard the footsteps. Small, quick steps. Something was wrong. Who was this?

Finally, light. The light at the end of the tunnel drew the contours of the person in front of him. It was a child. He stopped. He knew who it was. The sound of the footsteps faded.

What would he do? Go back or run after him? How could he explain this to him?

Go back or run after him? It was a calculated risk. He was just a child, with a vivid imagination. Who would believe him? But he was smart, maybe too smart, and people might trust him.

He went back to the room, continued to wrap the body, and waited until sunset to put the remains in the trunk of the car. He still didn't know what to do with her. What a mess he got himself in! This was murder.

Oh, God, this was murder! They would come after him. It had been a mistake to let the child go. He should have gone after him. But to do what? To persuade him not to tell? Would he kill him too?

The panic was so crippling. He was a man of reason, and he should be able to figure this out. Sitting behind the steering wheel of the car, he tried to calm down and find his peace of mind. Clara. Why couldn't he just keep her? Here. Forever.

He clenched his fists, dropped them on the steering wheel, almost hitting the horn, and let out a gust of frustration. With eyes closed, he tried to control his breathing. The sharpness of the mind returned, and within seconds the blast of neuron spikes painted a new image in his head. Yes, he knew what to do next. It could work; it should work. He got out of the car, locked it, and headed for the cabins.

* * *

The house of the Norman family had been out of the ordinary, but this impressed him even more. The two-story house stretched out over the wide lawns, now covered in snow. The large avenue leading to the house was planted on either side with tall, slender trees. As Magnus drove to the front door, he saw two Mercedes parked next to the house. Married to a venture capitalist, mother of two young boys, Marian Bergqvist, part-time fashion designer and socialite, had done well for herself. The woman who opened the door was in her mid-forties, blond, not too bad looking, and well groomed. She was pleasantly surprised by the handsome inspector standing at her front door. Maybe he was a little too old for her taste.

As he followed her to the living room down the impressive hallway, the excessive display of richness blew him away. It was like walking through a showroom: Chinese vases, Egyptian-style statues, large tapestries, and paintings decorated the cupboards, tables, and walls. But it felt like a sham. Why did people do that? It was a show to convince everyone how happy they were, and how well they had done in life. There was always something else hidden behind it.

The few photos that were displayed on the cabinet by the small window, opposite the seats where they took place, were mostly photos of her children. None of the husband. She offered him a cup of coffee, which he gladly accepted. While Marian went to get the coffee, he quickly checked his cell phone. There was still no word from his wife.

"You wanted to talk about my father, inspector," she said while she brought the tray and placed it on the glass table.

"Can I ask why?" she asked and handed him the cup.

"You must have heard about the dead girls in Sandviken."

She shook her head and said astonished: "Sandviken? My parents had a cabin there, and we spent most of our summer vacations in Sandviken."

"Yes, we know. That's why I contacted you. We believe this is the work of a serial killer who has been active for over thirty years."

"Thirty years, my goodness," she said.

Magnus took a sip of the coffee and continued: "We spoke with people who know the area: Alexander Nordin, Mats Norman, and Josip Radić, who suggested contacting you."

"Josip Radić! I haven't seen him for years. How is he doing these days? Wasn't he accused of abducting a girl?"

She wasn't completely honest with him. Josip had contacted her a few days earlier to meet, and yes, she had known what it was about. But for her, the case had been closed years ago, and she had refused to see him. Josip just had to forget everything and get on with his life as they all had.

"Yes," Magnus replied, "actually she was one of the girls we found in Sandviken."

For a moment, she didn't know what to say.

"Do you think he's guilty?"

"Josip Radić? I can't comment on this. But I wanted to talk to you about your time in Sandviken and ... about your father. It came to my attention that ..."

"No need to beat about the bush," she interrupted, "my father was a real bastard, a bully who mistreated my mother. He had no respect for women, and he is responsible for my sister's death."

The words came out so fast, as if she had bottled it up for years.

"Mrs. Mortensen ...," he started.

"Mrs. Bergqvist," she said, "Mortensen is my husband's name, not mine."

"Okay, sorry ... Mrs. Bergqvist, this is quite a bit of information. Can you tell me more?"

"Life at home was hell, especially for my mother. He hit her almost every day. And it got even worse when he got older. Even when my mother was already ill – she was diagnosed with cancer - he continued to treat her like crap. He treated all women badly, and unfortunately for him, for us, he had three daughters."

"Was he ever abusive toward you and your sisters?"

There was a silence. She got up and walked to the cabinet. He saw her elegant silhouette outlined against the sunlight pouring in through the window. What was she doing? She had triggered the question. She knew that. But after so many years, it was still so hard to talk about it, although she wanted to, she had to.

"Not against myself and Tasha ...," she started.

It was another lie.

"... but my youngest sister Elle, that's a different story. She was so beautiful, so lovely, but so vulnerable. She had always been his favorite, and somehow, we were jealous of the special relationship they had until we found out he had been raping her since she was six."

She paused. It was tough. There was so much regret. If only she had told Elle about the ordeal Tasha and herself had gone through all those years, if only they had realized that once their abuse had stopped, he had found another victim in their younger sister.

"By then it was too late. We couldn't help her anymore. Being in and out of psychiatric hospitals, she finally hanged herself in the bathroom of a cheap hotel, a few kilometers from here."

She stared at a photo, slightly hidden behind the ones of her sons. Her sister, her beautiful sister.

"You know what shocked me the most," she cried while holding it. Magnus shook his head.

"My mother defended him ... and she kept defending him until she died. Initially, Tasha and I broke all contact with my mother. We reconciled a few years before her death. But talking about Elle was taboo and would remain so until her death. We never reconnected with my father. Neither Tasha nor I were at his funeral."

"He died a few years ago, right?" Magnus interrupted.

"No, he passed away six months ago," she said, surprised.

"Six months ago, but I thought ..."

And he flipped through his notebook but couldn't find the information he was looking for. The background check of the Bergqvist family was missing. It had been a hearsay.

"He died all alone. I heard that only a few people attended his funeral." Because he had supposedly died before Stina Jonasson's abduction, Magnus had omitted Olav Bergqvist as a suspect, but now he was no longer convinced. Everything was open. Olav could have abducted and killed her before he died.

"How did he die?"

"Heart attack. They found him two days later after one of his neighbors alerted the police."

She sat down next to him and gave him the photo.

"This is my sister Elle when she was twenty," and she pointed at the young girl in the center, flanked by two other women, with the sea and a perfect blue sky in the background. He recognized Marian Bergqvist, but it was the third woman who caught his eye.

"Who is this?" Magnus asked, pointing at the woman on the left.

"That is my sister Tasha or Natasha. Why?"

"She has a daughter, Sara, right?"

"Yes, and a son."

Magnus had met Tasha before. She was the mother of Sara Norberg, Stina's best friend.

"Tell me about the cabin in Sandviken," he said, ignoring the confused look she gave him.

"Uh ... the property belonged to my grandparents. When they died, my father inherited it. In the nineties, but especially in the eighties, we often went there in the summers. There we met the other families: Norman, Nordin, and Radić. My sisters and I were much older than the other children, but that didn't matter. It was fun. At least for us, it was usually a time when my father was calmer and more behaved. After 2000, my parents rarely visited the place anymore. The past few years, my sister Tasha and her family used it for the holidays, but not as often as before. After my father's death and Tasha's divorce, we sold it."

"I am sorry to ask, but do you think your father might have abducted these girls and killed them?"

"He might have. He has a history of not only abusing his own children ... child, but ..."

A slip of the tongue. He had noticed it.

"He was charged with rape when he was a teenager. Even after that, there were rumors of him assaulting young women and girls. I wouldn't be surprised."

"They never arrested him?"

"No."

"There may have been rumors, but did you ever see any indications he was actually involved in these kinds of activities?"

"No, no ... maybe Mats Norman can tell you more. My father often went out with the professor. Mats was a bit of a womanizer. He probably knows more about what my father did on those nights out."

"Thank you. We will contact Professor Norman again. What about the other families? Nordin and Radić? Did you have a lot of contact with them?"

"Yes, we spent a lot of time with the children. Elle was fond of Alex. He was the youngest and still a toddler when we first met them. Elle loved to take care of him, like a mother. Josip was a different story. He was a wild boy, full of energy, but also full of anger. It wasn't too surprising he got into trouble."

She stopped and offered to pour him another cup of coffee, but he refused. Too much coffee would put him on edge.

"The Norman children - two boys and a girl - were always very charming, polite, always smiling. They looked too good to be true. Of course, the marriage was shaky. Everyone could see that. He went out to meet other women while she stayed at home and took care of the children. And like father, like son. His eldest son had a pretty turbulent love life himself, leaving his family for an eighteen-year-old girl, with whom he had a child. Of course, that didn't last. The number of women he had an affair with seems to be countless."

She didn't mention she had been one of them. It was a fling, which hadn't lasted long, but she had already been married. God, he had been exciting and so sexual, the first in a long line of young lovers. Her husband must have known, although he had never, not once in all these years, said a word about it.

"Mrs. Bergqvist, one last question, have there been, in all these years, strange things or events that caught your attention?"

"The red car," she said without hesitation.

"The red car? What do you mean?"

"I've always wondered ...," she mused.

In her younger years, she might have fitted the profile perfectly: slim, blue eyes, dark hair – she was blond now, but her real hair color was dark brown – and beautiful. Could she have been a target?

She continued: "It must have been more than twenty years ago. There was a time I had the impression I was being stalked."

"Why do you think that?"

"I saw a red car everywhere I went."

"It could have been a local," Magnus said.

Not a local. Why didn't she just tell him? Why tell him about the car and not the person? Because she wasn't sure at all.

"That's what I thought at first ... until there were a few incidents where the car followed me, slowly. I was so scared I remember running to the forest thinking he couldn't follow me. A second time, I rang the bell of a house nearby. Fortunately, people were home, and they let me in. The car drove off at high speed and that was the last time I saw it. I was afraid to tell my parents. They wouldn't have believed me, anyway. It wasn't until the following summer the subject of the red car came up again."

Why didn't she just tell him? If she told the story, she should just tell it all.

"What happened?"

"We were just walking around, just us… the children, and suddenly Alex mentioned he had seen the red car again. It was a shock ... I can tell you. The others didn't really know what he was talking about, but I did.

Later that day, I spoke to Alex again about the comment and he mentioned the man in the car had taken him for a ride and that he had enjoyed it. The man had told him he would come back and then he would also take his friends for a drive."

"He had talked to the man? He had seen him? Could he describe him?"

She smiled. She had asked the boy exactly that, but he couldn't tell her much, other than the man had a mustache, dark hair and a red cap. She realized he had been sitting in the back of the car, with no clear view of the driver. As she told the story to Magnus, she suddenly felt an adrenaline rush ... of fear. It was as if she was back there and then talking to Alex. She remembered how calm he had been, without showing the slightest sign of fear. But it felt like a threat, as if the man had wanted to let her know he could get to her friends anytime, anywhere.

"He mentioned he saw the car again. Is that correct?"

"Yes, but this time the car had followed him for a while as he walked to the village."

"What happened next?"

"I can tell you I was really scared that summer," she said, "but finally ... I didn't see the man and the car anymore. Alex never spoke about it again, and so I finally forgot all about it."

She kept staring at the ground for a while. This was the moment to confess. But the truth ... what was the truth? They wouldn't understand. She didn't understand it herself.

She let it pass.

"Mrs. Bergqvist, if there is nothing more you can think of, I'd like to thank you. If I have any more questions later, can I call you?"

"Yes, no problem," she replied.

It was nice to feel the fresh air outside, on his face, in his lungs. The past hour, every sense in his body had been challenged. The visual overload, the perfume so overpowering it had burned the hairs in his nostrils. But as with any scent, he finally got used to it. He took another deep breath. It was good to see the simplicity of the plain snow. He reached for his cell phone as he walked to his car. The missed call was from Isa. No message from Sophie. Isa needed him back in the office, but he didn't go to the police station. He drove back home.

* * *

The whiteboard was covered with pictures of the nine girls and protagonists. The scribbles next to the photographs were mostly Isa's. Facts, remarks, but sometimes even disconnected thoughts, written on post-its or written in felt-tip pen next to the photos. Nina looked at it in horror. She liked it to be more structured and systematic, but that wasn't Isa's style. Lars and Berger entered the room. The main room was open and bright, with many windows toward the outside and toward the hallway, which was not always practical as most passers-by could see everything: who was in the room, what presentations were being given and in this case the whiteboard with all the case information. Isa was sitting in the back, feet casually put on the table in front of her and the eyes fixed on the whiteboard. It irritated Nina even more. The careless style of her boss clashed completely with her own structured by-the-book way of working. This chaos wasn't efficient at all.

They were waiting for Isa to start the meeting, but she kept looking at the whiteboard. Magnus had failed to show up. He had sent a summary of the interview by email and had gone silent after that.

"Inspector Lindström?"

Isa suddenly jumped up and approached the board.

"Okay," she started, "something new?"

"Inspector Wieland talked about a red car, right?" Berger said.

"Yes, Marian Bergqvist was stalked by someone in a red car," Isa confirmed.

"Well, at one point the Nordin family owned a red Volvo. This was between 1990 and 1997."

"This makes little sense. It can't have been Peter Nordin. Why wouldn't his son recognize his own father? Or it must have been someone else in that red car."

"But there is more," Berger continued. "Remember in the Ida Nilsson's case they interrogated a man about the girl's disappearance?"

Isa nodded.

"Well, that man was Peter Nordin. Someone had seen him driving around the neighborhood when she disappeared. The police tracked down his car and interviewed him. He stated he was confused, and that he had been driving around without knowing where he was. This statement was later also backed by his wife and doctor. At that time, he was prescribed heavy medication to treat his depression. They admitted him to a psychiatric hospital shortly after the incident, where he stayed for six months."

"When was this?" Isa asked.

"Early 1992. I got the information from Janus."

There was a moment of silence while all eyes were back on Isa.

"So, let's recap ... last September, Alexander Nordin found the remains of Katrien Jans. Nine bodies were buried in Sandviken. Girls who had disappeared over thirty years. During that period four families regularly spent their summers together, near the area where the bodies were found: Nordin, Bergqvist, Norman, and Radić. Coincidence or not, the fact is that Josip Radić was arrested for the kidnapping of Katrien Jans, but later acquitted. The same Josip Radić recently disappeared after a mysterious phone call to Alexander Nordin, his longtime friend, requesting to meet him at his place to talk about ... something, we don't know what. Fact two is that one of the missing girls was the best friend of Natasha Bergqvist's daughter, Sara. Fact three is that Peter Nordin, Alexander's father, was seen in the neighborhood when Ida Nilsson went missing. Fact four: someone stalked the girls in the days and months before their disappearance."

"Fact five ... Peter Nordin worked as a salesperson at Ikea between 1985 and 1999 ... he quit his job when his mental health deteriorated," Nina added, "he would have access to plenty of plaids that were used to wrap the girls after their death."

"Peter Nordin, is he the one?" Isa asked.

"He died on 8 September 2016. Stina Jonasson was abducted on 7 September 2016, the day before. He could have taken her and killed her the same day and then taken his own life. He was mentally unstable. Maybe it was more than a depression. Maybe he was trying to fight these urges and ended up committing suicide ... out of guilt?"

"Okay, thanks, Nina. Let's see if we can get a search warrant based on these facts. Let's also talk to the psychiatrist who treated Peter Nordin. Maybe he knows something else. And Mrs. Nordin."

"She called," Nina replied.

Isa turned to her protégé, surprised.

"Why?"

"Alexander has yet to give his statement regarding the burglary, and she asked if she could bring him to the police station. She wanted to do that yesterday, but neither you nor inspector Wieland were available. So, they're coming this afternoon."

"Alright, I'll talk to her," Isa continued, and she stared at the photos again.

"Somehow ... it doesn't feel right," she whispered.

Nina joined her in front of the whiteboard.

"I know," Nina replied.

Isa turned around and addressed the young men.

"Have you found any other missing girl cases that could be related?"

"There are plenty of reports of missing teenage girls in the Uppsala area, mostly girls who ran away from home and were later found. Three cases may be interesting for us to take a closer look, but we haven't gotten the time yet to ..."

"Then do it quickly ... a life may be at stake," she yelled and left the room, with Nina running after her.

"Isa, it really makes little sense," she said, "Peter Nordin is dead ... if any of the abductions are related to this case, it can't be him."

"Damn ... I feel like ... if ...," Isa gasped, exhausted by the emotional stress. Nina was right, of course.

"As if we are being played," Nina said.

12

MOTHER AND SON ARRIVED at the police station that afternoon. Alexander was sitting next to his mother in the interrogation room and getting agitated. There was something disturbing about police rooms and police officers. It was as if his entire life was under scrutiny. Irene Nordin was calm and controlled in every way. Everything about her showed that she was a classy and educated woman, who had learned to be composed in every situation. She had been raised not to show unnecessary displays of emotion in confrontations like this, very different from her son, who had a hard time controlling his nervous tics. Anxiety was written all over his face.

Isa took a few deep breaths before entering the room. Control. She had to keep herself under control. No staring, no exuberant laughter or loud talking. But their eyes crossed, just for a second, and immediately she felt goosebumps running all over her body. No, this was not a good idea. How could she be focused when he was right in front of her?

He looked pale and tired, and part of his face was still all blue and swollen. He hadn't recovered from the concussion yet. It was too soon. Perhaps it was best to call off the interview and let him recover first. Yes, this would be so much better. For him ... and for her.

She was staring at him, a little too long to go completely unnoticed by Irene and Magnus. Alexander turned his eyes away and gawked at his hands again. He did this a lot lately. Like a little boy, feeling caught.

Ten fingers, six steps to the door, 342 steps to the car in the parking lot, 18 songs on the radio during the drive to the police station. It was all good.

"Mrs. Nordin, Mr. Nordin, aside from the burglary, we would like to ask both of you some questions about your late husband and father," Magnus started the conversation, "I hope this won't be a problem?"

"No ... we'll try to help in any way we can," Irene replied calmly. Her son was less restrained. Why did they want to talk about his father? Although he had never admitted it to himself, was there a chance his father was responsible for this? Did the police have any evidence? Why?

Inspector Wieland opened the file on the table, pulled out a pen and wrote down a few things, before addressing Alexander, who was diagonally opposite to him.

"You said Josip Radić contacted you a few days ago. When was this?"

"Five days ago. He called me in the evening, around nine or maybe even later. I don't quite remember anymore."

He tried to keep his eyes fixed on Magnus.

"What was the conversation about?"

"It was short. He said he wanted to talk, and if we could meet as soon as possible ... like the next day. It was urgent."

"Any idea what he wanted to talk about?" Magnus continued.

"No, not really."

"You didn't call him again to ask for more information?" Magnus asked.

"Not at that time, no," Alexander said, "but I tried to call him after the burglary to find out if he was fine. I got no reply. Every time it switched to voicemail."

"I see." Magnus wrote a few sentences on the paper in front of him. Alex's hands were trembling. He noticed Isa hadn't taken her eyes off him during the entire conversation. How could he be calm? What would inspector Wieland think? Maybe he had something to hide? Obviously, she had no problem with the unease of the whole situation. While he ... he felt like a love-stricken teenager who was ashamed of the stupid things he would do or say.

"And then what happened?"

"The next day, around 8 p.m., I walked to his apartment, rang a few times, but no one was there. If a woman hadn't entered the apartment building at that moment, I would have just left. But I slipped inside, took the elevator, and got out on the fourth floor. The door was unlocked, and a light was shining inside the room, so I entered. The room was a mess. Everywhere ... papers on the floor, chairs knocked over ... it took a few seconds to realize this was the scene of a burglary. And then I heard a sound coming from behind. I wanted to turn around, but at that moment someone hit me, and I lost consciousness."

"They found you outside of the apartment. How did you get there?"

"I, I don't know for certain. I think I must have crawled out."

"Or someone helped you," Magnus interrupted.

His gaze, stern and forceful, was intended to intimidate the witness.

Alexander remembered the blurry image of the bearded man. It was Josip. It must have been him. Josip had helped him, but he had run away and left him on the floor in front of his apartment. Why?

"No, no, I don't think so," he replied.

"Now, let's go back to why Josip might have called you. You see, the timing is quite interesting. Do you think he might have called you because he knew something about the girls?"

"Why would he do that?" Irene Nordin asked quickly. "What would he know?"

"He was directly involved in the disappearance of at least one of them. Maybe he remembered something ... something to do with your late husband?"

"What do you mean?" Irene asked.

"We have a few questions about your husband," Isa broke the silence. So far, she had let her partner lead the conversation.

"The police questioned your husband in 1992 about the disappearance of Ida Nilsson."

Irene was baffled, and she quickly turned her head away from her son when she heard him say, "Mom?"

She had never told Alex. It hadn't been one of Peter's finest moments. She still remembered him sitting at the table in the police office. That person hadn't been her husband. The mumbling, the bewildered look, the trembling of the hands, rocking back and forth in the chair. It had petrified her. How could a perfectly sane man spiral down to the mere shell of a madman, locked in a world of his own, oblivious to the people around him? Unmindful of her, his wife.

"This was all a misunderstanding. My husband was only questioned and never arrested."

"The story he told was rather strange and incoherent," Isa remarked, "claiming he was being followed."

"He was heavily under the influence of medication ... heavy medication to treat his depression. He was delusional, erratic, and disconnected. He should have been home, not driving around, but ... I lost sight of him. It was my fault."

She folded her hands and while her words sounded emotional, her posture was not.

"He admitted seeing the girl that afternoon?"

"That's all very well possible, but did your colleagues at that time have any proof that he was involved?"

There was a silence. Neither Isa nor Magnus said anything.

"I didn't think so. I remembered they searched his car, tried to find out his whereabouts that day. They even searched our home ... but nothing."

"You know, Mrs. Nordin, this doesn't seem like the behavior of a depressed person," Magnus intervened.

"Are you a medical doctor?" Irene said stoically, "I don't think you are qualified to make these statements."

The whole time, Alex had been still, watching the ping-pong conversation between his mother and the inspectors with increasing amazement.

"You owned a red Volvo in the early nineties. Correct?"

"Yes, it was the same car my husband was driving when he was questioned about the disappearance of the girl. How is this relevant?"

"We have a witness who claims a vehicle very similar to the one you and your husband owned was used to stalk a young girl in the beginning of the nineties ... in Sandviken."

After saying this, he turned to Alex. Would he remember?

There was no reaction.

"Who? And who would remember this after so many years? There are plenty of red cars. I don't think ..."

"Marian Bergqvist."

The next moment, he was back in that car. The passenger window in the back was half open, and he could feel the wind blowing through his hair and the sunshine on his face. He tried to put his hand out, but he was too small. The man in the front had his hands firmly on the steering wheel. He couldn't see the face and he didn't quite know who it was, but it all felt so familiar. He didn't feel scared at all. In the distance, he saw his friend Marian walking along the hiking trail, close to the trees. He wanted to call out to her, but then he saw how frightened she was when she turned around and noticed the car. She ran, and the car accelerated. The carefree feeling suddenly gave way to fear, and he threw himself in the backseat, his fingers firmly plunged into the leather cover. When he felt the car speed up, he cried. He wanted to get out.

* * *

He said nothing. There could be only one explanation ... it must have been his father. But he wasn't ready to give up on his dad just yet. It felt like disloyalty. Maybe he had misinterpreted the situation.

Irene went on the offensive.

"It was no secret we had a red car. Marian Bergqvist must have known. Why didn't she say anything?"

Magnus and Isa looked at each other. It was a mystery why she hadn't made the link with the Nordin family. Maybe Marian knew her stalker. Maybe she knew it hadn't been Peter.

Irene continued, "Well ... I see you have no proper explanation for that. Everything you told me is circumstantial, no direct evidence, just speculation."

"Stina Jonasson disappeared the day before your husband died. What happened those two days? After all those years, was Peter finally remorseful and did he take his own life?"

"I found my father," Alex interrupted.

And just like that, the conversation dropped dead. He pulled the strap of his watch. His fingers were trembling. Irene stared at it; everyone did. It seemed endlessly repetitive. She put her hand on his to stop him, but he pushed it away.

It seemed like yesterday when he put the key in the lock, turned it

144

and opened the front door. It was already dusk outside, but he didn't switch on the light. He knew perfectly well where everything was in the hall: the wardrobe to hang his coat, the table with the glass tray where everyone put the keys. His mother's keys were gone. That was strange. She had no plans to go out, not with his father being so ill. Where was she? It stayed quiet when he called his dad's name.

His eyes were not accustomed to the darkness yet. For a moment, he stood completely still. At the top of the stairs was a strange shadow he didn't recognize. It looked like a person, but then again not. It was as if a man were floating above the ground. He turned around to switch on the light. When he finally looked up ...

"He was hanging on the railing of the stairs ... in the hallway."

Did he just say this aloud? The words came out in an unstoppable flow.

"His face was all blue and the expression: it was ... horrible. I tried to get him down, but I couldn't. I couldn't get him down, I couldn't ... if I had been faster, he might still be alive. If I had come home earlier, I could have stopped him."

If, if, if.

That day, he hadn't counted the steps to the door. It could have been an odd number. The buttons of the coat hadn't faced the window, and it hadn't been perfectly aligned with the other jackets. It was all his fault. Why had he given up these habits?

Isa watched as the fingers of his right hand fumbled from his watch to the inside of his wrist. The scar she'd seen that night.

Suddenly she leaned forward and put her hands on his right hand. She wanted him to stop, and he did. Why did she touch him? Magnus stared at her hands. It was a simple gesture, but nothing had shocked him more. Alexander Nordin was not entitled to this kind of affection from her, but he was, and only he. It was inappropriate, but it felt so right. Her fingers slid over his. His heartbeat resonated through the layers of skin.

From the corner of her eye, she saw Magnus' bewildered expression and quickly removed her hands.

"Alex, the coroner's report says your father must have been dead for hours when you found him. You couldn't have saved him."

Alex? Since when was she on a first name basis with him? Magnus' anger, seeded by the glances they had exchanged and fueled even more by her compassionate attitude, had now grown to proportions he could barely contain. Alexander Nordin and his mother were suspects. If he could, he would have arrested him on the spot. Why? It didn't matter. It was jealousy whispering in his ears.

"But I'd like to know where your father was in the days leading up to his death," Magnus interrupted. "Mr. Nordin, since you were your father's keeper, maybe you can enlighten us about his activities. Did he leave the house?"

His reaction was slow. The words barely seemed to permeate.

"Mr. Nordin?"

"This is over a year ago, I don't know," Alex said, but he lied, and his mother knew. The days before his suicide, his father had gone missing on three occasions, each time for several hours. Even then, they had feared for his life, but he had returned home every time, not knowing where he had been, not knowing who he had spoken to. Alex now knew Peter had been in touch with GenoOne about the DNA analysis even the day before he died. But Peter had been melancholic and very emotional. He had told stories of older days, when life had been so much easier, and he had babbled about how he probably would have to do the most difficult thing in his entire life. His mother should have been home that day, but she wasn't, and Peter had carried out his suicide plans. Irene had never told her son where she had been. It was almost too horrendous to think she had left on purpose.

"Nothing comes to mind, Mr. Nordin?" Magnus asked again.

He shook his head.

"That is strange! Doctor Wikholm told us he saw Peter a few days before his death. He was alone, totally upset, and told the doctor his family probably didn't know where he was. You forgot to mention that it was you who came to pick him up."

"What else did Doctor Wikholm tell you?" Alex asked.

What did they know? They'd find out. Maybe he should just tell them everything.

"I am asking the questions ... not you," Magnus snapped, but on the other side of the table, neither mother nor son were impressed.

"Doctor Wikholm didn't tell them anything confidential if you're worried about that, Alex," his mother said calmly, "they need a court order to access medical records."

"On several occasions, your son called the good doctor to inquire if his father was there ... you lost sight of him, didn't you?"

"It still doesn't prove anything," Irene replied.

She felt strong and sure of herself. He wouldn't trick her into admitting anything.

"I see," Magnus sighed, "I guess we're done here."

He closed the file, got up and walked toward the door.

Before leaving, he turned around and looked at mother and son: "I can assure you, dear Nordin family, I will sort this out. We'll get that court order; we'll get access to his medical files, and we'll find out what sort of man Peter Nordin really was."

Magnus walked out the door and left Isa behind. He was so disappointed. It felt like betrayal. He didn't want to see or talk to her. How could she go so fast from loving him to having these feelings for another man? How easily he was replaced! Sophie didn't love him; Isa didn't love him. Who did?

* * *

"I believe this ends our interview. Thank you both for being here. I'll escort you to the exit."

It took Irene a moment to realize they expected her to get up and leave the room. Magnus had so unexpectedly cut off the interview. Inspector Lindström was waiting for them in the doorway. The old lady left the room, angry and disappointed, refusing to speak or look at Isa. She wanted to get out of the building as quickly as possible and started to walk to the exit with great determination, unaware that neither Isa nor her son was following her.

While leaving the room, Isa had stopped Alex.

"Alex, I need to talk to you," Isa whispered.

She touched his arm. Why did she do that?

"About what?" he asked and immediately added, "I don't think it's a good idea ... us talking ..."

"I really need your help," she pleaded.

"But inspector Wieland ...," he stammered.

"Forget about him. Call me and then we can arrange a meeting! Okay?"

She put the card with her phone number in his hand. He took it and left the room. His mother was already gone.

"I'll walk with you," Isa said.

In complete silence, they continued the walk down the long hallway to the exit. The interview had been strange. For the first time, his mother's attitude and the fierceness with which she had defended his father, had pleasantly surprised Alex. What had changed?

Alex was walking next to her. So far, yet so close, she could almost feel the warmth of his body. Why did she have to restrain herself from throwing him against the wall and kissing him with a passion she had never felt before? She was an easy victim of love. She knew that, but with all her previous lovers, including Magnus, it had taken months or even years before she could truly say she had been in love. What was it about Alex that distracted her and made her do stupid things whenever she saw him? It couldn't just be his fabulous looks. She wasn't that shallow. Was it this naïve innocence, this apparent vulnerability, and the mysterious, tortured glance? No, it was more than that. It should be more than that.

He seemed completely unaware of it. Something was occupying his thoughts. While they passed the big conference room, with its many windows, Alex caught a glimpse of the people inside. There was a small meeting between police officers, each of them attentively listening to the person in front of the room. It reminded him of the new seminar room at the university. Light, modern, and open for everyone to see what was happening in the room. No privacy, like animals in a zoo, to be looked at and judged. Suddenly Alex stopped and stared at the photos on the whiteboard in the room.

"What's wrong?" Isa asked.

"The photograph, the girl ... who is she?"

"You're not supposed to see that. These are the girls of Sandviken."

Neither the names nor the photos of the girls had been mentioned in the press, and only a few people knew the full list of victims.

"And who is she?" he pointed at the photo on the top left corner of the whiteboard.

"Ida Nilsson, the girl we talked about, but you didn't hear it from me."

He repeated the name a few times.

"What's wrong, Alex? Tell me. You know something."

"I have to get out of here," he said and ran to the exit, leaving Isa behind, puzzled about the sudden change in behavior.

His mother was waiting outside, near the car, getting impatient.

"Why did it take so long?" she complained.

"Take me home. I want to go home."

The pieces of a puzzle were slowly coming together, but it wasn't a pretty picture.

Ida Nilsson ... she was the girl in his dreams, lying on the floor in blood, partially wrapped in cloth, looking at him. Or maybe it wasn't her? It was all so unclear. It was her face, and then again it wasn't.

Irene opened the door of the car and got in. She waited for him to fasten his seatbelt and asked, "Are you okay?"

"Do I look okay?" he said, rather irritated.

She hit him in the face, so hard the headache came back in full force. It happened in a split second.

"What ...," he stammered and touched his cheek.

She slapped him a second time, even harder. His head hit the window on the passenger side.

"You don't talk to me like that," she yelled and started the car, "and you're not seeing that woman anymore."

There she was. This was his mother. His real mother. Dominant and abusive. There was always a reason in her mind to act the way she did. It made him feel small and stupid. For the first time in years, he felt that his mental state was no longer in balance. The lack of sleep, the anxiety, the fear, and the doubts were becoming too much.

This time he was determined not to let things get out of hand. But he had to get away from her ... as fast and far as possible. She always made him believe she had changed, that she cared for him and loved him. And every time he got hurt.

The US sounded so alluring again, but he couldn't leave until he got answers about his father's part in the killings. He looked at the card in his hand. Isa wanted to help him. Why not? But what did she want? Everyone always needed something.

CHAPTER

13

A SINGLE GUNSHOT ECHOED through the desolate snowy
landscape. She felt how he loosened his grip. His fingers slid through
hers and before she realized it, his lifeless body fell to the ground in front
of her, and the blood spattered the snow in all directions. Slowly the large
bloodstain, dripping from the wound in the back of his neck, stretched
further and further until all snow crystals in a twenty-centimeter
circumference were saturated with the bright red body fluid.

"Jonah? Oh my God, Jonah!"

She touched his face, but he didn't respond. What had happened?
Where did it come from? It was clearly a gunshot. A stray bullet?

She turned around. The trees, the deserted road, the rocky slope on the other side. Where did the shot come from?

And then she saw the red car parked fifty meters away, the window open, the arm of the man hanging outside. It was him. She had seen the car before. Passing by her school, driving by her house. It was him.

Run, Anna, run!

He started the engine, quietly pulled up and drove the car until it was only a few meters away from the girl who was frantically trying to find a way out. Her shoes had almost no grip on the snow, and with every step she felt herself slipping away, unable to get to a safe distance from her stalker.

The trees, I have to get to the trees.

But she was at the opposite side of the road where he could corner her. It was the calmness with which he controlled the situation that made it all so perverse. No roaring engine, no race car-like movements. He took his time. The chase was even more important than the prize. There was no one in the area. Not a soul would hear her desperate cries for help.

"Anna, don't make it hard on yourself," he said.

The car was now next to her. She turned her head. How did he know her name? Her foot hit a rock on the ground, and she fell on her face and lay still for a moment. Her nose was bleeding.

"Please, please ... don't do this!"

This was too easy. Begging wouldn't help. The car stopped, and she heard the door being opened.

Anna, don't stop! Get up! He's coming.

Desperately struggling to get away, kicking, screaming, and hitting, she felt his hands on her neck and shoulders. He put a handkerchief drenched in chloroform over her mouth and she lost consciousness.

This had been so exhilarating. His entire body was tingling with anticipation. Anticipation to possess her, to feel her and call her his ... forever.

The flowers had wilted. Carefully, he removed them from the grave, along with the thin layer of snow.

"Peter Oscar Nordin, beloved husband and father, died 8 September 2016."

His fingers skimmed over the letters on the tombstone. It was the first time he had visited his father's grave after the suicide. He wasn't a religious man and although he had thought a lot about his father over the past year, he had never felt the need to visit his grave and talk to him, until now.

"I don't understand any of this," he whispered.

After the police interview and the confrontation with Ida Nilsson's photograph, there had been so many doubts about his father's innocence.

The black book was a source of much more information than originally expected. Alex had linked at least six of the highlighted sections in the booklet to abductions of teenage girls over the past twenty years. What worried him was that there were more than nine highlighted entries in the book. More victims?

The dreams, the flashbacks, the documents he had found, it all pointed to his father being a serial killer, and it was tearing him apart.

"Dad ... how can I be the son of a murderer?" he said. "How did this happen?"

He looked around, ashamed of his emotional outburst. The cemetery was deserted. The place radiated peace and tranquility, but the anguish, festering and poisoning his mind every day a little more, couldn't be tamed. How did this happen? Of course, there was no logical explanation. No one had ever suspected Peter was capable of such atrocities. And he, himself, had been involved. Peter had involved his own son! How evil could people be?

The memories of the car when they had pursued Marian were real. So real he saw the car everywhere. Had he done anything to those girls? Had he cooperated willingly? Did he know what his father had been up to? Had he been an accomplice?

The dreams stressed him more than ever. They were the answer. But the more he tried to recall the details, the more his entire body and mind objected. The lack of sleep took its toll. He felt physically and mentally exhausted. His work was suffering and more and more he retreated into the silence. He recognized the signs. It wasn't the first time, but fighting those emerging dark thoughts took a lot of energy. Energy he didn't have.

The dreams and memories, were these signs he was destined to become a murderer too? Maybe it was hereditary, maybe his father had known and had tried to acquaint him with the horrors that would become a part of his life. His mother must have known. Was this why she hated him so much?

But maybe Peter wasn't his father after all? The mysterious GenoOne letter. Peter had been looking for answers too. The pieces of the puzzle weren't fitting. Parts were missing, big parts.

Maybe it was better to share everything he had found out about his father, and he had called inspector Lindström to talk about it. It was more therapeutic than the actual need to help her with the investigation. His mother would never approve, and that was why he didn't tell her. It would come out eventually, but right now he didn't want to confront her. He had avoided any confrontation with her since her violent outburst. There was nothing he wanted to say to her. He was tired of this love-hate relationship that gave him no stability or security.

He got up, shook the snow off his trousers, and walked to the exit of the cemetery. The ten minutes he had spent at this father's grave had given him some sense of clarity about what to do. No real answers. But as he walked home, he felt some relief and serenity.

* * *

"Magnus is worried about you," Dr. Ingrid Olsson said, while she took another bite of her lasagna. Her friend Isa was sitting on the opposite side of the table in the small but cozy Italian restaurant in the middle of Gävle. It wasn't particularly popular, but it was their place to hang out after work.

"Why?" Isa asked, apparently uninterested.

"He's concerned you're doing something stupid."

"Such as?" she asked, still fully focused and her eyes fixed on the plate of food in front of her. The risotto seemed more interesting than the conversation with her friend. It was a great dish, and she took the last bites when her friend confronted her with a topic, she wasn't too keen on discussing.

Ingrid hesitated, but she decided to throw all the cards on the table: "Like what you always do ... get too close and comfy with a suspect."

"He's not a suspect," Isa said calmly.

"So, you know who I'm talking about?"

"Well, it seems pretty simple to me since most protagonists in this story are old, dead or recovering alcoholics. Yes, of course, I know who you are referring to. Although you ... and Magnus for that matter, don't believe me, but I can assure you, you don't have to worry."

"Magnus seems to think otherwise. The incident during the interview upset him a lot."

"Magnus, Magnus, what the hell does he know? He should mind his own business. We are no longer a couple, so he has no right to make these statements ... about me."

"Isa, come on. He is really concerned. It's not the first time you ...," Ingrid said.

"His concern doesn't buy me anything, and okay, I'll admit Alex Nordin is good-looking, but that's all I can say ... and it's not ethical."

"Ethical ... that hasn't stopped you before," Ingrid continued. "He may not be a suspect, but his father is. I'm not only concerned about you, but even more about Mr. Nordin. I know you ... you can be selfish at times and hurt people."

"Selfish?" Isa called out annoyed. "When and where was I ever ...?"

"Eric, Johan, Marcel, Daniel, and Kristian. Shall I continue?"

"Those weren't really serious relationships," Isa laughed.

"My point exactly. You can't keep treating men like "throw away"-people. And Kristian got you into trouble last time, remember?"

"Listen, Ingrid, believe me: I would never cross that line again."

"Okay, but you always say that, and in the end, you can't resist."

"I hear you and I understand that both of you are concerned about me, but don't worry ... really," Isa said and smiled at her friend.

In all honesty, Magnus and Ingrid were right. She was interested in him, very much so. But the problem of Alex Nordin could be addressed. It was just a matter of self-control. She could have a perfectly normal conversation with him.

"I am against breaking up marriages, but you and Magnus were good together. He gave you some stability ... and so did Viktor."

The careless expression on Isa's face suddenly turned serious.

"Magnus wasn't my fault," Isa said softly.

"But Viktor was. How is he doing?"

There was no answer. Ingrid had pushed it too far. After all these years, it was still a sensitive topic, but Ingrid couldn't resist bringing it up. She had to; it was her responsibility as a friend and because it had so much more impact than on Isa and Viktor alone.

"This case is draining all my energy," Isa sighed, and with that comment, she tried to change the subject. Ingrid let it go.

"Do you think Peter Nordin is the killer?"

"No, Ingrid, no, I really don't."

"Why? Magnus is convinced. Why aren't you?"

"It's all too obvious. I agree, everything points to him, but it doesn't feel right."

"What are you going to do?" Ingrid asked.

"I want to go back to Sandviken. We didn't really search the area in detail."

In the meantime, the waiter removed the empty plates and brought the desserts.

"But what do you expect to find there?"

"I was wondering: the killer couldn't afford to transport the dead bodies over a long distance before burying them. This means that the girls were held captive somewhere close to the site where the bodies were found. I think we need to go back and screen that area."

"That could be. You're right, it might be good to search the cabins over there."

"But ... we still need a search warrant, and we won't get it. Not enough evidence. Just like Magnus tried to get access to Peter Nordin's medical file but failed."

She stirred the spoon in the chocolate mousse and took a bite.

"I know Doctor Wikholm well. He is a reasonable man, and he will give you something within the boundaries of what he can share. Just ask him."

"We've already done that, but it didn't help us much," Isa said, "but I guess it doesn't hurt to pay him a visit."

"What about the Croatian guy? Josip, right?"

"We still don't know where he is. He disappeared. I'm afraid something has happened to him. I don't think the people who broke into the apartment found what they were looking for."

"Or he can be hiding," Ingrid said and took a sip of the black coffee she had ordered five minutes earlier.

"Sure. He must know who is after him."

"He called Alexander Nordin. So, someone in the Nordin family is involved, Isa."

"Maybe. Or Josip Radić was looking for advice, or maybe he wanted to warn Alex."

"You won't know until you find him."

"Yes. We issued an APB, but, so far, nothing. But I have the feeling he might show up in the coming days. Dead or alive."

"What does Anders say about this?"

Isa shrugged. "What can he say? He is under a lot of pressure. The mayor wants to get this solved as soon as possible, and the Uppsala team is eager to take the case away from us. Finn Heimersson, man, that guy is a nuisance! He's effectively trying to sabotage the investigation."

"Maybe you should talk to him and tell him who's in charge," Ingrid suggested.

But it wasn't Finn Heimersson Isa was worried about. She was concerned about Josip Radić, who had been missing for a week. Why? Was he in danger? Was he still alive? If he was, how alone and scared he must be.

* * *

And scared he was. He should have told everything to Alex from the start, or better yet to the police, but it was too late now and there was no turning back. When he entered the cabin, he saw the same scene as the one he had witnessed in his apartment in Uppsala. Chairs, sliders, and papers were lying on the floor, some partially damaged. The computer was gone. He knew who had done this, and he also knew they wouldn't stop until he was dead unless he could come to an agreement. An agreement to save his life and the others. He tried to close the door, but the lock was forced, and it was no longer possible to completely close it. He couldn't stay here. Nor could he go to his parents or any of the few friends he still had left. He thought about it and made a final decision. As he took the cell phone out of his pocket and turned it on, he recalled how he had seen the lifeless body in front of his apartment the night of the burglary. How stunned he had been to find Alex lying on the floor and how he suddenly had realized that none of them were safe from then on. He dialed the number and heard the voice on the other end of the line.

"We need to talk," was the only thing he said. As the voice on the other end rambled on, he nodded but said nothing as he paced the room. The conversation lasted less than a minute and afterward, Josip left the cabin and walked along the trail to the main road. The snow and dusk made walking a lot harder, and he was exhausted when he reached the concrete of the driveway where he would take the bus to the city center. He had to hurry because it was already dark, and he didn't know how many busses were going to Uppsala that late.

* * *

Doctor Wikholm was charming, in his fifties but recently remarried and with a new baby on the way, he had never felt so young and alive. The inspectors, Isa and Nina, had been warned he was only allowed to share the details of the medical records if they had a court order, which was not the case, but given the severity of the matter, he was willing to talk to them.

"Thanks for meeting us," Isa started the conversation.

"How can I refuse such beautiful ladies a conversation," he laughed. His attempt at being witty and charming wasn't as successful as he had hoped. There was little reaction from the women.

"Peter Nordin was a patient of yours?" Nina asked.

The doctor, sitting comfortably in a leather chair specially bought for him when he had started his career at the hospital, looked at them. Both were rather pleasing to the eye. The lady sitting on the left was older and clearly the superior, but with her slightly curly hair, neatly pulled back in a ponytail, her remarkable eyes, a mix of blue and green, and the slender yet sporty figure, she was a beautiful presence he enjoyed watching.

"Yes, he was," he replied and smiled.

Isa didn't like him. He was too slick for her taste.

"And Mr. Nordin was being treated for depression?"

"I think there is no harm in saying this, but yes, he was. He was my patient for over twenty years. I became his psychiatrist just before the incident with the missing girl. Before that, he was the patient of my predecessor, Dr. Hinwald, who retired in 1991."

"So, he was under psychiatric care a while before you started treating him?"

"That's right. From 1987, he began to consult a doctor regularly."

"At any moment, during those twenty years or more, have you had any doubt he was anything other than depressed?"

His expression suddenly changed, and he waited a while before answering, weighing the words he was about to say.

"Yes, there was doubt. Many times."

"May I ask where this doubt came from?"

"I can't give all details as you know, but his symptoms weren't all characteristic of depression."

"Any other disease or state of mind you suspected?" Nina asked.

"Not really, it was rather that his symptoms could have fitted many psychiatric illnesses like schizophrenia, bipolar ... over the years, his behavior was changing so rapidly and ..."

He stopped and looked down at his hands, folded in his lap. He looked like a boy who suddenly realized he had said the wrong thing, thereby violating his patient's trust, and who was now ashamed of his indiscretion.

"You see. Depression typically manifests itself as a loss of energy, decreased interest in daily activities, irritability, concentration problems, changes in appetite, in the way of sleeping. People neglect their social network and withdraw from all activities. At least, in the beginning, Peter demonstrated this behavior but, as time passed, he could have these unbelievable manic periods full of activity, when he couldn't control himself."

And when he got violent against himself and his family, but he didn't say that out loud.

He got up and walked around, with Isa and Nina watching all his movements.

"So, it wasn't depression?" Nina added.

"And then, there were periods of delusional thinking, hearing voices, talking to oneself. It was all so atypical."

He stared at the diploma hanging on the wall. He remembered the frail man, sitting in the chair where now one of the ladies was sitting, frantically pulling his hair, and rocking back and forth. His speech was disjointed, the eyes bloodshot, and it seemed as if he hadn't eaten or slept in days. The conversation with him had been difficult, and Wikholm had become increasingly worried about his patient's well-being. The voices were a cause for concern. Those compulsory feelings of having to hurt someone had been there, but he couldn't imagine Peter acting on them until the police had questioned him about the disappearance of a young girl.

"It all happened so fast," he said, "it wasn't normal."

"But you had suspicions?" Isa mentioned.

He continued staring at the wall. Yes, he had his theories and so had Peter.

"Yes," he whispered, "I thought he was being drugged."

"Drugged? By whom?"

"The first thing I thought was that he was just taking drugs himself, but he came with a different theory. He was convinced someone was poisoning him."

"Really?" Isa said, excited by this somewhat new turn in the conversation. "Did he have any idea who wanted to do that to him?"

"I think so, but he didn't share it with me, and to be honest, I wasn't convinced. A toxicology screen test showed nothing. But the fact is he got better after his admission to the hospital ... and it went quickly. The delusions stopped, and he was lucid, normal, as if nothing had happened. But in the years that followed, after his discharge from the hospital, his health deteriorated again."

"So, he might have been right," Isa concluded.

"Munchausen by proxy has crossed my mind," the doctor said and looked at the inspector.

"Munch ... what?"

"Munchausen by proxy is a mental illness in which a person inflicts a physical or mental illness on another person to seek attention or gain sympathy. It is considered a form of abuse and usually involves a mother and a young child, but there are many cases where the victim is a spouse or a disabled adult."

"Who did you have in mind as possible culprit?"

"Mrs. Nordin, but she didn't show the typical behavior."

"Irene Nordin?"

"As I said, I found no evidence that she or anyone else for that matter was really trying to make him sick."

"But his health got better every time he was admitted?"

"Yes, but then again, that's what you would expect from intensive psychotherapy."

Dr. Wikholm walked to his desk and sat in the chair.

"I've already told you too much. His medical records now belong to his wife."

"I understand," Isa said, grateful for the information he had willing to share with them. He had gone beyond the boundaries of his profession ... far beyond.

"Thank you for sharing this with us," Nina said, "but before we leave, I want to ask you one more question."

The young woman scared him. From her attitude and the confidence with which she had addressed him, it was clear she was an ambitious woman. She respected her colleague, but she was ruthless and probably wouldn't hesitate to advance her career, even at the expense of others.

"Yes, what do you want to ask me?" the doctor said.

"In your opinion, as a doctor, but more so as a friend – can I say he was more than a patient ..."

"Yes, he was my friend," Wikholm admitted.

"In your opinion, could he have killed those girls?"

It was a shock to hear those words. He didn't know how to answer. He wanted nothing more than to spare the Nordin family, but he had to be honest.

"Yes," he said. The voice was so fragile and so soft it was barely audible to Isa and Nina.

"Doctor, sorry, what did you say?"

He sighed and said: "Yes, I believe he could have."

When they finally left the office of the doctor, Isa was in doubt again. She was torn between believing Peter Nordin's innocence and suspecting his guilt. The conversation hadn't put her mind at ease. All this time, it had been correct to focus the investigation on Peter Nordin. Irene knew more than she was telling, and Isa needed a strategy to get the old woman to give her more information. The son was probably the best way to get to her.

CHAPTER

14

WHEN HE ENTERED THE PUB, Isa was already sitting at a small table in the corner. Alex took off his coat and sat in the chair opposite her.

"This is not exactly the usual place for a police interview," he smiled.

"It can be done anywhere," Isa replied, gesturing the waitress to come and get their order.

"This was actually my favorite pub during my college years," she said.

"You studied in Uppsala?"

The waitress interrupted them before she could reply: "What do you want to drink?" They ordered two light beers and then the young woman left them to continue the conversation.

"So, you studied here?" he repeated.

"Yes, I have a bachelor's degree in linguistics," she admitted, and was curious to see his reaction.

"I guess the police academy was more exciting than linguistics," he said with an ironic twist to the words.

She looked at him and more and more she got bewildered by his amazing looks. This had to stop. He was a witness, and she had to treat him accordingly. But it was so refreshing to feel that way again after Magnus. Alex was more handsome and a lot younger, but Magnus had been her soulmate, her best friend, her everything.

"Yes, that and the fact that linguistics didn't really offer good job prospects," she continued, "and my husband didn't like it."

He was surprised: "You are married?"

"Was married. We got divorced a while ago and now he lives in London with our two children."

A decision she had made so many years ago. A difficult decision, but in her mind the best one for herself, and her son and daughter. She didn't know them, and they didn't know her, and they probably never would.

Why had she told him? It was so difficult to talk to her best friend Ingrid about Viktor and the children, and here she was, telling one of her darkest and most shameful secrets to a person she barely knew. Someone she couldn't even trust.

"That must be tough," he said with an unbelievable tenderness.

"Well, that was my decision. I have to live with it."

"Sometimes it's better not to have a parent than one who ...," he started, shook his head, and then kept quiet. She didn't need to know about his frustrations.

A sensitive topic, but for Isa the ultimate goal of the conversation. She wanted him to talk about his father. But it was too soon. He would completely shut down if she pushed it. So, she changed the topic: "And what about you? A girlfriend?"

"Oh, no ... no girlfriend."

"But how, you're so...," she stopped and felt stupid about her girlish comment.

"So what?"

It had sparked his curiosity.

"So good-looking," she said.

No one had ever said this so directly. Of course, he knew. He had often received admiring glances from women of all ages. Like the lady sitting near the exit who had looked up when he had entered, and who, for a split second that had lasted too long, had locked her eyes on him and then had overly compensated her interest by looking down at the plate of food and had started a rather loud conversation with the man in front of her. Or the waitress who had stood slightly closer than she should have, smiling as she took his order, while giving Isa a jealous and somewhat derogatory look.

"Uh, thank you, I guess," he felt ill at ease, "I've never felt the need to have a girlfriend or wife ... and it definitely doesn't help when you need to take care of a depressed father."

Now it was his turn to feel stupid and clumsy. Why had he told her? He took a sip of the beer the waitress had brought in the meantime.

"So, if you had the choice, would you go back to studying linguistics?" he changed the subject.

"I do have the choice," she answered indignantly, "and probably not."

"Why?"

"I like my life the way it is right now. Don't get me wrong, I still love to read and write. The power of the word can be tantalizingly beautiful and inspiring. It can sweep you away and take you to universes you can't even imagine."

He smiled and said: "That sounds great, but I prefer numbers myself."

The conversation changed topic again, and she asked him about Josip Radić.

"I was five when we first met in Sandviken. He must have been about ten years old. The family was Croatian but the father ... what was his name again?"

"Ivor," Isa said.

"Right, Ivor. He was quite an accomplished man. He had brought his family to Sweden before the civil war in Yugoslavia, and he has built a successful career over here. The family was and still is doing pretty well."

"What business is he in?"

"He's in real estate now. I'm not entirely sure about what he used to do before, but I think he had several restaurants in Dubrovnik."

"Quite a difference from real estate. Do you know why they came to Sweden?"

"No, not really," he answered.

"Did they have relatives in Sweden? Money problems? Maybe trouble with the police? Josip seemed to have had quite a few clashes with them."

There was a silence before Alex replied: "Josip just had bad friends when he got older. He had so much anger in him, it sometimes scared me. I couldn't understand where it came from. He has everything he could wish for. His parents are so ... well, they are loving, decent parents. You could tell they would do anything for their children."

What wouldn't he give for the solidarity and warmth he had seen in the Radić family? And Josip had thrown that all away. For what?

"Do you think he was involved in the murders?" Isa asked.

"I'm not the best person to judge this, but isn't he too young? The oldest dates to ... what? Thirty years ago."

"Yes, but what about father-son duo killers? It's not the first time this happens. Maybe Ivor killed the girls and later, his son helped him."

Alex sighed and shook his head.

"That's a bit far-fetched, no? Do you have any proof?"

"No, just a feeling," she said and looked at him. He didn't really look at her but was staring at the picture on the wall.

"You know ... I don't quite get it, but I have the feeling it has something to do with all of us ... and it worries me. It worries me a lot."

"And your own father?"

It was time to tackle the sensitive topic. There was terror in his eyes and his expression went from calm and controlled, to fearful and nervous.

"You said you didn't believe my father did it ...," he stammered.

"Yes, but I have to wonder. I'm a police officer and I have to look at the evidence."

"You have no idea," he snapped, while almost immediately regretting his outburst.

"Explain it then," she almost pleaded as she took his hand to calm him down. He remembered the soft touch of her hands, just like in the interrogation room. It hadn't been appropriate then, and it wasn't now. It wasn't compassion. It was manipulation. She just needed information about his father. He pushed her hand away. Well then, she would get what she wanted.

"Because I think he did it," he said and looked her in the eye.

It was almost like a confession, as if he had been the killer himself and he had carried the secret with him for a long time.

"Why? Why do you say that?"

"I have these memories, these dreams ... I think I was there."

"Tell me everything you know."

Faint-heartedly he described the memories of the red car, the stalking of Marian Bergqvist and the recurring dreams in which he saw the body of Ida Nilsson lying on the ground, covered in blood.

"This is indeed important, Alex, but have you ever seen the face of the man in the car or in the room? Was it really your father?"

He thought about it before answering: "No, but some things feel so familiar and comforting. The dreams are the most frightening. When I'm walking through the tunnel, it feels like someone is with me, leading me to the room. I'm not scared. It only gets terrifying when I enter and see the girl. There's a man's voice. A deep voice. I don't recognize it. So ... no, I'm not sure it's my father ... but who else could it be?"

"I don't know, Alex, you're the only one who can answer that."

There was a long pause before Isa continued the conversation: "Tell me more about your father. He was a troubled man, but only a few people really think he was capable of killing these girls. Most people saw him as a loving father and husband."

"Loving father and husband ... no, he was capable of violence," Alex replied to her surprise.

"Just to give you an example: I was twelve, and he had been delusional for months. He had been going to Dr. Wikholm for weeks, but there wasn't any improvement. He was hearing voices, seeing things that weren't there, and he started to talk to himself again. One night he entered my room. I can still remember the strange look on his face as if it were yesterday. Pure madness! Before I knew it, he had his hands around my throat, and he was strangling me. I remember trying to call my mom, but I couldn't make a sound, and no one came. All the time, he was yelling how I deserved to die. He really wanted to kill me."

"How did you escape?"

"He stopped ... as if he suddenly realized where he was, and who I was. As I gasped for breath, he looked at me, ashamed of what he had done, and he left the room. After that, I started locking my room at night. I know he wasn't himself, and I loved my father, but he terrified me."

The silence was a welcome respite. His posture revealed how demanding it had been to tell that story. He touched the glass in front of him, not to drink it, but simply because he needed a new point of focus. He turned the glass over and over so it would be nicely positioned in the center of the coaster, even though the wet traces on the beer mat weren't.

Symmetry, nice symmetry!

"Can I ask about the scar?"

Her voice was soft and calm. It suddenly occurred to her, while she had thought the scar on his arm had been self-inflicted, it could have been caused by one of his father's violent outbursts. What if the story had only been a tip of the iceberg?

He looked at his left arm and for a few moments, he was in doubt, but then he replied: "No."

"Why?"

"It's personal. It has nothing to do with the case ... and I don't really trust you."

"That's a very honest answer," she said, astonished.

"And so, let me be honest," she continued," if you don't tell me, someone else will and either way I'll find out ... that's my job."

There was little reaction from his side. It was a facade because he felt a sudden rush of panic when he heard that. It was a clear threat.

"And your mother?" Isa asked.

"What about my mother?"

"You seem to have a good relationship with her," Isa said.

Good relationship? If only she knew.

"What would you call good? She was never there. It was just me and him ... and now it's just me."

He could tell her so much more, but what was the point? His mother was great at manipulating others. In the end, it was his word against hers, and she always won.

"Why was she never there? Was she seeing someone else? Was she having an affair?"

"Maybe ... it has crossed my mind."

"Mats Norman?"

He looked at her in surprise.

"Mats? No, I don't think so. Why do you mention him?"

"Josip Radić told us you once caught Mats and your mother kissing when you were a child."

He shook his head and said: "Did I? I can't remember. Maybe ..."

He stopped talking and stared at the wall again. Mats? Could it be Mats?

"I think your mother knows more than she told us. The situation with your father is complicated and puzzling. My gut feeling says he didn't do this, but everything points in his direction. That's why I need your help."

"I'm not a detective ... what do you want me to do?" Alex asked.

"Talk to your mother. During the summers you all spent together, she must have noticed things. She knows your father's history better than you."

Talk to his mother? They weren't exactly on speaking terms. And he wasn't completely convinced, but the way she turned her head and looked at him was cute and he finally gave in. It worried him she could be mean and strict one minute, and so friendly and compassionate the next. Inspector Lindström was a dangerous woman who used her charms to get what she wanted, and it usually worked.

They spent the rest of the evening talking about family, friends, work, and life. It was a pleasant evening. Isa liked him a lot, and she was grateful he had shared some difficult personal things with her. But it was a risk to involve him, a risk she was willing to take.

* * *

"I think more snow is coming," Isa said softly.

Slowly, strolling a little, they walked to the parking lot. It was an open sky. The snow reflected the light of the moon. The daytime temperature had flirted with the zero-degree mark and here and there the snow had melted, but now an icy mush had formed as it was freezing again.

"I like snow," he said.

"Me too," she admitted and saw him kneel next to a pile of snow lying on the sidewalk. He took off his leather gloves, reached out and pulled a trail in the shallow snow. The tiny snowflakes on the tip of his fingers would be gone in no time, but he couldn't stop staring at them.

"Each one of them is so unique ... that shape ... it's perfection in every way. You know there's something called the Koch snowflake. It's one of the earliest fractal curves described ... already at the beginning of the twentieth century. It's just so fascinating."

The flakes had disappeared. Only a few drops of water remained, and they ran down the shafts of his finger. He turned around and saw her smile.

"For a moment I thought the romantic in you was going to get the upper hand, but I was wrong," she replied.

Why did he seem to disappoint everyone, all the time? People had expectations that he never seemed to fulfill. Why had he said this out loud? It must have seemed strange to her. But there was a moment between them. The same enchanting and tantalizing vibe he had felt in the apartment. He didn't know how to behave or respond to it. Was she expecting anything?

The concern on his face worried her. Maybe she had gone too far. They weren't friends; they weren't even acquaintances. He was so much harder to read than she had expected. Had she said something wrong?

"It's a joke," she explained.

"I know. I ... I need to go."

Escape was the only way.

"Let me drive you home," she proposed and walked over to him.

"My car isn't that far from here."

"No ... thank you ... I want to walk ... thanks again for a nice evening. I'll think about what you said."

With a faint smile on his face, he turned around and walked away from her. She watched him slowly disappear from view and then walked to her car.

* * *

Isa drove back to Gävle. She felt great, excited, and confident. It wasn't the case she felt happy about, but the man she had just spent more than three hours with. He was strange, but there was just something about him that made her want to know more. When she got home, she saw Magnus' car parked in front of the house. It was a small two-story house she had inherited from her grandmother, who had died ten years ago. She had let the house for a while but after the divorce, she had moved in herself. He got out of the car when he saw her car approaching the driveway.

"What's wrong?" she asked after getting out of the vehicle.

"Josip Radić was found dead an hour ago," he said.

"What? Where? How?"

"I tried to call you. His father found him in the apartment. It looks like a suicide, but Ingrid isn't convinced, and neither am I. Forensics are sweeping the apartment and tomorrow we should have a better view if this is suicide or murder."

"How did he die?" she asked as she put the key in the lock and opened the front door.

"Shot in the head." He switched on the light. He knew the house well. Not so long ago, he had practically lived there.

She took off her shoes and coat while he waited in the hallway.

"Don't just stand there, come in," she said, annoyed. Her good mood was gone.

He obeyed and entered the living room. It felt uncomfortable, almost like he was cheating on his wife again.

"Anything else I should know?"

"His phone seems to be missing, but otherwise nothing is gone or taken."

"Can we track his phone records? The phone is gone for a reason."

"He had a prepaid cell phone."

"But you know the number, so we can probably find out who he called in the last days."

"Do we know his number?" Magnus asked, surprised.

"Are you awake or sleeping?" she said sarcastically. "He called Alex and Josip's father probably would know too, no?"

"Alex?"

There he was again. Alex. He detested him.

"Alexander Nordin," she sighed. He kept quiet, not to trigger any further irritation from her side.

"What about the gun? Was it registered?"

"I'll find out," he said.

"I hate this case," she suddenly shouted.

"Now one of my prime suspects is dead! There are so many 'coincidences', which makes me believe this is all orchestrated so well. I feel like everyone is playing a role and I don't know who's behind it."

"I thought Peter Nordin was the prime suspect," Magnus added.

She plopped herself on the sofa. The wisps of hair fell gracefully over her neck and shoulder. He loved how she twisted the hairs around her finger, let go and repeated the movement over and over. Many times, when they had still been together, he had stood in the doorway, staring at her. He could watch her for hours.

"No, he's your suspect. Not mine. Don't forget, he's dead. Then who killed Josip?"

"Let's talk tomorrow. You're angry and disappointed right now and that clouds your judgment."

"Fine. See you tomorrow. You know the way out."

He left the house and got in his car, but he didn't start the engine. She was right. It felt like someone was directing all of this, someone in full control who was leaving pointers now and then but was leading them in a particular direction that wasn't the right one. A mastermind ... cold, but very calculated. And she was right: Peter Nordin didn't fit the profile. A confused and troubled man couldn't have planned this. Someone very much alive was in control. He started the engine and drove off, hoping that the next day would bring some clarity.

* * *

"Someone killed him," Ingrid said, "there is no gunpowder on his hands. This was done quite amateurishly. The bullet entered the right temporal lobe and caused severe hemorrhaging. He died almost instantly."

"There was no sign of a struggle," Magnus remarked.

"Yes, but he was very, very drunk. The alcohol level in his blood was almost 3 per mil, which suggests he wouldn't have been in control of his movements and senses."

"Probably he knew his killer and trusted him or her," Magnus continued.

He paced the room while Ingrid looked at him, following his every move. He seemed tired and worried.

"When did he die?"

"His father found him around nine in the evening. I'd say he must have been dead for three, maybe four hours."

"And the father? Has he been checked? Did he have gunpowder on his hands?"

"Yes, we checked him and no, he was clean. He was really in shock, and they had to take him to the hospital. I don't think he killed his son."

"This brings us back to square one."

He sighed and put his hands through his hair. She put her hand on his shoulder as a sign of understanding and comfort.

"Where's Isa?" she asked.

He shrugged and seemed very uninterested.

"Did you have a fight again?"

His face showed no emotion but was very serious.

"I don't know what she's doing, but I think she is getting onto thin ice."

"What are you talking about?"

"Alexander Nordin. I think she has been seeing him ... I am not sure what to think of it, but you know how she is."

Ingrid stood now in front of him.

"I've talked to her, don't worry, it's all okay," she whispered.

He still loved Isa, and this outburst of emotions was a mixture of jealousy and genuine concern for Isa's well-being. To Ingrid, Isa and Magnus were the perfect couple. They complemented each other. How did it all go wrong? Was it Isa's restlessness or Magnus' feeling of guilt and shame? Maybe Magnus was right to worry, and she had been too naïve to believe Isa.

"How are things at home?" she asked.

"Bad ... I don't know what to do."

"What do you mean?"

"Sophie doesn't want to talk to me. She ..."

There was no point in continuing. He couldn't find the words and talking about it was too exhausting. His marital troubles, his son, Isa, the case ... it was an overload of things to worry about. It had kept him awake for nights on end, swinging between an innocently stupid optimism and the most joy-depriving feelings. He understood Isa better now. How she had been fighting many times to muffle the magnitude of her mood swings. It was hard not to lose yourself in a spiral of paranoid anger and self-inflicted dejection.

"Take care and if there is anything I can do, just let me know," Ingrid said.

He nodded and said goodbye before walking back to his office. He followed up on Isa's request to investigate the phone records of Josip

Radić. Isa didn't show up and after lunch, Magnus called her. She didn't answer.

Where was she?

15

JELENA RADIĆ OPENED THE DOOR. Her movements were sluggish, her eyes bloodshot and rimmed with dark circles. She hadn't slept.

"Yes," she said in a hoarse voice.

"Mrs. Radić, I'm inspector Magnus Wieland, and this is Nina Kowalczyk, Gävle police. We are investigating the murder of your son, Josip. We would like to talk to your husband."

"Gävle? I thought ..."

"Your son's murder may be connected to the nine girls found in Sandviken."

She said nothing and let them in.

Ivor Radić was still sitting at the table in the kitchen, with a bowl of soup in front of him, slowly bringing the spoon to his mouth. He seemed almost twenty years older than the day before, when Magnus had seen him sitting in the apartment next to his son's dead body, paralyzed, confused, and unresponsive. The paramedics had taken him to the hospital before the police had been able to talk to him about his son's death.

"The doctor told us to avoid stress," his wife said.

"Igor Rajković," Magnus said.

The man stopped eating, sighed, and turned around to face them. Jelena stared at him open-mouthed.

"Now that is name, I haven't heard for long time," he whispered. He had a strong accent and was sometimes difficult to understand.

"You are Igor Rajković?" Nina asked.

Ivor looked at his wife as if he were asking for permission.

"No ... Igor Rajković is my brother. My real name is Roman Rajković."

"Can we sit down?" Magnus suggested.

Jelena invited them into the living room, which was small but cozy. She sat down next to her husband, who had stumbled from the kitchen to the old sofa, covered with stains, and slightly tattered.

"Igor, moj dragi Igor ... was my younger brother. He was a wild boy, always had been, since we were children. He had so much energy, but he was restless ... just like Josip."

Jelena took his hand.

"Igor had so much potential, but somehow, he always got into trouble. And he got himself in lot of trouble."

"Because of the girl he assaulted?" Nina continued.

"If he assaulted girl or not ... I don't know, but problem was not with the authorities, but with girl's family. They had ties with Russian mafia, and he thought they would come for him. I arranged for him, Jelena, and the kids to leave the country. We have some distant relatives in Sweden, and I knew people that could arrange these things. The false passports were ready, everything was carefully planned, but then Igor disappeared."

"This was in 1984?"

"Yes," Ivor replied.

"He just disappeared," Jelena mused.

"Igor was your husband and Josip's father?"

She nodded.

"What do you think happened to him?"

There was a moment of tension between Ivor and Jelena.

"I don't know, but we always wondered if he wasn't dead. He had many enemies."

"Why didn't you go to the police?"

"We were scared," Jelena said, "I feared for my children's lives and my own."

"So Roman Rajković became Ivor Radić and ..."

"You inherited your brother's family," Magnus intervened.

"Da ... although I wouldn't put it that way," Ivor admitted.

"And you never heard from your brother again?"

"Ne. I don't know what happened to him."

"And Josip?"

His expression became gloomy. And from one moment to the next the energetic man, who had talked about his brother and their escape to Sweden, turned into an old broken man again.

"What about Josip?" he asked, eyes cast down.

"Why were you there?"

"He called me. He wanted to talk, and we agreed to meet that evening at 9 p.m. in the apartment."

"There was a warrant issued for his arrest. You knew that. Why haven't you contacted us?"

"He was my son ... I hadn't talked to him for so long. There was so

180

much we had to sort out, and that he contacted us after so many years, it was just so ..."

He wiped the tears from his face and tried to regain his poise. Only then he felt how Jelena's hand was squeezing so hard that his fingers felt numb, and his entire hand was almost white.

"Why did he want to talk to you?"

"He didn't said. I just thought he wanted to make right."

"So you went to his apartment?" Nina asked.

"Yes, but I was disappointed he didn't open door. I wanted to go and then I remembered that I brought key."

"Key? You have a key to your son's apartment?"

"Da, he had given years ago when ... actually I made copy after I had found him drunk and full of drugs on the street once. We were afraid that he would do stupid things."

"And you entered the apartment?"

"Yes ... I ... I really can't..."

How could he describe the nauseating scent of blood he had smelled after entering the apartment, how his heart had pounded in his chest when he hesitantly had gone into the living room and how he had found the lifeless body of his son, an empty bottle on the table, gun still in his hand, head hanging sideways partially supported by the backrest of the sofa, the pieces of skull and brain scattered all over the fabric, floor and walls? He couldn't describe it, not even in his own mother tongue. Was this the image of the person he had considered his son that would be burned in his mind forever?

He got up but almost immediately felt the dizziness take hold of him. Jelena was there in time to catch him and support him.

"You need to leave!" Her voice sounded angry.

"But ...," Nina tried.

Magnus stopped her and got up.

"We'll leave. For now. But we still want to have a full statement from your husband."

"You know where door is," Jelena said and helped her husband to the bedroom.

Outside, Nina and Magnus walked in silence to the car.

"Do you think he killed his brother?" Nina asked as she got in the vehicle.

"Yes, but we can't prove it. Ever. It's hopeless after so many years."

"Or maybe he's Igor?"

"Igor did have an older brother, but most documents were lost and there's no way to prove who is who."

"I certainly think he's capable of murder," Nina sighed.

"Yes ... and his wife or sister-in-law, whatever you may call her, is protecting him."

* * *

That morning, Isa drove to Sandviken. Alone. She hadn't told anyone. It was just a hunch, maybe just a stupid thought, and instead of making a fool of herself when it turned out to be nothing, she had decided to go alone. She didn't need Magnus or Anders to tell her it might be a waste of time. Maybe it was, maybe it wasn't.

The road to the cabins was almost impassable for the thick layer of snow that covered most of the trail, and it took her a while to reach the area. It was so peaceful, and there was not the slightest hint of the gruesome discovery they had made there so many months ago. Everything was picture perfect. She stopped for a moment, looked at the site, and then walked uphill to the Nordin cabin. Through the snow, the color of the tree roots and branches was still visible. The path itself was unclear, and she ended up walking in the unsteady soil along the path leading to the cabin. She stopped halfway and closed her eyes. She really didn't hear a sound. This was just the perfect place to hide the girls. Remote, kilometers away from the habitable world.

But in the summers, it would have been full of life. She tried to imagine the children playing, running around, going on discovery trips. How could he have hidden the girls from everyone when there were so many people around? Or maybe he hadn't been that successful after all? Alex's recurring dream definitely pointed in that direction. As a boy, he might have witnessed Ida's murder without realizing it.

The Nordin cabin was deserted. She glanced through the window and saw the living room, pretty much in the same condition as the day she first interviewed Alexander. She continued on the path and after five minutes she reached a second cabin, which was the original goal of her trip. She remembered Alexander's remark that the cabin of the young couple was unoccupied most of the time, and she kept wondering if this was the cabin the Radić family had stayed in so many years ago. Maybe this had been Josip's hide-out. Why hadn't they thought of this before?

When she arrived, she found the door unlocked. Inside the cabin, drawers, pictures, and papers had been thrown on the floor, and chairs smashed as if there had been a fight. She was right. This cabin had been used recently. She walked through the mess on the floor to the next room. The second room in the back of the cabin was small, and among the papers on the floor, she found a pair of binoculars, and in the corner behind a closet a shotgun. When she went back to the living room, she saw the marks in the dust on the table. Maybe a laptop? It was gone now.

In the kitchen she found empty Scotch bottles, similar to what they had seen in Josip's apartment. Yes, Josip had been there. But also someone else. His killer? Was Josip killed because of something he had known? But what? He had insisted on talking to Alex, but then he hadn't turned up. He must have known he was in danger.

She looked through the window and saw the third cabin: Mats Norman's summer house to the east, a while further uphill. He had the best overview of the whole area. The former cabin of the Bergqvist family was halfway down the opposite hill at the same height as the house in which she stood.

"The best place to get an overview of the area," she said while looking again at the cabin of the Norman family. Mats Norman, the handsome professor, with a soft spot for women. Was he Irene Nordin's secret lover? Would he go so far as to kidnap innocent girls to satisfy his sexual appetite?

There was something mysterious and appealing about the house on top of the hill. She didn't know what exactly, but it was worth checking out.

The climb to that cottage was more difficult than the road to the other cabins because of the steepness of the slope. The road was a lot icier. The meltwater from the top of the hill, that now bathed in the faint light of the winter sun, had solidified on the way down as most of the path was covered by the shade of the trees. It took her at least fifteen minutes to reach the front door. The house was locked. She looked through one of the windows. The austerity of the interior struck her. In the center of the room there was a small wooden table with a black two-seater sofa close to the window and two smaller chairs on the other side of the table. Other than a decorated chandelier and few statues on the mantelpiece, there were no other ornaments. All the furniture was placed in an orderly and structured manner, as if it had been meticulously measured and positioned to reflect the highest amount of symmetry. As she walked around the house, a cold wind rose. It was treacherously slippery, and she had to be careful not to fall. About ten meters behind the house, there was an impenetrable tangle of branches and bushes. She tried to remove the smaller twigs but couldn't and she got herself injured along the way. For a while, she stood there staring at what looked like a wilderness, and after deciding that probably it wasn't worth investigating further, she turned around and started her way back. And then she saw the faint footsteps in the snow a few meters from where she was standing. The snow was melting and about to wipe some of them away. There were two sets of prints. The prints were different, but the nearly identical size and pattern showed they could have been made by the same person. It looked as if the person had stood there, waiting, a few meters away from the bushes as the footsteps were much deeper than anywhere else. The other pair continued on a path through the bushes. Now she saw the small opening in the twist of branches. The trampled ground indicated someone else had found a way through. Without hesitation, she tried to follow the same path. After a while, the road widened and ended in a track similar than the one connecting the different cabins. The forest was much denser here, and the amount of snow was scarcer. Probably the road had been cut off a while ago.

The footprints were gone. She wanted to continue, but without a reference, there was a high chance of getting lost, and with the darkness setting in, she didn't want to take that chance. Slowly, she made her way back. As she was standing in front of the cabin again, she tried to gather her thoughts. This discovery felt like something important, but she didn't know why. She had to report the robbery and everything she had found in the backyard of the house, but she decided to wait a little longer. She needed to bring Alex there. Maybe he would remember something or recognize what he had seen in his dreams. That evening she drove back home, for the first time with the feeling that they finally might have a chance of cracking the case.

Unnoticed, the red car had started to follow Isa's Volkswagen. She was so lost in thought she didn't notice how he slowly came closer ... first, a few hundreds of meters until the difference was only a dozen. The bumpers were almost touching. She heard an engine accelerate. Only then she noticed the car in the rearview mirror. A red car? Was it him? Where did he come from? The car was swaying over the road, barely avoiding a collision with hers. With trembling hands and the adrenaline pumping through her body, she shifted the gear stick and pressed the gas pedal. The car skidded off, but it felt like she had little control over it. The chaser responded almost immediately. He overtook her. The vehicle was now next to hers, the doors only a few centimeters apart. She couldn't see the driver's face. He got closer, and she felt trapped. The tires lost traction and slid. Frantically, she turned the wheel and hit the brakes, but she had lost all control. The car started spinning and drove off the road at high speed, only being slowed down by the deep snow beside the road, and it came to a stop a few meters in front of a large tree.

She felt the seat belt cut into her shoulder. For a moment she hung like a puppet between the seat and the belt. She couldn't move and she was shaking all over. What had just happened? Had someone tried to kill her? Her hands were still on the wheel, grasping it so tightly that her fingernails felt like bursting. She still couldn't move. What if he came back? She couldn't defend herself. She turned around, trying to scan the area outside, but the snow partly covered the windows, and it was so dark.

Think. She couldn't think straight. Everything was chaos. Disjointed thoughts were flying through her mind.

Take a deep breath! One step at a time.

Unbuckling the seat belt took a while and getting out of the car was even more tedious. Her legs sank in the snow. Every step was a chore, sucking up every bit of energy left in her body. It was so quiet, and so dark. It felt like she had been in that car for hours. Where was her attacker? There was no one. The red car was gone. But she wasn't sure, and she carefully inspected the area before turning her attention to the vehicle. At first glance, the damage to the car was minor, but it would be a lot harder to get it back on the road. There was little movement at first, but eventually the car slid back, and she could move it closer to the road. It took another few hours and some help from vehicle assistance to get her on the road back home again.

* * *

Josip Radić was buried in Uppsala two weeks later. The memorial service was short and sober and attended by only a handful of people. Josip's ex-wife and children were not present. His parents, Ivor and Jelena, and his younger brother Andrej with his family stood in front, around the coffin, while the priest began his sermon. Josip's death, let alone his murder, had seemed so unreal, hard to grasp. Jelena, supported by her husband, was staring at the floor, with tears running down her cheeks. She couldn't bear to look at the coffin. Her son, her beautiful son, was lying in there. Most of all, she wanted to run away, go home, and hide under the sheets of the bed or in a corner of the house, so she would never have to see anyone again. She wanted to be alone with her grief. There was no consolation here. There was only a merciless God, to whom she would never pray again.

Andrej was younger than Josip. He had looked up to him during his childhood, but then later, when things got bad for Josip, he had distanced himself. They had hardly spoken in recent years. Their worlds were so far apart that nothing seemed to bind them anymore. As he held his son's hand, his mind went in overdrive. There he was, his brother, whom he hadn't seen for years, suddenly at his front door, a few days before his death. He had nowhere to go, and he seemed desperate to find a safe place to stay. Couldn't he just stay with his brother for a while? Andrej had misinterpreted the situation and had done something he would regret for the rest of his life: he had refused. Ashamed of the shabby-looking person in front of him, his first thought was with his family. He didn't want to expose them to a world so obscure and dangerous, a world of alcoholism and drugs, where people made promises to change, but never kept them, where the need for the next fix was more important than family. How could he have known that his brother really wanted to change? He had given him no chance to explain, because in the quarrel that followed, accusations were thrown back and forth and Josip had left, disappointed and angry ... for the last time. The most devastating thing was that Andrej had felt no regret. In his eyes, he had lost his brother and he would never have considered reconciling. Now, he wanted a second chance to tell him he had been wrong. If he had helped him, maybe Josip would still be alive. He looked at his parents. How could he tell them he had caused Josip's death? No one would ever know, no one could ever tell him if he had done the right thing, and that made it so final and so hopeless.

"What do you think you'll find out by sitting here?" Magnus whispered. No one had noticed the two detectives sitting at the back of the church, hidden behind one of the marble pillars.

"I want to know who is coming to his funeral," Isa said while her gaze was locked on the family.

"Apparently only a few people," Magnus said and looked at his watch. He thought it was completely useless. It was a boring ceremony, and he wanted to check his cell phone, but Isa stopped him.

"At least show some respect," she reprimanded him.

This was so like her. At moments like these, when he least expected it, she was his conscience. But he knew that sense of morality was easily discarded in her private life. Magnus had often been the one to calm her down and had been the voice of reason. They kept each other in balance, which was why they worked well as a couple. Lately, he realized more and more that her absence had a greater impact on his mental sanity than he would have liked. He missed her.

The sound of high-heeled shoes on the stone floor suddenly echoed through the church, disturbing the serenity of the ceremony. Heads turned around to see who had entered.

"I was wrong," Magnus said, "this could become interesting."

CHAPTER

16

"MARIAN BERGQVIST," ISA SAID. She recognized her from the photos in the file.

"What is she doing here?" she whispered.

The woman, dressed in a long, black coat, sat down a few rows in front of them, at the back of the church. She looked around, searching for someone.

"Who is she looking for?" Isa asked.

A man entered the church. Just like Marian, he scanned the area and when he finally recognized her, sat down next to her.

"Who is that?"

"I don't know," Isa said.

The man was tall, blond, and well-groomed. His face looked familiar, but Isa couldn't pinpoint where she had seen him before.

The way Marian greeted the man showed that they knew each other well. They started a long conversation. Isa and Magnus were too far away to really understand what they were whispering about.

* * *

"I didn't think you'd come," Marian said and took a good look at the man next to her. The man sighed as he took off his gloves and put them in the pocket of his jacket.

"Amelia didn't want me to come ... she's alone with the baby," he said annoyed, "but here I am."

"Amelia? Ah, yes, how is your twenty-year-old wife doing? This is wife ... number?"

"No need to be sarcastic. You had your chance!"

Her face turned to a painful grimace. This wasn't the moment to pour all the frustrations of the past into the conversation.

"Why are we meeting here?" he asked.

"I don't know if this is the best place and time, but I need to talk to you. I'm scared. You see what happened to Josip?"

"You think he did this?" he asked. Was she serious? Suddenly his posture changed from arrogant to concerned. She was serious.

"Who else could it be?"

"I don't know. It's Josip, so it could be related to drugs and ... you know."

"They found those girls," she added, and wanted to see his reaction.

"Yes, I know. But there is no reason to link it to Josip's death."

"He called me a few weeks ago. After all these years, he wanted to talk about ... well, you know what. I told him to move on and forget about it. But maybe I was wrong and maybe something happened that made him rake up the story?"

"He called me too," he said, staring at the people sitting in front of the altar. How helpless and lost they looked!

"What?" Marian shouted and put her hand over her mouth, suddenly realizing her voice had sounded a little louder than expected.

Ivor turned around and saw them. The intensity with which he kept staring at them scared her. It was not until Jelena signaled him, he turned and faced the altar again, but he was clearly not happy with their presence.

"Michael, this is serious. Something is going on and we need to know what. What did he tell you?"

"Nothing. He just wanted to meet."

"And did you meet him?"

"No. Marian, don't freak out! Be calm and keep a low profile. I am sure this will blow over soon enough."

"It won't. Even if Josip's case is not a top priority for the police, there are nine dead girls. Do you really think this will blow over soon?"

"Marian, I don't see how these killings have anything to do with us," he said and took her hand to reassure her. She liked to feel his touch again after so many years. He was still a handsome man, but the heavy emotional baggage he was carrying had taken its toll and he looked older than his age. The soft features in his face had given way to deep lines running along the contours of his eyes and mouth. Three wives, four children and a myriad of mistresses whom he couldn't count on two hands anymore, was too much for even the most persistent Casanova among men.

"What about Alex?" she asked. She knew exactly how he would react, but she had to bring it up. It had been haunting her for nearly 25 years, and over the years it became harder to justify the actions of the past.

"What about him?"

"We have to tell him. We owe it to him."

"We owe him nothing. You know what will happen when we do that:

we will find ourselves in jail in no time," he said with a face that showed no emotion, and he let go of her hand.

She was startled and stammered: "But we did nothing!"

"Exactly," he said.

Out of the corner of his eye, he saw someone was standing next to him and he turned his head. It was Alex Nordin. For a moment, the words failed him, and he said nothing. Marian looked at him, confused and worried that Alex might have overheard the last part of the conversation.

"Marian, Michael, can I join you?" Alex asked and pointed at the free chair next to them.

"Sure," Michael replied. The rest of the funeral, they sat in silence. The arrival of Alex Nordin had ended the conversation abruptly. Marian didn't feel at ease. Her eyes went from the older man next to her to Alex, who was sitting one spot away. It had been nearly fifteen years since she had last seen him. He was all grown up now, taller, and more handsome than she could remember, but she still recognized the air of sadness that hung like a veil over him. She felt sorry for him. If only he knew. If only he remembered. But maybe it was better this way! A blissful ignorance.

* * *

The funeral was almost over. The priest concluded the ceremony with a few words of consolation for the parents and brother. It was the only truly emotional moment of the entire funeral service. Alex watched it with a mixed feeling of sadness and relief. Relief that his troubled friend would finally find some peace. But was this all that was left of him? A few people crying, the rest uninterested, an impersonal grave that no one would hardly visit. Forgotten. Even his violent death was insignificant, overshadowed by the murders of those nine girls. It made him think about his own death again. He seriously doubted anyone would display big emotions about his own passing-away. Like Josip, his death would go unnoticed.

* * *

Marian, Michael, and Alex got up and strolled to the exit. So far, he had only exchanged a few words with his former childhood friends, but Alex wondered why they had come and what had occupied them during the service. He had seen them in a busy discussion when he had entered. The conversation had been silenced by his own presence. It intrigued him.

It was a bright day and when they stepped outside, Marian closed her eyes for a moment to feel the warmth of the sunshine on her face. There they were, on the steps outside the church, ill at ease, when Marian suddenly said: "Good to see you, Alex. It has been, I don't know, how many years? You're all grown up now."

He smiled. It was a charming smile. He certainly had inherited his mother's beautiful looks. There was a softness in his face that struck her and at the same time, a melancholy that reminded her of his father Peter.

"I heard about your father," she continued, "I'm sorry I couldn't attend his funeral."

He answered with the standard polite comment he always used when people failed to admit that they were uncomfortable about his father's suicide: "That's fine, I understand."

"So why did you come to Josip's funeral?" Alex finally asked them. Michael looked away for a moment.

"I didn't realize you were that close."

"It's Josip," Michael replied, "we may have had our differences, but he's still one of our old friends."

Alex wasn't convinced of Michael's answer.

"How did you find out about his death? Did the family call you?"

The parents came outside, followed by the two inspectors.

An angry Ivor interrupted the conversation between Alex and Michael and shouted at them: "What are you doing here?"

The menacing tone with which he had addressed the three people stunned them.

"Hypocrites! How quickly you turned your back on him when he was still alive, and he needed his friends to stand up for him ... and now you pay respect. The audacity! None of you have right to be here!"

In his rage, Ivor struggled to find the words, and he reverted to his Croatian mother tongue: "Bog me pazi!"

"Ivor, zaustavi to! Ne na njegovu sprovodu!"

Jelena wanted to intervene, but Andrej took her arm and pulled her back.

"And you," he pointed at Alex, "you caused all this! You will pay for this one way or another!"

Suddenly Alex found himself in the center of the attention. With the finger of the old man threateningly pointed at him, he didn't know what to say or do. Where did this accusation come from? How was he to blame for Josip's death? Was this a desperate cry from a man, struck by the immense grief over his deceased son, or was there some reality in it? But how?

And then he saw her. He turned his head. The fact she had witnessed it made it so much worse. The glimpse on her face was a mixture of pity, confusion, and disappointment. He couldn't explain the old man's outburst and even if he tried, the accusation was out there, putting a seed of doubt about his credibility in everyone's mind.

Without saying a word, he took off in the direction of his car, leaving behind the small group of people outside the church. His head was empty. He could no longer think rationally as he felt a surge of emotions going through his body. He longed to be in the confined space of his car to let go.

There was someone walking behind him. It was her. She called his name.

"Please leave me alone," he said, and he increased the pace, but she caught up with him, a few meters before he could reach the car, and she jumped in front of him.

"What do you want?" He was angry, not with her, but with everyone else, with everything.

She said nothing and just stared at him. That silence was so revealing. It shocked him. Did she truly believe he was involved in Josip's murder?

"Do you really think I killed him?" he said.

His gaze was so intense it overwhelmed her. She couldn't let go; she didn't want to let go.

"As a police officer, I ...," she started.

"Do you think I killed him?" he repeated.

The tension between them was so high it seemed no longer tenable.

"No," she mumbled.

Her answer wasn't entirely satisfactory. The hesitation in her voice struck him. What had he hoped for? He had put her in a difficult situation by demanding a personal statement. She was the officer in charge of the police investigation, while he now seemed to have been upgraded to one of the suspects.

"Why would Ivor think I killed his son? Josip was my friend."

"What about the others? Marian Bergqvist and ... who was that man?"

"Michael Norman, Mats' oldest son. I don't know why they were there. Whatever they might claim, they have never been close to Josip."

"They had a lot to talk about," she remarked.

"Yes, I noticed. But why?"

"Alex, if you want answers, you have to help me. You need to talk to your mother. And ..."

She wasn't sure if it was the right time to bring it up, but she still wanted him to go to Sandviken with her.

"I've been thinking," she continued, "there are more answers to be found in Sandviken. I really believe he kept the girls close to where we found them. Your dreams, they mean something. Maybe you'll remember a lot more."

It seemed valid reasoning, but he doubted it would yield anything useful.

"Come to Sandviken with me," she proposed.

When he got into his car, he hadn't given her an answer. As she watched him drive off, it wasn't clear what she should think of it. It had been interesting, but confusing. More questions than answers.

* * *

It still took her some time to convince Alex to take the trip to Sandviken with her. Being alone with her got him stressed out and he tried to find excuses why he couldn't go. But he had to admit he was curious to find out if she was right about Sandviken. Maybe it could help him put these dreams and memories into perspective. A few days later, Isa and Alex finally drove to Sandviken. It was early in the afternoon. According to the weather forecast, a storm was coming that evening and Isa wanted to make sure they could get back home before the snowfall got too heavy. They drove in silence. Inspector Lindström looked very serious and seemed to be lost in thought. He focused all his attention on the road and landscape. The past days had been hectic, and the commotion at the funeral was still fresh in his mind, but the time to reflect had been good. The confusion, panic, and doubts had given way to more logical reasoning.

"How did he die?" he suddenly asked.

"Sorry, what did you say?" she turned to him as if he had awakened her from a dream.

"Josip. How did he really die?"

"Mr. Nordin, as you probably know, I cannot discuss this case with you."

Mr. Nordin? She was angry, and he didn't insist. He irritated her, and she preferred to continue the journey in silence. While Alex had given his father the benefit of the doubt, Isa had grown more suspicious of Peter Nordin and even his son. But she was desperate. She wanted to get rid of that perpetual mind swing. It hadn't been a lie when she had told him she didn't think he had killed Josip, but the Nordins were involved one way or another. She just had to know how.

The journey took about twenty minutes and Isa stopped the car on the road close to the cabin area. It had been months since he had been there. Since the bodies were found, the area had been off limits and the police demarcations, here and there already removed, had kept the looky-loos away. She hadn't reported the burglary yet or the mysterious site in the backyard of the Normans, and she had told no one about the accident involving the red car.

The road was familiar to him. Many times, they had played there as children. As the road was higher up, it gave a very nice overview of the area. There was almost no traffic and children from different parts of the area had gathered here to enjoy themselves. Locals and visitors. Many new friendships had developed there. But most of them had faded over the years. As people got older, interests and priorities changed and there was no room for childhood sentiment. But he also remembered it as the road where he had seen Marian, running frantically for her life. The memory was clear. It happened here.

"Why are we stopping?" he asked.

The feeling of discomfort grew stronger as he had absolutely no idea what her plans were.

"I want us to continue on foot," she said and opened the car door.

"Why?"

As he got out of the car, snow fell from the upper branches of the trees, and he couldn't dodge it. He tried to get the snow off his trousers and coat.

"Well, honestly I don't know."

For the first time since they had left Uppsala that morning, she dared to look him in the eye. Her face seemed softer now, but she was still annoyed with him. The more she thought about it, the more she realized she was only using this trip as an excuse to be with him. She didn't quite understand, but after all the drama of the past weeks and her growing doubts about his innocence, those feelings had intensified.

"Maybe we should ...," he started, but she intervened abruptly.

"I know you saw something ... in your dreams. I want you to take me there. This may be where the killer hid the girls ... this is the only thing I want you to do!"

The sudden reaction left him open-mouthed.

"I'm not sure I can, as I told you before," he said hesitantly, his blue eyes on her.

He continued: "Is there anything I have done to upset you?"

"Why do you think that?"

The answer was again curt and showed little affection. They were back to the situation of intimidating police officer and witness. Their hearty talk in the pub a few weeks ago seemed to have been forgotten, as if it had never happened. The incident at Josip's funeral surely had something to do with it.

"Never mind. Let's go then."

He walked to the small road that would lead them down to the cabin area. A feeling of sadness came over him as he kept on walking. He didn't know if she was following him, and he didn't care. The road was dangerously slippery, but he kept picking up the pace. The stillness of the landscape was soothing. How would he ever find the place he had seen in his dreams? He didn't even know if it had been anywhere near there. Everything looked so different and identical at the same time. The trees were bare and covered with snow. He could hardly distinguish the road from the treacherous wells, mud, and rocks. He had been here so many times. Surely, he would have recognized it sooner, even if the images had only recently become clearer. The memories he could recall were mostly about the girl, with few details about the surroundings.

He quickly turned around and saw Isa a few meters behind him.

"Where are you going?" he heard her scream. He slowed down and stopped, realizing he had been walking without a purpose.

"I want to go to the cottage of the Norman family," she said after catching up with him, and she pointed at the cabin, which was visible on the left, between the trees.

Seeing the doubt on his face, she immediately added: "I want to show you something."

There was no point in asking why or arguing with her, but he was sure there was nothing interesting there. They walked to the cabin. Immediately she made her way to the garden behind the house, with Alex following her.

As she looked around, there was no trace of the footsteps, neither hers nor anyone else's. It hadn't snowed in the past few days, nor had the temperatures been high enough to wipe away the snow that had covered the ground. No, someone had carefully removed the footprints. It showed that she was on the right track. But what lay behind the wall of dead branches and bushes, and why was it important?

Knowing nothing of the things Isa had discovered, Alex walked to the opening in the wall of twigs and branches. Pushing the dead wood aside, he continued his way with Isa coming behind him, calling his name.

"Alex, what are you doing?"

He turned around and said: "You were right. I recognize this place."

As he scanned the environment and tried to find a reference point, he recognized the darkness of the area. It looked like no one had been there for a while.

Isa came closer and touched his arm.

"Someone has been here recently," she said softly, "but they went to great lengths to remove the evidence."

"I've been here before," Alex said and walked on.

"When?"

"I don't know ... we usually never came here as children. Everyone knew the area was off-limits, too dangerous. Our parents didn't allow it."

"But you have been here, right?"

"Yes. I remember the stumps over there."

He pointed at the remnants of the trees, cut a while back. The wood was rotten, and it appeared to be housing many small animals now. He had difficulties orienting himself. Except for the stumps, all the trees looked alike, and it was easy to get lost.

He closed his eyes and tried to recall the images of the dream. It was summer. Leaves on the trees and the few rays of sunlight able to penetrate the dense foliage gave the area a completely different look. He remembered a big rock and part of the road covered with small rubble where some trees had been knocked over. The rock was still there, but there were many more fallen trees.

In the dream, he had run past it, and there had been a tunnel. It was long, poorly lit, and small. But here, there was no sight of it. Maybe he was wrong. Perhaps this had always been a figment of his imagination.

Isa watched him in silence. A few hours had passed since they had arrived. Although the snow had been predicted for the end of the day, clouds were already covering the sky. It was freezing cold. Alex, deep in thought, hadn't noticed, and she didn't want to disturb him.

"There should be a tunnel somewhere," he said.

"What kind of tunnel?"

"A long tunnel ... to a door where ... where there was a girl."

It gave her a chill. For the next fifteen minutes, they walked along the road but saw nothing special. The snow grew heavier, and she signaled him to go back. When they reached the cabin of the Norman family, the weather had turned so bad they could hardly see anything.

"We can't go back to the car," Isa shouted. He took her arm and dragged her down the path.

"The family cottage, let's go," he screamed.

She had a hard time keeping up with him, even though he held her hand and pulled so hard it almost felt like she had a dislocated shoulder. It took a while to find the key and when he finally opened the front door, they stumbled inside and nearly fell over each other's feet. Leaving traces of melted snow on the wooden floor, he walked to the back room. He turned on the electricity and started the electrical heaters in the living room.

"It'll be warm soon," he said while he opened the top drawer of the cupboard in the living room.

"Maybe we should light the fireplace," Isa suggested.

She tried to get the icy snowflakes out of her hair, as she felt the water slowly make its way from the head to the neck. It made her feel even colder than before.

"No, the chimney hasn't been cleaned in years."

The next ten minutes he was constantly running around with Isa calmly observing him, nonchalantly leaning against the leather chair.

"He's nervous," she thought, as he walked to the window and looked outside for the seventh time. It made her edgy too.

"Can you please sit down?" she finally said.

Ignoring her request, he stood in front of the window and stared outside.

"The snowfall is massive."

"Well, they predicted it," she replied.

"Only in the evening ... we need to get back. We really need to go back."

"It's probably going to get a lot worse," she whispered, "it's better to stay here."

"No, we really should ..."

The light, streaming in through the large window of the living room, emphasized his silhouette. He was so beautiful, just like the first time they had met. Every contour of his body was perfect. But he looked so sad, almost like a tragic hero. It was mysterious and sexy.

The temperature in the room was more pleasant now, and she took off her coat. Alex turned around. He had a strange look on his face. As she came closer, she said, while touching his hand: "Are you okay?"

His eyes were fixed on her. Her touch, as gentle as it was, stirred up too many feelings.

"We really ...," he whispered and then stopped.

While they had been dancing around this for months, avoiding each other and then wanting to be together, ignoring it and at the same time longing for it, now was the time to decide how far they wanted to go. He was about to lose himself in this tidal wave of emotions. His heart was racing. Their eyes were locked with such intensity that only the two of them seemed to exist. Her hand slid up his arm, over his shoulder to his face, all the time without saying a word and with him letting it happen. He knew what was coming. She pulled him closer and gently touched his lips with hers before she kissed him passionately, with an eagerness and bedevilment he had never experienced before. He took her face in his hands and kept kissing her. She pulled down the jacket he was still wearing. The gravity of the decision started to sink in, and he suddenly stopped her.

"Are you sure about this?" he whispered, still touching her face. She put her hand on his and said: "Yes." She lied. This was wrong and unethical in so many ways, but she couldn't resist the temptation anymore. What came next, she would deal with later. She continued to undress him, leaving the clothes scattered on the floor as he led her to the small bedroom.

* * *

He heard the man scream. The darkness led to disorientation. He kept turning around, trying to find a point of reference. The walls felt damp and cold. The voice came closer and as in the previous dreams he wanted to run to the light at the end of the tunnel, but he couldn't. Something pulled him back. Suddenly he was outside and for the first time, he was aware of the surroundings. In front of him, he saw a large distinctive oak tree, severely damaged on one side. In the distance, he recognized the big rock. Someone was carrying him, the arms so tight around him. He felt safe and warm. A soft hand was caressing his cheek and then he woke up.

He felt Isa's naked body lying next to him. As he tried to find his cell phone to check the time, he realized it was already dark. Outside it was still snowing. The phone, lying on the floor in the living room, showed it was 2 a.m. He went back to the bedroom. When he saw her lying there, so beautiful and serene, he panicked. There was no way to undo this. This made everything so complicated. He stared at her for a while and then decided to sleep in one of the chairs in the living room. In the morning, he would tell her what he had seen in his dream and how to find the way to the tunnel. The memory was burned in his mind. But in the morning, everything would be different.

CHAPTER

17

THAT NIGHT MAGNUS AND SOPHIE received a call from the intensive care unit of the hospital. In recent weeks, Toby's condition had deteriorated to the point that he had become a danger to himself and others. The voices in his head had sounded louder and more brutal than ever before, constantly criticizing and bullying him. He wanted it all to end. The days before the incident, Toby had been restrained to the bed and heavily medicated, continuously going in and out of consciousness. When they found him, he was lying against the wall, his head covered in blood, moaning, unable to speak. The restraints had been forced, and in his delirium, he had rammed his head against the wall with such incredible force that the plaster had cracked. That night, he slipped into a coma.

When the parents arrived at the hospital, it was clear from the CT scan, which showed a massive cerebral hemorrhage, that the damage to the brain was extensive and that his chance of survival was small.

Sitting in the hallway, outside the intensive care unit, they were waiting. Magnus looked at his wife Sophie, nervously biting her nails, getting up now and then to pace the hallway. He felt numb, a mere bystander. It was as if his body and mind were decoupled from the world around him. Where was the grief? The devastation? There was just a big void, like something or someone had drained all feelings from his being.

The nurse, who had received and taken them to the intensive care unit, had observed him since the moment they had arrived.

"Mr. Wieland?" she asked.

He looked at her but said nothing.

"Mr. Wieland?" she repeated. "Can I bring you something? When the doctor comes, I'm sure you and your wife will be able to see Toby for a few minutes."

"No, thank you," he whispered and let his eyes wander back to his wife.

They hadn't talked much since their quarrel in the hospital. Just like a few years ago, he felt her slipping away from him. He didn't know how to approach her. Every conversation ended in her walking away. There was a deafening silence that isolated him even more from her. He was finally punished for his affair. The ruins of his marriage lay before him, so very visible, and now he felt alone, alone with his grief. There was nothing anyone could do or say to help them. His family was no family anymore. Everything had fallen apart.

The neurologist told them a few hours later they had to resuscitate Toby several times and his brain had sustained further damage from the loss of oxygen. They now feared a complete cessation of all brain functions. But Magnus still couldn't react. He heard his wife burst into tears. The sobs, which lasted for minutes, with those high notes, felt like knives carving his eardrums. What was she whining about? She was the one who had insisted on admitting Toby to the hospital. She hadn't been strong enough to take care of him; she hadn't even wanted to ... and now Toby was going to die. She took his hand, but he pushed it away.

"It's your fault," he said.

He couldn't bear to look at her. His knuckles had turned white from clenching his fists, while he gritted his teeth to remain calm.

"What?"

"You couldn't be bothered to care for him, could you? And now, now he will die. Because of you!"

"I, I ... what? Why are you like that? I've done nothing wrong."

"You wanted to get rid of him from the day he was born," he shouted. "You are heartless, empty ... cold. You are incapable of loving anyone."

He wanted her to respond, tell him he was wrong. But she didn't.

Yes, maybe it was her fault. She tried so hard to tuck those feelings away. The pain and devastation of losing a child, a marriage, torn apart by grief and guilt. It would devour her, and it would be her demise.

The nurses, alarmed by the noise, rushed in and tried to calm the devastated father.

He had to get out of there, away from the woman sitting next to him. It was as if he was suffocating. The words to describe the anger and pain simply didn't exist. He got up and stumbled like a zombie to the door marking the exit. He didn't care she was still sitting there, recovering from his lash-out. He didn't want to talk to her; he didn't want to see her anymore.

* * *

When Isa woke up, it was freezing. The heating was switched off and the faint sunshine streaming through the window wasn't strong enough to heat the room. She looked around. The room was small and apart from a closet and bed, there was no furniture. She didn't know what time it was, but she didn't want to get up. She loved feeling the soft blanket on her naked body. The moment she got up, everything would become so complicated. The sex had been all-devouring, hot and intoxicating. The explosive end result of the addictive tension that had been sizzling between them for months. She had expected it to be gone, or at least watered down, but it wasn't. Far from it. Fortunately, he hadn't been there next to her when she had woken up. As she was trying to figure out what to say or do when she saw him again, she heard the signal on her mobile.

She got out of bed and grabbed the phone from the floor. Magnus had left her five messages scattered throughout the night and morning. She would listen to them later, but first, she had to face Alex. There was noise coming from the kitchen and the living room. Through the crack in the door, she saw him walking around. She loved to see him move. Even in the most worn-out jeans, he was still so desirable. His dark-brown hair was tousled as if he had just gotten out of bed. It was slightly too long and curled at the neck. The light-colored pullover drew the lines of his perfectly shaped upper body. It was so inviting. But no, she couldn't do that, she absolutely couldn't. The confrontation would be awkward enough, and she tried to delay the moment as long as possible. She found her clothes on the floor next to the bed. They felt cold and damp when she put them on. Ten minutes later, she entered the living room, trying to make as little noise as possible. Naively she thought she could stay unnoticed, but when she entered the room, he briefly stopped making coffee in the kitchen. The atmosphere was already tense. He avoided her glance as he continued with his morning task.

"Did you sleep well?" he asked.

"Yes, thank you," she answered," quite well."

There was an unpleasant silence. They didn't quite know how to start the conversation. Should they talk about what happened the day before?

Or carry on as if nothing had happened?

"I'm sorry, but I have nothing to eat. Just coffee. I hope that works."

"Yes, that's okay," she said and sat down in a chair by the window.

Outside, the sun was shining brightly. But it wasn't warm enough to melt the snow that was piled up against the window and door. The path to the car would be difficult to clear.

"I think we can try to get back home," she said.

He put the coffee on the table in front of her and took the chair on the other side. She felt him staring at her.

"You slept here?" she continued, seeing the blankets in one of the chairs.

"Yes," he said.

It was a short answer. He didn't want the conversation to wander from what he had in mind.

"Listen, Isa ...," he started, "we need to talk about yesterday."

There was no reply. She kept her eyes fixed on the window.

"I need to know. What ..."

What she was about to say, she had gone over in her head a few times, carefully phrased and rephrased, at least that was what she thought. But the words sounded so much harder and more insensitive than expected.

"It means nothing. Let's forget that this ever happened. Let's just leave it at that, okay?"

Without waiting for his reply, she got up and went to find her jacket. He was stunned. And she was shocked herself. Why had she said this? Just minutes ago, she would have jumped on him like a lioness on her prey. She would have lured him back in her bed and made love to him. But now ... she told herself it was all in his best interest to forget it all. Get him into bed and then move on. Throw-away people, as Ingrid had said.

Rejected ... again. Rejected by everyone. People never saw beyond the good looks. He was used and thrown away time and again. By everyone ...

and now she as well. He was in love with her, but this one sentence had destroyed everything. He couldn't figure out if her attitude were prompted by professional ethics or genuine feelings, and that this was just a selfish aspiration of hers to spend the night with him. The result was the same.

"We have to get out of here," she said, standing at the door.

He couldn't move. He couldn't speak. For one, almost non-existent moment, so brief and elusive, he had been happy, really happy. It was so difficult to put all those expectations aside and pretend to be okay with it. He felt nauseous.

She opened the door.

"Isa, there is something I ...," he got up and walked over to her.

"Mr. Nordin, there's nothing I want to talk about," she interrupted.

So, they were on a 'mister Nordin'-'inspector Lindström' basis again. How quickly they had gone from sharing the most intimate of human emotions to complete indifference!

Fine, if that was what she wanted!

"Not that. I think we should go back to the forest. I think I can find the way to the tunnel and the place where the girl was held ... if this still interests you ... inspector Lindström."

Inspector Lindström. The words sounded so harsh. Was this what she wanted? Could she really ignore the previous night? Could she ignore him?

"Yes, of course," she said.

"Okay. I'll get the shovels then. They're in the back room."

It took them a few hours to clear a path from the cabin to the upper road. The car was stuck in the snow, and it would take a few more hours to free it. No snowplow had passed, and even if they could remove most of the snow from the car, the road was still blocked. He would have to go back to the cabin and spend the rest of the day with her, waiting for the weather to clear up or for additional help to clear the roads. He couldn't bear the prospect of hours of complete silence and uncomfortable tension.

"There is nothing we can do here," he said, "maybe we can go back to the backyard of Mats' cabin."

"You think that might be easier," she questioned his proposal.

"Probably better than just standing here," he said angrily, and started making his way to the cabin of Mats Norman.

She sighed, took her cell phone, and tried to call Magnus. Her six attempts to reach him were unsuccessful. In all cases, she was redirected to his voice mail. The messages he had left for her during the night were short and gave little information, only mentioning that he wouldn't be at work for a few days due to urgent family matters.

Urgent family matters? Why didn't he call back? What was going on? It worried her. For a moment, she considered calling Sophie, but she quickly put that idea aside. A confrontation between wife and ex-mistress wasn't the best idea.

She put the phone back in the pocket of her coat and turned to check where Alex had gone. He was angry and she couldn't blame him. The way she had handled the situation hadn't been exactly an example of sensitivity and understanding. More and more, she doubted whether she had made the right decision. A decision she had made for the both of them, giving him no chance to talk about what he felt or wanted.

The way back to the cabin of the Norman family was difficult, as expected. From the footsteps in the snow, she noticed he had gotten off-track a few times, had slipped, and fallen. Finally, she found him near the rock they had seen yesterday.

"What are you looking for?" she asked.

"It should be close. I think it's more toward the west ... the image in my head is a bit fuzzy."

To her it seemed hopeless to find anything in this sea of whiteness, but she kept following him, prompted by a wrong and twisted feeling of remorse and pity.

Stepping through the deep snow took its toll. With every movement, he felt increasingly exhausted. By the time they reached the place he had been looking for, he was gasping for air and the pain in his limbs was agonizing.

Numerous branches and stones covered the entrance of the tunnel. He saw the oak and suddenly everything came flooding back. This was where he had seen the girl.

There it was. A dungeon in a forest, hidden behind the trees and rocks. Isa had had serious doubts about her companion's quest, but he had been right.

"We need to go in," he said and looked at her, seeking for approval. She said nothing and paced the area.

"Isa?"

"No, we need to get a forensics team here," she finally replied, "this is a crime scene."

She took the cell phone and dialed the number of the police station. The call took about ten minutes. Then she turned to Alex.

"There is no point in waiting here. At best, they'll be here in two hours. We can go back to your cabin or sit in a cold car. What do you prefer?"

He sighed. For a split second, he thought about stirring up the situation again by giving her a rather sarcastic and angry answer to the simple question she had asked, but he was tired, and he didn't have the energy to start a fight about something she had deemed non-existent and unimportant.

They returned to the cabin and stayed there until Ingrid's team arrived almost three hours later. The waiting happened in complete silence, avoiding each other. He stayed behind in the house while Isa joined the forensics team.

"Someone will come to take your statement," she said before leaving.

He nodded.

"I would appreciate it if you ...," she continued as she put on her coat and opened the door.

The frown on his face showed she had hit a sensitive note.

"Don't worry, I won't say anything about our ... whatever it is," he said angrily and turned around.

Her eyes followed his movements as he walked to the kitchen. Sleeping with him had been a mistake. In her head, she kept repeating it over and over, even though she didn't really believe it.

* * *

Carefully they removed the wood from the entrance and found a concrete tunnel that led to an underground room. It almost looked like a bunker built during the war. The tunnel, unlit and slippery because of the snow and ice, was long and small. On the other side, a metal door with several locks that could only be locked from outside. The door was open, and they entered. What they found behind it, was something none of them had expected, and it left them breathless.

"Finally, a breakthrough in the case," Isa thought, but the sheer horror of the scene had not yet subsided.

The room was small with only one basement window, a bed in one corner of the room, and a table and chair in the other one. The light was dim, but enough to see the traces of blood scattered over the room, dried out and absorbed by the porous structure of the concrete. In the wall, by the bed, thick metal chains with handcuffs had been placed. The smell was a mixture of moisture, sweat, urine, and the iron sniff of blood.

"Be careful not to contaminate anything," Ingrid said to the rest of the team. She looked at Isa, who was standing near the door, trying to make sense of it all. It put the Nordin family back into the spotlight. Alex had led her here, so he had been in this room. But why? What had he done there?

"Isa, how did you find this place?"

She hesitated for a moment and decided it was not the right time to go into the details.

"It's a rather long story. I'll tell you when we get back to the station."

"Well, that will take a while," Ingrid replied, while she unpacked the equipment.

"I saw that you are here with Alexander Nordin," Ingrid continued, trying to provoke a response from her friend. Isa kept her stance and ignored the comment, but her body language told the opposite. She felt the adrenaline rush through her veins.

"Well, yes ...," she stammered, "he helped me with the investigation."

"Right," Ingrid replied. Isa was nervous and clearly hiding something. She could probably guess what her friend had been keeping from her. It was disappointing. Hadn't she learned anything?

"Well, Ingrid, I need to go back. I think you can handle it here."

"The roads are probably still blocked. You may need to wait a little longer."

"I'll manage. See you at the station tomorrow!"

As she walked back to the cabin, she realized how stupid and rude she had been to Alex. She wanted to undo all of it. She stopped and closed her eyes. As she felt the cold air on her face, she remembered his touch, how he had run his fingers over her body, how he had kissed her, how they had made love, his body against hers. And it thrilled her. It was difficult to admit it, but she was actually falling for him. It was madness, irresponsible and so exciting.

When she entered, he was in the kitchen.

"And?" he asked.

"Yes, the girls were probably held there," she replied, while she saw his expression become more serious and gloomier. He kept staring straight ahead as he whispered: "So I was there. What does that mean? Did I see the murderer?"

"Possibly ...," she replied.

"Now what? Am I in danger? Just like Josip."

It had crossed her mind. They should keep an eye on him.

"I'll take you home. We'll talk again about this in the next days. Okay?"

It didn't put his mind at ease.

* * *

That afternoon they drove back to Uppsala. The atmosphere was anything but pleasant. The days after, he locked himself in his apartment, the way he had done many times before when things got too difficult to bear, and when the problems seemed insurmountable. Doubts about his father and his involvement in the murders were back, more pronounced than ever before. The fear he might be in danger, and the disappointment and the heartache over Isa had brought him to an all-time low.

* * *

It took the forensics team a week to examine the room. The DNA results were disappointing. There were few links to the murdered girls and there had been nothing useful to identify the murderer: no blood, no DNA, not a single fiber. Neither there in the bunker, nor in the cabin where Josip supposedly had stayed those last days before his death.

"Maybe we should consider hypnosis," Nina said.

Isa looked at her, with a grin on her face and a slight frowning of the eyebrows, as they walked back to her office. This had been the weirdest suggestion of Miss Kowalczyk so far.

"Are you serious?"

"Yes, there are several reports where it has been successful in retrieving long lost memories. It doesn't hurt to try."

"I don't think so," Isa answered and opened the door.

Talking to Alex wasn't exactly what she had in mind. Moreover, she had failed to convince Anders to put him under police surveillance and she had lost track of him. It wasn't okay. Their prime witness. And no one knew where he was. If only she could overcome that barrier of shame and guilt, she would go after him and make sure he was fine.

He was okay, wasn't he? Maybe she should check.

"I have the ballistic report of the Radić murder," Nina said and handed her the paper.

"So, the bullet that killed him came from the gun found at the crime scene."

Isa quickly went through the text.

"The gun is registered to a Nikolaj Blom and was reported stolen in 1992," Nina added.

"Who is Nikolaj Blom?" Isa asked, surprised.

"Let's discuss that later, but first I want to show you something else."

She put a file on the table and opened it. With a smooth twist, she put it in front of Isa, who had sat down on the other side of the desk.

"What am I looking at?"

"Alexander Nordin's file. Please look at the top of the page. As a baby, he was reported missing. This happened a few days after he was born. But look at the date."

"26 June 1987? This should ring a bell?"

"It's the day Clara Persson disappeared," Nina said.

Her boss looked up from the file and stared at her for a moment.

"What happened?"

"A nurse reported the disappearance. While Irene was sleeping, someone took the baby. That evening, however, he was found in a basket on the stairs outside the hospital ... unharmed. They never found out where he had been and what had happened to him during the eight hours he went missing."

"You think this has something to do with the case?" Isa asked.

"As you said before: the coincidences in this case are piling up until they are no longer coincidental. This family is at the center of it, but we still don't know why."

"Does he know?"

"What do you mean?" Nina asked.

"Does he know about all this? The kidnapping?"

"God, Isa, I assume so. I assume his parents told him, no?"

"How can someone just walk out of a hospital with a baby?"

Holding her head in her hands, Isa read the file again, looking for details and clues, but there was little useful information other than what Nina had already told her.

"No one would find it unusual for a father to take his baby for a walk, no?"

"Then Peter took him? But why?"

"A father and a baby ... wouldn't that inspire more trust than a man alone?"

"So, he used the child to get to Clara?"

"Maybe. It has been done before."

Isa got up and wandered around. This was a sign for Nina to keep quiet.

"I still don't understand why the disappearance was reported by the nurse, not by Irene."

"Maybe she was sound asleep," Nina tried to find an explanation.

"Really? You think she wouldn't notice if someone entered the room and took her baby. On the other hand, it might have nothing to do with our case."

Berger entered the room.

"I have news about the bunker," he started.

"Berger, please learn to knock," Isa reprimanded him.

"Sorry, boss. But I have information ..."

She signaled him to come to the point quickly, as she became impatient. The conversation with Nina had made it clear she needed to talk to Irene Nordin again. Alex hadn't given her much to work with. For some reason, he seemed reluctant to talk to his mother.

"The bunker is not a bunker, but part of a house. Construction began in 1979 but was halted by the local authorities in early 1980 because the region is protected, and the building was in fact illegal."

"Who was the owner?"

Berger examined the papers he was holding.

"The owner was Nikolaj Blom. He bought the property in 1985 from the first owner, a Dr. ... Karsegard. But here is something interesting ..."

"Nikolaj Blom disappeared in 1992," Nina interrupted.

"How ... how do you know?" Berger asked, surprised.

"The gun that killed Josip Radić was registered in his name."

"And he was pronounced dead in 2010. His grandchildren inherited the land, including the unfinished house."

"What happened to him?"

"Well, hard to say. Some thought he had run off and was lying low. Most of the family described him as a swindler and a lay-about, usually involved in shady business. Police reports show that there was an active search to find him, but they stopped looking after 18 months. Then the case was closed."

"Are you telling me Nikolaj Blom is our killer?" Isa asked, annoyed.

"Maybe," Berger answered cautiously.

"If he's still alive, he'll be ninety-five or so," Nina added, "probably not."

"Have you contacted the family about the house?" Nina asked Berger.

"Yes, they all said that no one in the family had seen the place in years. Since Nikolaj's disappearance, they aren't exactly on speaking terms. But one of the sons said someone must have expanded the place since the tunnel wasn't there originally."

"None of them knew?"

"Exactly, and Mats Norman and his family don't seem to know either. For years, everyone had assumed the place was off limits. Too dangerous for hiking because the ground is so unstable there."

"Seems indeed not the best place to build a house. Ideal for a killer, though. Is there anything else forensics found?"

Berger shrugged and answered: "I don't think so. Dr. Olsson only found DNA from the girls, but nothing else, surprisingly."

"He is very smart."

"Who reported the disappearance of the gun?"

Nina quickly checked the report.

"His son ... he reported it around the time Nikolaj went missing."

"Any connection between Nikolaj Blom and the Nordin family, or any of the others?"

"None we could find."

Isa sighed and stared at the window for a while. Nina and Berger were waiting for some reaction from her side. When she finally looked at them, she said: "Everything leads to the Nordins, but I'm not convinced that Peter Nordin is the killer. There is something else. I can't put my finger on it."

"Okay, I think it makes sense to talk to Irene Nordin again. I'll set up the meeting. I assume that inspector Wieland is still on leave?"

Isa nodded. Magnus had requested a leave of absence for family reasons. It was all very mysterious. No one, except Anders, knew what was really going on. He had ignored all of Isa's phone calls. He had simply disappeared, and Isa had given up trying to find out what was going on.

Nina got up, but before leaving the room, she turned around and asked: "And should we question the son again?"

That was what Isa dreaded even more. She had to face him at some point, but preferably on her own, not with her coworkers in the room.

218

"No, not now."

CHAPTER

18

LIESBETH HAD STOOD in front of that door so many times, touching the door handle, trying to enter, but never crossing that doorstep. The past fifteen years had been a nightmare for the family, not knowing if Katrien was still alive or not. She felt her heart beating fast. Breathing was superficial and was the only sign of the anxiety she was feeling. She opened the door. Only the cleaning lady had been in Katrien's room during the years she had gone missing. Today it was different. Today she had buried her husband, André. The emotions of the past months had worn him down until he had simply given up. Two funerals in the past four months. People pitied her, but strangely enough, the peace she felt was liberating. Yes, her daughter was dead. But at least she could lay her to rest, putting an end to the agonizing uncertainty they had lived with all those years. Yes, her husband was dead. The love she had felt for the man she had once considered her significant other, had been reduced to a mere pat on the back, a fleeting kiss on the cheek. Only now she realized how she had missed the passion and romance they had shared before. It was time to move on. As she stepped inside, she recalled happier times. She hadn't expected that. In those fifteen years, she had never allowed those feelings to surface.

Everything looked the same as so many years before: the posters, the dressing table with the make-up and perfume, her books and notes from the previous school year still lying on the desk. She had planned to go through them before starting the new school year. That was Katrien: serious, conscientious, but also very ambitious. She sat down on the neatly made bed, which no one had slept in for years. She sighed. Her job was to tidy up and put her daughter's stuff in boxes. It scared her. It was like she was going to put her daughter away forever. But she needed full closure. She had to move on with her life.

When she looked at the wedding ring on her finger, she knew she had to do the same with her marriage and she took it off, but the ring slipped from her hand, fell to the floor, and rolled under the bed. The gap between the edge of the bed and the floor was narrow, and it took her a while to get her arm under the bed. She felt the thick layer of dust under her fingertips, making it harder to find the lost ring. Suddenly her hand hit something, but it wasn't the cold and metallic surface of a ring. It felt like the pages of a book. Trying to grab the object, she tried to get her arm further under the bed. When she pulled it out, she saw it was a pack of letters. She wiped the dust off and sat on the bed. On some of them, she recognized her daughter's handwriting. Others weren't hers. The writing was majestic, elegant, and almost calligraphic. As she opened one, feelings of fear and despair took hold of her again. Why had Katrien hidden this? After all these years, would Liesbeth find the answers she had been looking for: why and who?

The letter began with, *"My love ..."*

Quickly she closed the letter. For five minutes, she sat on the bed, silent, motionless, in doubt if she really wanted to continue reading. Slowly she unfolded the letter. Her hands were shaking.

"My love, my dearest, I was so thrilled to hear from you. I feel the same way. Since I got your first letter, I can't get you out of my mind. I long to be with you. Although I am older than you, our love is true, and nothing should stand in our way. It's great news that you will be visiting Sweden in the summer. We can meet in person. Let me know when you will arrive ..."

Who was this? She looked at the back of the envelope. It mentioned no name. At the bottom of the letter, she found 'P', but no name. And while the address was handwritten, the rest was not. It was typed with an old-fashioned typewriter. Some letters were almost faded.

The rest of the letter was a continued and rather boring declaration of love. As she read more of them, she realized her beautiful daughter had made plans to run away from home, to be with her mystery man. Plans she ultimately had paid for with her life.

"Stupid, stupid girl," she shouted after reading the last letter in which her daughter had extensively complained about her family ... how they didn't understand her, how boring and insignificant her parents were, how stupid her brother and sister were.

The words were so confrontational and although she knew these were the frustrations of a teenage girl, feeling bad, troubled, doubting about the world and longing for that one true love, they were hurtful and devastating, nonetheless. If only she had known about her daughter's feelings. If she had been more attentive and accommodating, maybe Katrien would still be alive today. If, if, if ... that word haunted her again. Just after Katrien's disappearance, so many if-then scenarios had gone through her head. It had almost made her crazy until one day she had given up and had stopped blaming herself. Although he had never told her in so many words, Liesbeth knew her husband had struggled with the same things for so many years. He, on the other hand, could never get past that stage.

But now, seeing it in writing, they were to blame. It was their fault. Katrien hadn't been happy and they, her parents, hadn't known.

She closed the letter, put it on the pile, and wiped the tears from her face. She had to notify the police of this discovery. With the letters in hand, she left the room. It would be the last time she would set foot in that room. The memory of Katrien had been tainted, and it had finally and completely broken her.

* * *

As he walked to the entrance of the hospital, Alexander saw a familiar face. Seated on the bench in a small park, near the entrance, was inspector Wieland, with his hands supporting his head, and the eyes fixated on the ground in front of him. He hadn't noticed Alex, who was standing a few meters away from him, in doubt if he would say something. It was freezing and sitting outside seemed a bit of a drastic measure to escape from what was going on inside the hospital. Compassion was something else than the anger and resentment he had felt during the interrogation at the police office a few weeks ago. It was unspoken, but both men strongly disliked each other from the very beginning they had met in the cabin at Sandviken. They were competitors. But now, the sadness of the moment had caught Alex by surprise, and he felt compelled to say something. He knew what it was. He had struggled with it for years.

"Inspector Wieland," he said and stepped closer.

Magnus looked up. Surprised by the face staring back at him, he took a moment to gather his thoughts.

"Mr. Nordin ... what can I do for you?"

The bloodshed eyes showed he had been crying.

"Are you okay?" Alex asked hesitantly.

"Why wouldn't I be?" Magnus replied, irritated by the question.

"I'm sorry, but I saw you sitting here, and it looked like you were rather in despair."

Magnus sighed and looked at him more closely. He seemed genuinely concerned. But why would he talk about his grief with a stranger, let alone someone he distrusted?

"I'm fine. Thank you." Magnus got up, expecting the young man to leave, but he noticed Alex continued to stare at him.

"It helps to talk to someone about it. You shouldn't be facing this all alone."

"What ... what do you know about it?" Magnus cried and walked past Alex back to the hospital building.

"Maybe nothing ... but I've seen you here many times in the past months. In the psychiatric ward. It's one of your children, isn't it?"

Magnus stopped and turned around. He was angry and hurt, and he wanted to hit him. But he didn't and just stood there, amazed at the fact that his private life hadn't been so private and that what he tried so desperately to hide, had been open for anyone to see. At least one person had put the pieces together.

"I don't know the details ... and I shouldn't," Alex continued, "but I just want to give you some advice."

"Again ... what do you know about it? Why should I listen to you? What gives you the right to say all of this? Go away and leave me alone!"

Alex said calmly: "Yet, you're still here, talking to me. I know you're upset, and you probably don't want any advice, especially not from me, but I'll give it, anyway. Up to you to do something with it or not."

Emotions got the upper hand, and the tears rolled down his cheeks. Alex saw it but continued talking, "In your head, you've tried to make sense of it, but trust me, there's nothing you can think or do to make it right. This is something you need to accept. I've finally learned that a clear, objective view is essential to put things in the right perspective. So, my advice to you is to talk to someone, an outsider, but someone you trust. Someone who can put things into perspective, who can look at this with some distance and someone who has nothing to lose or gain from this. I'm really sorry I upset you. However, I hope this can help you in some way."

The one-sided conversation was disturbing, and Magnus needed time to let it all sink in. They had more in common than he originally thought. His son's schizophrenia, Peter Nordin's depression, the illness was different, but the pain and strain on their closest ones had been very much the same.

Alex turned around. He had said everything he wanted to say.

"Why are you here?" was the first thing Magnus could utter.

Without turning around, Alex said: "I never had someone to give me advice. If you want to know why I'm here, you can find me in the office of Dr. Wikholm."

As Alex walked away from him, Magnus realized that not only the father had been a patient of the good doctor, but the son too. A mental case, just like his father! And maybe a murderer, just like his father.

But at that moment, he didn't care. Inside that hospital room, his son was dying. Only he couldn't face the truth yet. His marriage was over, but he just couldn't give up on Toby. They all wanted him to turn off the machines that were breathing for him and keeping him alive. All of them ... the doctors, his wife. He didn't need advice about his son's illness; he needed advice about the decision to end his son's life. He needed Isa. The bond between them had always been so much stronger than the one he had shared with his wife. But she probably wouldn't even want to talk to him. He had created the distance between them, and now he didn't know how to mend it. When he went back inside, he saw Alex taking the elevator to the psychiatric ward of the hospital. Magnus made his way to the intensive care, where he would spend the rest of the day, with only the sound of the respiratory device and the monitor in the background, still not knowing what to do.

Toby, little Toby, his beautiful son. He would never forget the first time he took that fragile little human being in his arms. All his senses were so heightened now he could feel that first touch, smell that first scent of his newborn baby again. It was his second child, and one might be tempted to say the marvel of birth, of becoming a father for the second time, would be so much less magnificent than the first time, but it wasn't. Not for him.

He would never see him grow up, fall in love, get heartbroken, get married, have children of his own, sit next to him, and scarred by old age, take his hand and tell him, faced with death, that it was okay to let go. Life had been so disappointing. So unfair. He had never really gotten to know his son. It was partly his fault. He hadn't been there when he had taken his first steps, said his first word, when he had been scared and confused, when he had hurt himself, and when life had been so devastatingly cruel that he had seen no way out anymore. Sophie had. Why couldn't she see she held a treasure of memories that only belonged to her? He envied her; he hated her for it. She didn't deserve them.

Time was so limited, and none of them had known until it was too late. He closed his eyes and listened to the cadence of the respirator. It was soothing. The panic came in waves and the grief cut like a knife through his bones and mind. Alexander Nordin was right. It would consume him.

* * *

With the cell phone still in her hand, she opened the door. Irene Nordin had tried to call her son for days, but with little success. She had heard his voicemail more than ten times by now. The two ladies in front of her were no strangers.

"Inspectors, I didn't expect to see you here. What do you want?"

Her attitude changed. Irene Nordin was a resentful woman who categorically put people in two boxes: enemy or friend. There was no in-between.

"We want to ask you some more questions," Isa replied.

"Am I a suspect?" Irene asked defiantly.

"No, you're not," Isa admitted and was quickly interrupted by the older woman: "So I'm under no obligation to answer your questions. Good day!"

As she tried to close the front door, Nina reacted quickly by putting her foot between the door and the frame.

"It's about your son ... so we hope you can help us. Please."

"So now you're after my son," Mrs. Nordin said and looked at Isa. The stare made her feel uncomfortable. It was as if she saw right through her.

I know you used my son and now you'll pay.

Yes, Isa was definitely in Irene's enemy box.

Nina continued, "Mrs. Nordin, please, we need your help. We're not here to accuse anyone."

Nina was calm and finally convinced the old lady to let them in.

* * *

Sitting in the living room, Irene kept looking at the phone on the table and she didn't really pay attention to the questions, as they had to be repeated several times throughout the conversation. She didn't bother to offer them any coffee or tea. She wanted them out of her house as soon as possible.

"We asked your former neighbors in Sandviken, but as you may know from your son, we found the place where the girls were held and probably murdered. It seems strange to us no one has noticed anything wrong in all those years."

"Since I don't know exactly where this place is that you're talking about, since I haven't talked to my son yet, it's hard for me to make any statement about this," Irene said coldly.

"Where, where is your son? It has been a few weeks since the discovery. What's wrong?"

Alex, where are you?

Isa was worried. Did the murderer get to him?

The scar. She remembered the scar. Could he have done something stupid, just like he had in the past? No, she wasn't that important to him. She couldn't be. But he was important to her. For the first time, she could admit it. The surges of doubt, the barriers she had put up, now seemed so meaningless and so unbelievably absurd. It was as if she had suddenly woken up.

"You seem concerned, inspector?"

There was no answer as the women continued to look at each other. Nina felt the tension. There was more to it than what her boss wanted to share.

"My son is brilliant, but he is also very vulnerable and somewhat naïve," Irene continued, "people take advantage of that."

It was a direct attack.

"I don't know where he is. He usually locks himself up in his apartment when he's upset. I've called a few times, but no response. I'm not too worried ... it has happened before. So ... if you want to question him, feel free to try, but you have to find him first and convince him to talk to you."

With Isa not responding, Nina took over the conversation: "As I mentioned before, Mrs. Nordin, we're not accusing your son of anything. So far, he seems to be the only one who has helped us, and we need to investigate that further. He led us to the bunker, suggesting he must have been there before. The area behind the cabin of the Norman family, is quite secluded. Has it always been like that?"

"Is that the area where you found it?" Irene asked, and she became more interested.

"Yes, why?"

"That area has always been closed to the public ... since we've been going there. People in the neighborhood told us that there had been many mudslides over the years and that the area was just too unstable ... but ..."

She paused her story.

"But?"

"Oh, God, he was right ... and we didn't believe him," she looked at them, almost pleading for understanding and forgiveness.

"Your son told you before that he saw people there, didn't he?"

"Yes. He was so young, and such an inquisitive little boy, questioning everything, wanting to know everything. He was adventurous and I remember him sneaking out to explore all those hidden places, even the dangerous ones. That all changed later when he became more quiet, closed, and secretive. I guess because of his father. Anyway, I thought he made it up ... so I ... we didn't believe him when he said he had seen a man and a girl in a dark room out in the wilderness and that the girl was hurt. I should have believed him."

"So, you think he might have seen one of the girls?"

"Yes," she said surprised. "What else could it be?"

The two women in front of her exchanged a short glance with each other, which she noticed.

"I don't understand ... what else do you think happened?" she asked the inspectors.

"Who else had a particular interest in that area? Anyone you can remember?"

"I'm not sure. Everyone in the neighborhood had basically access to the area, but as far as I remember everyone tried to avoid it."

Nina took a small notebook from her purse and flipped through the pages after putting it on her lap.

"Nikolaj Blom, does that name ring a bell?" Nina said.

"Yes," the old lady called out. "Yes, ... I recently saw that name in one of my husband's papers or was it a file on his computer? I can't remember. Why?"

"What papers?"

"Uh ... I didn't look too closely, but I think it was about the rent of a house, several years ago."

"Where are the papers now? Can we have a look?"

"No, the papers are gone. Just like his laptop."

Nina sighed and turned to Isa, who straightened her back and leaned over to look at the older woman.

"Why are you so interested in this?"

"Mrs. Nordin, this is very important. Please try to remember what this was about! Are you sure that the name was Nikolaj Blom?"

"Yes, because it was a strange name, I had never heard or seen before."

"What house did it apply to?"

"I don't know anymore. It surprised me. I thought Peter had explored the options of buying or renting a house instead of a cabin so we could spend more time together as a family. Probably it was naïve of me to think that way. But I'm not sure anymore."

She closed her eyes and tried to recall the exact documents. Where had she seen the name? What had been the context? She had been so eager to get rid of Peter's things, all because she wanted to erase him from her life. She could have continued to pretend, but the last decade of their life together had been hell.

"Have you asked Mr. Blom?" Irene continued.

"Unfortunately, Mr. Blom is dead, or rather, he disappeared, and his family could not provide any useful information about the property."

"Where are the documents?" Nina asked.

"Uh ... in the dumpster. I threw them away months ago."

"And the computer?"

"No clue," she said, but she knew very well her son had taken the laptop with him a few weeks ago.

Nina turned a few pages in her notebook and asked: "Before we go, I'd like to ask you one more thing. There was an incident when your son was born. Is that correct?"

"Incident? What incident?"

Irene was astonished.

"He went missing. Someone had taken him and then brought him back a few hours later. What happened?"

For a moment, she couldn't respond. This wasn't something she had expected to be confronted with and she didn't quite know how to answer.

"Mrs. Nordin?" Nina asked again as she didn't get an immediate reaction.

"Uhm ... you caught me by surprise with this. What does this have to do with the murders?"

"Well ...," Nina wanted to reply, but was interrupted by Isa, who put her hand on Nina's arm as a sign of warning to stop talking.

"Can you please answer the question? What happened?"

The beep sound of Irene's phone indicated she had received a text message. She wanted to check it but knew that it probably wouldn't be appreciated by the ladies sitting on the opposite side of the living room.

"I don't know," she said hesitantly.

All those feelings came rushing back. How she didn't want to be a mother. How she wanted him gone. And the panic when he had been taken. She felt ashamed. She had tried to put it behind her, but when she was confronted with it again, she felt like the worst mother in the world.

"I woke up, and he was just ... gone. I've gone over it in my mind so many times. This is something that still haunts me, but I haven't heard and seen anything. I must have been fast asleep. I was terrified ... in a panic. Peter too. Luckily, they found him a few hours later ... outside, in front of the hospital."

"Do you think you could have been drugged?"

"Drugged? Yes, it has crossed my mind. I woke up drowsy, but they never checked it. It wasn't until much later that I realized this was probably why I didn't wake up or why I hadn't seen or heard anything."

"How do you think this could have happened?"

"Maybe through my meds. I had gestational diabetes during my pregnancy ... so I guess anyone from the hospital staff: nurses or doctors."

"A nurse named Anita Berenson discovered your son's disappearance. Could she have been involved?"

She sighed and looked quite desperate.

"I don't think so, but I may have missed a lot of clues."

"Right," Nina acknowledged, "they returned the baby, seemingly unharmed."

"According to you, why would anyone abduct a baby and then bring him back?" Isa asked.

"To scare or threaten us?"

"But why you? What's so special about your family?"

A new beep sound interrupted the conversation.

Finally, Alexander had returned his mother's messages. He was okay. She shouldn't worry, but he wasn't ready to talk to her or anyone else. This behavior she had experienced many times before. It had taken many years to understand him, but she knew if something wasn't right, if there was something bothering him, he needed time away to get everything sorted out.

She wasn't sure, but instinctively she felt it had something to do with his trip to Sandviken and with Isa Lindström. She disliked her; she hated her. When it came to women, her son had little experience. Aside from a few short-lived relationships with immature and – what Irene used to call – insignificant and mediocre women, he had shown little interest in the opposite sex, to the point that his mother had been concerned and had tried to pair him up with some of her friends' daughters. Without any success.

"Anything you want to share with us, Mrs. Nordin?"

She put the phone on the table again and said: "My son. He's okay."

"Where is he?"

"He didn't say, but I guess you'll find him in his apartment or at work."

"Going back to the kidnapping," Nina said, "does your son know what happened?"

"No," Irene admitted, "we have never told him. Why would we? No one harmed him."

"How did your husband react to the kidnapping?"

"Like any father would. He was in a panic, angry with the hospital, scared."

Nina wrote down a few lines and then closed the notebook. The old lady escorted them back to the front door and let them out.

* * *

As they walked back to the car parked a few blocks away, Nina said, "She was lying."

"Yes, I know," Isa replied and looked back at the house as they continued to walk to the car. Irene Nordin was peeking through the window.

"Anita Berenson told us they couldn't find Peter Nordin the day his son disappeared. Only in the evening, when the baby had already been found, he showed up. And as for her, nurse Anita had few good words. She described Irene as a distant, cold mother. The love for her son seemed almost forced, not real. After thirty years, this was one of the first things she said."

Isa kept looking at the woman, partly hidden behind the curtains, but still visible to them. It was as if Irene wanted to give them the signal, she would keep an eye on them and she would defend her family no matter what.

"You see ... I still don't understand why she would defend her husband with so much vigor. All I've heard about this marriage so far is that it wasn't a happy one."

The curtains were closed. Isa turned around and continued on her way to the car. Both women walked side by side in silence for a while. Isa didn't feel comfortable. There was this undefined, intangible feeling that worried her and grew stronger every day.

After five minutes, they finally arrived at the car. It was almost midday, and few people were on the street.

"Ah, something I forgot to mention," Nina said as she got in her boss' car, "we finally got access to Josip Radić' financials and something interesting came out."

"Tell me," Isa answered as she put the key in the ignition and drove off.

"Mr. Radić received a monthly payment of 10 000 SEK for the past few months. We haven't been able to find out where it came from, but Mr. Radić used it to pay his alimony and support his children. My theory is that this is probably blackmail. He knew who the killer was, and that probably cost him his life."

"But why now?" Isa remarked. "We need to find out where the money came from."

"The team is on it. I hope to have answers in the coming days."

"Perfect. What about the phone records? Still no news?"

"No, unfortunately not," Nina replied.

Her boss wasn't as talkative as usual. She was distracted and had been disinterested throughout the entire interview, except in one instance where the old lady had made a few statements directed against Isa. It was strange.

"Are you okay?" Nina asked.

Isa quickly looked at her as she turned the steering wheel to drive to the east of Uppsala.

It took a while to reply: "Yes, I'm fine. Do you know anything more about the letters from Belgium?"

"Well, they already sent us a few pictures of the handwriting for a first analysis. Probably the letters will arrive in a few days. Kenneth is on it."

"Good, I want them to analyze the handwriting as soon as possible. Do we have a sample of Peter's handwriting?"

"Yes, we have ... but Isa, can I ask you something? Why this sudden focus on Peter Nordin again? I don't think we should just focus on him."

"I'm not," Isa said angrily, "but so far he's our best lead."

Her boss was in one of those moods again, and then it was best to keep quiet.

CHAPTER

19

THE **POLAROID PHOTOGRAPH** in his hand was old, discolored from the sun and having carried it in his wallet for years. The face was barely visible anymore. Time had wiped out the details, but his imagination filled in the blanks, making it so much more idyllic than it had been. A misunderstood love, heartbreakingly beautiful and tragic. But there was nothing beautiful about the cold and dark bunker, the repeated assaults, the loneliness, and the emotional distress.

While he was waiting, he let the photo flip through his fingers a few times. When he saw her walking through the school gate with her friends, he put the photo back in his pocket. She resembled her mother, at least in her younger years. He detested the red hair she wore these days. And her aunt Marian, beautiful Marian ... how could he forget her?

The girls were laughing and talking loudly as they walked along the road toward the bus station. There was a crowd of people waiting for the 4 p.m. bus and he tried to hide in the back so they couldn't see him. It was perhaps too soon after Stina, but that girl had been a mistake, a regrettable mistake. He had no idea that it was Stina who had used the Sara243 account.

That evening, more than a year ago, it was too late to stop. At the rendezvous point, she had recognized him and, in that split second, he had made a drastic decision. She had to die. Instinctively, Stina knew something was wrong, and she tried to escape, but he cornered her. The blow to the head was severe. Her skull cracked as the branch hit her face, but she wasn't dead. Shocked and furious, he dragged her lifeless body to the car. When he arrived at the bunker, darkness had already set in, and he waited until it was pitch black to get her out of the car and take her to the room. As she lay on the floor, still unconscious, bleeding from the gaping wound on the left side of the head, he stared at her. Stina and Sara were much alike: same hair, same eye color, same height, same manners. But to him, they were so different.

He had met Sara in Sandviken, with her father, staying at the Bergqvist cabin for a few days. The family wanted to spend the summer there, but after a huge fight with her husband, Tasha had returned to Enköping with her son. Stina had been there too. But it was Sara who had caught his attention. The smile, the way she moved and walked, reminded him of Clara. She was Clara, the girl in the photo, the girl on the bed in the room, hidden away in the forest, all for him. All those other girls hadn't even come close. Those few days in Sandviken, he had watched her, learned everything he could about her. The girls had talked about the Facebook account, and he had assumed it was Sara's. But that evening in September, the girl lying on the cold floor in front of him wasn't Sara. She was insignificant, a problem he had to deal with. He put his hands around her neck and squeezed. There was little resistance as he continued to tighten his hands until she stopped breathing. Later that night, he disposed of her body, in the same way he had done so many times before. But it was a failure, the first one in a long line of mistakes.

* * *

The girls got on the bus. He had to get there without being noticed. Sara would surely recognize him. The old lady in front of him had problems climbing the stairs. He took her hand and tried to support her. No one had noticed that by doing so he had skipped the line and could get to one of the few remaining places on the bus. He was just a few meters away from the teenagers when the bus, fully packed, started moving and left almost ten people at the bus shelter. He could smell the scent of her perfume. It was exhilarating. The girls got off the bus six stops later. They hadn't noticed the man in the dark coat, with cap and scarf pulled so tightly over his head and face he would be unrecognizable even to his family. He saw his car parked some fifty meters away. He loved the thrill of the chase. The young girl, walking just a few meters in front of him, didn't know she was being followed. Sara, still talking enthusiastically to her friends, took a different route than he had expected, not going home, but accompanying one of the other girls to her house. Disappointed and irritated, he stopped and stared at them as the distance between him and the teenagers grew, and he finally saw them disappear behind the corner. His timing was off, as it had been so many times before in recent months. Was it misfortune or something more than that? It hadn't been a problem before. Maybe he didn't want it bad enough, maybe he was scared, maybe he felt remorse ... maybe he was tired, tired of everything. His hands were shaking, and he couldn't stop them. Some passersby gave him a concerned look. Quickly he turned around and walked to his car. Behind the steering wheel, he put his head in his hands. It wasn't the fact he couldn't get the girl, but it was the image of what he had become. For years, he had fought against these urges, but her voice had always drawn him back and persuaded him to give in. She had always been there. It was subtle and manipulative, at times seductive, arrogant, and demanding. He had to listen, but every day it was a struggle with himself and his demons.

In the car, behind the wheel, as darkness slowly fell over the city and people were busy with everyday life, he tried to regain control and confidence in what he had to do. He had to change his modus operandi. Yes, a new approach. That would do the trick.

* * *

It was almost 6 p.m. and Isa was still in doubt about what she was planning to do. As a stalker, she had been standing in front of the building for a few days. She knew he was home. One moment it had made so much sense, but the next, it had seemed such a mistake and she had backed off from the plan several times. There was no telling how he would react. She had shown no consideration for his feelings after their night together. She understood that now. Except for Magnus and her ex-husband, she had never been in a relationship where feelings mattered. It was usually nothing more than a casual fling. What this was, she still didn't know, but she had to find out.

Standing almost fifteen minutes in front of the apartment block, she saw the first opportunity to slip into the building. He would never let her in, angry and disappointed like he had been the last time.

An elderly woman in her seventies, packed with groceries, tried to open the door but struggled to manage the different bags. Isa suggested taking some of the load while the woman looked for the entrance key. Grateful for the help, the woman assumed she was a resident and said nothing when Isa entered the hallway and climbed the stairs to the second floor. The elevator was still broken, like it had been so many weeks ago.

She remembered helping him up the stairs after the attack in Josip's apartment. And then that crazy moment, full of sweet seduction!

Sitting at his computer, Alexander heard a soft knock on the door. Surprised, he looked up from the manuscript writing. He expected no one. His mother knew not to disturb him, and he had told everyone at the university he would work from home for a while. So much had happened in the past weeks he was cautious and considered remaining silent and pretending that he wasn't home.

"Alex, I know you're there. Please open the door. I need to talk to you."

It was a familiar voice that left him confused, happy and upset at the same time. It was quiet on both sides of the door. Still unable to get up, he wondered what he should do.

"Alex, please ... I want to apologize. I know I hurt you, but I want to explain. Please give me a chance."

Behind the door, in the safe and trusted environment of the confined space, where he had locked himself, for weeks now, Alex pondered about what to do. He was angry and didn't want to let her in. But if he let her leave now, she wouldn't be back, leaving him heartbroken for a second time.

Isa waited and then hesitantly the door was opened. He looked tired, and he probably hadn't shaven in days because it was the first time she saw him with a stubble. It made him look much older.

"Can I come in? I don't want to have this conversation in the hallway."

He said nothing, stepped aside and signaled her to come in. The living room was dark, the curtains drawn, with only the lamp on the desk to illuminate the small room. She looked around. It wasn't how she remembered it: instead of the simple, tidy and rather impersonal room, she saw papers scattered everywhere. On the table, desk, sofa and so many more on the floor. She bent over and took the one closest to her.

The scribbling made little sense to her. It was a mathematical formula. She held the paper in front of him to give it back.

"What is this?" she asked.

He took it, crumpled it, and buried it so deep in his hand as if he were trying to contain the surfacing anger.

"This is nonsense," he said, tossed the paper ball in the bin, and picked up the other pieces of paper from the floor.

"Why ..."

"This is what I do," he replied as he threw them in the basket next to the desk, "I'll probably start over tomorrow, and the day after and after that ... until I believe it's enough." And until his OCD took over.

Broken. The damage was so much larger than she could imagine. It was scary. She couldn't find the words. It was so much more difficult than she had imagined.

"Tell me you're okay," she whispered.

He suddenly stopped collecting the remaining scribbles from the desk and the sofa and looked up. His blue eyes were so dark and ominous.

"Do you think this is okay? Do you think I look okay?"

There was a painful silence.

"No, you don't. I'm sorry. I truly am. There is no excuse for the way I treated you."

"So, why did you?"

He kept staring at her, dozens of papers still in his hands. His fingers tightened the grip, crunching them, without even being fully aware of it. The way he reacted was his way of coping with setbacks, the way he had done all his life, using the one thing he understood best: mathematics. Structure, well-defined problems, with well-defined solutions, poured into symbols, plusses and minuses, integrals, and derivatives. With him it was usually all or nothing, black or white, one or zero. But emotions can't be put in beautiful formulas. They are messy and illogical. They are human.

"Look, Alex, I'm not good at relationships. I destroyed my marriage because I thought I needed something else. I don't think about the consequences of my actions. I just do, and that hurts people. I'm not good for you."

"So why did we have sex then? You just wanted to take what you liked? Is that what I am to you? I thought ..."

Emotion engulfed him like a tsunami and made him search for the words he couldn't find.

"I don't know what you are," she admitted.

At least that was an honest answer. Though not the answer he wanted. She stopped talking, walked over, and reached out to touch his face, but he blocked her and moved her hand away.

He walked back to get the last papers while she carefully observed him. She didn't know what to do. It was best she left. This was too early. Those big emotions got in the way of a more rational conversation, something that was barely possible anyway.

"I've upset you," she said, "it's best I leave."

She walked back to the door and opened it, but before she could step outside, she felt his hand touch her arm. He was standing behind her, so close that her heart skipped a beat, and she held her breath. Why had she told him she didn't know what he meant to her? This was what he was. This was what made him so much different from everyone else. His breath was warm, and she felt his soft lips touch the skin of her neck. Slowly, but with a determination that made it clear, he had started the game of seduction. It made her weak.

She turned around and touched his face. This time he let her. His fingers caressed her hand. The other hand ran down her back and he pulled her into the apartment. It was more sensual, seductive, and exciting than it had been in the cabin that evening in Sandviken. His touch ... she could feel every line, every unevenness of his skin. His scent was bewildering, and the kiss made her head turn. She lost all sense of reason.

* * *

"Thanks for meeting me this late," Nina said to the older man. He was holding a few letters in his gloved hands. The man was Dr. Kristian Riksand, a Finnish professor and world-renowned expert in forensic science and more specifically in graphology, who had left his home country almost thirty years ago to hold a faculty position at the University of Uppsala. His team of postdocs and students were all regarded as top-notch. He himself was a certified forensic document examiner who was regularly consulted in high-profile criminal cases.

"No problem. I'm used to that."

His smile was kind and pleasant.

"And any results?" Nina continued.

"Numerous fingerprints but I doubt they belong to our killer," he replied. Although his accent was still audible, the sentences and words were correct, and he had a certain eloquence that impressed her.

"And none of them match Peter Nordin's fingerprints," he continued.

"What about the writing? Is there a match?"

He put the letters in the box and walked over to the table in the far-left corner, with Nina following him.

The lab, an extension of the larger forensic lab, was austere, with a few scanners and computers on the desks by the window and a table on the other side of the room where only a pile of papers, a few pens, and an empty spectacle box were lying.

On the laptop in front of him, he pulled up two images of letters, written on white paper, one in blue ink and the other one in black ink.

"On the left, you will find parts of the letter your office sent. I think this was an older specimen collected from his home. And, on the right, the letter from the Stockholm office. This was sent to the Belgian girl in

2002."

He pointed to the image on the right side of the screen.

Nina nodded affirmatively. She felt like a young girl in a playground. It was all so interesting and thrilling. She wanted to learn more. In her department, she was regarded as someone with potential, but these days she doubted again whether this was really the career she envisioned. There was a persistent and unsatisfied hunger for knowledge and science that could never be fulfilled if she stayed where she was now.

"It was not easy. To most, they look identical, but the one on the right is a forgery. They are not written by the same person, but it is a superb forgery."

"Are you sure?" Nina asked.

"Yes. Do you see these lines here?"

He zoomed in on both texts and pointed to the loops of a few letters on the right and left specimen.

"They are different. Can you see it?"

"Yes."

There was a discrepancy, though small, in letter spacing, between the length and size of the loops, but there was more than she could see.

"Also ... the author of the right text tried to mimic the clockwise motion of the letter "o" as is done in the left specimen, but for him ... or her this is something unnatural, so this leads to hesitations in the natural flow of writing. You can see it: here and here."

The differences were subtle again, but they were obvious if you knew what to look for.

"The letter ratio and the pen pressure are different. Our 3D analysis shows the person on the left used moderate pressure, while the pen pressure in the right text is much heavier ... almost as if someone were angry."

"So, your conclusion is that these are written by two different people," Nina concluded.

"Yes, although there are natural variations in handwriting, especially between youth and old age, and handwriting can change even within the same document, these two letters were written by different people and one of them has gone to great lengths to make us believe they have been done by the same person. It takes skill and practice to write this forgery."

"Thank you, professor. Any match with the other samples?"

"These are the other suspects?"

"Yes, Ivor Radić, Olav Bergqvist, and Mats Norman," Nina added.

"The analysis is still ongoing, but so far I can conclude none of them match the letter from the Belgian girl."

She sighed in frustration, expecting at least one sample to give them more clues about the murderer.

"Inspector Lindström asked me to examine the last sample first," the professor continued.

"The last ... what?"

He closed the two documents and opened a new file on the computer.

"Now, why exactly did inspector Lindström want me to have a look at this?" he asked and looked up at the young woman.

She took a few seconds to reply.

"Uh ... I think she wanted to know if this sample could also be a match, I guess," she said, although she didn't understand what her boss was really up to these days. She was irritated that Isa hadn't involved her in all her ideas and suspicions. Perhaps she saw her as a threat rather than an asset to the team.

"Well, the handwriting doesn't match any of the two. The writing is bad and irregular, but it bears no resemblance."

She had no clue what he was talking about. Whose handwriting was this?

"Can you say anything more? Is it possible this person tried to mimic Peter Nordin's handwriting?"

"That's difficult to say. That would require a lot more analysis and more handwriting samples of the person. Judging from the text, this person has a writing impairment with difficulties forming letters. So, he should already be training himself quite a bit to forge someone else's handwriting."

He went on, "Actually, it looks like the writing of a child or someone who is pretending."

She looked at the letters on the screen. There was no link between them, each of them was separated and written in both upper and lower case, with different sizes, and some letters were unfinished.

"This is a typical case of dysgraphia," Kristian continued.

"Dysgraphia?"

"Dysgraphia is the inability to write coherently. The person may have a high IQ and can often read without difficulty but has difficulty with coordination and some finer motor skills to write properly. It is often associated with autism spectrum disorder."

"You say this person has autism ...," Nina said shocked. It sparked her interest.

"No, not necessarily, but it could be. I am not qualified to make that diagnosis."

"But he could have a high IQ, no? So, this person could still be smart enough to derail us from the truth?"

"In principle he can, but it seems unlikely. Maybe worth investigating further. Alexander Nordin. This is the son, right?"

Alexander Nordin. Why him? Someone wrote these letters in 2002. He was fifteen at that time.

The police hadn't taken any steps in the right direction to find the killer. They were all suspects and, at the same time, none of them were.

"Uh ... yes, it is. Anyway, thank you, professor. I think I have taken already too much of your time."

He got up and shook her hand.

"It was a pleasure," he said with a certain flair and what some people would call old-fashioned gallantry. She smiled and walked to the door. As she made her way to the exit, she checked her cell phone. Her boss hadn't responded to any of her messages. What was going on? Feeling irritated and disappointed, she got in her car and drove home.

* * *

Isa woke up. It was still dark. The space next to her was empty and cold. He had gotten out of bed a while ago. It was almost a déjà vu. She stepped out of the bed, still naked. The temperature in the room was pleasant, unlike the icy cabin where they had spent the first night. Through the narrow gap in the doorway, she saw a faint light shining from the living room. The door creaked when opened. Alexander, sitting at his computer in front of the large window looked up and smiled. The smile was so beautiful. He had always seemed so worried and sad before. There she was, standing in the doorway, shamelessly naked and seductive. As she walked over to him, she let her eyes slide over his bare-chested upper body. He was quite slim, not too muscular, just perfectly proportioned. As she ran her fingers through his hair, she realized she was falling for him. It was more than just sex. He was kind, sensitive and mysterious.

"What time is it?"

"After midnight, 1 a.m. or so ... go back to sleep," he said.

"What is that?" she asked, pointing to the file on the computer.

There was some hesitation, but he replied: "It's an application form."

She leaned forward and her face was now so close to his, that he could feel the excitement rushing through his body.

"For what?"

"For postdoc positions in the US," he replied reluctantly, afraid of how she would respond. He had expected none of this to happen. Now, he wasn't sure what to do. Stay in Sweden and be with her, or pursue an academic career in the US?

It was quiet, but he felt how her hands stopped caressing his back. He turned his face to her. There was no sign of disappointment or anger, as she said calmly, "And now you are not sure what to do?"

"Yes," he whispered.

She took his head in her hands and kissed him tenderly before throwing herself on the sofa.

"If that is important to you, then go ahead. I don't know where this, between you and me, is going, but we'll find out when the time comes."

He looked at the screen and closed the laptop.

"Would you come with me?" he asked.

There was no immediate answer, and he almost instantly regretted asking the question. Maybe he was better off not knowing. Everything was so perfect now. Why would he throw it all away?

"Maybe," she smiled.

It wasn't no, and it was good enough for him.

"I scared you," he said and stared at the floor.

"A bit," she replied.

"I know, it's weird and it might look strange and scary to people, but it's my way of dealing with ... stuff. It's the way I've always done it."

"Why?"

Amazed by her question, he turned his head and faced her.

"I ... I don't know."

The smile on his face was gone, replaced by the gloomy air that usually seemed to surround him.

Her attention was drawn to the scar on his arm that was now visible, and she stared at it. She hesitated for a moment, then got up, took his hand, and ran her fingers over the scar.

"Does it hurt?" she asked.

He followed every movement of her fingers.

"No," he whispered.

It was the emotional stress the scar represented that made it hard to talk about, and for years that threshold seemed so insurmountable.

"I tried to kill myself when I was fifteen."

Now it was out there. He didn't dare to look at her. He didn't want to see the horror nor the pity in her eyes. At times, the shame was so overwhelming that it blocked him in everything he did. No one could see it, nicely hidden under the sleeve of his T-shirt, but he knew that it was there. It was a reminder of the horrendous times he had survived but hadn't left behind him. On rare occasions, he had seen it as a victory, bust most of the time he regarded it as a way out, an option. And lately, he found himself converging toward the latter. The mood swings and the deepening sadness had become a state of perpetual being. This time he knew what it was, still, it felt like he couldn't stop the wave of depression. He didn't want to tell her. The pressure it would put on their relationship ... he wouldn't be able to deal with that and neither would she.

"I never really saw it coming," he continued, "there wasn't one thing that triggered it. It was just there, for months, years. I guess it was inevitable."

With her hand, she turned his head so she could see his face. Watery eyes, full of tears, he tried so desperately to keep inside. She wanted him to tell more. It was important. But trying to describe what he had felt, was impossible. He wanted to, but how could she relate to such a thing?

"Because of your father?" she asked, trying to wipe the tears from his cheeks.

If only it had been that, he could have managed, but he felt that no one had ever cared for him. He was a shadow, sometimes a ghost. Everyone around him was happy and took life at its greatest. Why couldn't he?

His relationship with his father had been troubling: at times dark and scary, but open and conversant most of the time. But his mother ...

"My mother hates me," he blurted.

It took her by surprise. She had been so focused on Peter Nordin and all his mental troubles she hadn't seen the complicated mother-son relationship.

"Why do you say that?"

When he had felt the blood pouring from his arm, fifteen years ago, alone in the bathroom of his parents' home, with the delirium already sinking in, he had seen her standing next to him, leaning forward, just staring at him. There had been no panic, no incentive to help him. It was his father who had finally rushed him to the hospital. Before that his mother had been the one, he had never doubted, after that there had been this growing distrust between them. Her actions that afternoon, in the bathroom, remained unspoken, but the way she had interacted with him, had changed. Maybe it hadn't changed, but maybe he had seen her in a different light. From that moment on, he felt subject to her erratic mood swings: loving mother on the one hand, mentally abusive and even violent on the other hand.

"Never mind."

Isa felt him clamming up again. It was too difficult to talk about it. The full story would eventually be told, but it took time, a lot of time, and she was patient.

"I'm better now," he said and pulled her hand away from his face, just to hold it in his hands.

He was still afraid she would run off. She was so beautiful. She made him happy, happier than he had ever been. But it intimidated him. It was so delicate. It could be gone in the blink of an eye. Was she real?

She changed position and sat on his lap, facing him. His head was now between her neck and breasts. He kissed her neck and felt the soft skin of her breasts against his bare chest. She pulled him away from the desk. There was no resistance as he followed her into the bedroom.

CHAPTER

20

"**WE HAVE TO TALK** about the case," Alex said as he reached out to give her the cup of coffee. She took it and sat down. He had nicely covered the table with plates and cups. In the basket were croissants he had bought in a small shop nearby before she got up. His insomnia had kept him awake most of the night. He was tired, but she seemed in worse shape than he was, yawning continuously. She wasn't a morning person.

"No, we don't. This is complicated enough. I could lose my job. Let me figure out what to do first."

She was in trouble again.

"Isa, I don't want any secrets between us," Alex replied as he poured another cup for himself.

"Secrets? What didn't you tell me?"

He had to tell her. Otherwise, he would never find peace.

"I haven't lied to you, but I haven't told you everything either, because ... I don't know what it all means."

"So, what didn't you tell me? Do you have an idea who's responsible for the murders?"

"No, no, of course not, but I feel like I may have some important pieces of the puzzle. It's just suspicions, and I don't know if it's relevant."

"What then?"

Why did he beat around the bush? Isa started to get irritated.

He put the cup down and walked to the living room. When he came back, he put the black book and the letter on the table in front of her.

"What is this?"

He sat down next to her in the only remaining chair in the kitchen, took the black booklet and opened it.

"I found it in my father's belongings when I helped my mother to clean up his stuff. It intrigued me. There are about fifty pages, full of dates, places, sometimes disjointed scribbles, but you can see he circled some dates."

He pointed to the lines as he flipped through the pages.

"Yes, but what does it mean?"

He read aloud the dates from the small piece of paper he had inserted in the back cover of the booklet some time ago: "26 June 1987, 31 December 1990, 10 July 2002, 19 June 2004, 12 January 2008, and 14 May 2010 ... does that ring a bell?"

Her expression turned from annoyed to baffled and then serious as he kept saying, "These six are the ones I could trace to girls who have disappeared. The others are illegible, the date is incomplete, or the place is missing. But Isa ... there are seven more entries that were highlighted in the booklet. Seven, not three."

She immediately understood what he tried to imply.

"There are four more bodies we haven't found."

"Could be ..."

He closed the book and handed it to her.

"Are you sure this is your father's handwriting?"

"It changes from page to page, but given his state of mind, I guess it might not be uncommon ... so yes, I think so."

Everything was out in the open. He awaited the verdict, but she disagreed. He didn't understand and grasp the significance of it all and to ease his mind, she interrupted him: "Do you think it is likely that a serial murderer of this magnitude is likely to track his exploits in this way?"

Surprised, he looked at her, while she kept staring at him and waited for an answer.

"I'm not sure ...," he faltered.

She leaned forward, nearly knocked over the cup of coffee on the table, kissed him and took his hand, trying to reassure him.

"Do you think your father did this? No, I don't think so. A serial killer usually takes personal items from his victims to collect and later, to relive the deed. Sometimes, he'll take photos, make videos ... but I have never seen a killer write about his murders so meticulously in the form of dates and places. This is too impersonal. A better explanation would be that your father was really onto something. He could have been tracking the killer already from the start."

She paused for a moment to say, "We have to consider that your father didn't kill himself but was murdered. I've studied his case. There wasn't much of an investigation after his death, due to his history of depression and mental illness, but there were a few entries in the file that were marked as anomalous."

"Such as?"

"Such as ... they found bruises on his head. It didn't match any injuries he could have sustained from the hanging itself ... but it could have been a blow to the head ... to render him unconscious."

As she continued to tell him about her suspicions, she felt the tension build in his hand and the rest of his body. It was all so confusing. One moment his father was the serial killer everyone was looking for, the next he was the victim.

"They found high levels of fluoxetine in his blood. The medication they gave him could explain it, but ..."

"He wasn't taking any medication ... not anymore," he said softly. "A few days before his death, I found out he had stopped years ago. I caught him throwing his pills in the toilet. I was so angry! He was getting worse again, so I thought ... and I begged him to get back on the meds, but he refused. I always thought my failure ..."

He got up and stood with his back to her for a while, trying to hide the consternation and the tears associated with the notion that the guilt he had carried for so long had been a deception. He couldn't remember the last time he truly cried. Had he ever? Maybe as a child, but he couldn't remember. He remembered little of his childhood. It was blank, like someone had erased it.

"That my failure had killed him," he continued.

"Alex, it was never your fault ... suicide or not. It wasn't your responsibility to save your father."

She got up, put her arms around him from behind and held him close, her head resting on his back. She didn't want to let him go, and she wished they could stay in this moment forever. He put his hand on hers, closed his eyes, and he slowly bent his head sideways to touch hers.

"My father ... isn't my father," he whispered as if he couldn't say it aloud yet, as if it were a blasphemy to admit it.

Isa let him go and turned to see his face, which was wet with tears. She loved him, but was she really the woman he needed? Did she have the strength and courage to help him with all these demons from the past and the ones that might still come to haunt him? He wasn't as strong as

Magnus. Many times, Magnus had kept her from falling apart, but here the tables were reversed. She had to take care of him, and she wasn't sure she wanted that responsibility.

"You think Peter wasn't your father? Why?"

As he pointed to the table, she saw the letter lying next to the black book. It was the GenoOne letter. She quickly scanned through it.

"How can you be so sure this refers to you and your father? Do you have anything more?"

Disappointed, he replied: "I don't ... I tried to get more information from GenoOne, but they just told me they had sent the information to my father the day before he died."

"Alex, maybe he was looking for some other information that has nothing to do with you. Maybe he was trying to prove his suspect was a killer. Has that ever crossed your mind?"

Considering what she had just told him, this was a more plausible explanation. It could also be the reason his father had to die. The killer could have discovered what Peter was planning to do or what he knew.

"No, it didn't," he had to admit.

Tunnel vision had laid out a trap for his mind to overvalue his father's part in the whole story.

"I'll try to get a warrant to get all information from GenoOne, but I need something more than this to build a case for it. Can I take the book and letter with me?"

He nodded and kept his eyes fixed on her as she put the two things in the pocket of her jacket. There was no point in looking for fingerprints on the book and letter. Too many people had handled them. As she put on her coat to leave, a sudden feeling of fear overtook her, and she stopped and looked at him. There was something that frightened her. It wasn't him, but the mere idea that by loving him there was also the possibility of losing him. She didn't want to feel like that. Was this really what she wanted? It scared her so.

He was quiet and gloomy, but a faint smile appeared on his face as she kissed him softly on the cheek.

"Thank you for sharing this with me," she said, "it's extremely helpful. I have to go now to make sure we analyze this as soon as possible. But I'll see you this evening, right? Here?"

"Yes ... but Isa, before you leave, I want to give you something." He wasn't sure if it was the most appropriate moment. He went back to the desk in the living room and pulled out a book.

"What's this?" she asked as he handed it to her. She examined it. It was thin, with a simple blue cover and white lettering, slightly curled corners and solid sheets that resembled yellowish, old parchment paper.

"The winter poems by Beatris Ivenson," she read and turned it back and forth in her hands before she opened it.

"I don't know the writer," she continued.

"It was my grandmother," he said.

"Really?! Wow ... but why ...," she said and closed the book.

He smiled.

"I want you to have it. I think you'll appreciate it more than I do. She gave it when I was ten, just before she died. It was the only book she ever published."

"How come?"

"She got married after publishing it and then my father was born. It marked the end of her writing career."

"That's really sad."

"I'm not sure if she saw it that way."

"Thank you," she said and kissed him, "I'll see you this evening."

"Okay," he said and watched her leave the apartment.

The coffee was already cold, and he made another before going to university. His hiding had lasted long enough.

* * *

She walked back to her car, which she had parked the evening before, a few blocks away from the apartment building. She had missed several messages from Nina and Magnus. Nina had explained to her in a few sentences how that the handwriting in the letters didn't match Peter's, and what the professor had concluded from Alex's scribbles.

"Autism?"

She had encountered many autistic people in her life, even in her own family, but Alex hadn't struck her as the typical case ... although there had been some peculiarities of her new lover, his obsessive cleanliness, and the urge to have everything symmetrical and ordered in a certain way, which had not gone unnoticed. But these were more likely the symptoms of a person with OCD. The scribbling had been something else. That had been frightening. Either way, it didn't seem relevant to her at the moment.

Magnus' message was more cryptic: "Can you come to the hospital in Uppsala? Send me a message when you will arrive."

It had been sent just before she had left the apartment. She sighed and tried to control her growing irritation. What was he up to? Why the hospital?

Amid one of the biggest and most important cases they had ever faced, he had taken off without so much as an explanation. Just like their relationship. He still owed her one. But she found herself, against her better judgment, driving to the hospital where he was waiting for her at the entrance.

"Magnus, what is this? Why do we meet here? What did you find out?"

"Good morning to you too," he said ironically, "that was fast ... I suggest you come inside. It's too cold here."

Giving him the angry look, she stepped inside and in the main hall, he took her hand. For the first time, it made her feel uncomfortable.

"It has nothing to do with the case," he said calmly.

As expected, it upset her, and she shouted: "What? I really don't have time for this."

"Please be patient with me. Let me explain why I haven't been there lately ... I need to," his voice trembled, and she had rarely seen him so emotional.

"Magnus, what's going on?"

Her anger and annoyance had suddenly disappeared, but she was afraid of getting caught in another emotional rollercoaster.

"Come with me," he said.

They walked in silence down the long hallway for about five minutes, eventually reaching an elevator. They went up to the third floor, to the palliative care unit where they had moved his son the day before.

Magnus led her to the room at the far end of another long corridor. The nurses they passed on the way all seemed to know Magnus, smiling and nodding friendly. The nod was respectful and showed compassion.

Isa had never liked hospitals and deep down she didn't like where this was going. When she stepped inside the room, she heard the repeating sound of the breathing apparatus. The curtains were open, and the weak sunrays were streaming in through the window, but the room felt dark. The boy, lying in the bed, was motionless and his face was difficult to see because of the many tubes and lines hanging around his body.

"This is my son Toby," Magnus said and looked at the ten-year-old.

Intuitively she had known, although Isa had never met any of his children before, not even when they were a couple. Magnus had made sure of that, and she had never felt the need to get to know them. She struggled with her own situation, being separated from her children.

The whole situation frightened her: the room, the machines, the person in the bed.

"What happened to him?" she asked with a soft voice, almost afraid to wake him up.

"He had a brain hemorrhage a few weeks ago ... the doctors think he will never recover. They declared him brain dead."

"Magnus, I'm so sorry. Why didn't you tell us?"

She took his arm as a sign of compassion, but that made it so much harder to keep his emotions under control. He took a moment to recover his thoughts. The last few days, he had been rehearsing the conversation repeatedly, but when the time had finally been there, he had never realized how heartbreakingly difficult it would be for him to tell anyone, even her.

"Then I also had to tell you he has been ill all his life, and that he did this to himself. He's one of the reasons I left my wife ... my family. But he is also the reason I left you to go back to them."

"I see," she said, almost emotionless.

She let go of his arm. How could she have been so stupid to believe it was because of her?

"I'm sorry," he said, expecting nothing.

She walked to the bed, away from Magnus. That young boy she had never met, who she had never known, was now the reason for all the heartache and pain he had put her through that last year. No, she couldn't believe that. How could Magnus put all this on his son?

"What's wrong with him?"

"He has schizophrenia. Most of the time he hears voices and sees things that are not really there. Sometimes he doesn't recognize us, or he thinks we are the enemy, trying to kill or hurt him. It's ..."

It had been tearing him apart, bit by bit, until there was nothing left. He gazed at his son for a moment, while he tried to remember better times. Were there better times? It was all so tainted by the outbursts, the yelling, the hallucinations, and the rejection.

Isa no longer knew what to say and how to feel. Should she be offended that he had kept a secret from her all along? Should she be angry that he had kept quiet about the real reason for their break-up? Should she feel sorry for this man, she had once loved passionately and who was now facing one of the most difficult moments in his life?

"Why are you telling me this now?" she asked softly.

He turned around and faced her.

"Because I need you, Isa! I need you now more than ever to get through this. I can't do this alone anymore."

"What about Sophie? You made your choice a while ago ... and it wasn't me."

Her words sounded so cold and angry.

"We broke up ... for good," Magnus said calmly, and he walked over to her.

What she wouldn't have given to hear that six months ago, but now these words had lost so much of their meaning. It made her even angrier, and for the first time, she realized she would always be second for Magnus. He would never put her first, and this was no longer enough.

He pulled her close and kissed her. In her head, she compared him to Alex, and the excitement she had felt for the past days was far more thrilling than what she was feeling right now.

"Magnus, I can't do this," she said as she pushed him away.

"Why?" he asked surprised, but he already knew the answer.

"I have moved on ...," she mumbled, "and I'm not the right woman for you."

He let her go, disappointed and angry.

"Ah, pretty Mr. Nordin," he called out with enough sarcasm to get a reaction from her.

"Leave him out of this."

"No, no, that ... we can't do. He's exactly why we're having this fight."

"Magnus, this is between you and me, and why every time I feel like I'm being put in second or third place in your life. Alex has nothing to do with this, and I will not discuss my relationship with him."

"Relationship?! Isa, we've seen all of this before. This is not a relationship. You'll get bored with him, just like so many before him. You'll move on, and he'll be forgotten."

"Like I got bored with you," she said.

It was enough to calm him down. He stood there, rooted to the spot.

"Yes," she continued, "I've cheated on you several times in the two years we've been together."

But his response was different from what she had expected.

"I know," he said calmly, "but I've forgiven you."

This was new. She hadn't realized he had always known.

"You knew? Why didn't you say anything?"

"Because this is what you do … this is what you always do," he said, "and I didn't want to lose you."

Was this really what she was? An unstable, fickle, and untrustworthy woman who had a hard time to remain faithful to her lovers. Was this the image he had of her? Maybe he was right.

"He won't understand," he added, "he won't."

"He's different," she whispered, "he needs me."

"Why? Because he looks damaged and fragile? I can tell you that Mr. Nordin has a few things up his sleeve. Do you know pretty boy has a few sessions a week with his daddy's psychiatrist? I wonder why?"

"Magnus, please! I don't want to have this conversation in front of your dying son. We need to talk about this, but not now."

And she pointed to the child who was still lying motionless in the hospital bed.

She was right. This was neither the time nor the place to argue about this. But he had to tell her, "Is … can't you see … I love you. I would do anything for you."

I love you. Those three words. Was he serious? How could he love her? Those words meant nothing to her. Easy to say, empty of meaning.

"Do you? Really?"

Isa's phone rang. She had forgotten to turn it off. But it was a necessary distraction. On the display, she saw Nina was calling.

"I ... it's Nina. I have to take this."

Magnus said nothing. It gave him some time to calm down.

"Nina, what's up?"

The voice on the other side of the line sounded agitated and spoke quickly.

"Nina, calm down! What happened?"

The expression on Isa's face turned serious and at the end of the conversation, she said: "Natasha Bergqvist's daughter Sara has disappeared."

"What? Are they sure? She didn't run away or something?"

As she put the cell phone in her pocket, she shook no.

"We have to go. Are you coming?"

"Where are they? Gävle?"

"No, Uppsala. We have to go, Magnus. Are you coming or not?"

He hesitated. He hadn't left Toby's side for weeks, knowing that Isa and the team could handle the case perfectly without him, but now Isa would need all the help she could get. They had to put their disagreement aside for a while. He could do that. He took his son's hand, kissed it, and reached for the jacket he had put over one of the chairs in the room.

"What else do we know?" he asked as he followed Isa.

"Not much. Sara left for school this morning but never arrived there. Her mother got a message around 9 a.m. asking why her daughter wasn't at school that day. And none of her friends saw her today. This means she was probably abducted in the time it took to get from her home to the bus station."

"Do you think it's him?"

"We shouldn't assume anything, but I wouldn't rule it out," she opened the car door and got behind the wheel.

"And I can tell you, it wasn't your "pretty" Mr. Nordin because he was with me this morning," she said, hinting at their conversation in the hospital.

"Okay. Fine. I'll follow you in my car."

He closed the door and saw her drive away. Fifteen minutes later, he also arrived at the police station.

CHAPTER

21

TASHA BERGQVIST WALKED up and down the interrogation room. Apart from a few chairs, there was only a small table in the center of the room. The cup of tea, brought by one of the officers, was the only thing standing on the table. By now, the tea was lukewarm. Tasha was distracted. She wanted to know where her daughter was. Why were the police not searching for her?

Someone opened the door. They were the same police inspectors who had visited her home to talk about Stina Jonasson.

"Did you find Sara?" she asked immediately.

"Ms. Bergqvist, please sit down," Isa invited her to take a seat in front of her.

"Please tell us again what happened," she continued.

"I have already told this to your colleagues. Why do I have to repeat it? Why aren't you looking for my daughter? You're wasting precious time!"

Tasha sounded frustrated and angry. She was at breaking point and Isa tried to calm the devastated mother.

"My team are searching the streets and the neighborhood near your house to find clues and witnesses who might have seen Sara this morning. So, we have to be patient, but you are right. Every second counts, and so we need you to tell us about the circumstances in as much detail as possible. Okay?"

Tasha's breathing slowed down.

"Take us step by step through the events."

Trying to put order in her line of reasoning, she kept staring at the almost empty table for a while.

"There was really nothing special," she said. "I woke up Sara at 6:30 a.m. She showered, didn't eat much, as usual these days, and then she went to school. She was dawdling, and I was afraid she would miss the 7:45 a.m. bus, so I was ..."

She gasped for air. What if this had been the last time she had seen her daughter? This is not how she would like to remember her. This is not how she would like Sara to remember her mother: a frustrated, ill-minded, middle-aged woman who couldn't find joy and was annoyed by the slightest thing. She hadn't told her she loved her and how proud she was of her. Why did every day's annoyances always get the upper hand?

"I yelled at her," the voice nearly broke, but she pulled herself together and continued to explain to the inspectors how after Sara had left the house, she had gone to work where the principal called her an hour later to tell that Sara was not in school.

"Does Sara always go to school by bus?" Magnus asked as he wrote down the statements.

"No, usually my husband ... ex-husband or I take her to school in the morning. In the afternoon she takes the bus."

"And why did she take the bus this morning?" Magnus asked.

"My ex-husband Frank was supposed to take her to school, but he couldn't ... probably he was too busy entertaining his new girlfriend," she sneered.

"And you?"

"I had an early meeting at 8 a.m., which I couldn't miss. You can ask my colleagues."

"Does Sara have a cell phone?"

"Yes, but I've already called several times," Tasha said, "and no answer."

"Do you remember seeing anything strange in the last few days or weeks? Strange people or things that might have happened and were out of place."

After some thought, she said: "Not really. But then again, Sara lives with her father every other week. It might be good to talk to him too."

Magnus closed the notebook and got up.

"Very well, Ms. Bergqvist. Thank you. May I ask you to stay close in case we have more questions and new information to share with you?"

"My son ... someone should take care of him when he gets home from school."

"Can you call a neighbor?" Isa proposed.

Tasha nodded. That would do. It was all she could do. She felt so helpless.

The police officer, who entered the room after Isa and Magnus had left, asked her if she could bring her more tea. Tasha refused. She didn't need anything to drink or eat; she just needed her daughter back.

"How did the kidnapper know Sara was going to take the bus to school this morning?" Magnus asked as they walked down the hallway to the office Isa had been using when she was in Uppsala. Nina had told them earlier that Frank Norberg, Sara's father, and Tasha Bergqvist's ex-husband, had arrived at the police station. On Isa's request, they had taken him to the office. Isa didn't want any confrontation between the former spouses. At least, not yet.

"He didn't," Isa answered, "but he has probably been watching her for a while. Remember, he's a stalker!"

"Someone must have seen him lingering about," Magnus concluded.

"Exactly. We just need to find that witness."

When they entered Isa's office, they saw a man sitting in the chair by the window. Isa estimated he was in his mid-forties, not too bad looking, well dressed in a dark blue tailored suit and busy checking emails on his cell phone. He got up when he saw the inspectors enter the room.

"Any news?" was the first thing he asked.

"Mr. Norberg, please have a seat," Isa started.

Magnus took a chair and pushed it in front of the desk.

"This is inspector Wieland, and my name is Isa Lindström. We are overseeing the investigation into your daughter's disappearance. Let me get right to the point: we spoke to your ex-wife, who told us you were supposed to take Sara to school this morning, but you couldn't. Is that correct?"

The man sat down next to Magnus, who, with paper and pen in hand, was ready to note down his statement.

"That is right. I couldn't bring her because I was spending the night in Enköping ... with my girlfriend. Tasha moved to Uppsala after the divorce, which is easier for her work. We have joint custody. Therefore, I recently moved to a small apartment in Uppsala so I can have the kids every other week. I usually take Sara and Steyn to school during the weeks they stay with Tasha, but it's getting harder because I have ... other commitments."

He felt guilty. He had just admitted that he had put his new love above his children. If he had brought Sara to school, she wouldn't have disappeared. He stared at the desk. Tasha would never forgive him. He wouldn't forgive himself if something happened to Sara.

"I see," Isa replied. By no means did she want to judge the man in front of her. She had also made some bad choices in her life.

"Anything strange you might have noticed during the last weeks when you took Sara to school or picked her up?"

"No, not really," he said.

Isa sighed, disillusioned with how little new information they had received from Tasha Bergqvist and Frank Norberg. She could only hope this was the same perpetrator. At least then Sara would still have a chance.

"Thank you, Mr. Norberg. Just like your ex-wife, I'd like you to stay around in case we need to ask you more questions. My assistant will come to pick you up."

Isa got up and Magnus followed her, but when they were almost out of the office, Frank said: "Wait, I am not sure if this has anything to do with it, but I saw this guy again recently at Tasha's house ... when I went to pick up Sara."

Isa turned around, surprised by the sudden revelation.

"What guy?" she asked and walked back to the man still sitting in the chair next to the desk.

"Well, that guy. I don't know his name ... he was in Sandviken almost two years ago during the summer holidays. He was there with his family. Tasha may know who it is. I saw him a few times, sitting in his car. Like he was waiting for someone. I thought he lived nearby. I didn't think ..."

Isa walked to the door, opened it, and yelled: "Bring me Natasha Bergqvist."

The young officer who had been waiting in the hallway immediately returned to the interrogation room.

"And call Marian Bergqvist," she said to Magnus.

"Why?" he asked, surprised.

"Because she knows ... I think she has always known."

* * *

"Hey man, you're back!"

Alex looked up from his computer and saw Robin staring at him.

"Yes, obviously," Alex said ironically.

"We've missed you. Lorens gave an appalling seminar last Friday. You could have done it so much better."

"Robin, just give him a break. He has just started. He still has a lot to learn."

"Right, and where have you been?"

Standing in front of the desk, Robin kept looking at him, by his sheer presence demanding an explanation why the man, which he considered a friend, had disappeared for weeks without even telling him.

"I haven't been feeling well ... I had to take time off, but I'm better now," Alex explained, hoping Robin would leave it at that.

"You were so ill you couldn't call me to let me know? I thought we were friends?"

"Robin, we are, but there was so much stuff going on. I'm sorry, okay?"

The young man, not entirely pleased with the apologies, returned to his own desk.

"Okay, fine, but you're acting strange these days," Robin continued as he turned on the computer.

"Strange? I'm always strange," Alex laughed.

"Hmm, yes, you are," Robin had to admit.

They were good again. Robin was a strange bird. They all were. Socially inadequate, but super intelligent. Living in their own universe of mathematical symbols and codes, they were incomprehensible to the average human, but Alex felt at ease there. He didn't have to pretend; he didn't need to find out why people behaved the way they did, and why he was so bad at interpreting their behavior. He loved the endless but passionate conversations, the scientific competition and the strange solidarity that was beyond comprehension for outsiders. And it was only at moments like these he understood that Robin, in his own quirky way, was trying to convey he considered him his best friend.

They worked in silence for a while, until Robin suddenly said: "Ah, by the way, Professor Norman called for you. Several times."

"What? Mats Norman called here? Why?"

"Don't know, he wouldn't say," Robin said without looking up from his computer.

"Why didn't he call my cell phone?" Alex asked and stopped typing. He took off his glasses and put them next to the computer.

"Maybe he did," Robin replied.

His cell phone was still in the pocket of his coat, hanging on the rack in the room. The battery had died the night before and he had forgotten to turn it on after charging. He had several missed calls from his mother and from Mats Norman. His mother had to wait, but the professor's urgency to talk to him was intriguing. They had agreed to meet that afternoon again to talk about the postdoc position, although he now had serious doubts whether he would go through with it.

He called the professor back. As the phone rang, an uneasy feeling took hold of him, a feeling he couldn't explain.

The man on the other end of the line mentioned his name. For a few seconds, he didn't know what to say.

"Professor Norman? It's Alex. You called me?"

"Ah, yes, Alexander. I tried to tell you I can't make it this afternoon. We have to reschedule."

"Okay," Alex answered, "when?"

It was quiet for a while.

"Professor Norman?"

"Alexander ... I can't right now. We'll talk later."

"Did you talk to my mother?" Alex began to worry his mother had convinced Mats Norman not to help him.

"No," the voice on the other side sounded cheerless as he continued: "Alexander, I'll always put your interest first ... no matter what. Never forget that."

And then there was no sound anymore. Mats had switched off the phone. It had been a strange conversation. For a moment he remained dumbfounded, with the phone still in his hand. Robin hadn't noticed. Maybe he read too much in it. He went to the coat rack and put the phone back.

And then he saw the photos. All this time he had carried them with him. The photo of Mats with the baby caught his attention every time. He was convinced he was the baby, but why was Mats holding him? Why take a picture of an acquaintance, someone you didn't even consider a friend with your newborn baby? Somehow, he already knew the answer. He had known the answer all along. This was his real father. He remembered everything. He had seen them together many times. Peter knew. He had always known. It was only normal that Peter had hated him. He had raised the son of another man. Perhaps this had caused his depression and eventually led to his death. But when Alex looked at the rest of the photos, there was so much more.

"Alexander!"

He turned around. Robin was sitting at his desk, facing the computer screen, fully focused on his work. Where did the voice come from? Was he going mad? It was as if he was thrown back in time to those summer days when he was a child in the forests of Sandviken.

It was Mats Norman ... the man in the car, chasing Marian Bergqvist down the forest path, the man in the bunker. He had observed Professor Norman taking supplies to his backyard. He had seen the girls through the small window, locked in their dungeon of terror, crying, yelling, desperately trying to get out.

Alex was gasping for air. His heart was racing, pumping his blood through every capillary of his body at a rate he didn't think was possible. He wasn't feeling well. He really was the son of a murderer, and he had known it all along. Why hadn't he told anyone what he had seen? Maybe he had, maybe they hadn't believed him. He couldn't remember. He should have been more convincing. It was his fault. He could have saved them.

He was suffocating and needed to get out. He grabbed his coat and ran down the hallway, leaving behind a startled Robin, who wondered where his weird colleague suddenly had run off to again.

Outside, in the cold, he came to his senses, but the clarity of mind was gone. Like so many times before, the tunnel vision gave him a twisted view of the reality in which he always saw himself as the accused in the dock. Isa! How could he explain it to her?

He picked up his phone to call her. He let it ring for a while until he heard the voicemail take over. He hesitated, but then left a message: "Isa, it's me, Alex. I know who the killer is ... it's Mats Norman."

He needed a moment, conflicted as he was about what he was up to.

"I know you'll talk me out of it, but I have to confront him. I need to know why he got me involved in this perverted game he has been playing for all those years. I really need to know."

He closed his eyes. The images were still there: Clara, lifeless on the ground in front of Mats, Ida, looking straight at him, pitiful, compassionate but gasping for her last breath. She reached out to touch him. He tried to grab her hand but couldn't. A final blow and she was dead. He felt the blood splash on his face. And then ...

"Oh, God!"

"Now, who do we have here? Nice, very nice ..."

The voice was so loud, pounding in his head. The pain he felt in his stomach paralyzed him. It was so clear. The nauseating sensation was too strong, and he gagged. He leaned against the wall of the building. Minutes he stared straight ahead. What he remembered was beyond words and reason. He now understood why he was the way he was. The phone had been recording silence for the past few minutes. He brought it closer to his mouth and ended, "... I ... I'm sorry. I'm so sorry."

While he shut off the phone, he walked to the parking lot, on autopilot. This had hunted him for most of his life: the dreams, the incomplete and lost memories. This was horrific, but he was afraid that there was so much more he didn't remember. He felt it. But maybe he would finally get clarity. He got into the car. There was an indefinable feeling that had grown stronger and stronger, and that seemed to tell him he was about to make a big mistake. But just as he had done in Josip's apartment, he completely ignored his inner voice and drove to Mats Norman's house.

* * *

"I don't know," Tasha stammered. "Don't put such a pressure on me! Let me think!"

Angry and frustrated, she looked at the inspectors and her ex-husband. She remembered the last summer in Sandviken, where she had decided her marriage was over, where she had put herself first in this loveless engagement. She had once been in love with the dashingly handsome Frank Norberg, but the marriage had been hollow, without passion and commitment from the beginning. They had found those things with other people for a while, but it was getting harder and harder to pretend to themselves and to the children. She had pulled the plug after a terrible fight at the beginning of their stay in Sandviken in the summer of 2016. The fight was about nothing, but all the frustrations and pain of the sixteen-year-old marriage had been poured into that terrible hour of yelling.

Yes, they hadn't been there alone. There were familiar faces, people she had known almost her entire life. Her father had even shown up, drunk and ill-mannered as always, complaining that his daughters were systematically banishing him from his grandchildren's lives. Who else had been there? Everyone: Peter, Irene and their son Alex, Mats, Annette and their two sons, and even Ivor Radić and his wife had turned up for a while. It had almost felt like a reunion. But not a happy one.

"They were all there," she shouted.

"Mr. Norberg, any more info you can give us?" Isa asked.

"Do you think this has anything to do with the kidnapping?" he asked, impressed by the sudden sense of urgency and seriousness with which the investigators had treated his remark.

The austere look on Isa's face answered his question, and he sighed. It was a sigh of frustration as he couldn't remember the name, but there was something else: people hadn't called the man by his name, but by his ...

"Professor," he said, "it was the professor ... that's what everyone called him."

With that one word, he had thrown a bomb into the conversation.

"Mats Norman," Tasha said, surprised.

At that moment, Marian entered the room.

"Yes ... you're right. The distinguished older man who owns the cabin at the top. I saw him either pass by in an old red Volvo or wait outside one of the apartment buildings close to where Tasha lives."

"Red car," Isa whispered and went through her notes.

Nowhere it was mentioned that Mats Norman owned a red car. She found a photo of the Sandviken vacationers Irene Nordin had given her, forgotten, and tucked away in the back of the file. She put the photo on the desk in front of Frank Norberg.

"Which one?" she asked.

He immediately pointed to Mats Norman, the man in the top left corner. He had his hand on Peter Nordin's shoulder.

"You knew," Isa said and looked at Marian. She saw the fear in the woman's eyes as Marian quickly glanced at her sister, who was standing in the corner.

"I didn't, I suspected it," Marian stammered.

"All this could have been avoided if you had come forward," Isa yelled.

She looked at Magnus and got up. "Jesus, this was so simple. Why didn't we see it? He has the bunker right in his backyard. Let's assemble two teams: one to go to Sandviken ... Magnus, you'll take the lead. Nina and I will take a squad to his home in Uppsala. We need to hurry."

The ringtone of a cell phone echoed across the room. Magnus took the phone out of his pocket and glanced at it with growing amazement, his finger hovering over the accept button.

"Magnus?"

"I ... I," he said hesitantly while the annoying sound continued.

"The hospital?"

He turned it off and said: "It's nothing. Don't worry."

It was quiet. Everyone else was still trying to come to terms with the revelation. For years they had socialized with a murderer. This man had been so clever, so cunning to deceive them.

Finally, Isa said, "We'll try to get your daughter back safely!"

* * *

The team that Nina had assembled in a short time was impressive: several dozen well-trained police officers and snipers. Magnus had already left the police station for Sandviken with a squad of ten police officers. The local police would accompany them later.

"So, Mats Norman," Nina said when both women stepped in the car. Before buckling up, Isa checked her gun.

"Do you think that will be necessary?" Nina said, surprised.

"Nina, he killed nine girls and maybe even more. He's dangerous."

It was the first time Nina had been involved in this type of intervention. She had been trained for this, but she knew that reality was often different from the staged situations they used to practice.

"Nina, start the car! We have no time to lose."

"Of course," the young woman said and drove south. The mansion of the Norman family was situated a few kilometers outside Uppsala, direction Gävle.

"We've been so blind," Isa said during the fifteen-minute-drive.

"He is a prominent member of society. Nobody really expects that."

"That's exactly why he should have been on our radar. These are usually the people who have something to hide. I hope we're not too late. Let me check with Magnus where he is. It's at least a one-hour drive for him."

The cell phone display showed a missed call and a message from Alex. She ignored it and called Magnus. She couldn't reach him but was finally able to talk to one of the other police officers. The team had taken the liberty of ignoring any speed limits, but it would take them at least another half an hour to reach Sandviken. Isa watched the buildings pass by, while Nina's attention was fixed on the road. In the rearview mirror, she saw the string of police cars following them. She was scared. What if they were too late? Her incompetence had probably cost this young girl's life. She couldn't deny it: she had been too pre-occupied lately, with other things. Alex!

She took her phone again and looked at the icon that indicated she had a new voicemail. Maybe she should listen to it. It would take another ten minutes to get there. She had time. As she listened to the message, her expression changed. His words were clear, but in the long silence that followed she felt his distress and she interpreted the final words as a goodbye. What was he going to do?

She shouted: "Damn it, Alex! Nina, drive faster, we have to get there as soon as possible!"

Nina was concerned: "What happened?"

"Someone is about to make a huge mistake. Drive!"

The multiple attempts to call him back were all in vain. He had turned off the cell phone, but she couldn't stop trying and for the next ten minutes, she kept pressing the redial button.

* * *

Alex had arrived fifteen minutes earlier at the house of the Norman family. The gate to the house was open, but he parked the car on the street near the house and walked to the mansion.

He had only been here a few times. The recent years, when he needed advice on some scientific projects or decisions, he had consulted Mats, but he had never visited the house when he was a child. He had only seen him in Sandviken or at his parents' home.

As he approached the house, he saw the red Volvo parked in the driveway to the house. It startled him to see the old car, an old-timer by now. He could still feel how frightened he had been, sitting in the back, feeling how the car sped up and drove with an unbelievable speed down the small forest road. When he saw the reflection of the man in the rearview mirror, Mats Norman, and the almost diabolic expression on his face, he began to cry. Shocked by the sobbing of the young boy, Mats turned around. The car lost speed and came to a hold. Meanwhile, the young girl had disappeared into the woods and the boy had crawled into a corner between the car door and the back seat. His son, his beautiful son! He liked him more than any of his other children. His love child. His and Irene's! How he had loved her! Beautiful Irene.

Alex looked at the house. It seemed very deserted. No lights. Some curtains were still drawn. The front door was ajar and the many footsteps in the snow showed the recent activity around the house.

He pushed open the door and stepped inside, shouting, "Professor Norman? Is somebody home?"

The small puddles of water in the hallway, up the stairs and toward the living room showed someone was still in the house. He felt the adrenaline rushing through his veins. Why did he want to confront Mats? What would he say when he finally saw him? He hadn't thought it through. He just should leave it to the police. But then he heard a crackling sound coming from the living room.

Slowly he walked to the door and opened it. On the large sofa in front of him, he saw someone sitting, showing only the back of the head. It wasn't Mats Norman.

"I'm sorry. I wasn't sure if anyone would be home, and the door was open ..."

There was no reply, and he walked toward the sofa to face the person, but as he approached, he saw the blood on the floor. There was a large wound on the side of the head and so much more blood on the sofa. It was Annette Norman. Her skin was so pale. The eyes were still open, her face frozen in a snapshot of fear and surprise. The killer was probably still inside the house, and he instinctively felt that someone was behind him. Mats wouldn't kill him. He couldn't; he was his son.

He turned around and faced the person who was pointing a gun at him. The surprise and disbelief were unimaginable when he felt the bullet pierce through his body. He fell to the ground. There was no pain, only emptiness. He used to read that people typically saw those life-defining moments pass by in slow motion when the end was near, but there was nothing, just a tear running down his cheeks. He couldn't move. He still felt no pain, only sadness. Mother ... father, Isa.

And then the pain came, in all its fierceness. Like a tsunami, it took over his entire body. He had never felt anything like it.

Make it stop!

The pain was so crushing. He wanted to get away, but his body didn't comply. The person was now standing over him, gun pointed at his head. No, he didn't want to die. Not now.

"Please ...," he pleaded with the few gusts of breath that remained. His voice so quiet, broken like china. And then everything turned black.

CHAPTER

22

GRANDMA, NANA.

I love you so much. Don't cry for me when I'm gone. I had a great life thanks to you. More than I could ever have imagined. I don't know how long I still have. He hasn't visited me in weeks. At least, I think it's weeks. It's hard to know. Every day is the same, an endless succession of meaningless moments, nothing to do. Just me and my thoughts. I sleep most of the time or I write. At least I have that.

You know I'm not a religious person, but I've been praying that someone would find me, and that this nightmare would be over. But no one came. No one will come.

It's freezing here, in this basement or whatever it is. The blankets are not enough, and I estimate I have just enough food and water for another week. After that, I don't know anymore. When you read this, if you ever read this, I'm probably dead. But don't be sad, don't cry. You believe in an afterlife where we will meet again. I have to believe the same. I need to. It's the only thing that keeps me going. I love you. Forever.

Your Elin.

* * *

They didn't notice the small black car parked in the street when the police squad arrived at the mansion of Mats and Annette Norman. The sirens and lights were switched off, and only a handful of officers took up positions outside the front gate of the house, while the others tried to get to the back through the adjacent properties. Isa was eager to go inside. Sara had to come first, she knew that, but all she could think about was Alex. Was he safe?

"Nina, we're going through the front door. I need you to cover me. Okay?"

Nina felt the pressure increase. She couldn't tell her boss she was far from prepared for this type of intervention and that she questioned her ability to protect her colleagues. This wasn't the time.

"Isa, can't we ..."

"We have no time to waste. There are people in danger."

"We should wait for the intervention squad ...," Nina tried, but off her boss went. Isa couldn't wait a second longer.

Guns in hand, they walked up the path to the house, and carefully scanned the surroundings. Apart from a few trees and the red car parked close to the house, there was little to hide them from the sight of anyone in the house. Isa moved fast, and it was difficult for Nina to keep up. She quickly glanced at the red car. It could be the car that drove her off the road in Sandviken that day. She wasn't sure.

The front door was unlocked and half open. Isa stood behind the door and signaled her colleague she would go in. The young woman moved to the other side and entered the house soon after Isa had gone inside.

The floor of the hallway was still dirty with small puddles of melted snow. There were wet footprints leading to the living room. While Nina took position in the corner behind the living room door, Isa entered, soon followed by her colleague.

Just as Alex had immediately spotted the woman sitting on the sofa, her presence took Isa by surprise, and she pointed the gun at the motionless person.

"Police ... slowly get up and put your hands in the air," Isa shouted. At that moment, Nina moved behind her and scanned the room.

There was no reaction, even after a second warning. Isa slowly approached until she realized the woman was dead. Aside from the large head injury, the woman on the sofa appeared to have been shot several times. The severe blood loss had stained the fabric of the sofa, and the blood splatters on the floor had dried out.

When Isa turned around, she saw a second body: a man lying on the floor a few meters away, his face turned the other way so she couldn't see it. The traces of blood on the ground suggested he had tried to crawl away. But now he lay motionless in a pile of blood, and a few steps away from the body, there was a gun on the floor.

Her heart was beating out of control, and she felt sick. She recognized the jacket. She ran to him, put her own gun down and turned him over.

"Alex, my God, Alex," she cried in a panic. He didn't respond. His coat was soaked with blood and the stain covered almost the entire right side of his chest. The blood loss seemed massive. Her hands trembled as she frantically tried to feel his pulse. The heartbeat was very weak, but it was there, and she immediately took the phone out of her pocket to call for medical help.

The whole situation had distracted Nina and when Mats slipped into the room behind her, he was holding a knife against the throat of the

282

frightened teenage girl.

In a reflex, Isa took her gun from the floor and pointed it at him. Nina, startled by the reaction, turned around and did the same. She was angry with herself. He had sneaked up behind her and he could have killed her. She had been careless.

"Mats, what are you doing?" Isa spoke to him. Her voice, calm and reassuring, showed no sign of the fear she felt. She knew he was erratic. With nothing to lose, he could easily kill the girl and himself.

"Mats, you are a man of reason. Listen to me. You don't want to hurt Sara. You love her, don't you?"

He looked at the girl he was holding in his arms. Meanwhile, he heard the police officers coming in behind him, surrounding him and aiming their guns.

"Yes ... but I loved them all ... and they are still dead. I did that, I did that!"

"Let me help you. Let me help Sara and Alex ... I'm sure you didn't want to hurt them. It was an accident, right? You would never hurt your son. I understand what happened."

Isa tried to reassure him, tried to appeal to the emotions and love he had felt for his son and the girls.

But the expression on Mats' face changed as he stared at the body next to Isa. This was unexpected. It almost looked like he was surprised and shocked.

"Alexander ...," he mumbled, as the inspectors saw how he loosened the grip on the knife.

He shot Alexander, or maybe not? He couldn't remember. Sara started to cry. He needed to have a clear head. Her sobs annoyed him.

"Shut up," he shouted and put his other hand around her neck.

The police officers sharpened their aim.

"Mats, please, we are running out of time," Isa pleaded, "we can help you."

The words meant nothing to him. How could she help him? He had killed all these girls; he had shot his own son, the person he had promised never to hurt was now bleeding to death on his living room floor ... his wife's body lay on the sofa; she was probably dead. Why couldn't he remember? Was it her again? The voice in his head?

What was there to live for? He wanted to end it all, but that small fraction of humanity that still lingered inside him now kept him from cutting Sara's throat and killing himself on the way. There was no way around it; he had to decide.

As he looked at the fragile girl in his arms, he ran his fingers down her cheek and neck. How he loved her ... forever!

He let go of the knife and immediately felt her break away from him, leaving him at the mercy of the police officers, who threw him on the floor. It was over; he had given up.

While they handcuffed him, Isa turned to Alex and tried to call for help. His skin was even paler than before. She was afraid it was too late. As they dragged the suspect away and secured the house, the paramedics, three young men, entered the room. There was nothing more they could do for Annette Norman. She had been dead for several hours. They focused on Alex Nordin, who was now clearly in danger.

"How does it look?" Isa asked as she watched them administer oxygen. They put him on a stretcher and carried him outside.

"Not good. His pulse is very weak. He lost a lot of blood. I'm not sure he'll make it."

The young man quickly followed his colleagues outside. Until then, she had been running on autopilot, suppressing her pain and the guilt she felt for not being there on time. She ran after the paramedics, with Nina behind her.

"Isa, Isa, wait," she shouted.

"Nina, just leave me, I have to go with them," Isa replied without turning around. Nina caught up with her when they reached the ambulance.

"Isa, it's no use," Nina continued and took her arm.

Angry, Isa continued her way and ignored her.

"I'm coming with you," she told the paramedic as she got in the ambulance and left a startled Nina behind. As the ambulance drove off, Nina turned around and saw how Mats Norman, hands tied behind his back, was led to one of the police cars. It all felt so unreal. The case was finally solved after so many months. This was a victory, but it hadn't felt like it. Too many people had died. Could they have prevented it? She studied the teenage girl sitting in the remaining ambulance, pale, terrified, almost looking like a zombie ... surrounded by so many people, but still alone. The psychological damage had been done. It would take years to recover from this. She would need the support of family and friends, and she would have to find the strength to live with this all her life. It would define her; it would determine the choices she would make during the rest of her life.

She turned around and looked at the space where the other ambulance had been. Isa and Alexander Nordin ... somehow, she wasn't surprised. There had always been a tension between them, a chemistry she had rarely witnessed between two people.

She walked to one of the cars, parked closest to the gate, and asked to take her back to the station. She called Magnus Wieland and told him about the arrest of Mats Norman. Then she called Ingrid. Isa would need all the support she could get from her best friend.

* * *

The drive to the hospital only took fifteen minutes, but it seemed as if they had been driving for hours. Isa, sitting next to the gurney, looked at Alex. The medics had stripped off the coat and shirt to expose the gunshot wound. Wires were attached to his chest to monitor his vital signs, and the medic was taking his blood pressure.

"He is not stable," the paramedic said, who had noticed her looking at the monitor. The heartbeat was irregular, and the blood pressure was jumping up and down.

She said nothing. It was as if her brain had shut down, and she was only an observer. They had said goodbye that morning. He was so happy ... for the first time. She had to believe it was because of her. It was the first time in a long time that life hadn't been that complicated. Now, there was no telling how it would end. She took his hand, hoping he would notice, hoping he would fight to keep alive. Their time together had been so brief that she hadn't told him he was important to her. She wanted to say it out loud, but at that moment, the monitor beeps changed into a nauseating flatline sound, alerting the paramedics. When they started resuscitation, she let go of his hand. All she could hear was the continuous sound of the heart monitor, while they frantically tried to revive him.

The ambulance arrived at the hospital almost ten minutes later. By then, they were still trying to get his heart started.

"Stop," Isa said quietly, but they didn't hear it.

"Stop," she repeated, "stop ... he's gone."

They were almost out of breath from the intense attempts to save the life of the man lying on the gurney. The young paramedic who had been handling the defibrillator stopped and stared at her, disappointed and defeated.

"Let him go ... it's okay," Isa said and put her hand on his arm to comfort him.

Alex was dead. She got up and kissed his forehead. So many wires and tubes were hanging around him, but he looked peaceful and so beautiful.

"I'm so sorry," she whispered and kissed him again.

Her breathing was superficial, and she started to sweat. Where did this come from? Breathing became difficult, very difficult. Just a few more seconds and she would faint. The cold air rushed in as she opened the door. Outside, doctors and nurses were standing around the ambulance. They would take him away from her. Forever. She couldn't move. She didn't want to move when they removed the stretcher from the ambulance. It was like he was sleeping, so peacefully. She didn't see the blood and the gunshot wound anymore. She wanted to crawl next to him and tell him everything would be all right. Hold him, kiss him. But he was no longer there.

Ingrid was standing close to the entrance of the ER, and when she saw her friend sitting in the ambulance, she approached.

"Isa, what ...," she asked.

"He's dead," Isa said, and to her surprise, she heard her voice tremble and suddenly nothing else came out but those three words.

Shocked by her friend's announcement, Ingrid said: "Isa, I'm sorry ... so sorry. Is there anything I can do? Isa?"

She clung to one of the metal bars in the ambulance. She could no longer stop the flood of emotions and thoughts.

"The book. Where is the book?"

Frantically Isa looked around and moved things as if she were looking for something.

"What book? What are you talking about?"

She hadn't heard anything and as if in a flurry of panic, she kept on moving about in the ambulance while shouting, "His book ... the book he gave me. Where is the book?"

Outside, the paramedics were waiting to claim their vehicle, but Ingrid signaled them to be patient.

"Is, stop," Ingrid yelled and touched her friend's arm.

She turned around, the face all red and covered in tears. Never in her life, had she experienced such a dramatic downfall.

"Let's get out of the ambulance," Ingrid said and offered her a hand, which she took. The crowd around the car had grown to about ten people who had witnessed her breakdown. They looked at her with pity. In other circumstances, she would have been embarrassed, and told them to back off and leave her alone, but now she didn't have the courage to pay attention to them.

"Isa, let me help you."

"Can you please take care of him?" Isa said between moments of silence in which she tried not to fall back in a flood of panic and painful thoughts. Ingrid had never seen her friend so distraught. She didn't know what to say.

"Of course. But you know we have to do an autopsy in this case."

Still struggling to find the words, Isa nodded yes.

"Thank you ... I need to go to the police station," Isa breathed.

"No, Isa, you are in shock. You are in no condition to go anywhere. Let me call Magnus."

"No, no, I don't want to talk to him. He ..."

And then she saw the big red stain on the white blouse she was wearing. It was Alex's blood. She had Alex's blood on her. She kept staring at it.

"Isa, you need to go home. I'm sorry to say it, but when Anders finds out you had a relationship with Alexander Nordin, he'll suspend you."

"That's why I have to be there," she was determined and closed her jacket so she could no longer see the bloodstain. It was as if he was still there with her.

She had to focus on the job. It would be fine. She would be fine.

"I'll call Magnus," Isa said, "but I need him to take me to the station."

"Okay, if that is what you want. I still don't think it's a good idea."

Isa took out her phone and called Magnus, who was on his way back from Sandviken. Ingrid, knowing she couldn't change Isa's mind, went back inside.

It took Magnus another thirty minutes to pick her up at the hospital and drive her to the police station.

Maybe it hadn't been such a good idea. She wanted to see Alex. Maybe he wasn't dead. Maybe they had made a mistake. She stood in front of the entrance, about to go in, and then she stopped. No, he was dead, and seeing him like that would make things worse.

* * *

"They took him to P2. I told Anders we'll join as soon as we arrive. I've heard there's one dead and one person wounded," Magnus said as he drove off with Isa beside him.

"Two ... two people were killed," she said.

Looking straight ahead at the road, his mind only occupied with the investigation, he hadn't noticed how quiet she was.

"Oh, I must have been misinformed. Who?"

"Annette Norman ...," she said, "and Alex."

His head suddenly turned toward her. She looked pale and tired, and she was almost frantically holding the two ends of her jacket over her chest.

"Isa ... I didn't..."

"Say nothing. I just want to focus on the investigation."

She looked outside. She couldn't and wouldn't work up the courage and effort to keep the conversation going. The speed of the car, the sight of the trees, houses, and cars as they passed by, was soothing, but it wasn't enough to distract her. Angry, in despair and confused. So many emotions. Too many of them. She went over the events in her head. If only she had listened to his message earlier, she could have saved him. Why had he gone there? She could only guess he wanted answers, answers to questions he had been struggling with.

But it all made little sense. How could she have misjudged Mats' intentions? She wanted to look him in the eye and ask him why he had killed his son. Was it a mistake or was it a calculated murder?

CHAPTER

23

WHEN MAGNUS PARKED THE CAR at the Uppsala police station, they hadn't spoken a word during the entire trip. He had never seen her so defeated. She was running on an emotional autopilot, oblivious to the world around her, and dulling every sense and glimpse of the pain that would soon overtake her.

Building P2 on the other side of the road was old and grizzled. The renovation of the police station, over five years ago, hadn't been extended to this part of the complex. But this was where they brought the high-profile criminals for questioning, usually to keep them away from the press or public attention.

The murders had been the subject of much debate and criticism over the last months. The public opinion had been harsh on the inspectors, accusing them of incompetence and laxity. Superintendent Anders had always defended his team, but it had come at a price. The constant pressure had affected his social life and health. When he met his chief inspectors in the hall of building P2, he was a relieved man. Proud that they had finally solved the case.

"We've been waiting for you," he said, and looked at Magnus and Isa.

"I'm doing the interview ... Isa can observe from behind the one-way glass," Magnus blurted and turned to her.

She said nothing. It was his way of protecting her, and he wanted at all costs to prevent Mats Norman from using her indiscretion to overturn the charges.

"Are you sure?" Anders asked.

"I can handle it. I think Isa could use some rest after the intervention. Where's Nina?"

"We'll handle it," a deep voice said.

Inspector Finn Heimersson joined them. He was an impressive figure, almost two meters in height, towering above the Gävle police officers. Middle-aged, but physically in top shape, with clever eyes and a somewhat mischievous smile around his mouth.

"But this is still our case," Magnus stammered.

"And you're on my turf now. Don't forget my team's valuable contribution in solving this case. Without them ..."

"Look, let's argue about who's taking credit for what later. Right now, there's a serial killer in that room, and we need to get him to talk. As fast as possible."

Finn, rudely interrupted by Magnus, stared at him for a while, before the sternness turned into a faint smirk. Why were these small-town inspectors always so aggressive, so arrogant? As if they had to prove something all the time.

"Okay then. Give it your best shot!"

Nina, standing outside the interrogation room, had been waiting for her superiors. When Magnus finally joined her, she was unaware of the argument with inspector Heimersson.

"I'll do the interview with you," Magnus told her.

"How is she?" she whispered and pointed to Isa.

"She'll be fine, but you know she can't run this interview," he said softly, "I won't risk compromising the investigation."

"I know. Mr. Norman is inside. Forensics have screened him. They took his clothes for examination. But he's refusing a lawyer."

"Okay, let's go in," Magnus said, and before he entered the room, he quickly glanced at his partner, who looked so fragile and beaten, far from the strong, passionate and ambitious woman she was. Why did it affect her so much? Would she have reacted differently if it had been him lying in the morgue? He couldn't help her. He could only be there for her and hope it was enough.

The man sitting at the table in the room looked as defeated as Isa, and so much older than Magnus remembered from the visit a few months earlier, when the flamboyant and lively professor had talked about his family and the summers in Sandviken.

"Mr. Norman, before starting the interview, let me remind you that you have the right to legal representation," Magnus started while Nina turned on the recorder.

"Are you sure you want to continue the interview without your lawyer present?"

"Yes."

"Right. Professor Norman, you are accused of the abduction and murder of Clara Persson, Anna Falk, Ida Nilsson, Anna Berg, Katrien Jans, Lise Ekström, Ella Nyman, Elin Dahlberg, and Stina Jonasson. The abduction of Sara Norberg and the murder of Josip Radić, Annette Norman-Peterson, and Alexander Nordin. How do you plead?"

The old man continued to stare at his hands, handcuffed and resting on the table. An oversized plastic overall partially covered his wrists. Almost emotionless, he had listened to the accusations.

"You forgot a few," he said calmly.

"What? You mean there are more?"

Watching from behind the glass wall, Isa touched the pocket of her jacket. The black booklet Alex had given her in the morning was still there.

"Four more bodies ...," she whispered and took out the booklet, while being closely watched by Anders.

"Inspector Lindström, what is this?" he asked and pointed to the object she was holding in her hand.

She sighed. It was time to tell him about Alex.

"Alex Nordin gave me the book."

"Alex Nordin? Why? What is it about?"

"This is Peter Nordin's diary. It contains dates and places. Several of them correspond to dates when girls went missing. Six, but there are seven more entries that I believe are significant. Seven more, thirteen in total."

"Thirteen ...," Anders repeated and turned his head toward the glass.

"Professor Norman, are there more?" Magnus asked again.

"Yes, but it's all irrelevant," Mats replied and stared at him.

His attitude was changing. Instead of the defeated and insecure gaze he had shown at the beginning of the interview, he was gradually adopting a more controlled and superior poise. It was the glance of a predator, not the demeanor of an esteemed professor who had been admired by so many.

"Who are the girls and where are they buried?"

"I buried them in the area behind the cabin, close to the bunker ... but it doesn't matter."

"Mr. Norman, who were the girls?"

"It's irrelevant," Mats yelled, and in his anger, he jumped up. The alarmed police officer at the door ran to the table.

Magnus stopped him and gestured the officer to go back.

"Why?" Magnus said, while Mats calmed down and sat down again.

"Only one matters ... my Clara," he sighed, and his posture turned from arrogant to sad.

He couldn't control the emotions taking him to highs and lows. He realized he had lost his temper. They had finally seen a glimpse of his other side. A side that was short-tempered and violent.

"Your Clara? Clara Persson?"

"Inspector, have you ever loved someone to the extent that it entirely consumed you, that you could only breathe them, that the longing is so ... so maddening that you lose yourself completely?"

Isa, behind the glass, had watched the whole scene. But the memory of a great love was too much to bear, and she left the room, with Anders going after her.

"Inspector Lindström, what's going on?"

She wanted to tell him; she tried to find the words, but no sound came out.

"Oh, I see ... how long has this been going on?" he said.

More than disappointment, his entire attitude radiated compassion.

"Not long ... but long enough," she stammered.

"I understand now why Magnus didn't want you in that room. It can jeopardize everything. Isa, I really hope this doesn't come out. It can damage both our careers. You're lucky that Finn Heimersson isn't here to witness this."

"But I have to be in that room. This is my case. I need to end it," she pleaded.

"You're too emotional, and if he suspects any conflict of interest from your side, the case is done. He can go for a mistrial, and everything will be lost. You better go home and take time to grieve. Go home, right now!"

There was no point in arguing. But she couldn't go home. She was afraid of being alone, with her thoughts about Alex, with the what-ifs, the things she could have done differently, things that could have saved him.

Anders went back inside and left her in the hall. Five minutes later, inspector Heimersson joined him.

* * *

"What happened to Clara?" Magnus asked. "How did she die?"

"I don't know ... she just died. I guess I killed her."

"You guess you killed her? Can you explain that?"

"Okay, I killed her," he sighed, "yes, I killed her because she told me to."

"She? Who is she?"

Slowly Mats lifted his finger and pointed to his head: "She's always there ... in my head. She doesn't like the girls ... she doesn't like Alexander. There is nothing I can do."

"Are you telling me you hear things? That you have to obey the voice in your head?"

Mats said nothing, but just stared at the inspectors.

"Stop the interview, we'll take a break," Magnus yelled and ran out of the room.

He was angry and disappointed.

"Seriously?! He's hearing voices. Do we really believe that? He's not getting away with this."

Anders and Finn met him in the hallway.

"Inspector Wieland, calm down! We'll request a psychiatric evaluation."

Inspector Heimersson's deep voice echoed down the nearly empty hallway.

"We need to go back in," Nina suggested.

Magnus ignored her and paced about.

"He won't give us any information," he shouted.

"Magnus, go back and find out what happened to those girls. There are four more. They are still being missed by their mother and father. We have to find them."

"You need to talk to Marian Bergqvist and Michael Norman," Isa interrupted the conversation.

Magnus and Nina looked at her in surprise.

"Why?"

"I think they know more about what's going on," Isa answered.

"Marian is still here. We can talk to her."

* * *

Marian was sitting in the interrogation room, constantly moving her hands through the strands of hair that were blocking her view, emotionally exhausted and scared. She knew exactly what would be coming. She didn't need a lawyer or anyone else to defend her. She was responsible for a large part of the mess they were in now. When the inspectors entered the room, she quickly looked up. It was the handsome man who had come to her house a while back to talk about her father, and a much younger looking woman, whom she gathered was his assistant.

"Did you find Sara?" she asked.

Tasha didn't want to talk to her anymore. The mere thought that her own sister had known the murderer all along, and that her own daughter had been in danger as a result, had left her outraged. Tasha had yelled and cried. She had rejected Marian's explanation. It had been no explanation at all. Just a few words that meant nothing to her.

"We have found her; she's safe," Nina replied.

Marian let out a deep sigh, and her body, cramped with stress and anxiety, seemed to loosen up. It was such a burden that fell off her shoulders.

Magnus and Nina sat down in front of her, with Isa again following everything from behind the glass wall. She wanted to stay. It kept her mind off the things she didn't want to think about.

"Mrs. Bergqvist, we have arrested Mats Norman on suspicion of abduction and murder. But Mr. Norman is not very responsive."

"We believe you can help us," Nina said.

Suddenly all the blood seemed to drain from her face, and she hid it in her hands. A few seconds later she started to cry, her body shaking violently with every moan she pushed out.

"Mrs. Bergqvist?"

The words didn't come out in a flowing wave of rhetoric; she was stuttering, and she couldn't find the right way to tell them the story that had happened over twenty years ago.

"I know nothing about those girls ... you have to believe me," she pleaded.

She was never that emotional, but this secret she ... they had carried with them for so long, had haunted her, in everything she had done, in every decision she had made until then.

"But Mats Norman didn't kill Ida Nilsson."

"Why do you say that?" Magnus asked.

Isa, listening and watching from the other room, felt a surge of adrenaline going through her body.

"Nikolaj Blom ...," she started. "At that time, he hung around Sandviken a lot. He was a disgusting old man who harassed young girls. Tasha and I have experienced it more than once. He often inappropriately touched our legs or breasts, but since we thought he was a good friend of Mats, we didn't dare to complain."

"You said he was a friend of Mats?"

"Yes, that's what we thought since they were always together ... at least that summer in 1992."

"Had you seen him before?"

"No, never, but he mentioned he had a house in the neighborhood."

"What has Nikolaj Blom got to do with this story?" Nina continued.

"Well, he liked his girls young," Marian replied, "... but his boys even younger."

Isa gasped. She knew what would follow. Marian burst into tears again.

"When we found them, Ida was already dead and ... Alex, he was unconscious and so beaten up we thought he was going to die. Nikolaj had sexually assaulted them."

An uncomfortable silence followed. Magnus looked at the window. Isa had heard everything.

"I carried him outside and ran as fast as I could to the cabin of Mats Norman to get help."

"Where did you find them?"

"Alex had been missing for hours. We couldn't find him until Josip remembered seeing him in the backyard of the house. It was a remote area. Everyone said it was too dangerous, but Alex loved to play there ... so we went looking for him."

"We?"

"Josip, Michael and I," she answered and pulled out a handkerchief to wipe the tears from her face.

"It was a wilderness out there, and I was about to give up until I heard the soft moans of a child. It surprised me to find a bunker hidden behind the branches and rocks. I found Alex halfway through the tunnel leading up to ..."

With that part of the story, she still had so many difficulties.

"Up to what, Mrs. Bergqvist?"

"Up to a room ... where I found the girl. She ... she ... her face was covered in blood; her eyes were open and staring ahead. The clothes were ripped off her body and the marks and bruises on her thighs and breasts showed she had been ..." She took a deep breath before continuing, "... well, someone had raped her."

She used the handkerchief again to wipe the remaining tears from her face.

"Oh, God, it was awful! I tried to find a pulse, but she was dead. And in the corner of the room, I saw Alex's trousers on the floor. Then I knew someone had also ... hurt him."

"What happened next?" Magnus asked.

"We took Alex to the cabin. He was badly injured, going in and out of consciousness all the time. Mats was there and so was Alex's mother, Irene. Annette wasn't. Maybe I should have seen it then, but Mats was more interested in finding out what had happened to the dead girl than calling the police or bringing Alex to the hospital. Josip showed him where we found Ida while I stayed behind to take care of little Alex."

"But how did Alex end up in the bunker?"

"Honestly, this is still a mystery," she admitted, "because the room had a steel door with several locks. I always thought Nikolaj must have taken them and locked them up in the room."

"Nikolaj Blom disappeared in 1992. Do you know what happened to him?"

Until now, Magnus had done all the talking, while Nina had carefully taken notes. She took the file, until then lying unopened on the table, and handed it to Magnus.

"They never found his body," Magnus said, while he flipped through the pages.

"That evening Nikolaj came to visit Mats. Josip, Michael, Irene, and I were still in the back room with Alex, who was in a lot of pain. Mats still hadn't allowed Irene to take him to the doctor. At one point, they started screaming. I can still hear Mats yelling at Nikolaj that he had hurt Alex and that he would pay for what he had done. Nikolaj laughed. I left the room, and then I heard the knock and that sickening sound of a skull being cracked open."

For a moment, she stared ahead as she continued, "I had never seen or heard anything like that before ... it is..."

"So, Mats killed Nikolaj?"

"Yes, the man was lying on the floor. There was so much blood I felt sick and threw up. Mats was crying. He kept saying he hadn't wanted to kill him. He was in shock."

"And what happened next?

"Ivor Radić was called to help, and they buried Nikolaj close to the bunker where he still lies, I guess. What happened to the girl, I never knew, until now. The next day, they had cleaned up everything. There was no trace anymore of what had happened ... except we knew. And Alex recovered, but Alex was no longer Alex after that. He became timid, secluded, sad. He stayed inside most of the time and never spoke about it. I don't think he really knew. And we never told him, but we should have, we really should have."

"Why didn't anyone go to the police?" Nina asked indignantly.

"Josip was eleven, Michael was fourteen, and I was nineteen ... we were scared. We were really scared. I've thought about it a lot, but then Mats made sure we wouldn't go. He had his ways of terrorizing us. He used to follow me with his red car to show me he could get to me anywhere, anytime. Besides ... Nikolaj was the bad guy: he had hurt Alex and the girl. So, to some extent, he deserved to be punished. Only now ... I think this was all a hoax."

"Why do you believe that?"

"Nine girls. There have been girls before Ida Nilsson, and there have been girls after Ida. Nikolaj can't be responsible for all these murders. Mats set this whole thing up."

"With what purpose?"

"To get rid of Nikolaj Blom."

A surprising statement that raised the eyebrows of the people in the room and Isa, who was still behind the glass wall.

What had happened to Alex was horrible. But now she understood where this vulnerability had come from. The depressions, his suicide attempt, they had all been manifestations of this unresolved, lingering trauma from his childhood. He hadn't known, which maybe had been for the best. At least she hoped he hadn't known.

"Why would Mats want to get rid of Nikolaj Blom?"

"Josip called me a few weeks ago before his death. He wanted to talk about the death of Nikolaj Blom. I wasn't particularly interested in meeting him. He seemed agitated and aggressive. He was almost begging to talk to me because he suspected it had been a set-up for us to believe Nikolaj deserved to die. I switched off the phone, and he never called me again, but he also contacted Michael, and wanted to talk to him about the same thing."

"Do you think this was the reason someone killed Josip?"

She shrugged. The interview had drained all the energy from her, and she felt numb.

"What is going to happen now?" she asked hesitantly.

"We will talk to Michael Norman and Irene Nordin, but it's likely that they will charge you with obstruction of justice and withholding of information."

She sighed. It was a mild punishment for keeping such a secret for over twenty years. It was time to make amends.

"I can go?" she asked.

"Yes, for now," Nina said.

"Can I talk to Alex about this?" she asked as she was about to get up, "I'd rather tell this myself before he hears it from someone else."

Nina and Magnus exchanged a glance before Magnus told her:

"That won't be possible, Mrs. Bergqvist. Alexander Nordin is dead."

That was it. She would live with this for the rest of her life. No possibility to explain it to him, no possibility to ask forgiveness and penance. She felt ashamed. Not one moment in all these years she had tried to find out how he was doing. What his life had been like. Could it have made a difference? Perhaps it had put things in perspective and given meaning to the insecurities and downfalls he had experienced in his short life. But she didn't know that ... how could she? Only now, when there had been no way out, she had finally admitted everything, but it was too late.

She was such a coward.

CHAPTER

24

ISA WAS BITTER. The evil they faced now was so much worse and darker than she ever expected. Had Mats really sacrificed his son to destroy Nikolaj? She couldn't wait any longer. She had to talk to him in person. It was easy. The police officer in front of the interrogation room let her in without any problems.

Mats looked up as he heard her enter the room. She closed the door and waited for a while, back against the wall. The way he stared at her made her uneasy until she noticed that he wasn't looking at her but at the bloodstains on her blouse, which she had tried so carefully to hide.

"It's his blood," she said.

He kept staring and said nothing.

"I don't understand. Explain why you would kill your wife and son! Why? Say something!"

The woman, standing before him, was nothing like the confident and intelligent inspector who had interviewed him a while ago. She was more unsettled than she should be. He didn't understand.

"My wife ... she was sweet and caring ... and Alexander, he was charming, handsome, and so smart, but he was ... damaged. I tried to help him whenever I could, but Irene didn't want me to. You know, I chose his name? Irene didn't like it, and neither did Peter."

"Peter knew?"

"Yes, he suspected it. He didn't want me to see my son. Irene too at first. They kept him hidden from me, but I took him."

"Yes, you did, didn't you," Isa said calmly, remembering the story of Alex's abduction as a child.

"He was so small, so tiny. I took him to see Clara. It was so nice."

The memories were so vivid and pleasant that he smiled.

"No. It wasn't nice. You used him to trick Clara and kidnap her. It wasn't nice at all."

It was time to confront him with the atrocities he had committed, but he kept smiling. The words barely got through to him.

"What is this?" Isa showed him the black book.

He laughed loudly, alarming her colleagues in the hall. When Magnus and Nina returned to the room, Isa was standing only a few meters away from the door, a black book in her hands.

"What are you doing here?" Magnus said surprised and took her arm. She didn't look at him and kept staring at the old man. The smile on his face was so insulting and ridiculing that it irritated her and made her angry.

"What is this?" she repeated.

"Peter thought he could outsmart me, but he couldn't. These are just incoherent scribbles of a man who was slowly but surely losing his mind. These mean nothing."

"They are accurate. Places, dates ... was he following you? He suspected something, didn't he?"

His expression changed, and he looked at her sharply.

Isa flipped through the pages and read out loud: "11 October 1993, 28 March 1997, 19 February 2000 and 17 April 2006. These dates refer to other girls. Who were those girls?"

"They are irrelevant," Mats replied.

"As irrelevant as your wife and son you so coldly killed?"

Eyes cast down, looking at his hands again, he said: "I didn't want to kill them, but she didn't like them. She's very persistent."

"Who the hell is she?" Isa yelled and glanced at her partner Magnus.

"She tells me what to do. She wanted them dead."

"There is no she! It's all you, only you. Admit it! Just like you set up everything to kill Nikolaj Blom."

His response was alarming. He looked up, eyes full of rage.

"He deserved to die!" His voice sounded terrifying, and as he went on, his whole demeanor changed again from the weak and pitiful man, he wanted his interrogators to believe he was, to the assertive and powerful manipulator he really was.

"Why?" Isa yelled, almost out of breath.

He had his eyes fixed on her.

"Why are you so upset?" he asked.

His piercing glance almost seemed to cut away the layers of defense behind which she was hiding her devastation over Alex's death. It was time to intervene, and Magnus tried to get the conversation back to the essence of the matter.

"Why did Nikolaj Blom deserve to die?" Magnus repeated.

He wanted Mats to focus on him instead of Isa. It worked. Mats let go of his fixation on Isa and turned to Magnus:

"You have been talking to Michael and Marian. And so, you know that this disgrace of a man attacked my son. My pure, beautiful son! He was so innocent, and he took that away from him. He took everything. He had so much potential!"

This man loved his son. He would never have sacrificed him. Marian was mistaken. Mats had killed him in a fit of anger. It wasn't to hide anything.

The audacity with which Nikolaj had told Mats that night how he had found Ida and Alex in the bunker. And that for the first time he had given into the perverse desires he had long cherished but never had dared to admit. Things had gotten out of hand, and when he had been confronted with Ida's lifeless body, he knew he couldn't let the little boy go.

When Nikolaj told the tormented father about the details of the horror he had inflicted on the toddler, something broke in Mats and he grabbed the first thing he could find to hit him. The poker struck him on the left side of the head. The hundred-kilos heavy man fell to the floor. The blood poured from the open wound in his skull, but he was still alive. He hit him again and again. Marian, who had come out to see what the turmoil was about, had witnessed the horrific scene. No, he had felt no remorse. He still felt no remorse.

"Something is not clear," Magnus continued, "why would Nikolaj come to you to talk about this?"

His demeanor changed again. He leaned back as if he had all the time in the world. He was not immediately inclined to just throw everything on the table. He wouldn't make it easy for them.

Magnus had been great, Isa thought. He had been considerate, but also strict and clever. She was grateful he had been there, while she had treated him so badly.

"Ah, I see," Magnus finally said. "Nikolaj had found out about the girls, hadn't he? He was blackmailing you. What did you give him? Money?"

Mats' silence was a sign he was on the right track. Suddenly it occurred to him that Mats had only talked about Alex. Ida's death had been incidental.

"No, you promised him the girls. You promised him Ida. Only, he found in that room a little more than a teenage girl. Something he liked even more. I'm right, aren't I?"

"Alexander shouldn't have been there," Mats whispered.

This was too much. It was more than Isa could deal with at that moment and she, until then still leaning against the wall, left the room.

"Let's go back to today. Why Sara Norberg? You must have known you took an enormous risk by abducting Tasha's daughter. It would eventually be traced back to you. Frank Norberg saw you hanging around the house several times. You were sloppy."

After the attack on Alexander, he had wanted to stop so many times. He knew well it had been his fault, but the flesh was too weak. The longing was too strong. With every girl, he promised he would keep these impulses under control, but he never could. Nobody even knew until Alexander found the remains of the girls. Undiscovered for more than thirty years, it made him superhuman, invincible, having lost all touch with reality. Until that day in September. This was a sign. A sign to end it all.

"You wanted us to stop you," Nina said as if she had been reading his mind.

"Is that why you took Sara?" Magnus added.

"Yes."

"What happened after you kidnapped Sara?"

Mats sighed. He was tired of answering all these, in his opinion, stupid questions.

"Did your wife Annette catch you red-handed? Did she have to die because of that?"

"I didn't kill my wife, and I didn't kill Alexander."

"But you admitted to killing them half an hour ago ... if you didn't ... then who did?" Nina asked.

"You were the only one in the house ... it can only be you," Magnus said.

"I didn't kill them."

Mats' voice was louder than before, and the heightened anxiety was noticeable in his manner.

"That's not what you mentioned earlier. The voice in your head made you kill them ... that's what you told us."

"No, no, no," he yelled and started to hit his head.

"Mr. Norman, stop," Magnus shouted and tried to grab his arm when the hitting escalated, but he couldn't avoid that Mats' elbow landed against his chest and he fell to the floor. Three police officers stormed into the room and with brute force pinned him on the table. Eventually, they had to sedate him and carry him out of the interrogation room.

* * *

"How can an intelligent and highly respected man get that far?" Nina said, while she sat at the table again. In the tumult, she had taken shelter in the corner of the room, while the paramedics and police officers had taken Mats Norman outside.

"There are plenty of cases like that," Magnus replied.

"Yes," Nina said, clearly distracted.

"He hasn't really confessed. It will be harder to get a conviction without his confession. What are we going to tell the families? There are so many questions he doesn't want to answer."

"I know," Magnus said softly.

He collected the papers from the table and floor, and went outside, with Nina behind him.

"We need to get him talking," Nina declared.

"You won't get any further than an incoherent rambling. The question is if he is faking it or if it's real."

He stopped. He had to say something to Isa.

"Isa, Isa, I want to tell you ...," he said when he walked over to her.

"What?" she said.

"I just wanted to say I'm sorry for what happened to Alex."

"Sure, you do," she said ironically. "I'll leave ... you don't need me here anymore."

She left her partner in the corridor of the police station. She knew exactly where to go; she knew exactly where she wanted to be.

The walk to the hospital would take a while, but it was exactly what she needed. There were so many things in her head that made little sense. She couldn't work like that. In her life, she had never faced loss and tragedy before, and now the death of someone she barely knew, made such a huge impact on her. It was confusing. She didn't want to be in the middle of it. How come everything looked so futile? That morning her biggest concern had been her job and how she had for the umpteenth time crossed the line of professional ethics. Now ... it wasn't about her anymore.

How she wanted to touch and kiss him one more time! Hold him one more time and tell him she loved him. Would they have had a future together?

But there was no future ... not anymore.

Thirty minutes later she reached the hospital. By that time, darkness was already setting in. The cold was penetrating her limbs, but she didn't want to go inside. Not yet.

The phone rang. It was Ingrid. For a moment, she stared at it. While the ringtone continued its most annoying and insisting lamentation, she watched the passers-by. People just got on with their daily lives. How was this possible while her world stood still? It seemed like an eternity before the ringtone finally stopped. She walked around the hospital for a least an hour before entering.

Ingrid had waited patiently for her in the morgue. And while her Uppsala colleagues had left home, she had called her husband and children to tell them that she would be late that evening. Her best friend needed her.

When Isa finally sat down on the bench next to the postmortem room, Ingrid was sitting by her side. The silence, vibrating through the dark hallway, was unworldly and drenched with so much sadness. The scent of dead bodies and embalming fluids was so pungent it nauseated her. It never bothered her before, but now it did.

"There's no one around this time of day," Ingrid said.

She took her hand and held it tight as if she were afraid of losing her.

"His mother didn't come in yet. You'll be the first."

"Tell me, Ingrid, did he suffer?" Isa said and turned to her friend.

When she saw the doubt and hesitation on Ingrid's face, she continued to say, "Please ... be honest with me."

"Yes, he probably did. The bullet caused significant damage to his stomach, liver, and part of his lungs. I'm surprised he could still move."

She felt Isa's grip tighten.

"Could ...," her voice broke, and she needed a moment to continue. "Could I have saved him?"

"Maybe ... but I doubt it. The blood loss was so substantial and only if you had been there when he was shot, you might have gotten him to the hospital in time and even then ..."

She couldn't hold back the tears. Ingrid had never seen her like this.

"He's in the next room. You can go in. Take all the time you need."

She still doubted whether to go in. It would make it all so final. She just wanted to dwell a little longer in the illusion that this was all a dream, and that she would wake up in bed next to him.

She got up and walked to the door. The doorknob was cold and when she entered the room, she saw an autopsy table in the center with a body covered up to the neck by a white sheet. Only the head was visible, with the dark hair sticking out.

Slowly she walked over to the table, but when she recognized the contours of his face, she stopped for a moment. It was even worse than she had imagined. She came closer and caressed his forehead and hair. He felt so cold and looked so pale, yet so handsome, even in death.

"If only I had known that our time together would be so limited, I wouldn't have hesitated. I wouldn't have made such a mess after Sandviken. Because I knew ... from the first day I met you. And I should have told you."

In the room next door, Ingrid heard her friend crying.

She stayed with him through the night, looking at him, touching him, talking to him and just being quiet. When she left the next morning, she thought she had felt everything and had said everything that needed to be said, but she was wrong. For months and years to come, she would struggle with the senselessness of his death and the reminiscence of what could have been.

* * *

"It has been a long day," Nina said, kicking off her shoes. It was after midnight when they arrived at the Gävle police station. Nina and Magnus were the only people in the room. It was so quiet. Maybe it was time to go home. It had been an emotionally exhausting day, and they both needed sleep.

Nina remembered how scared she had been in the house when Mats had sneaked up on them. She had endangered her colleagues, civilians, and herself, and that should never happen again. The more she thought about it, the more convinced she became that this wasn't the career she wanted to pursue. Magnus and Isa wouldn't appreciate her decision, but after the case she would hand in her resignation and go back to school.

"What is this?" Magnus pointed at the file on his desk.

Nina turned around and said, "The phone records of Josip Radić."

"And this?"

He took the thick, light-brown, medium-sized envelope in his hands and felt its weight. Only paper, he thought, but there was a lot.

"This has been on your desk for weeks now," Nina replied, "they delivered it in your absence, I think."

It was addressed to him. There was no name or address of the sender mentioned anywhere. Interesting. With some hesitation, he took the letter opener and slid it down one side of the envelope. When he took out the bunch of papers, he was glad it hadn't been white powder or a cut-off finger. There were about ten pages of handwritten text.

"What is it?" Nina asked as he began to read, at first with a rather indifferent glance on his face, but that soon turned to frowning of the eyebrows and an expression that radiated anxiety.

He didn't answer, but quickly scanned the papers and reread it from the beginning.

"What is it?"

When he still didn't answer, she got up and walked to his desk.

"Does Isa know about this?" was the first thing he asked when he saw her standing next to him.

There was a look of concern in his eyes.

"No, what has this got to do with it?"

"Just keep it quiet and don't tell her."

"Look, Magnus, Isa's behavior was far from professional, so I'm not inclined to share any information with her. Someone has to report her relationship with Alexander Nordin."

She rattled on. It wasn't exactly what he wanted to talk about.

"Let me handle it," he said, annoyed.

"Yes, you should, because if you don't, I will."

It almost sounded like a threat.

"Nina, this is the least of my worries. We should look at this letter."

"Why?"

He handed her the document, and she quickly scanned through the papers. Like Magnus, her attitude changed immediately.

"This is a letter from Josip Radić," she said, surprised.

The envelope had been on his desk for a while. They could have solved the case so many weeks ago if he had been there, if he hadn't run away and abandoned his colleagues saying nothing. How was he going to explain this to Isa? And the family of all those victims?

"Read it," he said. "This case is not closed yet. We have to talk to one more person."

CHAPTER

25

"**G**OOD MORNING, MRS. NORDIN,**" Magnus said when he entered the room. The past few days had been hectic, and he needed a big shot of caffeine to stay awake and focused. Dividing his time between the hospital and work was wearing him down. He put the large cup of coffee in front of him as he sat down. It was still hot, with a light fume rising from the cup.

Mrs. Nordin had brought her lawyer. Mr. Hansen was a short, bald man, in his fifties, who didn't look too smart. He was constantly flipping through his notebook. It irritated Irene Nordin, who gave him a disapproving glance.

"Shall we start?" the man asked, his eyes still fixed on the papers.

"My colleague will join us in a few minutes. In the meantime, I have to tell you we'll be recording this interview."

Nina entered the room, coffee in one hand and a pile of papers in the other.

Mrs. Nordin, dressed in black, looked carefully at the young woman as she entered the room. She had expected to see someone else and seemed disappointed.

"What am I doing here?"

The tone of her voice was harsh. "My son just died. I shouldn't be here. I should be planning a funeral and you should be talking to the man who murdered him."

"My condolences, Mrs. Nordin, with the loss of your son," Magnus started, "but then again, it seems strange that you haven't even visited him, let alone even asked to see him. He died three days ago."

"It's just a dead body," she replied, "it's not my son anymore."

Even though she was right, it wasn't exactly an example of compassion and sensitivity, and it left the other people in the room stunned.

"What Mrs. Nordin means is ...," her lawyer tried to explain.

"My words need no explanation, Mr. Hansen. They were clear enough."

It was also clear who was in charge. He would be the one listening, while she would make the decisions. He was there for form's sake.

"Okay, I see," Magnus said and reviewed his notes.

He flipped through the pages until he stopped on a page halfway through the file and pulled out a relatively old-looking paper.

"Tell me about your relationship with Mats Norman!"

Her eyes were fixed on the paper he had put on the table next to the folder.

"Mrs. Nordin?"

"What do you want to know?" she said.

"I had a look at your file. It was interesting to learn that you were an administrative clerk at the University of Uppsala in 1981, before your marriage. At that time, the brilliant and handsome Mats Norman was working as a doctorate student in the physics department. Did your affair start at that point? An affair that lasted until now. He was already married, and you were engaged to the decent but boring Peter Nordin. Am I right about the relationship?"

"If you say so," she snapped.

"If you've been in a relationship that long, I would be surprised that you didn't know about his dark side. I think you knew he had a soft spot for beautiful women and young girls and that you even used that to tie him to you."

"No, you're wrong," she shouted," there are plenty of examples where people very close to serial killers had no idea what they had done until the moment of arrest. Where is the evidence?"

"I'll get to that, but I believe you found out about his dark fantasies early on and instead of breaking all connections, you encouraged him to give into them. But you made sure you were in full control. You helped him abduct the girls and hold them captive. That way you made sure he would never leave you. You married Peter to keep up appearances, and he was the perfect scapegoat. He was mentally unstable, and you made sure he would start to question his mental state more and more, first through simple suggestions, later probably through drugs you administered without his knowing."

"Again speculation, you have no proof," she said proudly.

Mr. Hansen had been monitoring the conversation carefully, but he said nothing.

"And then things got more complicated than you expected because you got pregnant with Mats' child, Alex."

She laughed. Not a kind smile, but a denigrating derision. This wasn't the response they had expected.

"Oh, come on! Alex wasn't Mats' son; he was Peter's son. Mats so badly wanted Alex to be his, he believed it even though I told him repeatedly this wasn't the case. And Peter ... I'm sorry to say, but he was even disappointed when he found out from that stupid GenoOne analysis that Alex wasn't Mats'. How much would he have given to find that one reason to reject Alex? But he couldn't."

"I think you left both men in the dark about Alex's real father so you could manipulate them," Magnus added.

"But Alex is Mats' son," Nina declared and pulled out a paper.

"DNA analysis shows Mats and Alex are father and son," she concluded.

"In fact, the GenoOne test showed Peter wasn't Alex's father. After all these years, he finally got the confirmation he was looking for."

Irene sighed and turned her eyes away. She almost looked disappointed.

"When Mats' fantasies became so tenacious and there was no way to stop him, you offered to help him. With your son."

"The kidnapping of Alex as a baby was an example," Nina said. "It was Mats who took the baby and used him to lure Clara in his car, with your permission."

"What's not clear is to what extent Peter was involved," Magnus continued.

Nina put the black book on the table. The last time Irene saw it, was in Alex's apartment. For a moment, she had been tempted to take it.

"He suspected you from the start, didn't he? That's why he kept some kind of notebook, a diary. Did he feel threatened?"

"But he couldn't keep it a secret from you. He was too weak, and you just let him do it. He had low credibility anyway and this would just look like the writing of a madman ... until your son found it. And he linked it to the kidnappings."

There was no reply. Mr. Hansen took the book and flipped through it.

"It doesn't say much," he said. "How can this be linked to my client?"

"Do you know what this is?" Magnus put the light brown envelope on the table.

Mr. Hansen shook his head.

"It's a letter from Josip Radić, written a few days before his disappearance. Its authenticity has been verified by our forensic team. He had given it to a friend, a bank clerk, for safekeeping. In case something would happen to him, she had to post it."

"It is very interesting reading, Mrs. Nordin," Nina added. "He mainly talks about the events of the summer in 1992. For years, he had doubts about how they all had interpreted the dramatic incident, but he had become more and more convinced you had set up the whole thing."

"Mats had hidden the girls in the house of Nikolaj Blom you rented under Peter's name. But Nikolaj found out about the girls and blackmailed Mats. So, you had to get rid of him ... but not just him."

"Alex, only five years old, was a very inquisitive child, and he had discovered the hiding place of the girls. He had seen how Mats brought the girls food and he had told you, his mother. He probably thought it was a game. You also knew that Nikolaj had a reputation for molesting young boys and girls. I have his file here that says he was fired for sexual harassment."

"The plan you had was cunning and would never be traced back to you. That afternoon you took Alex to the bunker and left him there with poor Ida. Mats had promised Nikolaj that he could spend time with the girl. But when he saw Alex there, he couldn't resist. You knew very well when Mats found out, he would kill Nikolaj and ... he did. Only, Alex didn't die in the attack."

Irene remained stoic about the accusations against her. There was nothing in her attitude that showed any emotional connection to the story.

"Luckily for you, he remembered nothing, and although the emotional stress took its toll, he would never really know what had happened to him."

"But Josip had seen you that afternoon with Alex. While Mats psychologically terrorized the witnesses to Nikolaj's murder, you kept a close eye on Josip for years. You knew he would connect the dots at some point, so you had to intervene."

There was still no response from her side, and Magnus continued: "The kidnapping of Katrien Jans was the perfect opportunity to catch two birds with one stone. You were there when Katrien took off. Mats waited for her outside the museum, and you made sure she got in his car. The consternation caused by the quarrel between Katrien and Josip played completely in your cards. You could discredit him as a result, and even if he were eventually cleared of the crime, it would have eroded his reputation to the point that no one would believe him anymore. It almost destroyed him, until they found the remains of the girls last year, and he put all the pieces together. He contacted you and he wanted money, which you paid him in the beginning, but you couldn't rely on him keeping quiet, especially after your son said he got a call from Josip to meet him. He also contacted Marian and Michael because he wanted to come clean and tell Alex everything. And he had evidence he kept in a safe deposit box at the bank, to be opened after his death. The burglary of his apartment and the cabin was supposed to scare him, but when he disappeared and threatened to go to the police, you had to kill him. That night you made him drunk, put the gun to his head and pulled the trigger."

"All speculations," Irene laughed ironically.

"The night of his death, Josip called an unregistered phone number."

"So, you can't trace it back to my client," Mr. Hansen intervened, "all circumstantial, no real evidence."

The inspectors became increasingly frustrated. Nothing seemed to elicit a real reaction from her they could work with. The self-discipline and control were amazing.

"And here I have a statement from a witness who was questioned at the time of Katrien Jans' disappearance. It's from a woman called ... Irene Kirkegard."

She shuffled restlessly in her chair.

Finally, some reaction, Magnus thought.

"Irene Kirkegard. That's your maiden name, Mrs. Nordin."

"May I have a word with my client?" Mr. Hansen interrupted.

"I'm fine," Irene stated and ignored her neighbor's attempt to give her some time to think about her defense.

She had regained full control of her emotions and she put up the impenetrable facade again she mastered so well.

"Maybe you should listen to your counselor," Nina said.

"So, I was there. It doesn't prove I was involved in the abduction and the alleged attempt to discredit Josip Radić. He did that all by himself."

Magnus had to admit that, except for the letter and the files on the USB stick they found in the deposit box, they had little evidence to go on. There was too much coincidence to ignore it, but it was all indirect.

"Let's go back to your husband. Peter had a hunch, but his mental state was so bad that for most years he couldn't put it together until he stopped taking his medication. He became more lucid, and it confirmed what he had been expecting all along: that you had changed his meds and had replaced them with something that made him more aggressive and mentally unstable. It worried him. His son thought it was because of his refusal to take medication, but he feared for his own life and Alex's. He confronted you with the DNA test. He probably didn't understand why you had lied to him and Mats for years about who Alex's real father was. Did you have a fight, and did you kill him? You couldn't have hanged him by yourself. Did you call Mats to come and help you?"

"I didn't kill Peter," she said.

"What about Alex?"

"What about him?" she answered angrily.

"Did you love your son?"

"What do you mean? Of course, I loved him. He wasn't the most sociable person, but he was kind and smart."

"And he was a man," Nina added.

"What?"

"Your son was being treated by Dr. Wikholm for a bunch of neuroses, but what stood out was that while Alex seemed to have been severely affected by his father's illness and death, it was the emotional bullying and even the physical aggression by you, his mother, who pushed him into loneliness and self-doubt. He told the doctor you regretted having a son because men are scum. They hurt women and treat them like second-class people ... and he was just one of them."

"You talked to Dr. Wikholm? You have no right!"

"Oh, we do. This is a criminal investigation, and we have access to the medical records of both your son and your husband."

"When you were ten years old, you witnessed your father beat your mother to death. That must have left its impact."

"How would you know?" she said sarcastically. "You can't imagine what it's like when you see your father trying to strangle your mother and then, with his bare fists, beat her repeatedly until you feel the spatters of blood, her blood, on your face, arms, and hands ..."

The run-up to the event had been so futile: a mere argument about her school results. She hadn't done well in school, and her father blamed her mother. Usually, it ended with yelling and a few punches, but this time he had been drunk, very drunk, and although his rage had been against Irene in the first place, her mother had intervened, and she had paid for it with her life. After her mother's death, Irene promised herself that she would never again be in a situation where a man would determine her fate. She could handle lovers and a husband. They meant nothing to her, but her son had put her in a dilemma. As a mother, she was supposed to love and protect her child, but her hatred of men had been so overpowering that she could only see him as the next generation oppressor of women.

* * *

"I don't pretend to know, Mrs. Nordin. My only concern is how this affected the bond with your son. Alex's sessions with Dr. Wikholm worried you, didn't they? Because he might remember, and to some extent he did. Dr. Wikholm's notes suggest Alex had dreams and memories he couldn't put into context. The nightmares started years ago when he was a teenager."

"They could have," she said, but didn't want to elaborate further.

"Tell me about the suicide attempts."

"So, you know about that too? Fine, there's not much to say. The first time he tried to take his father's medication. They had to pump his stomach, but it wasn't too serious. The second time my husband found him on the bathroom floor. He had cut his wrist. In retrospect, it wasn't very serious either, and he was out of the hospital within a few days. A pathetic cry for attention! Though, child protection services forced us to go to family counseling."

"He was only ten the first time and fifteen at the second attempt. The hospital records show he lost so much blood by slitting his wrist they had to resuscitate him twice in the ER. But in this story, the question is: where were you?"

"In his statement, Peter mentioned that, while he had assumed you were home that afternoon, you weren't. He was worried about Alex's mental state for a while and wanted you to stay home with him. Alex was lucky his father came home earlier and found him. Otherwise, he would have been dead."

"And where were you the first time?" Magnus asked.

"What are you exactly saying, inspector?" Mr. Hansen asked.

"That your client, on purpose, was absent, and that she didn't help a person in need. On the contrary, she made sure the chances were high he would die."

"Speculations," he said.

"He ran away from home when he was seventeen," Nina continued.

"With his so-called girlfriend," Irene said scornfully. "She had a terrible influence on him. I cut off the relationship, and he came back to us."

Nina listened to her open-mouthed. The way Irene kept talking about her son was so stomach-churning. She felt nothing but pity for Alexander Nordin.

"Let's go back to the present. Mats called you three days ago. We have phone records to prove it. He had abducted Sara and didn't know what to do. You had always been the mastermind. I think it was you who planned the kidnappings, but this time he acted rashly. He was in a panic, and he needed your help."

"No, he called to say Annette couldn't meet me that day," she replied. "Her mother's condition was getting worse, and she wanted to stay with her, so we had to reschedule our shopping trip."

Magnus sighed. It wasn't going well. They needed evidence. There was no one who could place her at the home of Annette and Mats Norman that morning. The only possibility was that the search would yield something: clothes stained with blood or gun powder marks, letters, diaries about her relationship with Mats.

"When you got there, Mats was upstairs, busy with the girl. And then Annette came home. It was unexpected because she should have been with her mother in the hospital, but her sister told us she wanted to go home to pick up clothes, books and so on because she was going to be staying longer than expected. What happened when she got home and saw you there? Did you kill her in cold blood, or did you have her sit down, had a nice chat with her and then killed her? Did she confront you with the suspicions she had for years about your relationship with her husband?"

"And what did Mats do? Was he shocked? Did you tell him it was an accident, or did you try to convince him he was responsible?"

There was no answer.

"Annette left the hospital around 8:30 a.m. and presumably died between 9 a.m. and 11 a.m. Alex arrived at the mansion around noon. His colleague at the university confirmed the timeline."

He watched her closely. She had everything under control, no emotions, stoic.

"What did you think when you saw your son enter the house? Was it premeditated? Phone records indicate that Alex called Mats' cell phone that morning. Did you ask Mats to lure him to the house?"

She sighed and looked bored. Magnus had given up getting a response from her.

"It was you who killed Alex, wasn't it? Finally, after all these years, the perfect opportunity to get rid of him. Did you hate him that much?"

"You accuse my client of killing her own son ... and not only killing him but also planning to kill him," Mr. Hansen said. "Again, where is the evidence?'

There was none. The only prints found on the gun were Mats'. It was his gun. There was no way he could link it to Irene.

But he wanted to appeal to her mother's instinct to confess. Only, he realized she was ice cold, calculated and extremely smart and manipulative, and she would never confess to anything.

"That was an entertaining story, but you give me too much credit," she said. "I deny everything. Unless you charge me with something, I'd say this conversation is over."

She signaled Mr. Hansen, next to her, to leave, while she got up and took the coat from the chair. Disheartened by the entire interview, Nina and Magnus said nothing.

"Oh, please send my regards to inspector Lindström," she turned just before leaving the room. The sudden, seemingly kind words surprised Magnus.

"Please convey to her I will file a complaint about her with the disciplinary committee. I think her involvement with my son has clouded her judgment. A conflict of interest that will cost you the case."

"What is your proof?" Nina asked.

"I have a witness," the old woman said.

"Someone saw inspector Isa Lindström enter my son's apartment a few days ago around 6 p.m. in the evening and leave only the morning after. Now, tell me why would a young woman spend the night in a man's apartment? I guess it wasn't to question him about the case."

Oh, my God, Magnus thought, she kept track of his every move.

She has spies everywhere!

"So, you'll be hearing from me," she concluded and left the room, followed by Mr. Hansen.

"That woman should be locked up," Nina concluded, "as soon as possible."

Magnus threw his head back and looked up at the ceiling. She was always one step ahead of them. He felt like an amateur.

"It will be tough," he said and closed his eyes.

"Yes, and now even more than before. I told you Isa would be a liability."

Her voice was serious and angry.

"Anders put her on non-active, Nina. Leave her alone!"

"I don't understand how she could get herself involved like that," she continued, "and you keep defending her."

He said nothing, opened his eyes and looked at the papers in front of him. All these girls! They couldn't give up. Never.

CHAPTER

26

THE FUNERAL TOOK PLACE ON a Tuesday late March. Although the temperature had risen the week before, that day snow fell from the sky again.

Mats Norman had finally confessed to murdering the girls and Nikolaj Blom, but about his other victims, Josip, Annette, and Alex he kept quiet, much to the dismay of their families and not in the least his own children.

The case was extensively covered in the media and many people showed up to pay their last respects to Alexander Nordin, a victim of the serial killer who had roamed the area for over thirty years. Family, neighbors, and especially colleagues filled the cathedral in Uppsala, but also people the family had never even heard of. Isa and Magnus were sitting in the back.

"Are you okay?" Magnus asked and took her hand. It was a kind gesture, a gesture from a friend trying to comfort another friend. He continued to hold her hand throughout the ceremony.

"No, I'm not," she whispered.

Her voice broke with emotion. She closed her eyes. Alex was still haunting her. The nights, all alone in bed, she imagined how he lay beside her. There was no talking, just the two of them, lying in silence. He had been a troubled man; she knew that. Few people really knew him as the sensitive, fragile, and ever worrying man he had been. He had questioned his existence, looking up to a father who had struggled to accept him, and longing for the love of a mother who had used him in the most pernicious way possible. Pure unselfish love he had never experienced. He barely had time to figure out his relationship with the beautiful, extrovert and ambitious inspector Isa, who had been so different. Maybe in her mind, it was more than it had been in reality, but she had to believe it had been the most beautiful romance ever. She had so little of him, so few tangible things. There were memories, but memories would fade and details like his smell, his voice, his touch, she couldn't even recall anymore.

The past weeks had been difficult. A succession of sadness, anger, and shame had taken control of her. Losing herself in police work was not possible, as Anders had suspended her for an indefinite time. She had locked herself in the house with the music so loud at times that she no longer heard it. His last moments kept playing in her head all day and night until she finally fell asleep from sheer exhaustion. She stared for hours at the photos she found of him on the Internet. They weren't of great quality, but it helped her sharpen the memories that were already fading. She replayed the YouTube videos of his seminars over and over, just to watch him move and hear him speak until the pain was too much to bear and she screamed until she had no voice or breath anymore.

Robin Gilmore was the only person he had considered a friend, and it had been a turning point for her when she met him. He liked to reminisce about the quirks of his desk buddy, his insecurities, especially with women, and he talked about how Alex had always struggled with his low self-esteem and purpose in life. But he had been happy that final day. As a friend, he had felt it and, for the first time, he had seen him carefree, and it had meant a lot to her to know. She saw him sitting a few rows in the front, with other colleagues. You only need one. One good friend, who will remember you and tell the world who you have been after your death.

* * *

In the front of the church, Irene Nordin was sitting with her sister and family next to her. She looked tired and worn-out. But she wasn't emotional, no one expected that from her. That was just the woman she was.

Before the ceremony, Isa had observed her. The elegant, slender woman, dressed in black, had walked around, had talked to family and friends, as if nothing had happened.

"I don't understand how a mother can kill her child," she said.

Magnus looked at her, somewhat preoccupied.

"I don't know, Isa, but you're a mother. Why do mothers reject their sons? Why have you decided not to be part of your children's lives?"

It was hard. She hadn't expected that from him. He felt how her fingernails clenched into his hand. He had always challenged her about that decision; she knew that, but to bring it up at that moment was surprising. She didn't understand that he projected his own situation. Sophie's rejection of their son Toby was inexplicable to him. He had looked for reasons; he had blamed himself, but finally, he had given up.

"You know I only want to protect them," she said.

"I think you truly believe that, but it's wrong. Children need their parents. How messed up the parents may be, children deserve to know their parents."

"As messed up as she is," she pointed to Irene.

"You're not Irene, and ... you're not Sophie."

It was all about her, and not once had she asked him how he was. He was at the hospital every day, even though he was drowning in work. Now that Isa was suspended and Nina had resigned, he was the one pushing the case forward. It had kept him from making the decision he didn't want to make. He still couldn't let his son go. At home, his wife avoided him. They lived side by side with no interaction. Later that day, he would tell Sophie he had found a small apartment near the center of Uppsala, and he would move out of the house at the end of April. A divorce would be best for them. He was willing to share custody of Anna and Toby if she agreed.

"Think about what you could give them. Isa, this is important for yourself and your children. Spend some time with them."

She smiled, not completely convinced by his words, but she valued his advice. The frustration and anger she had felt over their break-up seemed now so far away. He was the only real friend she had.

For the rest of the ceremony, she let herself be carried away by the music that was modern and uplifting rather than sad, and the endless speeches of colleagues and so-called friends, some more articulate than others, some more emotional than others. But it all remained superficial. It was a church full of people, but few had really cared about Alex. It wasn't that different from Josip's funeral.

* * *

"I can't remember inviting you."

Irene had seen the inspectors sitting in the back of the church when she passed by after the ceremony. Outside, in the square in front of the

331

cathedral, she confronted Isa and Magnus.

"I believe it's a free country, so I think we are allowed to pay your son our respects," Magnus replied.

"Don't come near me, don't come to his grave ... ever," she said threateningly and walked away.

"I can't believe that woman is still walking free," Isa said.

"There's no direct evidence against her."

"I know. You need Mats to admit she was his accomplice. Prove her involvement with the girls. I just want to put her behind bars."

"He's still protecting her," Magnus said as they walked from the church across the square to the other side.

"That may change if he's convinced of her involvement in Alex's death. You need to talk to him again. Try to get through to him."

"I'm not sure, Isa."

"If he realizes she lied to him about almost everything, then maybe he will tell the truth."

"She has visited him five times in the past weeks. I'm sure she has been whispering enough lies in his ears to confuse him and make him believe that he killed Josip, Annette, and Alex. We need to make a plan of attack here, and honestly, Isa, I don't know how to do that."

"We need solid evidence," she replied.

They walked through small, quiet streets to the old cemetery. He had promised her not to follow the same path as the funeral procession. She couldn't handle a second confrontation with Alex's mother. It would take them much longer to get there, but it gave them more time to talk.

"What are you going to do?" he asked after a while.

"I don't know, Magnus. I want my job back, but I think she'll come after me with everything she has. I need to be prepared."

"I don't know where Anders stands, but if he's put under pressure, he will have no choice. You need to defend yourself."

"No illusions there," she said, and took his arm.

She felt comfortable talking to him. It was as if they hadn't gone through painful break-up fights and periods of silence and unresolved anger for the past year.

"Look, Isa, I have been thinking, maybe you should consider playing down your relationship with Alex."

She stopped walking and stared at him. Had she understood him correctly?

"Playing down?! What are you saying? That I have to deny my relationship with Alex. You are asking me to lie?"

He took her hands in his. He knew she would react that way. What he wanted to ask her was against all the rules. It went against every sense of decency and professional ethics.

"Hear me out. It's not just about you anymore. I want justice for all those girls. And to do that, we cannot fail. And for that to happen, we may need to resort to something that is maybe less morally correct."

"You are asking me to lie?" she repeated.

He sighed, stared at the ground for a while and then looked up, saying: "Yes."

"Magnus, everyone knows. Ingrid, Anders, you. If put on a stand to testify, these people will not lie."

"But there is no proof ... you didn't admit it."

"Magnus, please," she pleaded.

She was disappointed. How could he even have suggested such a thing?

"Okay. Whatever you do, I'll help you," he said.

She stopped again and looked at him. The collar of his coat wasn't right, and she straightened it. It was an intimate moment they hadn't shared in a long time.

"Thank you, Magnus."

Her voice sounded soft and fragile.

* * *

The grave was new. For now, it was a pile of sand with a simple cross. No stone or picture to identify it as the last resting place of Alexander Nordin. Magnus stood next to her as she kept on staring at the grave. She kneeled and touched the soil. That was it. Now she had to get on with her life.

"I didn't particularly like him," Magnus said without reservation, "but he was good to you."

"Yes, he was ... but I wasn't good to him," she said, got up and took his hand again.

He felt how she sank back into a black pit full of emotions and what-ifs.

"You'll be fine," he said. "We'll both be fine. I promise I'll put his murderer behind bars. I promise."

"Thank you," she smiled, looked at the grave one more time and walked back to the exit.

Magnus didn't immediately follow her. He stared at the grave. As soon as Isa had turned her back on him, his expression changed completely. So, there they were: victim and ... murderer.

* * *

In the commotion of the past weeks, nobody had noticed that Magnus had arrived in Sandviken more than thirty minutes later than his Uppsala colleagues on the day of Mats' arrest. But he was inspector Magnus Wieland, and no one questioned his integrity. Behind the steering wheel of his car, Alex Nordin had called him that day when he couldn't reach Isa. He had so many doubts. He had stopped so many times during the short trip to Mats' house. He needed advice. Was he doing the right thing? Magnus had ignored the call at first but had called him back a few minutes later before driving to Sandviken. Until then, there had been no plan. But the hatred had been growing in his mind to such a proportion Magnus was scared of his own thoughts. All those lonely evenings and nights in the hospital by his son's bed had given him plenty of time to reflect on his relationship with Isa. He wanted her back, no matter what. But when Isa had so openly rejected him that morning, something had snapped inside him. Alex differed from all the flings she had ever had. He would take her away from him forever. So, Alex had to go.

Yes, he would join him at the mansion of Mats Norman. Yes, they would face Mats together and he would tell Isa.

He didn't drive to Sandviken but arrived at the house of the Norman family before Isa and Nina, and even Alex. He knew the shortcuts. And he was surprised to find the door unlocked and no one in the house. It was so quiet. He found Annette in the living room. Dead, with the gun on the floor next to her. He picked it up, leaving no prints because of the gloves he was wearing. It was then that he saw Alex approaching the house. After so many weeks, he still didn't know what possessed him to hide behind the living room door, waiting for his rival to come in. It was such a great opportunity. They would accuse Mats of the crime. No one would ever know he had been there. Alex's phone gone, his message erased from Magnus' phone, the conversations between them erased from the records. It was that easy. He aimed. Even now, he still wondered what had tipped him over that threshold from being an ordinary man, who loved his family and work, to a cold-hearted murderer. When Alex turned around, his hand was shaking so hard that his aim was completely off. Two seconds. And in that short time, the all-consuming hatred for the man in front of him wiped away any restraints he still had, and he pulled the trigger.

Except Alex wasn't dead. Two more seconds to get over the shock. As he stood over the body and looked at the man on the floor, gasping for air, touching the wound, looking at the blood on his fingers and begging for his life, he pointed the gun at his head. His hand was no longer trembling. Alex Nordin had to die.

Upstairs, someone was crying. It was Sara. She was slamming her fists on the door of the room. He heard someone enter through the front door. It was Mats.

He dropped the gun and made his way to the kitchen and then went through the back door to the backyard. Via the garden of a neighbor, he reached the street. He was so scared. If Alex survived, he would surely reveal that Magnus had shot him. Did Mats Norman see him? Had he left evidence behind? What if people had seen him flee the neighborhood? As he drove away, he saw police cars approaching the house. Isa and Nina were there. The drive to Sandviken had seemed so much longer than expected, and he often panicked during the journey. What had he done? What had he done to his family? He expected to be arrested the moment he arrived in Sandviken. But Alex died, and no one came after him. He got away with murder. And a strange thing happened. The panic and initial remorse for his actions made room for a sense of superiority and absence of accountability. Everything turned in his favor. Irene was a factor he hadn't considered but would serve his cause well and the public opinion had been so biased that, no matter what, Mats would be the obvious culprit.

* * *

Isa was waiting for him at the exit of the cemetery. It would be a matter of time before she was his again. She would eventually get over Alex and he would be a small footnote in her life.

She smiled as he approached. He took her hand and kissed it gently.

"Is there something wrong?" she asked.

"No, everything is fine," he said, "let's go home."

THE END

Printed in Poland
by Amazon Fulfillment
Poland Sp. z o.o., Wrocław
08 December 2022